Wrath of Olympus
Volume 3

Oath Breaker

By

Brian Tripp

IMPRINTS

Copyright © 2025 Brian Tripp
ISBN: 978-1-945567-56-8
Library of Congress: 2025934338
Interior Design: Ruth Souther
Cover Design: Emily's World of Design
Printed in USA

Dedication

To Dawn, whose unwavering support for my writing has meant the world to me.

Look Dawn, I wrote a book!

ACKNOWLEDGMENTS

I really want to thank my family and friends for how supportive and incredible they have been as I have started my writing journey. This entire process is possible thanks to you, and for building up my confidence as a new writer as I learn and evolve my writing style. Thank you as well to Ruth for helping to guide me through the publishing process, and to Karen for just how incredibly supportive she has been with spreading my writing to as many people as she can.

I would also like to give a special shoutout to Adriana for helping me test read and edit, to Dawn for not hesitating for even a second to support me when she learned I wrote books, as well as finding unique ways to encourage me to hit soft deadlines I set for myself, and to Jordyn and Brittany for just being positive parts of my life. I am so grateful for you all.

Oath Breaker

Prologue

As she stood at the precipice of Stormhaven's towering walls, a warm breeze teasing the loose leather straps of her tunic. Below, the city lay in its usual quiet order, but beyond its borders, the world was anything but ordinary.

The sky was a breathtaking canvas, its colors shifting and blending in an endless, hypnotic dance. A chaotic explosion of oranges, purples, and pinks streaked across the horizon, swirling as if painted by Apollo himself. The hues burned with such intensity they seemed almost alive, pulsing and writhing in a frenzied rhythm.

The ground below was equally surreal. Once-verdant fields, where the grass swayed in the ever-present breeze, had transformed into a vast meadow of bioluminescent flowers, carpeting the vibrant soil as far as the eye could see. Their sweet, heady fragrance hung thick in the air, teetering on the edge of overwhelming—both intoxicating and suffocating at once.

The city itself was deathly quiet as if the hundreds of people within its walls had fallen asleep at once or perhaps something even more sinister. Though she stood upon the walls ringing the civilization, Ashe knew that attempting to enter the city was impossible. She had been in this dream many times before, and an invisible force kept her from any sort of exploration each time.

"They're coming," a man's familiar voice strained beside her ear.

Ashe whirled around, looking for the source of the voice, yet all was as it had been, how it always was when she was dragged into this liminal space. Though she often referred to this place as a dream, lately she wondered if nightmare was a more apt description.

Every time she came here, she was stuck, rooted to this spot on the wall for what felt like hours on end, choking down the sickly scent of the flowers and waiting for something that never came. At first, she thought it beautiful, watching the colors shift in the sky. Now, it simply nauseated her. It was as though the world was moving around her at speeds she could not comprehend, and the motion began to make her feel sick.

"They're coming!" the voice called out again, the initial strain giving way to a rising, unsettling urgency.

"Who is coming?" She spun around, trying desperately to make some sense of why she was there.

A large bang thundered across the sky as if on cue, shaking Ashe's vision or perhaps the world around her.

"THEY'RE COMING!" The voice wailed now, adding to the already unsettling nature of the scene around her.

Once more, the world trembled as a mighty force struck the heavens, shattering the swirling colors and replacing them with a web of shimmering gold. Ashe's breath caught as recognition dawned—the dome woven from the strands of Fate upon her return to Stormhaven.

Its purpose was singular, absolute: to herald the return of the Olympians to the Mortal Realm. And if they were revealing themselves to her now, it could mean only one thing.

The wall beneath her feet shuddered violently, sending Ashe to her knees as three more concussive blasts slammed home around her. Just beyond the golden net, she could see a series of cracks snaking their way across the sky, splitting the already confusing world into a disarray of colors and shapes like a kaleidoscope. Then, just as soon as the disruptions had begun, they stopped, blanketing everything with an unnatural silence.

"They're here."

A brilliant jolt of violet lightning punched through the cracks in the sky, tearing a gash in Ashe's threads and sending translucent shards of essence cascading down upon the city below her. She could only watch in horror as bolt after bolt rained down, slamming into the world, tearing up chunks of earth and debris clouds, and leaving smoldering ash craters in its place.

A hideous chorus of laughter broke out, echoing across the sky like the cackle of hyenas. Ashe could do nothing but watch as the land around her was ripped away one piece at a time until, finally, it was her turn. She watched in terror as everything disintegrated into nothingness.

~~~

Ashe gasped as she sat up in bed, her platinum hair plastered to the side of her neck, thick with sweat. Though cool, autumn air drifted into the dark room through a cracked window; her body felt feverish, as though a small fire was lit just beneath the surface of her skin.

After a few steadying breaths, Ashe pushed aside the tangle of thoughts racing through her mind and rose from the bed. Moving lightly, she crossed the chamber toward an oil lamp mounted on the far wall. Normally, she despised the rough cobbled stone beneath her feet, always careful to muffle the sound of each step. But tonight, she welcomed the cool touch of the rock, each step sending soothing waves through the lingering burn in her skin.

It was not until the lamp was lit and she was sitting back on the edge of her bed that she felt the warm sensation of blood upon her upper lip. Gingerly, she reached up to the liquid and lightly touched it, pulling her hand away and examining her fingertips. Her eyes widened as, instead of red, she saw her blood streaked with gold, running down the length of her finger.

Ever since she had taken the entirety of Fate within her from the Tower, she felt feverish. Though she hoped it was simply taking time for her body to acclimate to the new, intense power, she lately had started to fear that perhaps it was too much for her alone to bear.

Her mind felt as though it were constantly being pulled in a million different directions, as if Fate were trying to weave new futures from within her head. There was a small part of her that wondered if the hallucinations she had been having were delusions of madness rather than simple dreams or even visions. For the first time since meeting Hestia, Ashe felt as though her power was consuming her, and that thought terrified her.

She missed Quinn now more than she had at any other point in her life. Even when she was within the Tower and thought she would never see him again, she still had her memories and the confidence that what she was doing was good and right.

Now, however, she had begun to feel as though she were unraveling under the weight of her power, and with Quinn and Levy off on a mission of their own, she felt incredibly alone. For the thousandth time, she pleaded silently for them to return home soon.

With a deep breath, she forced her mind back to the matter at hand, burying her fears for another time. Delusions of madness or not, she was the only one who could warn everyone when the Olympians were coming.

If what she saw in her dream was not a clear indication the time was nigh, nothing would be. Ashe had a job to do, and her fears could not get in the way of that.

She pulled her tunic over her head, tightened the laces in the front, and splashed some cool water in her face from the bowl she kept upon her desk. With one more deep breath, she briskly left her quarters behind, pushing essence into the rune carved in the talisman she wore around her neck.

Each council member had a similar one on their person so that when an emergency required their attention, they could be quickly notified. With that done, she made her way into their meeting spot and waited for each to trickle in.

Though none seemed too happy with being woken up in the darkest hour of the night, all understood the importance of what it meant when they were summoned in such a manner. As Lend, the last of them, entered and claimed a seat at the table, eyes bleary and hair a mess of cowlicks and tangles, Ashe stood, looking each of them in the eye. With a deep breath, she readied herself to deliver the unfortunate news. It was time to get to work.

Oath Breaker

Chapter 1
Levy

An ear-shattering howl raked down Levy's spine, leaving discomfort and goosebumps in its wake. He dove to the left, wincing as sharp gravel scraped along his shoulder and back, narrowly avoiding the dagger-sharp claws from the massive black paw that slammed into the ground where he stood just a moment before.

"Relax Quinn! I already took care of the guard dog, Quinn!" his friend mocked from a few feet away, using his shadowy cloak to blunt a strike from one of the monster's ugly heads.

Levy clenched his fists, not taking his eye from the threat in front of him. Though Quinn's words were sharp, Levy could see the twinkle in his eyes, and the smile and exhilaration splayed across his face as he controlled his Chaos.

"Well, how was I supposed to know that Cerberus would return to the Underworld when I killed it instead of just disappearing like the rest of the monsters?"

The duo had not been in the Underworld for longer than an hour before the massive canine had risen from the shadows at their feet, as though it were wearing a certain mask the two of them knew all too well.

Cerberus had certainly seen better days. Though it was not in the greatest of shape the first time Levy had killed it, it at least resembled a dog.

Now, however, the grotesque and nightmarish creature that stood before them was only recognizable by its three massive heads. Its body was a jagged assemblage of skeletal bones, held together by scraps of putrid muscles and tendons visible to the eye.

Greasy patches of black, matted fur were scattered in clumps around its body, coarse and unkempt. They hung loosely, giving the beast the overall impression of neglect and decay.

All three mouths were gaping maws of terror, filled with sharp and uneven teeth. Thick strands of saliva dripped from its jaws, leaving a stinking, slimy trail as it moved.

All six red eyes pierced through the glumness of the Underworld with an otherworldly glow, reflecting the beastly malevolence that resided within.

The heads lifted as one, loosing another shrieking howl that echoed across the empty fields of Asphodel. From this close, it was all Levy could do to keep his vision from blurring at the intense pain inside his ears.

"LEVY, MOVE!" Quinn roared as Cerberus lunged forward, picking him out as the weaker of the two.

Realizing he did not have time to dive out of the way again, Levy forced his essence into his core, arms, and legs. His muscles bulged with enhanced strength, ready for the impending crash.

The monster's jaws snapped down at him, intending to bite him in half, but with trained reflexes, Levy reached out, grabbing hold of the dog's open mouth and wrenching it apart.

Realizing the danger it was in, the middle head reared around, attempting to sink its teeth into Levy's abdomen. However, just before it could make contact, Quinn was there, pushing Levy out of harm's way.

Levy watched in awe as his friend, now fully wielding the Primordial power of Chaos, entered into combat with the guardian of the Underworld.

Quinn moved like a wraith, seamlessly blending with the shadows as he evaded the beast's snapping jaws. He conjured chaotic illusions, confusing Cerberus momentarily. Shadows danced around the dog, distorting the monster's perception of reality.

Not to be outdone, Levy charged the beast, his movements swift and powerful. With a mighty swing, he aimed to strike Cerberus across its skeletal frame. Levy felt the trickle of warm blood slide from his knuckles down his wrist as the smack of muscle against bone echoed through the desolate landscape. Cerberus retaliated with a swipe of its gnarled claws, forcing Levy to somersault backward to avoid the attack.

Seeing Cerberus momentarily distracted, Quinn seized the opportunity, casting shadowy tendrils from his cloak that ensnared Cerberus' three heads. The creature roared in frustration, unable to break free from the ethereal grasp.

Levy took advantage of the moment, rushing in to deliver powerful blows to the trapped guardian. His muscles strained against his essence-filled strikes, each hit shaking the ground around them.

Cerberus was not easily subdued. With a surge of dark energy, Quinn intensified the shadows, amplifying the chaos within. The monster thrashed wildly, breaking free from his entanglement.

Now enraged, the beast turned all three heads toward Quinn. A desperate hunger gleamed within its scarlet, hate-filled eyes. Sensing a moment of urgency, Levy summoned his strength for what he hoped would be a final, decisive blow.

The two friends' eyes met for the briefest of seconds, and instantly, an understanding built from years of training passed between them. In a synchronized effort, Quinn unleashed a surge of Chaotic energy, engulfing all three of the dog's heads, while Levy pushed all of his essence into one devastating strike.

He could feel the monster's ribcage shatter beneath the might of his blow. The combination of shadows and brute force overwhelmed Cerberus, causing it to collapse into a tangle of bones and fur.

They stood in silence—Quinn gazing down at the heap of monster while Levy bent over, hands on his knees, gulping in the warm, stagnant air of the Underworld.

"Did you just fight Cerberus with your fists?"

Quinn stared at him, one eyebrow arched—a perfect blend of astonishment and reluctant annoyance at being impressed.

Levy glanced down at his blood-soaked hands, only now realizing what he had done. The jagged bone had torn deep into the thin skin of his knuckles, leaving behind raw, angry gashes. The sting that had begun to settle shifted into a slow, searing burn. Grimacing, he gave his hand a sharp shake, hoping to shake off the discomfort.

"I guess I did. Didn't really think about it—just acted on instinct.

"You have a sword strapped to your back," Quinn replied dryly. "I know you're making progress with controlling the strength Hestia's essence gives you, but don't make rash decisions.

"You may feel pressured to prove yourself to everyone else after everything that has transpired, but you don't have to prove anything to me."

The two friends locked eyes briefly before Levy casually looked away. Since coming to terms with his own inner turmoil, his friend had transformed into what Levy would have considered a true hero straight out of one of the myths the Masters used to have him study growing up.

Gone was the boy filled to the brim with self-doubt and trepidation. In his place was a man, lean and strong, with clear eyes and the confidence to lead without a second thought. Once upon a time, Quinn had looked up to Levy, but as they stood here now, deep in the realm of Hades, Levy couldn't help but smile as he realized the roles had been reversed.

"You're right," he smiled, patting Quinn on the back. "Sometimes I need the reminder that the world is not placed squarely on my shoulders. Thank you."

Quinn smiled back, walking up next to him so they could both stare at the endless expanse before them, stretching infinitely into the distance. These moments of peace were a rare commodity lately, and it was nice to taste the nostalgia of times long past.

Beneath them, the Underworld stretched endlessly, a vast expanse where time itself seemed to hold its breath. The air was unexpectedly warm, heavy with the scent of ancient earth and lingering decay. Overhead, the sky glowed a hazy red, as if the sun had been trapped just beyond the horizon, casting an eternal twilight over the realm.

Oath Breaker

Levy's eye followed the fields of Asphodel toward their destination: Their delicate, ghostly petals coloring the ground in muted, grey hues. Amongst the flora walked many shades, their eyes glassy, no longer knowing who or where they were.

Shadows danced along the landscape, their movements slow and languid. Every so often, faint murmurs and mournful whispers tickled Levy's ears, the voices of the departed souls who inhabited this realm.

Though he could not see the water, a shimmering mist rose from the banks of the many rivers that snaked their way through this realm, shrouding the world in a ghostly blanket. Despite its desolate appearance, he couldn't help but feel that there was a certain eerie beauty to the Underworld. It was a place where the past lingered, forever bound to the shadows of the afterlife.

Just as his adrenaline began to fade, Levy sensed a shift in the air. It was subtle—a slight drop in temperature, enough to send a shiver down his spine. He glanced at Quinn, who stood rigid, his expression grave, every muscle tense like a startled cat with its hackles raised.

"What is it?" Levy asked, his voice low.

Quinn's eyes narrowed, his senses on high alert.

"Hades. He's getting closer." His words were clipped, his voice terse. "We need to move."

Without hesitation, Levy nodded, and they turned from Cerberus's lifeless form, their pace quickening as they pressed deeper into the fields toward their objective. Though he felt more confident in his control over Hestia's gift, the memory of his battle with Ares still lingered—the brutal beatdown he had suffered was not so easily forgotten.

His fingers drifted unconsciously to the black eyepatch covering the place where his left eye had once been. Even Quinn, growing stronger by the day, would struggle against Hades alone. It had taken all three of them—Levy, Quinn, and Ashe—to bring down a single Olympian.

They moved swiftly through the waist-high plants, the shades drifting aside yet eyeing them with a strange, guarded wariness—half-curious, half-hostile as if they sensed the intruders did not belong. With every step, the unease thickened, pressing down like an unseen weight.

The air grew heavy, charged with an unspoken dread. Shadows twisted and stretched unnaturally, flickering along the swaying asphodel like silent omens. A low hum vibrated through the air, subtle at first but rising in intensity with each hurried stride.

Though Levy lacked Quinn's sharpened senses, even he could feel the presence closing in—the unmistakable weight of Hades' power bleeding through the very fabric of the Underworld.

"There!" Quinn called, pointing toward a towering archway of black-and-white speckled granite, its surface worn smooth by time. Beyond it, the River Styx thundered, its inky waters churning with a relentless, unforgiving current.

"I'm supposed to get in that?!" Levy yelled. His words were barely audible over the river.

"This was your idea!" Quinn fired back, his eyes scanning the way they came for any sign of the vengeful god on their trail. "And we don't have a lot of time. If you don't want to do this, say the word, and I will take us out now. But decide quickly."

Levy stepped up to the archway, his gaze fixed on the churning, murky waters beyond. Quinn was right—this had been his idea. And not just that, but it had taken considerable effort to get his friend to agree.

Quinn had been adamantly against it at first, refusing outright until Levy had finally worn him down through sheer persistence—a skill he had, ironically, learned from Quinn himself.

He had made countless mistakes—reaching for power he had not earned and chasing causes he did not truly believe in. But this time, he knew in his heart it was different.

As he was now, he was no match for the Olympians. His battle with Ares had made that painfully clear. Quinn wielded the power of an ancient Primordial, and Ashe, the power of Fate. If he was to stand against Zeus, he needed more.

But not out of selfish ambition, as he once had. Not even for the sake of humanity.

No, this time, he sought power for one reason alone—to protect his friends. The ones who had risked everything for him, time and time again. Now, it was his turn to repay that debt.

Levy stared into the water, remembering the ancient tale of

Oath Breaker

Achilles, dipped into the river as a baby and made practically invulnerable. The fact that Ashe and Quinn had agreed to bring him here showed the depths of their trust in him. He would succeed in this. He had to.

"I'm going in." He turned back to Quinn, firm in his convictions.

"No." An oily voice rasped. Its very existence shook the realm around them with untamed power. "You are not."

A point of darkness coalesced at the edge of the field, expanding and twisting until a massive, seething gateway yawned open in the air. From its depths, an army of the dead emerged—putrid and decayed, their hollow sockets glowing with eerie, sickly green light.

Among them prowled dozens of braying hellhounds, smaller and leaner than Cerberus, yet no less menacing. Their razor-sharp teeth gleamed as they snapped at the air, their claws carving deep gouges into the chalky soil with every step. Last of all, the god of the Underworld himself stepped through.

Hades was just as pale and slick with grease as Levy remembered. His sleek black hair curled past his gaunt, lifeless face, framing eyes as dark as the abyss, smoldering with undisguised contempt. Only his sneer, curling with bitter amusement, surpassed the disdain in his gaze.

He wore a black breastplate over flowing fur-lined robes, an ostentatious blend of opulence and militarism that only he could make look effortless. In one hand, he gripped a long onyx bident, its shaft inlaid with emeralds and rubies that gleamed like trapped fire in the dim Underworld light.

The army halted just fifty yards from where Quinn stood, restrained only by the silent command of Hades' raised hand. The hellhounds prowled the front lines, pacing restlessly, their lean bodies coiled with barely contained anticipation, eager for the order to strike.

"I do not know what possessed you boys with the courage to infiltrate my realm and kill my guard dog." His eyes flitted to Levy, "*Again.*"

He looked back at Quinn, a predatory smile slowly spreading across his face. "But when I am done with you, I will be sure you spend an eternity of pain in the pits of Tartarus, where you are so far beyond help, even the darkness cannot reach you."

Levy stepped toward Hades, the wounds on his knuckles reopening as he reached for the sword on his back, but his friend stopped him with a quick shake of his head.

From within Quinn, dark tendrils of crackling power sprang to life, enveloping him in his shadowy cloak. His sword had already found his hand, and the very air around him was distorted with raw power.

"Go," he muttered, flicking his wrist toward the river. Without a second glance, he stepped forward, resolute, ready to face the impossible.

Chapter 2
Quinn

Quinn spared his friend only the briefest glance, relieved to see that Levy had trusted him enough to obey without question, stepping into the river and leaving the Olympian and his undead army in Quinn's hands.

In the past, Levy would have hesitated—argued that Quinn wasn't strong enough to face such a threat alone. But now, he had turned away without a moment's doubt. It was proof of how much they had endured together, how their trials had forged an unshakable bond.

The power of Chaos crackled around him, its tendrils whipping around in an invisible wind. Quinn felt a smile creep along his face. The thought of going against one of the elder Olympians and his undead army should have terrified him.

Instead, he was filled to the brim with anticipation and a lust for battle. Quinn wasn't sure if that was the last dregs of Chaos' personality within the power or if it was his own excitement over finally getting to unleash it to the fullest degree he dared. Still, his muscles tensed against the adrenaline now coursing through him. Hades was not prepared for what was coming his way.

"Listen, boy," Hades began, but Quinn had no interest in idle conversation.

Without hesitation, he pushed off the ground, becoming nothing more than a streak of black as he tore through the wall of the dead that stood between him and his target. The legion barely had time to react before he was upon the god himself.

Before Hades could so much as lift a hand, Quinn's palm slammed into his face, fingers gripping tight. Using the full force of his descent, he drove the Olympian backward, sending him crashing into the ashen earth with a resounding impact.

Quinn grinned, satisfaction flickering in his eyes as he looked down at the stunned god—wide-eyed and speechless, staring up at him through the gaps in his fingers.

Hades let out a roar of pure malice, his fury manifesting as a powerful essence that crackled in the air, raising the hairs on the back of Quinn's neck. Recognizing the danger, he flung himself backward just in time—mere moments before a surge of sickly purple energy exploded outward from the god, ripping through the space where he had stood.

Hades rose to his feet, seething, wisps of dark essence still clinging to his cloak like ghostly embers. Gone was the lazy arrogance of an Olympian facing a mortal. In its place burned something far more dangerous—unrestrained, primal rage.

"Bring me his head," Hades spoke, his voice quiet yet edged with undeniable severity. "So that I may drink my nectar from his skull for the rest of eternity."

As one, the hellhounds threw back their heads, unleashing a chorus of piercing howls that shattered the stillness of the dead air. Their cries were a call to war, and the corpses answered.

With a sickening lurch, the undead surged forward toward their master's foe. Like a rotting tide, they charged—limbs clawing, bones grinding—churning over one another in a relentless wave of decayed flesh and putrid bone.

Quinn tightened his grip on his sword, feeling the familiar hum of Chaos energy thrumming beneath his skin. He exhaled slowly, steadying himself. This was more than just another battle—it was his first true test since facing Ares. A proving ground for the power he now claimed as his own.

He let the black energy unfurl from within, rolling out in waves.

Oath Breaker

The energy surged around him, a living storm mirrored the unshakable resolve burning in his chest. This was the land of the dead, but he had no intention of joining their ranks.

As the first wave of corpses lunged for him, he moved—fluid, effortless—his sword an extension of his will. Each strike was precise, every arc of the blade slicing through the undead with lethal ease. Around him, the tendrils of Chaos writhed and lashed like whips, tearing through the horde with savage ferocity, a relentless force that matched the fire in his soul.

A hellhound lunged at his leg, jaws snapping, but Quinn was quicker. He sidestepped the beast, bringing his sword down in a swift arc. The blade connected with a sickening crunch, severing the creature's head from its body. As the hound fell, two more took its place, their growls rumbling like distant thunder.

Quinn's cloak flared, its tendrils unfurling and writhing like a nest of serpents poised to strike. He spun, the Chaos answering his silent command with perfect harmony, and unleashed a wave of force to rival Hades' own. The eruption sent hellhounds tumbling through the air, their yelps lost in the deafening roar of power.

The battlefield reeked of decay, the putrid stench thick in the air. All around him, the guttural cries of the undead filled the void— twisted wails of agony as they were torn apart, scattered like dust within the maelstrom of Chaos.

Yet, despite his prowess, the onslaught was unending. For every foe Quinn struck down, another emerged from the shadows, surging forward like a relentless tide of darkness. The ground beneath him became a seething mass of writhing limbs and snapping jaws, an ocean of death that threatened to swallow him whole.

A sudden shift in the air was his only warning. A hellhound lunged at him from behind, its fangs bared in a vicious snarl. Instinct took over—he twisted sharply, barely avoiding its crushing bite, and brought his sword up in a fluid motion, deflecting the beast's attack in a shower of splintered bone.

Quinn's breath came in ragged gasps, his muscles burning with exertion. Sweat mingled with the ichor that spattered his face, but still, he fought on. His energy surged and pulsed, providing him with a layer of protection against the ferocity of the horde, but it was a double-edged sword.

Its power was wild and difficult to control. He could feel it straining against him, like a beast trying to break free of its chains.

Amidst the chaos, Quinn caught a glimpse of Hades, watching with an infuriating smirk. The god's presence was a constant, oppressive weight, a reminder of the stakes of this battle. Quinn gritted his teeth, pushing himself harder. He had to win and prove that he could master the Chaos within him. At least until Levy came back from his dip in the Styx.

A particularly large undead warrior clad in corroded armor charged him with a mighty roar. Quinn met the challenge head-on, their swords clashing in a shower of sparks. The impact jarred his arm, but he held firm, pushing back with a surge of Chaos that shattered the undead's weapon and sent it reeling.

As Quinn dispatched the warrior, a hellhound managed to slip through his defenses, its fangs sinking into his leg. He cried out in pain, the Chaos energy flickering around him as he struggled to maintain his focus.

He lashed out with a tendril of energy, flinging the beast away, but the damage was done. Blood flowed from the wound, and Quinn's leg trembled under the strain.

He staggered, his energy dimming as his strength waned. The horde, sensing his weakness, closed in like vultures. For a moment, doubt flickered in Quinn's mind. The sheer numbers were overwhelming, and the pain was clouding his thoughts. Then he heard Hades' mocking laughter, a cold, disdainful sound that cut through the haze of battle.

No. It would not end like this—not in this bleak abyss of death and sorrow. He refused to let Hades claim victory.

He thought of Ashe, the warmth in her eyes, and the soft, knowing smile that would greet him upon returning to the Citadel. The image burned in his mind, pushing back the shadows threatening to consume him. And in that moment, he felt it—his embers rekindling, the fire within him blazing back to life.

With a roar of defiance, Quinn drew upon the deepest reserves of his power. The Chaos energy flared, stronger than ever before. Tendrils burst forth, expanding into a swirling vortex of darkness. He channeled everything he had into a single, devastating attack. The air around him seemed to shudder, and then the energy exploded outward in a blinding flash.

The shockwave tore through the horde, disintegrating the undead and blasting the hellhounds into nothingness. The clearing was shadowed in deep, chaotic hues, and for a moment, everything was silent. As the energy faded, Quinn stood alone amidst the carnage, panting and bloodied.

Hades' smirk vanished, replaced by cold fury. The god's eyes burned with a promise of retribution. Quinn staggered, barely able to stay on his feet. The Chaos energy was gone, leaving him feeling drained and hollow. He looked around the ruined battlefield, the bodies of the dead dissolving into dust. He turned and met the cold, dead eyes of Hades. The god smiled.

"Now it's my turn."

Chapter 3
Levy

There was nothing but darkness as far as the eye could see. No water, no landscape, not even a horizon. It was also bitterly cold. Levy didn't know what had happened or how he had gotten here.

One second, he had been running into the water of the Styx, hoping to dip in quickly and then rush back out to help Quinn fight. The next, he was in this black abyss.

He wasn't even sure if he was floating in place or falling. What he did know was that he needed to get back. He just had no idea of how to do that.

"Hello?" he called out into the darkness. He didn't have Quinn's heightened ability to sense when powers drew near, but he had been around enough gods and monsters in his time to know the feeling of being watched by something powerful. He had also not been blind to the distinct pop of his eardrums, signifying he had entered a separate domain.

"How curious," a woman's voice reverberated around the abyss. "It has been quite some time since a mortal has tried to drown themselves in my river."

The speaker's voice was light and melodic, almost hypnotic. And yet, there was no mistaking the severe undertones. Whomever it belonged to was dangerous, Levy was certain.

Oath Breaker

"Well? Speak mortal. Or perhaps you are here as a sacrifice instead?"

"I'm sorry," Levy replied, trying to gather himself. He wasn't usually the one that dealt with speaking to the immortals. Where was Ashe when he needed her? Even Quinn would have been better suited for this. "I don't quite understand where I am."

"You walked into my river willingly yet have no idea where you are?" the woman laughed, her voice enchanting and full of mirth.

Oh yeah, Levy thought, *this one is very dangerous indeed.*

"Come then, and speak with me face to face," she said, amusement still lacing her voice.

There was a loud snap, followed by another pop of Levy's eardrums. Suddenly, the world began to spin rapidly. When his dizziness subsided, the abyss was gone.

Levy found himself standing in a mesmerizing courtyard, forged entirely from shimmering onyx, the very essence of the underworld resonating in every polished surface.

The air was thick with an ancient stillness, the expanse drained of color, replaced by a palette of infinite shades of grey and black, painting an eerie, otherworldly scene.

The ground beneath him was made of smooth, faintly reflective black tile, capturing distorted silhouettes of the domain's endless shadows. Each tile was etched with intricate patterns, arcane runes that pulsed faintly with silver light as if imbued with what was left of the Underworld's forgotten souls.

Towering columns of jagged onyx rose like dark sentinels, supporting archways carved with flowing forms of ancient, serpentine creatures, their eyes gleaming faintly with a cold, silvery glow.

Between the columns, sheer curtains of shadow wavered like veils, their inky blackness occasionally rippling as if alive, blurring the boundaries between where he stood and the deeper realms of death.

A vast fountain formed from solid black marble stood at the heart of the courtyard. A slow cascade of thick, tar-like liquid spilled out from the center, oozing with a rhythmic trickle. The liquid glimmered under the ghostly light, blacker than night, swirling in an endless spiral as it pooled into the shallow basin at its base.

Above, the sky was a void- no stars, no moon- only a vast, oppressive expanse of swirling greys, mirroring the endless depths of the Styx's waters. From time to time, faint, ephemeral shapes would drift across; the souls of the underworld, trapped in a silent, eternal march.

In the corners of the courtyard, dark, gnarled, and ancient trees rose like skeletal hands, their branches bare and twisted, stretching toward the sky as if in mourning. Their dark bark glinted like polished ebony. Thin, silver mist clung to their roots, weaving through the cracks in the onyx ground.

"It has been many years since a mortal has seen these halls." The voice from earlier spoke, snapping Levy out of his thoughts. "It has been many more since a mortal left here alive."

From the shadows emerged the goddess Styx, her presence slamming into Levy, who didn't need Quinn's finely tuned senses to know she was powerful indeed. She stood tall, towering above Levy with a regal, commanding grace.

Her long, chestnut hair cascaded in wild waves down her back, shimmering like dark water in the moonlight. Her eyes, deep and brown, gleamed with an intensity that seemed to peer into the very souls of those who dared meet her gaze.

There was power in her stare, one that spoke of ancient oaths and unbreakable bonds, the kind that could unravel even the bravest of hearts. Though beautiful, she was no gentle deity. Her features were sharp, her lips set in a hard line, and her movements deliberate, like the slow, inevitable flow of the river, she ruled.

She was clad in a dark, flowing gown that hugged her lithe form, woven from fabrics as black as the midnight sky and adorned with shimmering silver threads as if the stars themselves had been sewn into the cloth. The edges of the dress swirled like mist, alive with the shadows that clung to her.

A silver belt cinched her waist, carved with intricate designs of serpents and rivers, symbols of her dominion. Her arms, bare except for glittering silver bracers, held the quiet strength of someone who command both gods and mortals alike. The air around her crackled with latent energy, a dangerous force waiting to be unleashed.

Levy realized that she was not merely a goddess of the

Oath Breaker

Underworld; she was the embodiment of its unforgiving might—beautiful, yes, but in the same way a storm is beautiful, with terrible power lurking just beneath the surface.

It was this power that left Levy feeling shaken to his core. He blanched in her presence, faltering back a step. The goddess' eyes locked onto him, a predatory smile creeping slowly across her face.

"I can smell your fear, hero. I thought you were supposed to be the brave one. No wonder she chose your friend."

As her words washed over him, the fear that had found him in her presence faded as quickly as it had come. A wide smile split Levy's face then, fueled by both humor and a more primal side of him, rage.

Styx seemed puzzled by his sudden change in demeanor.

"You find humor in being rejected?" A dangerous glint lit her eye.

Levy couldn't help but find it amusing. "After millennia upon millennia of existence, every immortal I meet seems fixated on the same trivial detail of my life."

He stepped forward, forcing himself to relax as he faced the goddess directly. "Is immortality so devoid of pleasure that the love life of a single man is the height of your interest? Or perhaps you're showing interest yourself?"

The goddess blinked before loosing a hearty laugh, her voice rich and melodic, with an allure that seemed to echo through the air like a tempting song. Levy swallowed; Styx was dangerous indeed.

"I like you, boy." She said, all previous threats gone from her posture. "Not many mortals have a spine steel enough to sass me. Perhaps I will give you my blessing after all. I assume that is why you are here?"

Levy nodded, all humor fading from him.

"As I am now, I won't be able to help my friends, let alone humanity, against Zeus. I need more."

Styx looked deep into his eye as if reading his very soul.

"Is that need for power not what got you to where you are now?"

A chill crept up Levy's neck, the cold fingers of shame embracing him.

"It's different this time. Before, I was determined to be the hero.

To put the world on my back and carry humanity forward. I wanted the recognition. I was selfish."

"And now?"

"Now, I simply wish to be able to stand side by side with Quinn and Ashe and face the threat together. I let my desires consume me, and when it didn't go my way, I lost myself. That will not happen again."

"I wonder about that."

Styx stepped up to him, cupping his chin and lifting his face so that his eye met hers, her essence swirling within them as if searching for something.

"Very well." She released him, raising her hand. You wish for the same boon I granted Achilles so many years ago. Prove to me you are worth it."

Her pale hand rose, and with it, the air shimmered. Slowly, a portal formed before him, swirling with dark, watery light. Beyond it, he could see Quinn standing with his back to him among a field of shattered corpses.

For a moment, his friend stiffened and began to turn as if sensing the portal's presence. But before he could, his attention was pulled back to Hades as the god said something with an ugly sneer.

"Do you understand mortal? I offer you a chance few would ever receive. You will possess the strength of Achilles, his power, his invulnerability. All it will cost is a single act. One life. A small price for such greatness."

"One life?" Levy asked, horror dawning on him as he began to understand what she was asking.

"All you must do," Styx continued. "Is plunge your blade through the portal and into his back. Do this, and Achilles' power is yours." She paused, her eyes gleaming as if savoring the weight of the moment. "But should you fail, your soul will join the countless others in my waters."

Levy stared at the portal, heart thundering in his chest. This was not how this was supposed to go. Quinn, who had fought for him in front of the others, bled for him, trusted him when he damn well did not deserve it.

The blade in his hand felt heavier than ever. He wanted this power desperately so that he could stand against the Olympians and make up for his mistakes. He had sworn to his friends, the council, and the people that he would not make the same mistakes as before in pursuit of power. Yet now, if he did not do this, his soul would be sacrificed to the churning depths of the Styx.

"It is a simple choice," Styx said, her voice like a serpent coiling around his thoughts. "You seek power. You wish to be invincible, yes? Then act.

"Only the strong deserve such gifts. And who will know? The Underworld is a dangerous place. You will return with the sad news of your friend's demise while fighting the god of death, and in return, you can stand toe to toe with the Olympians."

He could feel her eyes boring into him, the pressure mounting with each passing second. The portal flickered. The image of Quinn was clear as day. His hand tightened around the hilt of his sword. He could step through, end it with a single strike, and become everything he ever wanted to be.

But the thought twisted in his mind. Was this power worth the price? Could he truly go back on his word again, even if it was for the sake of humanity?

"You hesitate." Styx's voice was colder now, sharper. "Do not pretend you are above this. The world is not kind to the weak, and neither am I. Do it. Or are you not as strong as you believe?"

His hand trembled, the sword wavering in his grip. He took a step towards the portal and then stopped, his breath catching in his throat. The river Styx bubbled and churned somewhere off in the distance, where he knew the souls of the damned writhed just beneath its corrosive surface; their faces twisted in silent agony. It was the fate she had promised him if he failed.

Something stirred within him then—a defiance, a rejection of the choice she laid before him. His gaze flickered back to the goddess.

Her lips curled in a knowing smile. She was pushing him, daring him to give into the darkness of his past. He blew air from his nose in a forceful sigh before sheathing his blade and facing her again.

"I won't do it," his voice was quiet yet firm. He stepped back from the portal, readying himself for the inevitable. "No power is worth this. Not even if it costs me my soul."

For a moment, there was silence. Styx's smile faded, replaced by something more unreadable. Then, a low chuckle escaped her lips, dark and melodic, like the current of her river. And suddenly, he understood. She didn't want him to succeed—not in the way she had made it seem. The real test was not striking down Quinn. It was refusing.

"Very good," she said softly, the portal behind him dissolving into nothingness. "You have passed."

Levy blinked, his heart still racing, unsure of what had just happened.

"You did not truly think I desired you to betray him, did you?" Styx's voice dripped with amusement. "The power of Achilles is not given to the treacherous. It is a gift reserved for those strong enough to resist their basest instincts."

As she spoke, a strange warmth flowed through him, the aches and pains of his journey fading away. He felt different. Stronger, invincible, as though his skin had become a shield unto itself.

"Remember this," Styx said, her eyes locking onto his as the realm around them began to fade, along with herself. "True strength lies not in the blade you wield but in the choices you make.

"Stay true to yourself, and this power shall never abandon you. Lose your way, as poor, sweet Achilles did, and watch your world crumble. Go now, and bear my gift well."

Her words trailed off as she finished speaking, her figure dissolving into the shadows of the underworld, leaving Levy standing alone on the banks of where he had first stepped foot in the river, the weight of the goddess' words settling upon him like a cloak.

Oath Breaker

Chapter 4
Ashe

"When will Quinn and Levy retuuuuurn?"

Ashe, Mallory, and Andra entered the courtyard, the air greeting them with a delicate sweetness carried by the abundance of blooming flowers. If their world weren't crashing in around them any day now, Ashe may have actually felt at peace here.

The sun hung low, casting a soft, golden glow that kissed every petal and leaf. Along the stone path beneath their feet, vines thick with purple wisteria draped lazily over an old wooden trellis, swaying gently with the calm breeze. The trio's footsteps were hushed, their soles pressing against the cobblestones warmed by the day's lingering heat.

On either side of the path, a rainbow of flowers painted the landscape: beds of marigolds the color of ripe oranges, peonies heavy with blossoms in soft blush pinks, and tall sunflowers reaching toward the sky in shades of deep saffron. The air was filled with the hum of bees weaving between clusters of lavender and foxglove, their wings shimmering in the golden light.

"Any day now, I suspect," Ashe replied, just as she had every day before in response to Mallory's persistent questioning. In truth, she had no real idea how much longer they would be gone. She knew the basics of their mission to the Underworld, but the details—especially the timing—remained uncertain.

They had all hoped it would be as simple as opening a portal, taking a quick swim, and returning just as swiftly. By now, they understood all too well—nothing ever went as planned when the Olympians were involved.

"That's what you said yesterday, the day before that, and the day before that!" Mallory pouted, pushing out her lower lip to obscene proportions.

"And it is likely what she will say tomorrow when you inevitably ask again." Andra smiled, her eyes lingering on a cluster of delicate lilies, their ivory petals tinged with pale gold as if they had soaked in the last rays of the sun.

She breathed deeply, savoring the heady fragrance of the roses, lush and velvety, lining the courtyard's edge in a wild array of crimson and burgundy. Horacio, her black and white Drakon, followed along behind her, nipping at any of the bees that came too close. He had grown large enough in the past few months that he could no longer fit wrapped around her shoulders.

"I know, I know, I'm sorry. I just get anxious, not knowing what's going on." Mallory sighed as she let her fingers trail over the tops of the blooms as they passed.

She loved brushing the velvety soft petals and the feathery fronds of ferns, feeling the pulse of life within the garden. The wind rustled through the leaves of nearby magnolia trees, their enormous white blossoms gleaming like stars in the twilight.

"Honestly, I just miss them when they aren't here, and I worry for their safety with the Olympians out for blood."

"Them?" Ashe asked, quirking an eyebrow.

She had seen how Mallory's eyes stayed glued to Levy up until the moment he and Quinn had gone on their secret mission. Though she assured Ashe it was to keep an eye on him should he revert to his old ways.

Yet there was no mistaking the giggles that passed her lips as they talked or the not-so-casual way she played with her hair while she watched him spar when she thought nobody else was looking.

Mallory stopped in her tracks, a warm red flushing her cheeks. "That's not what I meant. I mean, obviously, both of them. We need all the help we can get if we're going to defeat the gods. Besides, Quinn is all alone with him. What if he decides to turn on us again, and nobody is there to watch his back?"

"I assure you, Quinn is more than capable of looking out for himself." Andra grinned, sneaking up behind Mallory and jabbing her in the ribs. "You just miss watching Levy work out with his shirt off."

Mallory choked on the air, trying and failing to speak a thousand different protests at once. "It's not like thaaaaat," she insisted, once again sticking out her lower lip and throwing a pleading look towards Ashe. "He is the last man I would ever want after what he did to you."

Ashe smiled, enjoying this fleeting moment of peace. "It's okay if you have feelings for him, Mallory. I know him better than almost anybody. I'd argue even better than Quinn. He has a good heart despite everything he has done. I understand feeling conflicted, but with everything that is to come, nobody would shame you for finding what happiness you can."

"You truly believe in him, in his change of heart, after everything he has put both of our people through?" Andra asked, stopping her walk and turning a serious eye on Ashe.

Ashe paused by a cluster of violets, the deep purple blooms almost glowing in the fading light. In the distance, a fountain murmured softly, the sound of water bubbling and cascading down stone tiers, adding a sense of calm to the already serene setting.

"What Levy did cannot be so easily forgiven by most, and I understand that. More importantly, however, he understands that."

Ashe reached out, tucking an errant strand of Andra's prismatic hair behind her ear. Andra's eyes met hers, and Ashe was once again struck by the mix of hope, caution, and anger that was always at war behind the eyes of this girl who was forced to grow up too fast.

The recent loss of Nes still ate at her, yet she shouldered the burden of grief and led her people extraordinarily well.

"I understand that we are recent allies, so if you're unsure about taking my word for it, listen to Quinn's. He put his life on the line for him."

Andra let a look of pleading enter her eyes, still not breaking their stare. "It's BECAUSE I know Quinn so well that I want your opinion on it. Quinn is a good man, but his heart is soft. He wants to see the best in everybody, especially those he loves."

"And you think I'm different?" Ashe asked, the corner of her mouth rising slightly.

"I think you're logical and able to put your thoughts ahead of your feelings in ways Quinn cannot. And that is not a dig at him. I think that trait is beautiful. But that is also a trait he shared with Nes," her eyes glistened as she spoke, her voice carrying the faintest quiver.

"And he died because of it. We are already balancing on the edge of destruction, and the last thing we need is to implode because of a betrayal that could have been avoided."

Ashe smiled, pulling the smaller girl into a warm embrace. She held her until Andra's shaking subsided, stroking her hair. Every time Ashe spoke with the leader of the Abyssillian people, she was blown away by her wisdom and strength.

"There is nothing to fear with Levy. He recognizes his mistakes and will work tirelessly to rectify the damage he has caused. He and Quinn will come back stronger than they were when they left and give us an advantage against the Olympians they won't see coming.

"But should he falter again, you have my word that Quinn and I will not allow him to destroy the progress we have made here. This I swear to you."

A sudden force slammed into the side of them as Mallory wrapped her arms around them both, adding her own warmth to the hug, threatening to topple the three to the ground.

"And don't forget, as your second, I have just as much reason to watch his every move as well, and I will be keeping a very close eye on him. One step out of line, and he'll be getting the Mallory Pow-Pow Special," she said, holding up her two fists.

Andra smirked, disentangling herself from their embrace. "The Pow-Pow special, huh? Is that what you call your private sparring sessions?"

Mallory's face flushed beet red. "ANDRAAAA STOOOOP! IT'S NOT LIKE THAT! Ashe, tell her it's not like that!"

"Andra, it's not like that," Ashe confirmed. "I'm sure there is a happy ending after her Pow-Pow Special."

"ASHE!" Mallory wailed, her face turning an even brighter red.

Oath Breaker

"Et tu, Bruté? I cannot believe this betrayal."

Ashe couldn't help but laugh as her friends continued their verbal sparring behind her, their banter light but familiar. The courtyard was alive with the scent of blooming flowers and the soft hum of nature, a tranquil escape from the chaos looming on the horizon. She closed her eyes for a moment, letting the sun's warmth bathe her face, soaking in this fleeting moment of peace.

But deep down, she knew better. Her dreams had already shown her what was to come, vivid images of devastation and the weight of Fate pressing heavily on her shoulders. The world would soon come crashing down around them, and this serenity would be little more than a memory.

For now, though, she allowed herself to stay in the present, surrounded by laughter, sunlight, and the faint hope that they could hold onto this a little longer.

"Ashe," Lend's voice cut into her thoughts, shattering the tranquility around her. He looked out of breath, his dark green hair tousled by the wind as he sprinted to find her. "We have a visitor at the gates. You need to come right away."

"Who is it?"

"Cyrus."

Ashe's eyes widened. "Andra…"

But she had already taken off at a dead sprint, Horacio keeping pace behind her, roaring with their shared rage.

Chapter 5
Quinn

Quinn stood amongst the field littered with broken bodies and shattered bones, the undead faces frozen in twisted agony or whatever was left of them. Ichor soaked the barren ground, pooling in the cracks of the earth like golden rivers.

The air was heavy and thick with the stench of death and the ever-present gloom of the Underworld. Even the sky, if one could call it that, was a swirling mass of ashen clouds, casting its eternal twilight over the barren, grey land.

Quinn stood at the center, breathing heavily, his hands clenching his blade tightly. His body was bruised and battered, but he had triumphed over Hades' initial attack. Around him, the slain forces of the Underworld lay shattered remnants of his ferocity. The silence that followed the massacre was deafening, oppressive.

A cold, palpable energy surged behind him, more powerful than anything he had felt in the fight. It was raw, ancient, and filled with malice. His muscles tensed, instinct driving him to turn, to face whatever new threat loomed at his back, but before he could react, the rough voice of Hades cut through the silence like a blade.

"Impressive, Quinn. But tell me, did you tire yourself out with the small ones, or is there more fight left in you?"

The words slithered into his mind, mocking yet drenched with the kind of confidence only a god could possess. Quinn remained still, noting the foreign energy behind him fade as quickly as it had appeared, slipping back into the void from which it had come.

"The energy within me is primal, powerful. Far more powerful than the paltry essence of a god."

Though that was true, and Quinn knew with enough time spent training, he could potentially outmatch an immortal, his words now were nothing more than bluff, meant only to rile Hades up and hopefully keep him off balance.

To his satisfaction, Hades snarled, bearing his pointed teeth. Though Quinn still had the embers of his essence stoked within him, his body was exhausted, and he wasn't sure how much more he could keep up against the onslaught of the god of Death.

Hades extended his arm, his dark cloak flowing like smoke. His eyes glowed faintly in the dim light, sharp and unforgiving. In his hand, his black bident coalesced from shadows. The weapon's aura pulsed as if it was alive, hungry for blood.

"You've made quite the mess," Hades remarked, a smirk pulling at the corners of his lips. "Shall we clean it up together?"

Without another word, Quinn pulled on the reserves of his smoldering energy, igniting his body once more with swirling chaos. Dark tendrils of energy spiraled around him, forming another cloak that flickered like an erratic flame. He extended his blade out in front of him, the edge of the weapon crackling.

The two stood at a distance, their energy reaching out and filling the space between them. Then, in a blur, Hades lunged forward, his shadowy bident aimed at Quinn's chest. Metal clashed against metal with a deafening ring. Quinn parried, the force of Hades' strike sending a shockwave through the field of corpses.

Energy flared from Quinn's blade, a searing pulse that exploded outwards, slamming into Hades. But the god of the Underworld only laughed, stepping back, his eyes gleaming with anticipation. Each strike of Quinn's blade sent arcs of darkness spiraling outwards, tearing through the earth, a volatile extension of his will.

Hades moved like a shadow, his every motion fluid, effortless. His strikes calculated and precise. For every blow Quinn landed, Hades returned it with greater force, their weapons sparking with divine fury. Neither relented, neither gave ground, on the field of corpses that had become their stage, god and mortal dancing the steps of battle.

As the seconds turned into minutes, Quinn's breathing grew heavier, and the chaotic energy that had once surged around him began to flicker and dim. With each exchange, Quinn felt the tides of battle shift in Hades' favor. The god's strikes became more precise and punishing, testing Quinn's endurance limits. Yet, even as fatigue began to creep in, Quinn refused to yield.

He ducked beneath a sweeping strike, retaliating with a thrust aimed at Hades' side. The blade, infused with his chaotic energy, bit deep into the god's flesh, leaving a wound that pulsed with an unnatural light, followed by a spurt of pure Olympian ichor.

Hades staggered slightly, a flicker of surprise crossing his face. For a moment, respect flashed in his eyes, admiration for the mortal who dared to challenge him in his own domain.

But that flicker was fleeting. Quinn pressed forward, unleashing a flurry of attacks, each more desperate than the last. Hades met him with equal ferocity, their weapons clashing, sending shockwaves rippling across the field. Quinn fought like a tempest, drawing on every ounce of his strength, but Hades was an ancient, relentless storm of his own.

The longer the battle raged, Quinn felt his energy draining, the essence he commanded slipping through his fingers like sand.

Please, Levy, I can't do this on my own. Please be okay.

Hades capitalized on every moment of weakness, pushing Quinn back, forcing him to the edge of exhaustion. With each strike, the Olympian seemed to grow stronger, the shadows around him thickening, swirling like a dark mist.

Suddenly, Quinn felt a bone crunch under his next step, causing his foot to slide on the uneven ground. As Quinn faltered, Hades seized his opportunity. With a swift and powerful motion, he called forth the energy that thrummed with the weight of ages, gathering it between the two prongs of his bident.

"You have fought valiantly, mortal. More valiantly than any of the scum that has come before you." Hades taunted, his voice echoing with thunderous resonance. "But this is where your defiance ends!"

In one fluid motion, Hades unleashed the energy in a

devastating arc. A dark wave sliced through the air with terrifying speed. Quinn barely had time to react as the force struck him like a battering ram, the impact sending him sprawling across the battlefield and through the long grasses of Asphodel. Had it not been for the cloak around him, blunting as much of the impact as it possibly could, he would have died upon the first impact.

As it was, he tumbled through the air, the world blurring around him, until he crashed violently against the ghostly gates of Elysium. The ancient doors groaned under the weight of his body, splintering as he came to a jarring stop.

Dazed, Quinn looked up to see the ethereal light of the Elysian fields glimmering just beyond the gates, a stark contrast to the dead landscape of the rest of the Underworld.

Even more surprising was the shimmering forms of the army that stood massed on the other side. And standing at the head of the company were two faces Quinn thought he would never see again. As he begrudgingly pushed himself back onto his feet, readying himself for one more stand against Death, the figure with the overly large ears yelled, "CHARGE!"

Chapter 6
Ashe

Ashe burst from the courtyard, the scent of crushed blossoms still clinging to her skin. It had only been moments ago that she, Mallory, and Andra had been walking in relative peace among the gardens, the afternoon sun casting a golden light across the rows of newly planted flowers.

The vibrant colors had been a rare comfort in a world still engulfed in chaos. According to Mallory, Andra had been quieter than usual since Nes' death, her grief barely masked beneath her surface calm.

Though new allies, they shared a common bond with Quinn, and Ashe had taken a liking to his younger protégé. As a favor to him and their budding friendship, Ashe had been keeping a close eye on Andra, sensing the storm within her younger companion.

When the news of Cyrus' arrival reached them, it was as though something coiled tightly inside Andra had snapped. Without a word, she had taken off, sprinting for the town gates, leaving Ashe and Mallory standing amidst the flowers, stunned for only a heartbeat before instinct took over.

Now, Ashe was running full tilt through the streets of Stormhaven, her mind racing almost as fast as her feet. The power of Fate within had shown her so many images, all of which flashed through her mind constantly, at a maddening pace. In many of them stood Cyrus.

Ashe knew he had an important role to play in what was to come, but what role that was relied on far too many variables for her to be sure so early into the final confrontation with the Olympians. In some, he was necessary, and in others...Ashe shuddered at the thought.

The town had changed so much in such a short time. Rebuilt stone walls rose strong and proud where rubble had once lain. The air was thick with the smell of fresh timber and the metallic tang of iron from the blacksmiths working hard to reforge what had been broken. Warriors trained in open yards, their grunts and clash of weapons filling the air as they honed their skills, preparing for the fight to come.

As Ashe ran past them, a few heads turned, and whispers followed. She was no stranger to attention. After her return from the realm of Fate's Tower, she had become one of the most influential figures in Stormhaven. With the power of Fate now residing in her, many believed their fate, as well as the fate of the world, rested entirely upon her shoulders. It sickened her how not far off they were.

People stepped aside as she passed, recognizing the urgency in her stride and how her jaw was set in determination. But there was more than just wary anticipation in their eyes as they watched her. There was respect and perhaps even a flicker of hope. She had a duty to these people and to all of Humanity. She would not let them down, no matter what it took.

Hurry back to me, Quinn, she thought as she ran. *I can't do this without you at my side.*

She caught glimpses of the townspeople's daily lives as she sprinted past. A baker, covered in flour, stood at the doorway of her shop, gazing out as the scent of freshly baked bread mixed with the sharper smells of the street.

A woman in the marketplace cradled a basket of fruit, her eyes following Ashe's every move. A child, no more than five of six, tugged at his father's sleeve, pointing at Ashe with wide, admiring eyes. A part of Ashe warmed inside, remembering all the times

Quinn looked at her that exact same way as they grew up together.

Fuck she missed him. The town was returning to life, but she knew it was built on fragile foundations and perhaps borrowed time if some of the futures Fate had shown her were to be believed. One misstep could undo everything that they had fought for.

Ashe's heart pounded in her chest, both from the sprint and the weight of what lay ahead. It wasn't that she was of shape, but rather the strain the power of Fate put on her body had started to make her feel as though she was unraveling at the seams as it burned through her. So much power was not meant to be contained in a body that was not fully immortal.

She knew she had to reach Andra before the ruler of the Abyssillians did something she couldn't take back. Grief could make a person reckless. Ashe knew that all too well.

She had seen it consume others, had watched it twist even the best of people into something unrecognizable. The town gates loomed ahead, tall and imposing against a clear sky, and that's when she saw them.

Andra stood just outside the entrance, her posture tense and unyielding, a long, silver blade clutched tightly in her hand. Horacio crouched at her side. The Drakon had grown into a formidable creature, now the size of a large tiger, and his scaled hide shimmered like obsidian in the sunlight. He snarled low, his keen eyes trained on the man standing across from them. Cyrus.

Ashe's breath caught at the sight of him. Cyrus looked entirely too comfortable for someone who had walked into enemy territory. His light brown hair was ruffled by the breeze, and his lips curled into a smile as if this entire confrontation was a game to him. The scythe of Demeter, the weapon Nes had died trying to secure, was strapped to the former Master's back, its divinity seeming to have taken all of the age lines from Cyrus' face.

His light brown eyes shone with amusement. His hands rested casually at his sides, but Ashe didn't trust the nonchalance. There was always a calculation behind his actions, a reason for everything. Mallory had warned her of that.

"Andra!" Ashe called, closing the distance between them, though she could tell by the rigidity in Andra's body and the wild gleam in her eyes that the younger woman had no intention of backing down. She was trembling, not from fear, but from the raw, unchecked anger that seethed inside her.

Cyrus had taken Nes from her—ripped him away without remorse—and now he had the audacity to stand here, amused, as if he hadn't shattered her world.

"Andra, listen to me," Ashe said, reaching for her shoulder. Her fingers pressed into Andra's arm, firm but gentle, trying to ground her in the moment. "You can't do this. Not yet."

The girl turned slightly, just enough for Ashe to see the tear-streaked fury in her eyes before a wild strand of pearlescent hair fell in front of them.

"He killed him, Ashe," she hissed. "Nes is gone, and he's just standing there, laughing."

Cyrus tilted his head, clearly entertained by the exchange. "I wasn't aware I was such a topic of importance. But I am here for a conversation, not a fight. If a fight is what I had wanted, I would not be standing here without my weapon drawn."

Ashe's golden eyes narrowed, her voice sharp as ice. "You don't get to speak so casually after what you've done."

Cyrus raised a hand in mock surrender, his grin unfaltering. "Sacrifices must sometimes be made for the world to continue as it must. And the boy was such an eager volunteer.

"However, I am only here to talk, nothing more. Though I must admit, the welcome has been warmer than expected." His voice was still smooth, his tone gravelly, despite the circumstances.

Ashe ignored him for the moment, turning back to Andra, whose fists were clenched tight, knuckles white. "I know you want to make him pay. I know it feels like nothing will ever be enough until you do. But this is not the time. If you strike him down now, we might never know why he's here."

Visions flashed by her eyes in rapid succession. Fate showing her all the many outcomes this visit could lead to. Though she would love nothing more than to loose Andra upon this arrogant man, one thing was certain to her; his survival through this meeting was important. Their chances of success went to zero should he die here.

"We need answers, Andra. Not blood. Not yet."

Andra's chest heaved, her breath coming in ragged gasps. For a long, agonizing moment, she didn't move. Horacio's growl deepened, his tail lashing the ground in agitation, kicking up dirt and leaving deep gouges in the earth. Then, with a shaky exhale, Andra's fists loosened, though her gaze never wavered from Cyrus.

Venom lacing every word, she said, "By the time this is over, I swear I'll feed you to my Drakon—every last piece of you. And when you're nothing but the shit he leaves behind, your only legacy will be as fertilizer…though I doubt anything worth looking at will grow from it."

Ashe exhaled in quiet relief, but she wasn't done. She shifted her stance, placing herself slightly between Andra and Cyrus, her expression hardening as she fixed the former Master with a cold, unflinching stare.

"You have five minutes to say what you came here to say. After that, I suggest you leave. And if I have even the slightest inclination you are lying about anything, I will personally see to it that you do not leave here at all."

She allowed an aura of golden fire to envelope her, the scorching heat directed at Cyrus, a warning to back her threat.

Cyrus chuckled, but there was a dangerous glint in his eye. "Fair enough. Though I think you will find what I have to say…enlightening."

"Then say it and be gone."

Cyrus stood with an air of supreme confidence, his smirk never faltering as he glanced between Ashe and Andra. The tension in the air was palpable, and though he seemed at ease, Ashe knew better. Every word from him was calculated, every gesture intended to provoke a reaction.

"You're both wondering something," Cyrus began, his voice smooth. He let the silence stretch just long enough to make the next words sink in.

"Why hasn't Zeus broken through what remains of that precious barrier of yours yet? Why hasn't he wiped Stormhaven, and all of you with it, off the map?"

Ashe's expression remained impassive, her eyes narrowed, giving nothing away. She would not allow him the satisfaction of knowing how close his guess was to the truth. Beside her, Andra shifted, her fingers twitching as if aching to reach once more for her blade, but Ashe kept her focus steady.

Oath Breaker

When neither of them responded, Cyrus continued, his voice dripping with arrogance. "Ah, the silence of denial. But you know it is true, don't you? It does not take a genius to figure out that Zeus could crush this place at any moment. And yet...he hasn't."

Cyrus stepped forward just enough to make his presence feel heavier. Horacio let out a deep growl, but Andra laid a calming hand on the Drakon's side, likely out of pure instinct.

"The reason," Cyrus continued, "is quite simple. Zeus wants something. Something we Masters had locked away a long time ago deep inside the northern vaults—the same ones where young Levy found Hades' little trinket."

His eyes flicked to Ashe, gauging her reaction at the mention of the Orb and of Levy. "It is not just any item, though. It is something far more important. An artifact with a quite tragic history. And it is tragedy that breeds unwavering strength. With it in his possession, Zeus can ensure that humanity will never rise against the gods again. Ever."

The air felt colder as his words sank in. Ashe's eyes narrowed further, but her thoughts were racing. An item with a powerful, tragic past. As if in response to this new information, the Fate within her began to show her exactly what would happen with this new item introduced into the equation, should it fall into Zeus' hands. But why would Cyrus warn them of this?

Cyrus smiled, seeing the weight of what he had told them take hold. "Aphrodite will soon be on her way to the vaults. Now that the barrier is as weakened as it is, it is easy for an Olympian to slip through. And Zeus trusts her far more than many of his other allies. She is...persuasive."

He flashed her a knowing grin. "But I didn't come here just to gloat. I came to warn you. That item cannot—*must not*—fall into Zeus' hands. With it, he will become unstoppable."

Ashe's skepticism was clear in the way she crossed her arms, her gaze never leaving Cyrus. "Why would you warn us about this, Cyrus? You betrayed Nes. You stole the Scythe of Demeter. You have done everything within your power to support Zeus. And now you expect us to believe you've been on *our* side all along?"

Andra's breath hitched at the mention of Nes, her rage still barely contained. She glared at Cyrus with pure hatred. Ashe's steady presence was all that kept her from acting on it.

Cyrus chuckled, shaking his head as if the accusation amused him. "Oh, dear Ashe. You think this is as simple as picking sides? I am not loyal to Zeus. I am *using* him. You think I care about the gods' petty squabbles? I don't.

"I have been playing my own game from the beginning, and the death of Nes, tragic though it may seem, was necessary. Without it, I could never have earned Zeus' trust. Now I am deep enough in Olympus' ranks to undermine him from the inside."

His smile faded slightly, his expression hardening. "I am on the side of humanity, whether you believe me or not. Zeus wants absolute control, and this artifact will give him exactly that. If you do not stop Aphrodite, everything you have fought for will be lost."

Ashe studied him, her mind working through every angle, scanning every possible outcome Fate showed her until her head felt as though it would burst. Could he be telling the truth? It seemed too convenient, too perfect.

But the urgency in his words…it felt genuine. Still, trust was not something she could afford to give him, at least without running it by the others of the council first.

Not after everything that had happened.

"You expect us to believe you?" Ashe asked coldly. "After all the blood you've spilled?"

Cyrus shrugged, his smile returning. "Believe me or do not. That is up to you. But if you let Aphrodite retrieve that artifact, you will see soon enough how wrong you were."

Andra took a step forward, her hand drifting to the hilt of her blade once more. "You bastard," she spat. "You think you can just stand here and-"

Before Ashe could stop her, Andra lunged, her blade flashing in the sunlight. It was a swift, deadly strike aimed directly at Cyrus' chest.

But the blade passed through him as if he were nothing but mist.

Cyrus laughed, a sharp, mocking sound that echoed off the stone walls around them. "I am impressed you managed to hold off so long. You didn't really think I would be stupid enough to show up in person, did you?"

His form shimmered slightly, beginning to fade, a distant echo of the man standing in front of them. "I do enjoy these little meetings, though. So full of passion. Should the world fall under Olympian subjugation once again, I would miss that."

Ashe's eyes flared. Before Cyrus could vanish completely, she reached out with her mind, grasping the strands of Fate that wove through the world around her. With a flick of her hand, those invisible threads tightened around Cyrus, pulling him back and holding him in place.

His form flickered, and for the first time, his expression faltered. Fear twinkled in his eyes as he found himself trapped by the power Ashe wielded.

"You underestimate me, Cyrus," Ashe said quietly, her voice laced with warning. "You might have fooled Zeus, but don't forget that I control something far more ancient and dangerous than he does. If you ever show your face again—in person or otherwise—I *will* kill you."

Cyrus' expression twisted into something more serious, his smirk gone. He looked at Ashe, truly seeing her for what she was, perhaps for the first time.

Ashe held his gaze, unflinching. "Now, run back to Zeus like a good dog."

With a final flick of her hand, she released him, the strands of Fate unraveling. Cyrus' form immediately began to dissipate, the last traces of him fading into nothingness.

Andra stood beside her, her hand still clenched around her sword, her knuckles white. Horacio growled low, his eyes fixed on the spot where Cyrus had stood moments before. Ashe exhaled slowly, her gaze hard. "We need to move quickly. Aphrodite can't be allowed to beat us to those vaults."

She didn't respond at first, still seething, but finally, Andra nodded. "We'll make sure of it."

Ashe looked toward the sky as if she could see the cracks in the barrier she knew were slowly spreading. Her thoughts were already turning toward the battle ahead.

"Quinn and Levy will be home soon; I can see it. Once they arrive, we will determine our next steps. For now, let's inform the others what we've learned."

Together, they turned back towards Stormhaven, the sense of

dread tightening in Ashe as the heavy gates swung shut behind her, blocking out the sun.

Chapter 7
Talius

Talius lay in the dark, swallowed by the suffocating blackness that pressed down on him from all sides. The air was thick with the smell of wet earth and stone, every breath heavy in the dampness of the cold cavern. Water dripped somewhere near him, the sound echoing in his ears, faint but constant, like a heartbeat to the endless void around him.

He could feel the weight of the chains biting into his skin, pressing against bone. His wrists were bound, hooked even, his ankles shackled. His chest compressed beneath the weight of metal that seemed to draw more than just his physical strength.

It siphoned his essence, pulling from him in slow, agonizing waves, feeding into the very walls of Stormhaven. Every pulse of power that left him sent a fresh wave of burning pain through his body, like fire coursing through his veins.

Talius barely remembered who he was anymore. There were brief moments, fleeting flashes of clarity where he could grasp the edges of his mind, but they slipped away too quickly, leaving only agony in their wake.

His thoughts were fractured, like broken glass scattered across the floor of his mind. But there was one thought that persisted, that lingered even through the haze of torment: if this was the pain Athena had endured because of him—because of his betrayal—then he finally understood.

He understood why she had punished them all. Why her wrath had been so absolute when she broke free. If this was even a fraction of what she had suffered, then perhaps she had been merciful.

Talius' body convulsed as another surge of pain ripped through him, searing and all-encompassing. His muscles tensed, his breath caught in his throat, and he felt himself slipping away again, the agony pulling him under, dragging him into the abyss.

But then, just as he was about to lose himself completely, there was a voice. Soft, soothing, like a balm to the raw edges of his soul.

"Stay strong, Talius," the voice whispered, a woman's voice, familiar yet distant. "The time is almost upon us."

The pain receded, if only for a moment, enough for him to breathe again, enough for him to think. The voice soothed him and brought a brief reprieve to the endless suffering. He tried to focus, tried to grasp what remained of his fleeting clarity.

Who was she? Who was the one speaking to him? Deep down, in the farthest corners of his mind, he knew her. Hestia. But the knowledge was like a dream, elusive and fading as soon as he reached for it.

"You have one last purpose to fulfill," she continued, her tone gentle but firm. "For the sake of humanity."

Humanity. The word resonated with him, even through the fog of his pain. He had always fought for them and always believed in their potential and strength. Even if he had made mistakes in how he went about it.

When he betrayed Athena to power his walls or committed atrocities to bring the heroes of prophecy within his grasp—it had all been for them. But what was left of him now? Could he still serve, still save, when he was little more than a vessel for the power that protected Stormhaven?

The voice faded, and with it, the pain surged back. Talius clenched his jaws, his teeth long since having fallen out from the pressure of his bite, his body wracked with convulsions as the torment threatened to consume him once more. The brief reprieve Hestia had given him was gone, and all that remained was the burning, all-encompassing agony that had become his only constant.

The darkness closed in again, and with it, the clarity that had briefly touched him vanished, leaving him adrift in a sea of pain. And though he could no longer think clearly, no longer remember who he was, a single thought lingered in the back of his mind:

The time had almost come, at last.

Chapter 8
Levy

Levy stumbled onto the banks of the Styx, the murky waters behind him reflecting a faint sheen of the Underworld's oppressive atmosphere. His skin tingled as if alive with newfound power—the invulnerability Styx had bestowed upon him.

The sensation was unfamiliar and foreign, as if his very body struggled to grasp the weight of it. He rolled his shoulders, shaking off the disorientation of crossing between domains. His breaths came in uneven spurts, and as he steadied himself, he became acutely aware of the scene around him.

The air reeked of death and rotting flesh. Strewn about the ground were the remnants of Hades' army: twisted, half-rotten corpses, skeletal remains shattered into heaps, and the carcasses of hellhounds, their blood a sticky gold that seeped into the dirt.

The air felt heavy with the lingering essence of what had transpired. The metallic tang of blood, mixed with the stench of decay, assaulted Levy's senses. His boots squelched through the gore as he surveyed the battlefield.

Despite his attempts, he could not stop his racing heart as his panic began to rise. Quinn. Where was Quinn?

Scanning the area frantically, he locked onto a trail of destruction—smashed bones, shattered weapons, and deep furrows gouged into the trampled fields of grass, marking where someone had seemingly cut through the horde. Levy's heart leaped into his throat.

Quinn, it had to be. The trail led towards the gates of Elysium, distant but unmistakable, looming with an ethereal glow on the horizon.

He didn't waste another second. Ignoring the fatigue lingering in his limbs, Levy sprinted in the direction the trail led, his feet carrying him with newfound speed. The power of Achilles pulsed through his veins, a tingling, almost electrifying sensation, making him feel as if nothing could touch him.

The perfect shield for his friends, just as he intended. Styx's warning echoed in his mind. *Falter in your beliefs, and the power will fail. If that happens, there will be no saving you.*

It was good then that he had no intention to go back on his word. Quinn, Ashe, even Mallory, who had refused to leave his side since Quinn had brought him back within the fold. Her beautiful eyes squinted at him as though he were a magic trick she had been trying to figure out. He would protect them all, no matter the cost.

As he neared the gates, a low rumble reached his ears—distant at first but steadily growing. The unmistakable sounds of battle.

Levy narrowed his eyes, his vision sharpening against the haze. In the distance, beyond the gates, pale green hues of energy pulsed and flickered, illuminating the battlefield like ghostly fire. His pulse quickened as realization struck—he was witnessing the ongoing clash between the spirits of Elysium and Hades' undead legions. A war between the honored dead and the damned, raging just beyond his reach.

The gates loomed larger now, and the battlefield came into full view before them. In the heart of the chaos stood Hades, a familiar purple orb clutched in one hand. Even as his forces were struck down, the orb pulsed with dark light, and the fallen rose again, bones snapping back together, corpses dragging themselves upright.

But that wasn't what captured Levy's attention. His breath caught in his throat as he saw Quinn, ragged yet locked in combat with Hades, his form darting like a shadow, cloaked in the energy of Chaos. And Quinn was not alone. Two figures fought at his side— ghostly warriors, their forms shimmering within the pale light of

Brian Tripp

Elysium.

Levy's brow furrowed. They were familiar, yet he could not place them. One was smaller, with large ears and quick, precise movements. He looked young, as though he had died far too early in life. The other was a muscular warrior, his body lined with scars that seemed to glow faintly with each motion.

Levy felt a pang of jealousy twist in his chest. These warriors, these ghosts—whoever they were—fought alongside Quinn with perfect synchronicity. He had seen Quinn fight before, but never with such harmony. After all these wasted years on the wrong side of this fight, where did that leave him?

His fists clenched his disappointment in himself over the pang of jealousy souring in his gut. He shook his head, forcing the feeling down. Styx's warning crept back into his mind again, all the more potent.

One moment of weakness.

One moment of weakness and the power would fail him. That would not happen. Quinn needed him now, and that was what mattered.

Steeling himself, Levy charged into the battle. The first wave of undead came at him—a large group of rotting corpses, skeletal figures wielding rusted weapons. He met them head-on, smashing through them with ease. His fists were infused with his new strength. He shattered bone on contact, sending skulls and limbs flying. Yet, as he fought, he noted another effect of his new power.

The undead, numerous as they were, struck back. Blades, claws, and jagged bone-tipped weapons slashed at him, aiming to tear through his flesh. But levy barely felt them. He watched as weapons hit him, leaving long, deep gouges in his armor, the metal screeching and ripping under the force of their blows.

His skin remained untouched. The blades glanced off him as if his body were forged from steel, the power of Achilles rendering him untouchable. Not even the sharpest strike left a mark on his flesh.

He was invincible.

The realization hit him all at once. As he moved through the horde, their weapons clattered against his body with a hollow thud. A spear drove toward his chest, the point hurdling straight for his heart. He didn't flinch.

The spear's tip snapped on impact, splintering in two as if it had struck a wall of iron. Another warrior slashed his arm, but the blade only left a jagged tear in his armor, the flesh underneath unscathed.

Levy grinned, his confidence surging with every strike. He was unstoppable. He felt as if his very bones were forged from the same divine energy that now thrummed through his blood.

His movements became faster as he got more confident and more brutal. Each punch, each strike, shattered bones and ripped apart undead bodies with frightening ease. Their blows were useless, mere whispers against the impact of his strength.

With a fierce shout, Levy threw himself deeper into the fray, bludgeoning down the undead in his path. Each step brought him closer to Hades, the orb in the god's hand glowing even brighter. The power coursing around him was intoxicating, the taste of invincibility like a burning fire in his chest.

He was both a weapon and a shield now, a perfect Aegis. And he was ready to face down the god of Death.

Levy burst from the heart of the battle, leaving a whirl of dust in his wake as he locked eyes with Quinn. A flash of gratitude lit his friend's exhausted face.

His heart pounded at the sight of the towering figure ahead. Hades exuded a malice that was as ancient as it was overwhelming. As he drew closer, the young-looking ghostly warrior let loose a fierce snarl, telling Levy that his arrival was unwelcome.

"What the fuck is this guy doing here?" Sen spat, his eyes narrowing so far in disbelief they may as well have been shut.

And in a flash, Levy remembered where he had seen his face before. The bitter memories of the past hung heavy between them, of a time when Levy's hand had controlled the dark orb and Sen had fallen in battle under its cursed influence.

Quinn, ever the voice of reason, raised a hand to halt the tension. "Levy is with us. There's a story here, but it can wait. First, we need to bring Hades down."

Sen and Nes exchanged doubtful glances, but with Hades towering before them and his undead forced encroaching fast, there was little time to argue. Their resolve hardened, and in a moment of silent understanding, the four turned to face the Olympian once more.

Hade's chilling laughter cut through the battlefield. "Oh, how heartwarming. A reunion of flimsy alliances and forgotten betrayals. Simply enchanting."

He sneered, raising his hand, and a fresh wave of undead surged from the ground. His other hand gripped the orb, pulsing with an unnatural glow as he channeled his power into it.

The skeletal forms around him strengthened, their broken bones and tattered flesh reassembling with unnatural speed.

"Keep him occupied!" Quinn barked, his cloak of chaotic energy flaring as he swung his blade, cutting down two undead soldiers in a single blow. Nes and Sen flanked him, Sen's blade and Nes' axe dancing through the horde as they advanced.

Levy took a deep breath, feeling the power of Achilles pulsing through him once more, raw and unyielding. This was his chance to prove himself to Quinn, Sen and Nes, and himself. With a growl, he rushed forward, charging into the fray beside Quinn and pounding back the undead as they tried to block their path to Hades.

They were upon the god faster than should have been possible with the sheer number of bodies in their way. Hades barely had time to raise his arm before Quinn lunged, his blade arcing through the air. It was a brilliant move, one which awarded a direct hit. Hades staggered back, a deep gash marring his chest. Brighter than the brightest gold, Ichor cascaded from the wound, the god's eyes flashing with fury.

With Hades momentarily distracted, Levy saw his opening. He darted forward and drove his heel into Hades' hand, knocking the orb loose from his grip. The sphere hurtled into the air, spinning as it rose, its dark energy spiraling out in waves around it.

Sen and Nes didn't hesitate, leaping toward the orb.

"Mine!" Sen shouted.

In a blink, his hand closed around it, wrenching it free from the power Hades had poured into it. A shudder ran through the battlefield, and the undead army began to falter, their movements slowing as the energy holding them unraveled.

Hades roared in frustration, his eyes darting toward the orb as Sen and Nes worked together to sever the ties of energy he'd been feeding into it. In a moment of desperation, he lunged, his arms outstretched, fingers clawing through the air to reach the orb.

Levy intercepted him before he could reach it, stepping directly into Hades' path with an unyielding stance. He braced himself, then threw his first punch, the impact echoing across the field.

Hades reeled back, a flash of shock across his face. Levy wasn't sure, but he'd be willing to bet he was the first mortal to sucker punch a god. He pressed forward, each strike landing with unyielding force- a blend of Hestia's essence and the power of the Styx- driving Hades back with every blow.

The Olympian stumbled, ichor and fury mingling in his gaze, but Levy gave him no quarter. His fists flew in a relentless rhythm, years of frustration at the hands of the gods pouring off him. Each strike tore at Hades' defenses until the god's once proud figure was reduced to a beaten, bloody shadow of itself.

With the orb cut off from Hades' influence, the undead collapsed in waves, their bodies finally surrendering to the earth. The once chaotic battlefield became silent around them, save for his and Quinn's heavy breaths. With the horde no longer a threat, Quinn, Nes, and Sen regrouped around Levy, their eyes now fixed on Hades, who knelt, weakened and seething.

Quinn stepped forward, his shadowy cloak still flying around him in an invisible breeze, looking every bit the part of Primordial. "Your reign over the dead has come to an end, Hades."

Nes stepped forward as well, Hades' orb secured firmly in his grasp. His tone was laced with quiet fury. "You've treated us souls in the Underworld like playthings. No more." He met Hades' gaze with unwavering defiance. "From now on, the Underworld is under new management."

The warriors of Elysium around him roared their approval at his proclamation.

Hades' eyes, though dulled with pain, gleamed with hatred. "This isn't the end," he spat, his voice a dark promise. His trembling hand reached into the air, summoning a portal that rippled with a ghastly light.

Before they could react, he dragged himself through, his figure vanishing into the void with a final, haunting glare. The portal snapped shut, leaving the battlefield empty of his presence but heavy with the promise of retribution.

The silence that followed was electric. Slowly, Levy turned to face the others, his chest still heaving with adrenaline. Sen looked at him, a storm of emotions flickering across his face; pain, confusion, and perhaps the barest hint of grudging respect.

"Guess you weren't here to betray everyone this time," Sen muttered, his voice less sharp but still wary.

Levy met his gaze, giving a nod of understanding. "Not this time."

"Levy," Quinn broke into the loaded silence. "Didn't I just tell you earlier to stop punching your opponents?"

"Ah, give him a break Quinn. The guy just beat the shit out of an Olympian with nothing but his fists." Nes joined the group, a look of wary concern betraying the levity of his words.

Levy watched as Quinn caught up with his old friends, filling them in on everything that had transpired since their time in the Underworld. A small feeling of melancholy crept into his heart as he noticed the clear respect and comradery the three held for one another. He wondered if that would have been extended to him had he never lost his way.

He held his ground, aware of the cautious stares Sen and Nes cast his way as Quinn relayed Levy's journey: his regrets, his split from Ares, his decision to turn back towards humanity, and his choice to stand beside his friends once more.

Sen's gaze softened, though he remained wary, his voice clipped but respectful. "Seems you finally chose a side. Can't say I understand it, but I trust Quinn."

Nes nodded, his previously guarded expression tempered by something almost resembling relief. "You helped us turn the tide here, Levy. That's something I won't forget. But we have been outside Elysium's gates too long. It's time for us to return."

His hand brushed his chest lightly as if feeling the faintest flicker of life waning. Around him, the warriors of Elysium seemed to waver, their translucent forms fading, barely held together.

Then, to Levy's surprise, Nes stepped forward, holding out the orb of Hades. The dark sphere pulsed faintly with a new green energy, as opposed to the deep purple it had once been. He placed it into Levy's hands, his fingers lingering as if reluctant to release it.

"You already know how to use this," his voice firm and even.

"When Zeus finally comes, summon us. The warriors of Elysium will answer."

Levy nodded, his fingers curling around the orb, feeling its weight as if it were his own burden. There was a silent understanding in Nes' gaze, an unspoken warning, and a sliver of trust.

He looked at the scarred warrior, his voice barely more of a whisper. "Thank you. I won't let you down."

Nes took a step back, a faint smile playing on his lips. "See that you don't."

As the gates of Elysium flickered into view, green and grand against the drab "sky," the warriors began to fade, slipping back to their eternal realm. Levy watched as Nes and Sen lingered a moment longer, their faces etched with eternal wisdom, that which betrayed their youth.

A wisdom that only the dead might claim. Then they, too, stepped through, and the gates closed behind them with a thunderous finality.

Quinn exhaled a long breath and gave Levy a slap on the shoulder, a friendly grin breaking the tension. "Not bad for a supposed enemy of humanity."

"Ex-enemy of humanity, thank you very much." Levy couldn't help but chuckle, feeling a warmth he hadn't felt in what seemed like ages. "Guess there's hope for me yet, right?"

His friend's grin widened. "There is. Just try not to go rogue again. We don't have that many allies left to spare, and I'd hate to catch an uppercut from whatever kind of steel fists you're rocking now."

He glanced over the empty battlefield before reaching into the air and tearing open a portal. Behind it, Stormhaven waited, the distant spires of the Citadel a comforting sight.

"Come on," Quinn said, nodding toward the portal. "Time to go home."

Levy took a last look at the closed gates of Elysium, feeling the weight of his responsibility settling over him. But with Quinn and Ashe by his side and perhaps the slightest measure of faith from Sen and Nes, he felt stronger than he had in a long time.

Together, they stepped through, leaving the Underworld behind.

Chapter 9
Hades

The portal twisted open with a shudder, spitting Hades into the shadows of his own throne room. He crawled forward, hands grappling the cold, polished obsidian of the floor as he dragged himself from the gateway, his breaths labored and wheezing.

The scent of smoke and sulfur hung in the air, thicker here than anywhere else in his realm, mingling with the metallic taste of old blood that seemed permanently embedded in the stone. In every corner, torches flickered with blue-black flames, casting distorted shadows across his palace's ghastly, gothic splendor.

The throne room was cavernous, a sprawling expanse of onyx pillars stretching up to a domed ceiling painted with scenes of eternal suffering, just as Hades liked it. Overhead, engravings of lost souls writhing in torment seemed to move in the dark.

Gargantuan chains draped across the walls like vines in a twisted forest, interwoven with clusters of obsidian spikes. Hades' throne sat upon a raised platform of black marble, its surface veined with eerie streaks of scarlet and bone white. Carved into the throne were hundreds of faces, each mouth open in a silent scream, each set of eyes frozen in eternal horror.

Hades staggered to his feet, gritting his teeth against the dull throb of wounds that even a god could not easily heal. He stumbled forward, every step a battle against weakness as he made his way toward the throne. A dark, rank chill filled the air, and with every breath he drew, he tasted centuries-old rot. He sank into the carved throne with a guttural growl, his fingers digging into the stone arms as he glared into the shadows.

"Curse them…curse them all," he grumbled, his voice raw. "Quinn…Levy…all of them—the damn warriors of Elysium, those ungrateful wretches."

His mind churned with fury, each name becoming a sharpened weapon in his thoughts. "I will make sure they feel every torment this realm has to offer. I will tear their flesh and bind them in chains hotter than the sun itself, let them scream until they have no voices left. Until silence is the only mercy left to them."

He could already picture it: Quinn, struggling against fiery restraints that sank into bone and soul alike, his defiance eroded to dust. Levy clawing at his own flesh as endless lashes of darkness stripped away his pride, his dignity, his very being. Hades' gaze darkened further, a twisted smile curving his lips.

"And when their spirits are broken, I will cast them down into Tartarus, where even the damned fear to tread. There, they will learn what true eternity feels like."

A low, mocking chuckle slithered out from a dark corner of the throne room. Hades' eyes snapped to the sound, his hand instinctively curling into a fist. Out of the shadows, a pair of caramel-brown eyes gleamed, unblinking, watching him with an unsettling calm.

A figure emerged, smooth and silent, until Cyrus stood fully visible, his figure silhouetted against the dim torchlight, his eyes still locked onto Hades with a chilling intensity. Hades' heart gave an unexpected lurch, a primal flicker of unease jolting through him before he scolded himself, a sharp bark of laughter escaping his lips.

"Hah! Shaking at the sight of a once mortal man? Ridiculous," he muttered to himself, his gaze hardening. "What is it, Cyrus? Has my brother loosened your leash, or are you here to deliver a message like a good little pet?"

Cyrus merely inclined his head, a thin smile ghosting across his face. "Mortal? It seems to me that the mortals of the world seem to haunt even you. Tell me, how *are* Quinn and Levy?"

His voice held a mocking edge, and though he laughed again, the glint in his eyes remained void of amusement.

Hades bristled, the crackling torches seeming to dim. "What do you want, Cyrus? And be wise in how you answer, for trespassing here without invitation comes at a cost."

Unfazed, Cyrus' expression remained eerily calm. "Zeus is displeased," he said, his voice a sinister purr. "He has grown tired of your oversights and your failures. So, he sent me to correct them."

Hades let out a scoff, crossing his arms. "My brother sent you?" His laugh rumbled through the room, dripping with contempt. "The arrogance—that you should dole out my punishment."

But Cyrus only smiled, a wolfish gleam flashing in his eyes as he stepped closer, raising his hand. The room suddenly pulsed with thick and heavy energy that pinned Hades to his throne with crushing force.

Hades' eyes widened as he struggled, a glimmer of fear creeping into his gaze. The essence enveloping him felt unmistakably like Hera's, mixed with Ares'- sharp, potent, and filled with rage. But that was impossible. Hera and Ares were dead.

Cyrus tilted his head, his expression sharp and unforgiving. "Perhaps you should have considered Zeus' patience," he whispered, his voice dark as the shadows clinging to the walls. Reaching over his shoulder, he pulled a long, curved weapon from his back. The scythe of Demeter gleamed in the dim torchlight.

Hades' jaw clenched, his every instinct screaming at him to fight, but he was still too injured from his last battle, and the power around him held him firm. He could only watch, helpless, as Cyrus approached with a look of grim satisfaction.

"Don't worry, *Lord* Hades," Cyrus drawled, his tone mocking. He let the scythe hover just over the god's flesh. "It could be over quickly…"

Then he smiled widely, eyes narrowing. "But it won't."

With a slow, deliberate swing, Cyrus brought the scythe down, its blade slicing into Hades' flesh. A scream tore from Hades' throat, filling the vast expanse of the throne room, as the blade cut not just his body but his very essence.

His form flickered, weakened, fragments of his power flaking away like ash caught in the wind and siphoning into Cyrus. Every slice burned like fire and ice, shredding him from within, peeling away the god he was, and scattering his strength like leaves in a storm.

Cyrus leaned in close, his smile never faltering as he watched the agony twist across Hades' face. His voice dripped with mockery, smooth as poisoned honey. "So much for the mighty Lord of the Dead."

The throne room echoed with Hades' wails, his cries reverberating off the walls until, finally, the sounds ceased, cut off in an instant. The silence that followed was as deep as the grave.

Chapter 10
Ashe

In the depths of slumber, Ashe drifted, yet she was not truly lost. Even in this dismal place of shadows and dread, she knew this was no ordinary dream. Her heart sank as the unmistakable feeling of Fate's tendrils brushed against her mind, coaxing open her awareness with a sense of what might come to pass.

This haunting world of fire and ruin was the future that lay before her, or the one currently most likely. She stood rooted as the vision unfolded around her.

The world was ablaze everywhere, and all of it was drowning in furious, golden flames that licked the sky and curled around her. Ash rained down from above in torrents, coating her hair and skin, clinging to her lips and tongue.

It filled her mouth, carrying the bitter taste of destruction and failure, like swallowing despair itself. Around her, the ashes fell heavier, settling over the broken ground littered with the remains of those she had led- those she had hoped to save.

She tried to move, but her feet wouldn't budge, her body anchored in place as if bound by chains made from the very sorrow that gripped her heart. She looked around, desperate for signs of life. Yet all she saw were corpses, the fallen armies of humanity and Abyssillian alike, stacked in macabre heaps across the ravaged earth. *Familiar faces lay in the dust, eyes dull and lifeless, comrades and friends alike.*

And then there was Quinn.

Suspended above her, his body dangled like a lifeless marionette, a spear driven clean through his chest, the dark stain of blood streaming through the cracks in his armor. He did not breathe. His chest no longer rose, but his eyes, locked onto hers, seemed painfully alive.

His gaze bore into her, filled with a silent question and unspoken accusation: How could you let this happen?

Ashe staggered, pressing a hand to her heart as if to still its wild beat, but there was no stopping the panic that surged within her, clawing at her insides.

What had she done? Or, rather, what had she failed to do that had brought them to this?

A shudder ripped through her as her eyes landed on another figure. Levy, her steadfast, stubborn friend, was slumped on his knees nearby, his head resting some cruel distance away. She took a step back, recoiling from the reality painted so vividly before her.

This future clawed at her soul. She had thought herself ready to see the worst of her nightmares, but nothing could have prepared her for this.

A sinister glint caught her eye, flickering from within the golden flames. And then she saw them, those dreadful eyes. Cold, gleeful, and brimming with a wicked satisfaction. They watched her, pinned her in place with the cruelty of someone who knew exactly how much it would cost her to look upon this scene.

"You thought you could change it," came the voice, familiar in its contemptuous drawl. *It snaked through her mind, rich with venom.* *"But you are nothing, Weaver. This ruin is your future."*

Her hands shook, her body straining under the crushing weight of his words. She fought to breathe as despair wrapped around her lungs, her throat tight as she struggled for air.

"No," she whispered, her voice barely more than a broken breath. She could hear her pulse pounding, drumming like a death knell in her ears. *"No, I...I would never let this happen. Not like this."*

The laughter that answered was icy, a chilling mockery that seemed to echo through the flames and the ash-laden air. *"Oh, you can try,"* the voice hissed, taunting.

"But your fate was sealed long ago, and your theft of a power you cannot hope to contain will not change that. You can struggle and claw at every step, but it will still bring you here, and you will watch your world burn."

She could feel the power of Fate within her, coiling and twisting as if writhing in response to his words, wishing to break free. Panic churned inside her, desperation boiling over, and she reached for it, for that force that had always seemed so boundless, so beyond her full control.

But now, in her anguish, it responded with a terrifying intensity, rising within her, breaking free from the frail vessel she was. She could feel it tearing through her flesh, a torrent of pure, searing light bleeding from her skin.

As her body began to tremble, she recalled Clotho's distant words, long since spoken but never forgotten. *Sometimes, you must choose the best of the worst in the hopes that from the ashes, new light will rise.*

Had she been that light? Or had she simply been the best of the worst?

The realization came too late. The power surged, spiraling out of control, overwhelming her entirely. She could feel herself being torn apart, as if her very essence was unraveling, her mortal form unable to bear Fate's might. Light flooded the world, bright and relentless, consuming all she could see.

"No!" she screamed, her voice raw with agony, a desperate plea lost in the raging inferno.

That cold laughter rose once more, echoing through the blinding, all-consuming light. It lingered, triumphant, even as her scream faded, swallowed by the final shattering of her soul.

Ashe's body jolted awake, a violent gasp escaping her lips as she wrenched herself from the horror of that blazing, desolate world. Her heart thundered in her chest, beating so fast it felt as though it might tear free from her ribs.

She tried to steady her breath, but the vivid remnants of golden flames, twisted faces, and sinister laughter still clung to her mind. Everything seemed dark until she felt warmth grounding her. Strong hands gently cupped her shoulders, bringing her back to the here and now, pulling her away from that dreadful future.

"Easy, Ashe. It's just me," came a soft, familiar voice, rich and steady, spreading over her like a balm.

Her gaze lifted, her tear-filled eyes landing on Quinn. Sweet, beautiful Quinn finally returned from his journey to the Underworld. In the silvery light filtering through the narrow window, he looked almost ethereal, like a dream-made flesh. His raven-black hair fell messily across his brow, framing those crimson eyes that glowed with quiet strength and deep tenderness.

One corner of his mouth turned up in that soft, reassuring smile of his, and his hand moved slowly along her back in small, soothing circles, just as he always did when they lay tangled together, falling asleep in each other's arms.

She felt her heart steady, her pulse slowing beneath the gentle rhythm of his touch. But the pain of the vision lingered, and she felt a tear slip free, golden and shimmering, as it traced down her cheek. Quinn's gaze softened, and he reached out, catching the tear on his fingertip, a flicker of wonder crossing his face.

"I've missed you more than you will ever know," he murmured, his voice low and unsteady with feeling that wrapped itself around her. "Every hour, every breath, my heart was yours, Ashe. Even across the realms."

His words struck her, stirring an ache in her chest that only he could soothe. She felt her control splinter, and she flew forward, throwing her arms around him, pressing herself against him as though afraid he might vanish.

She slid into his lap, wrapping her arms around his neck, clinging to him with fierce desperation. The solid warmth of his body steadied her, chasing away the remnants of the nightmare, and she buried her face in his shoulder, breathing in his scent, the faint hints of cedar, of steel and leather, of *home*.

This was real. *He* was real.

Quinn stroked her hair, his fingers gliding through the tangled strands with a gentleness that nearly undid her. She could feel the steady rise and fall of his chest beneath her cheek, the familiar cadence of his breath. He whispered soft assurances, pressing a kiss to her neck as he held her close, grounding her back in the present, in him.

Finally, she pulled back just enough to look up at him, her eyes tracing his face as if memorizing every detail all over again. She brushed her fingers over his cheek, and unable to hold herself back, she leaned in and pressed her lips to his, firm and unyielding, savoring the taste of him.

The warmth and strength and sweetness that she had missed with a fierceness she could scarcely contain. His kiss was tender and unhurried, as though he was savoring the feel of her, grounding himself in her just as she did with him.

For a long, lingering moment, she stayed there, feeling his hand slide along her jaw, cradling her face as if she were something precious and irreplaceable. She pulled away just enough to look into his eyes, breathless, her thumb tracing his cheek.

"I couldn't lose you," she whispered, her voice raw and low. "I don't think I'd survive it, Quinn."

His gaze softened further, a mixture of love and fierce devotion lighting his crimson eyes. "You don't need to carry it all, Ashe. Not alone," he replied, his voice like a promise woven in the moonlight. "No matter where I am, no matter where you are, you'll have my strength. And I will always find my way back to you."

"Do you promise?" she whispered, though she already knew his answer.

His fingers traced gentle lines along her arm, his voice soft but unwavering. "I swear on all of my essence, now and for the rest of time, and whatever comes after, you will have me. All of me."

She sighed, sinking back into his chest, letting his warmth chase away the lingering shadows of Fate's haunting vision. She wanted only to be here, to feel him close and real.

Then his hand slipped under her chin, lifting her gaze back to his. His eyes softened as they searched hers.

"Now tell me," he murmured, his thumb brushing her cheek. "How long have you been crying golden tears?"

Chapter 11
Mallory

Under the twilight glow of Stormhaven's streets, the city's usual hum was layered with the distant murmur of townsfolk finishing up the day's work. Mallory, Andra, and Kael strolled side by side, each lost in thought as they took in the sight of the city's flickering lamps against the darkening sky. The recent revival of the Wastes weighed heavily on their minds, and their plans for what might come next hung in the air between them.

"We could send a group back." Kael tossed his bright red hair out of his eyes, fixing an intense gaze on Andra.

His voice brimmed with energy. Each word was charged with the fiery passion he brought to every battlefield. Mallory admired his talent for combat and his ability to lead a unit, though she found his political skills less impressive.

"Just enough to begin rebuilding Petram. Our people deserve something to return to when this is all over."

Mallory shook her head slowly, her eyes flicking from the cobbled streets up toward the city walls, where a familiar figure stood against the backdrop of a star-speckled sky.

"It's too soon. We can't spare anyone, not with Zeus still looming over us. We need every able-bodied person here for what's coming. If we win this war, Stormhaven can provide for us a little longer; long enough to begin again."

Kael's jaw tensed, his gaze hardening. "Even if Stormhaven opens its gates for us now, tensions will rise. Feeding so many of us will strain resources, and once the threat has passed, prejudices will return. They always do. The Abyssillians will be the first cast aside."

Andra's stride slowed as she turned to Kael, her voice carrying the steady resolve that earned her continued respect as a leader.

"You're right to be cautious, Kael, but you are wrong to assume we will be abandoned. Friends don't just protect each other in battle; they help each other heal. And we are among friends here. I understand what you're saying, truly, but strides cannot be made if we cling to the fears of the past."

Though Kael's eyes softened at her words, the line of tension across his brow remained. Andra gave him a small nod. "For now, I agree with Mallory. Sending a group of your soldiers back to Petram would be a mistake, but I won't ignore your wishes, either.

"We will send a small, handpicked group- no warriors, save for two for protection. Let them assess the land and see what can be salvaged. If there is even a chance of something good, it will be worth the effort."

Kael's stance eased, and he nodded his appreciation to Andra. "Thank you. It will mean much to all of our people, knowing that Petram isn't just a memory."

Mallory, silent for a moment, glanced up to where that same figure sat atop the walls, his face softened by a rare moment of vulnerability. Levy's gaze was trained upon the stars as if the vastness above held the answers to unspoken questions. Though she had been around him plenty by this point, Mallory still found herself caught off guard by the quiet strength of his body.

Andra's lips curved in a knowing smile as she observed Mallory's lingering stare. She nudged her friend gently, snapping her attention away from the brooding warrior.

"Distracted, are we? Maybe some plans of your own for the evening?"

Mallory frowned, a playful scowl hiding a flicker of embarrassment. "It isn't like that between us," she muttered, casting Andra an indignant look. "Levy's...complicated. Everything he is clashes with everything he's done. I don't need any of your matchmaking nonsense." She finished, sticking her tongue out.

Andra laughed softly, her expression full of amusement. "Oh, Mallory, I would never dream of meddling."

Her expression became serious, a deep pain behind her eyes. "But take it from me, go after what you want sooner rather than later. You'll have that much more time with your happiness before everything goes to shit."

Collecting herself, she smiled again, though Mallory could see the sorrow still lingering behind the cracked façade. Hooking her arm in Kael's so that she might lead him away, she said, "Go on, take the night. You might even enjoy it."

With a reluctant grin and a muttered reply, Mallory finally relented, parting ways with her friends. She headed toward the stairs that climbed the wall to where Levy still sat, her heartbeat quickening slightly despite her efforts to brush it off. She climbed the stairs, her footsteps soft against the stone, as Levy's gaze remained focused on the heavens.

As Mallory reached the top of the stairs, Levy's silhouette stood against the night, still and silent. The silver accents on his black eyepatch caught the faint starlight, and his one visible eye held a gleam she couldn't quite place. Before she could say anything, he spoke without turning to face her.

"Are you planning to stalk me all night now that I'm back, Mallory?" His tone carried a jest, though, beneath it, there was a weariness she hadn't heard from him before. "Or would you like to join me and speak face-to-face for a change?"

Mallory raised an eyebrow, trying to hide her surprise at his words. "Stalking? Hardly. Someone has to keep an eye on you to make sure you don't pull any funny business."

She'd meant it as a lighthearted retort, but the words tasted wrong the moment they left her mouth. The hint of sadness in Levy's expression deepened, and she wished she could take them back.

He gave her a small, sad smile. "A smart call. But if someone has to keep watch, I can't complain that it's you. You're easy on the eye." He said, tapping his patch. His eye flicked to her briefly, his faint smile not quite reaching it.

For a moment, she forgot her attempt to maintain composure,

feeling a blush creep up her cheeks. She was thankful for the darkness hiding it. "Do you mind if I sit with you?" she asked, breaking the silence.

"Please," he said, gesturing beside him. She took a seat, close enough to feel his presence but careful not to look directly at him, giving them both a comfortable distance. They sat in silence, looking up at the heavens.

The night stretched out above them, a sprawling tapestry of stars woven against a deep indigo sky. Some were bold, casting silvery gleams across the landscape, while others were faint, shimmering like tiny fragments of glass suspended in the dark.

A faint, misty arc, the edges of some constellation, cut through the sky, its beauty untouched by the turmoil of the world below. The stars seemed close, as if they leaned toward Stormhaven, casting their silent light in approval, or maybe, she wondered quiet empathy.

Finally, Mallory broke the silence. "When did you and Quinn get back?"

"Only just now," he said, his eye never leaving the stars. "Quinn went running off to see Ashe. Didn't even look back." There was a glimmer of fondness in his voice, a warmth she hadn't heard from him in all of the time she'd known him.

"Must be nice, having someone that devoted to you," Mallory said, her tone a mixture of jest and wistfulness.

Levy's gaze softened. "It is."

He looked at her, and for a moment, she saw something in his eye she couldn't quite place, something that mirrored her own feelings.

"Everyone deserves that kind of love."

Mallory gave him a small nod, her eyes catching the faint glow of stars reflected in his eyepatch. "You seem different than you were when you left," she said, keeping her tone gentle. She didn't want to pry, but something about the way he carried himself had changed.

Levy's face darkened slightly, his gaze turning inward. He told her about everything that had happened, everything he and Quinn had gone through.

She knew they would be talking more about it tomorrow with the rest of the council, but she couldn't imagine how seeing Nes and Sen, good people who had died because of him, must have made him feel.

"The Underworld does that to a person, I think," he finished, though Mallory hadn't heard what had led him to that statement. "Seeing it all, the despair, the trapped souls. It's not something you walk away from unscathed."

Mallory frowned, shaking her head gently. "That's not what I meant, though I am sure it was hard."

She searched his expression, seeing the weight he carried so clearly in the lines of his face. "I meant you, Levy. I see how much you're carrying. You can't keep holding onto it all. You have to let it go."

He turned to her, his look one of disbelief mixed with something almost vulnerable. The look broke her heart. "How can I do that, Mallory, when nobody else can either? Even you said you feel as though you have to watch over me."

Her cheeks warmed again, a stubborn flush of shame she couldn't hide this time. "There are other reasons for watching someone," she replied softly.

At that, he smiled, really smiled. The sadness retreated momentarily. "Thank you, Mallory," he said, his voice low. "For sitting with me. For speaking with me."

Without another word, he rose and left, footsteps fading into the night. Mallory watched him disappear down the stairs before returning her gaze to the stars above. Something in her heart stirred, a quiet resolve taking root.

She would make sure that from now on, Levy knew he had someone other than Ashe and Quinn by his side. He would never have to bear his burdens alone.

Chapter 12
Quinn

The chamber was heavy with silence, its stone walls aglow with the flickering light of torches and casting shadows across the faces of the council. A chill lingered in the air, underscoring the weight of what was about to be discussed. Quinn could feel the scrutiny from each member around the table, their gazes sharpened by the unknowns that had trailed him and Levy since they had been gone.

Levy shifted beside him, rolling the Orb of Hades over his knuckles. Its dark, stormy light glowed dimly, and the faint hum of its power filled the silence like a whispered promise.

Quinn could see Ashe, the only other person who had known of their journey, watching everyone with a calm, expectant gaze as though she were measuring each of them for what was to come.

Since she had told him the night before of how Fate had been showing her mixed visions of the future, he wondered if every conversation changed something and if she was bracing for that now.

"As some of you may have guessed by now, Levy and I made a journey to the Underworld." Quinn let the weight of his words settle over the room. "Our purpose was specific: Sneak in, get what we needed, and sneak back out without alerting Hades. Unfortunately, we were only lucky on two of those three fronts."

He paused, studying their reactions, making sure they understood the risk. "We went to gain something that could tip the scales in our favor. Something we felt was worth the danger."

He watched as their expressions shifted, each member absorbing the weight of his words differently. Andra's gaze was fixed on the orb with a quiet intensity, as though she was remembering the past and yet seeing the future and the possibilities the orb offered at the same time.

But Quinn knew her too well; the recognition in her eyes and what it meant was not something she would speak aloud, at least not to a group.

"Our purpose was to reach the River Styx," Levy added, his voice a low rumble as he continued to roll the orb in his hand. "For me to swim in its water and gain the strength of Achilles. A power with which I can shield the people of Stormhaven from even the mightiest blows."

There was a trace of darkness in his eyes, memories of the agony that had surged through him as he took on the goddess' trial, memories that bound him to her relentless power.

He held up the orb, letting its dim green glow cast eerie shadows over the table. "But that wasn't all we came back with."

A ripple of unease passed through the room as Levy turned the orb slowly in his hand, its dark core pulsing with restless energy. "This is the Orb of Hades. It holds the power to call forth the dead."

"We remember." Lend cut in, unmasked anger on his face as he undoubtedly was assaulted by his memories of the last time Levy held the orb.

Levy shot him an apologetic look before continuing. "In this case, the warriors of Elysium have offered their support for when Zeus strikes." He paused, allowing the implications to settle. "This was Hades' own creation. We have inherited it, and with it, those warriors now fight with us."

Andra's gaze deepened though she remained silent. The orb held a potential reunion with Nes, a reunion she dared not hope for, but Quinn could see the glint in her eyes. He turned his attention to the rest, waiting to gauge their responses.

Avery, Lend's personal assistant and right hand, shifted uncomfortably, a frown creasing his brow. Lend, however, didn't hold back. His voice was tight, his expression a mask of restrained frustration.

"So, you not only went to the Underworld without informing us but also returned with powers that could be catastrophic if held in the wrong hands."

Though he did not state explicitly what he meant, Quinn could see Levy's shoulders droop slightly beside him.

Quinn met his gaze, holding steady. "We didn't make the decision lightly. There was a high risk that we wouldn't even make it back, let alone succeed. Telling everyone would have only caused more worry for something that could have ended in failure. This was Levy's risk to take."

Lend clenched his jaw, his disapproval evident. "But it is not just his risk now, Quinn. You've brought it back here to all of us."

He looked at Levy. "And you, after everything you have been through, you decided to throw yourself at the mercy of the Styx? To accept a power you knew hardly anything about? What if it had corrupted you? What if it had destroyed you?"

Levy's eye was unwavering, his voice steady as he replied. "I know my past, Lend. I know I have made mistakes, but every moment since I have returned has been spent working to make up for them. This power was a choice I made for Stormhaven."

He shifted his gaze to each member. "To protect all of you."

Kael, who had remained silent until now, rose to his feet. "And that choice, given your history—you didn't think to consult any of us?" His eyes were dark as he regarded Levy. "You should have never made this decision without asking our permission."

Quinn felt a flash of anger flare in his chest, ready to defend Levy, but Mallory's voice rang out, clear and unyielding, before he could respond.

"With respect, Kael," she said, her tone firm, "Levy is as much one of us as anybody else at this point, and he is most certainly not a child who needs to ask permission to be granted him when he makes decisions in his personal life. "

"He has done nothing but prove himself since he has been here. He's been training our soldiers, dedicating every waking moment to ensuring our survival. You may remember his past, but I've seen his passion for this firsthand."

Oath Breaker

A light flush crept up her neck. "Levy deserves our trust."

Kael's mouth opened to retort, but Andra raised a hand, her voice carrying the weight of command. "That's enough, Kael."

Her tone left no room for argument, and though her gaze softened when she looked at Mallory, she didn't allow others to see the deeper emotion hiding there. "Stormhaven is stronger because of him, not in spite of him."

Mallory flashed her a thankful grin in return.

The silence that followed was thick with unresolved tension, the council teetering on a delicate edge between discord and unity. Finally, Ashe spoke, her voice a calm but commanding presence that anchored them.

"We've been through so much, and yet there is still more to come. This power," she gestured to the orb, "is dangerous, but it is also a weapon that we will need in future fights. Quinn and Levy have returned with more power and a true fighting chance, not just for themselves but for all of us."

Another silence settled over the table as Kael looked away, his brow furrowed with silent distrust. Avery, however, cleared his throat, his tone measured, though it was impossible to miss the cautious skepticism there.

"I understand the reasoning, Quinn," Avery began, choosing his words carefully, "but the stakes are too high to act without the council's input. It's not a matter of questioning your judgment or Ashe's. It's the potential consequences for us all."

Quinn exhaled a slow sigh, keeping his voice level as he looked between Avery, Kael, and Lend. "I hear you," he replied, weary but resolute. "But you must know by now, Levy can be trusted. He chose his path to stand with us, not against us.

"He was the difference between victory and defeat in both the fight with Ares and Hades. And after everything he has done to prepare Stormhaven and train our warriors, he's earned that trust."

Ashe placed a firm hand on the table, her voice soft but commanding. "We cannot afford to fracture ourselves, not while we're up against Zeus."

Her gaze swept over the room. "Every disagreement, every moment we spend doubting one another, only gives Zeus the advantage. We need to be a unified front."

Quinn nodded, watching Kael and Avery. "If we spar every time Levy is involved, this council will tear itself apart from the inside out. There's no time for division. Eventually, you'll need to trust both myself and Ashe and in turn, Levy. Our enemy is Zeus, not one another."

Lend's expression softened slightly, and he rubbed a hand over his face, the anger fading into a look of shared exhaustion. "You're right, Quinn," he admitted with a sigh. "We're all on edge; it's been a long fight."

His gaze shifted toward Levy, holding for a beat longer than usual. Then, in a gesture that surprised even Quinn, Lend stood, walked around the table, and extended his hand to Levy.

"From this moment on, I will see you as an ally," he spoke, his voice solid with conviction, "not a suspect."

Quinn noticed the subtle easing in Levy's posture, a hint of relief in his eye. Levy took Lend's hand, and though he said nothing, his nod spoke volumes.

The room fell into a tense silence, though Kael kept his gaze averted. Quinn took note, already deciding to challenge the young man to a sparring match after the meeting. Sometimes, the best way to reach a soldier wasn't through words—but through battle.

The tension gradually ebbed, replaced by a thoughtful silence, broken only when Ashe cleared her throat, drawing the room's attention back to her.

"Now that the details of your mission are clear," she said, her tone grave. "There's another pressing matter to discuss. While you and Levy were away, we received a visit from Cyrus."

Quinn felt a familiar surge of irritation at the mention of the Master's name, his jaw tightening instinctively. He glanced at Ashe, who looked just as wary.

"What did he want?" he asked, his tone edged with caution.

Ashe's expression darkened. "He brought word that Zeus is searching for an artifact of immense power—one hidden deep within the vault where Levy first discovered Hades' orb. Supposedly, it holds the power to end us for good."

Quinn frowned, a cold weight settling in his chest. "Is there any clue as to what this item could be or what it might do?"

Ashe shook her head, her expression far away, as though she

were flipping through the future for information. "We don't know. It could be anything, but everyone here agrees it's not something we should ignore. If Zeus gets his hands on it..."

Levy's brows knit together as he leaned forward. "What if it's a trap? Zeus could be counting on us to chase this down."

"That's possible," Andra acknowledged.

"Likely even," Mallory chimed in as if they had had this exact discussion many times already.

"But," Andra continued. "We also can't ignore it. If it's real and falls into his hands, we would regret it."

Lend ran his hand through his hair, fidgeting with the strip of fabric that tied it back. "We've searched the libraries thoroughly, but there is no record of anything that sounds remotely like this. It's likely older than the texts we have."

Levy's head snapped up, his eyes widening as a thought struck him. "There might be a source who knows more."

He scanned the faces around the table before his gaze settled on Ashe, the weight of his idea reflected in his expression. "But it would be dangerous."

"As dangerous as taking a secret trip into the Underworld and fighting the god of Death on his home turf?" Mallory deadpanned.

"Even more so," Levy replied, his face losing some of its color.

"Oh." Mallory leaned back in her chair. "Neat."

Levy, his eyes still locked on Ashe, continued. "Clotho, the Weaver before Ashe, is being held within the dungeons of Olympus."

Ashe straightened, her eyes piercing as she put the pieces together aloud. "An ancient Fate, and an immortal no less. If anyone would know of an item of such power and what it may be capable of, it would be her."

She turned to the rest of the council. "And if she is in the dungeons of Olympus, she is likely one of our few remaining allies who could hold that sort of knowledge."

Lend folded his arms. "So, we're faced with two missions. Finding this item and, potentially, extracting a prisoner from Olympus." His voice was gruff, pragmatic as he weighed the risks.

Andra spoke up, her tone steady. "As much as we'd want any knowledge Clotho holds, right now, our priority has to be the item itself. If Zeus is after it, then we can't waste time or resources on anything else."

Levy cut in; his voice edged with quiet urgency. "The last time I saw Clotho, she was wasting away. I know she's immortal, but if she's kept in those conditions much longer, she may not even be coherent by the time we get to her. And if Zeus realizes we're close to the item first, he'll know better than to keep her alive after that."

The room tensed as Levy's words sank in. If they tried to rescue Clotho first, they risked losing the item entirely. But if they ignored her until after they secured it, she might be lost or silenced forever.

Quinn leaned forward, feeling the weight of the decision settle in his bones. "Then we split our forces," he said, a plan beginning to take shape.

"I can portal a team to the northern vaults and cut travel time. Then I'll go to Olympus with one other to free Clotho before Zeus even knows we are aware of his scheme."

Kael gave a dry scoff. "Oh, you mean like you 'snuck' into the Underworld?"

Quinn's eyes narrowed. "That was different. The Underworld was one god's domain. A foreign intrusion is easily detectable, as I learned. Olympus is an amalgamation of different essences, the realm itself belonging to no one god individually. They will not notice another one."

He hoped.

Kael looked as if he was going to speak again, but it was Mallory who silenced him with a sharp glare. "He got the job done, didn't he?"

Kael looked away, chastened, but the air remained thick.

Ashe picked up on the plan, her voice steady. "If I go with the group to the vaults, my control over Fate *could* potentially guide us to the item faster. We'd have an edge."

But Quinn shook his head, his answer firm. "No, I won't be apart from you again."

Ashe met his gaze, her lips curving into a small, thankful smile. Mallory raised an eyebrow and pretended to swoon, a hand over her heart. "Oh, the devotion, I might faint."

The tension eased for a moment as laughter rippled through the group. Finally, the decision was clear.

Oath Breaker

"Mallory, Andra, Kael, and Levy will take my portal to the vaults," Quinn commanded. "Find this artifact and keep it out of Zeus's hands—no matter the cost. Meanwhile, Ashe and I will infiltrate Olympus and bring Clotho back."

His gaze shifted to Lend and Avery. "Keep things steady here. The people are restless—they'll need a guiding hand."

Each member nodded in agreement, though Quinn could feel the gravity in their expressions. The risks were high, but each of them understood the stakes.

As the council members rose, stretching their legs after what felt like an eternity of discussion, Quinn's voice sliced through the movement—calm yet unwavering.

"Kael," he called, his tone carrying just enough authority to turn heads. "Meet me in the sparring yard. We need to have a chat."

As he strode out of the room without glancing back to see if Kael was following, he caught the sound of Mallory's teasing voice drifting through the air.

"Ooooooh, you're in troubleeee."

Chapter 13
Kael

The training grounds hummed with quiet energy though only a small crowd had gathered. In the sanded pit, Kael tightened his grip on his wooden staff, his knuckles whitening as he faced Quinn.

Despite the measured calm in Quinn's gaze, Kael could feel the sheer weight of his opponent's experience pressing down on him—a silent, undeniable force. A pang of irritation flared within him, but he forced it down, focusing instead on the match ahead.

In the stands, Mallory lounged with a grin, a bucket of popcorn balanced in her lap. Sensing the rising tension, she lifted a handful of popcorn in the air like a toast and called out, her voice brimming with amusement.

"Let's go, Kael! Show us what an Abyssillian general can do!"

"Where did you even get popcorn?" Andra asked, not seeing any vendors or food stalls in the immediate area. Mallory simply winked, offering her a handful of warm, buttery goodness.

Kael's mind was a firestorm of emotions, each one fueling his every movement as he took a steadying breath and lunged. His staff carved through the air—powerful, fast, each strike carrying the full weight of his strength and determination.

Yet, no matter how well-timed his swings or precise his thrusts, Quinn was too fluid. Too effortless. He moved like water, slipping through Kael's attacks as though they were nothing more than raindrops in a storm. Every strike was met with an almost lazy deflection, sending harmless vibrations up Kael's staff while frustration coiled tighter in his chest.

Kael swung harder, faster, letting his emotions fuel him. But Quinn was relentless in his ease, tapping Kael's ribs, his shoulder, his hip- a steady rhythm that felt like a mocking beat, hammering into Kael's pride with every touch. The heat of Kael's anger built with each failed blow, each a reminder that strength alone wasn't enough.

Mallory cackled, tossing a kernel into her mouth with a smirk. "That's six for Quinn! You might want to consider actually hitting him, Kael!"

Kael clenched his teeth, feeling his composure slip. Quinn noticed it as well. Pausing just enough to meet Kael's burning gaze, he spoke. "Tell me, Kael, why do you hate Levy so much?"

The words struck a nerve. Kael's grip on his staff tightened, and he felt a spark of raw fury he'd tried so hard to keep buried. "

Why do I hate him?" he bit out, his voice harsh, trembling with barely restrained rage. "Because he led an army of the dead against my people. Against my parents. They never stood a chance.

"I didn't have a chance to save them. They were overrun, slaughtered by the same undead he called from their graves. And for what? Power? He doesn't even deserve to breathe."

Kael surged forward, his anger fueling his strikes with an intensity that bordered on reckless. Each blow was a piece of his grief, a shard of bitterness, and Quinn met each one with calm resilience.

The impact of their staves sent splinters into the air, and the wooden rods began to crack under the strain of Kael's unrestrained fury. Every deflection, every block, only added to the pressure inside him until it felt ready to burst.

Quinn let Kael's emotions run their course, allowing the barrage to push him back just enough to let Kael reach his tipping point. And then, in a moment of startling gentleness, Quinn held up a hand, lifting his shirt to show a scar over his heart- a faint mark, but a deep one.

"Levy stabbed me here," Quinn said, voice calm but full of

something Kael couldn't quite name. "His choices, his mistakes, cost me, too. They tore apart Stormhaven. Strained bonds between Ashe and I that I thought could never be strained."

The confession quieted Kael's fury, his staff lowering as he listened, chest heaving, feeling the weight of Quinn's words in the aching silence that followed.

"But he is not the same man," Quinn continued, eyes steady on Kael. "He fought beside me against Ares. Saved my life when I thought it was over. He fought harder than anybody could expect against Hades. He's earned the respect of Nes and Sen enough that they entrusted him with the orb. He has his own regrets, his own wounds."

Kael stared at him, breathing heavily, something unfamiliar gnawing at the edges of his anger. But before he could respond, Quinn dropped low, sweeping Kael's feet out from under him in a flash. Kael hit the ground with a dull thud, his head spinning as Quinn's staff pressed gently but firmly against his throat.

"You don't have to forget, Kael. I would never ask that of you," Quinn murmured, his voice as steady as his hand. "But maybe, in time, you can forgive. At least until all of this is over. We can't lose any more of the people we care about. Not if we are going to face what's coming. That means working as a team. One cohesive unit."

Kael's anger ebbed, replaced by a deep, reluctant understanding. The weight of his resentment felt different, quieter, as he stared up at Quinn, hearing the unspoken truth. If he could let go of some of his pain, maybe they could work as a team. It didn't mean he had to forgive the bastard completely, but perhaps he could hear him out.

As Quinn extended a hand, Kael hesitated for only a moment before grasping it, feeling the firm, steady grip of not an opponent but an equal—a fellow warrior, a brother-in-arms. He pulled himself up, brushed the dust from his clothes, and met Quinn's gaze with a silent nod of respect.

Without a word, Quinn turned and strode toward the exit, leaving Kael standing alone in the training pit, his thoughts swirling like embers in the aftermath of a fire.

For a second, Kael felt a glimmer of possibility where only bitterness had been. He could watch Levy on their upcoming mission and see for himself if there was any truth to Quinn's words. He could even, tentatively, work with him, fight beside him if necessary, and let himself judge Levy by what he saw with his own eyes.

The idea of it didn't seem as impossible as it once had. Perhaps, just this once, he could set aside the weight of the past and see what the present had to offer.

That, however, would be entirely up to Levy.

Chapter 14
Olympus

The throne room of Olympus stood, crumbling and faded, a ghost of its former splendor. Once gleaming marble now bore deep cracks, jagged fissures that split across the floor like ancient wounds refusing to heal.

Shadows pooled in those cracks, swallowing up what remained of the pale, flickering light that cast the hall in a sickly glow, half-dead and unsteady as the god who commanded it. The air itself seemed heavy and damp, charged with the volatile energy of a storm on the edge of breaking, thrumming like a live wire, waiting for a single spark to turn it loose.

High columns bearing once-proud carvings seemed to slump, their details worn to blurred remnants by the passage of time and the weight of neglect. A cold wind stirred through the chamber, setting the torches to sputter and dance, casting grotesque shadows across the room.

It was as if the gods themselves, beaten down by the constant storms of Zeus' anger, had drained the room of its former glory. Tension roiled in every corner, seething just beneath the surface.

The gods stood in silent assembly around the hall, each casting wary, sidelong glances at their king. Zeus sat upon his immense throne, his presence brooding. The very air around him thickened with the threat of lightning, barely restrained.

His piercing blue gaze was fixed on Cyrus, the lone figure standing before him, confident and poised. None dared speak; the gods watched, tense, waiting for the storm they all felt in the air to break.

Zeus' eyes blazed as he watched Cyrus, his voice rumbling low and ominous. "What did you find?" Each word dripped with barely suppressed fury like a thundercloud waiting to let loose.

Cyrus met his gaze, showing neither fear nor hesitation, the faintest hint of a smirk tugging at his mouth. A daring amusement, as if the king's wrath was nothing more than a passing curiosity.

"I found Hades," he said, letting the words drop into the silence like stones into a dark well. "And I found him dead."

A murmur rippled through the gods, each shifting uneasily, yet none dared look directly at Zeus.

"Defeated?" Zeus' voice was sharp as a blade, his hands tightening on the arms of his throne until sparks danced around his knuckles. "By whom?"

"By those who dare oppose you," Cyrus replied, almost lazily. "Levy and Quinn. Levy took a swim in the Styx, and Quinn holds the power of Chaos himself. Together, they killed your brother."

The silence that followed was deeper than before, like the eye of a storm, stretching and building until Zeus' rage erupted. He stood, unleashing a torrent of thunder and fury, lightning exploding outward from his palm in blinding arcs, sending cracks snaking further across the marble floor.

The walls seemed to shudder as if they, too, feared his wrath, and the pillars groaned under the strain. Each Olympian in the room recoiled, heads ducked, averting their eyes from the storm in his gaze.

"Insolent wretches!" he roared, the sound rolling through the hall like a breaking wave, a wrath older than mountains and fiercer than fire. "They meddle in realms beyond their comprehension. They kill gods as if we are vermin!"

Poseidon, seated nearest to him, kept his gaze lowered, his expression set in a rigid line. Artemis, ever defiant, hid her unease beneath a fierce scowl, her fingers tightening around her bow. Demeter looked ready to flinch with each flash of lightning as if she had been singed by his outbursts before.

Even Hermes, usually quick with a jest, seemed visibly uncomfortable, shifting from foot to foot. The gods bore witness to their king's fury as one might watch an inevitable disaster, and none dared move until the storm had passed.

At last, Zeus forced himself to still, slowly lowering himself back onto the throne, his grip on the armrests loosening, though anger still simmered in his eyes. Each breath he took was slow and deliberate, forcing the violent energy back into some semblance of control.

"Report," he demanded when he noticed Cyrus still standing before him.

Unfazed, Cyrus straightened and, with that same calm amusement, continued. "The mortals of Stormhaven have taken the bait, my lord," he said with undisguised pleasure. "They are on their way to the vaults to retrieve the treasure, just as planned. Aphrodite is already there, awaiting them."

This news seemed to soften the rage in Zeus' eyes, replaced by a flicker of satisfaction that darkened into something more sinister. He leaned back in his throne, a faint smile curling at the corners of his mouth.

"Two prizes, then," he muttered, low enough for the gods to catch the words but not the intent behind them. "They will deliver the box to Aphrodite, along with Levy."

A tense, strained silence followed his words. Poseidon glanced sidelong at his brother, barely concealing a grim frown. Hermes gave a nervous glance at Apollo, who only stared at Zeus with a calm but calculating expression. The other gods exchanged looks, each bearing their own measure of discomfort.

"Do none of you have the courage to speak your mind?" Zeus asked, as though he hadn't recently killed his own wife for doing just that.

It was Artemis who finally broke the silence. She stepped forward, graceful and poised, her brown curls catching the pale, flickering light. Her eyes held undisguised suspicion, her stance filled with the strength of a huntress on edge, ready to draw at the slightest provocation. If she were going to die, she would at least put up a fight.

Oath Breaker

"What purpose do you have for bringing him back?" she asked, not bothering to conceal the disdain in her tone. "That human trash has killed two of us, betraying your trust in him, has he not?

"What makes you think he would ever willingly come back into the fold? What use could you possibly have for one who has already proven himself a traitor twice?"

Artemis' words lingered in the air, laden with venom. Her contempt for the mortal was clear in her expression, her lip curling in barely disguised disgust. She gripped her bow, her fingers tapping lightly on the shaft, betraying her brave demeanor.

Zeus' eyes met hers, his smile twisting into something unreadable, something dark. "Who said it will be his choice to make?" His words were soft, each holding an ominous weight.

His gaze flickered with hidden knowledge, a plan none of them could fully see, and he seemed to revel in that fact.

Unease rippled through the room again. Even Dionysus, who had maintained a mask of detached amusement until now, wore an expression of something closer to suspicion. Hephaestus' hand tightened around the hammer at his side, his brow furrowing.

Artemis opened her mouth to question him further, but a flicker of warning in Zeus' stare stilled her tongue. Around her, the Olympians stood frozen, unable to shake the feeling that their king was slipping further from reason, sinking into a darkness none dared to confront.

The hall remained silent, and as Zeus' dark smile persisted, each god wondered who among them might be next to face his wrath.

Chapter 15
Ashe

The first rays of dawn brushed over Stormhaven, casting long shadows across the high stone walls, illuminating where the council would soon gather. The last couple of days had been spent preparing to set this mission in motion, a mission that could very well determine the fate of all who stood against Zeus.

They spoke of the risks, each of them, and acknowledged the perils in their own silent ways. Yet now, with morning creeping steadily forward, there was no room left for lingering doubts.

Ashe stood alone in her quarters, Quinn having left some time earlier to don his armor as well. A slant of light from the small, square window cast a warm gleam over her as she prepared.

She took a deep breath, steadying herself, and reached for the strip of worn leather resting atop her dresser. It was an old scrap of armor salvaged from something Quinn had worn long ago. Its edges were frayed, softened over time, but the faint scent of him still clung to it, a comfort she hadn't realized she would come to rely on.

She wound the leather around her platinum hair, tying it into place with practiced ease, feeling the familiarity of it settle over her like a shield against the weight of what lay ahead. A faint smile tugged at her lips, knowing that Quinn had likely kept this leather band close by on purpose, knowing she'd take it and wear it.

Oath Breaker

Pulling her focus back to her armor, Ashe reached for the black leather tunic resting on the bed. It was well-worn, crafted with reinforced seams, and fitted perfectly to her frame, but it was nothing like the gleaming silver plate she typically wore into battle.

Today was not for grand displays of strength, not for the rallying calls of war. Today was for quiet steps in the dark, for merging with the shadows as they infiltrated the heart of Olympus itself. She ran her fingers over the leather, her mind drifting back to Quinn again.

He, too, favored this type of armor, more subtle, more suited to slipping unseen past guarded perimeters. The image of his body suspended in the air, a spear sticking through his chest, flashed quickly through her mind, but she shook it off, making a mental note to have a new chest plate crafted for him.

As she fastened the straps across her chest, Ashe felt the faint throb of her heartbeat in her fingertips, each pulse a reminder of the time ticking away. They would meet outside the gates soon, and from there, there was no turning back.

She wondered for the millionth time if she was leading them down the right path, the path Clotho's prophecy had laid out for them, or if she was instead leading her world, and all of humanity, to ruin.

A tap at the door interrupted her thoughts. "Ashe?" came a familiar voice, low but warm, carrying a note of hesitation.

She glanced over, spotting Mallory's form shadowed in the doorway. Her dark hair was also tied back, though two long strands fell on either side, framing her heart-shaped face.

Her eyes held the kind of steel that spoke of a sleepless night and countless battles ahead. Ashe nodded for her to enter, and Mallory stepped in, her gaze flicking over Ashe's armor with a smirk.

"Gone for Quinn's look, have you? The couple that dresses together stays together?"

Ashe shrugged. "Stealth mission. Figured plate armor wasn't exactly the wisest choice."

Mallory snorted. "Hardly," she replied, humor lacing the word. "But I imagine Quinn will be pleased."

They shared a laugh before the room fell silent again. There was something in the silence that held them both; an understanding, unspoken but heavy, of what this mission meant and the likelihood of what could happen associated with the risk involved. They had been through battles, sieges, moments of loss, and victory, yet this felt different. Its weight pressed down on them both, heavier than they cared to admit.

Mallory surged forward, wrapping her arms around Ashe and squeezing tightly as if she feared Ashe might slip away again. Ashe returned the embrace just as fiercely.

"I only just got you back," Mallory whispered. "It feels so unfair that I might lose you again."

Ashe gently patted her friend's back. "I know, Mallory. I feel the same. But we'll make it through, and when we do, we will stick it to Zeus and the rest of the Olympians together."

After a lingering moment, Mallory finally loosened her grip, stepping back and wiping a phantom tear from her eye.

"Levy and Andra are already outside, along with Kael," she murmured. "They're ready."

Ashe nodded, feeling a shift within her as she took a final look around her room, anchoring herself in the familiar before stepping into the unknown. "I'll be right there."

With a last, lingering glance, Mallory left the room, leaving Ashe alone once more. Fastening the final straps on her tunic, Ashe reached for her cloak. It was crafted from thick, dark fabric that draped fluidly over her shoulders, falling to just below her knees. She pulled the hood up, adjusting it until her bright hair was hidden beneath its shadows, another layer of anonymity to aid in the stealth their mission demanded.

Steeling herself, Ashe stepped out into the cool morning air. The gates loomed high into the distance; their stone arches silhouetted against the pale light of dawn. As she arrived, she saw a collection of figures gathered there, each distinct in form and posture.

Levy stood with his usual calm demeanor, his gaze turned toward the mountains in the distance, though he greeted her with a warm smile and a friendly nod as he saw her approach. Andra knelt beside him, scratching Horacio beneath the chin, Mallory giggling as the young Drakon purred, trickling flame out of his nostrils. He was not yet old enough to spew fire, but it had begun generating deep within his gullet.

Kael was a dark presence, silent and brooding as ever, his attention fixed on the ground as if calculating each step of the mission in his mind. He reminded Ashe a lot of Quinn back in their early days at the Citadel.

Quinn was the last to join them, striding forward with quiet confidence, his gaze passing over each of them in turn, lingering a moment longer on Ashe. His presence was a beautiful death, a shadow draped in black leather armor that hugged his form as if it were a second skin.

The thin blade strapped across his back spoke of lethal intent, and his dark hair, catching the first light of dawn, gleamed like polished obsidian. Dangerous, poised, and effortlessly gorgeous, he looked as if he could cut down gods and keep walking, leaving only whispers in his wake.

He inclined his head slightly, something like pride in his eyes, acknowledging her choice of attire with a small smile.

"Everyone ready?" he asked, his voice carrying a calm that steadied them all.

Nods followed, firm and resolute.

Quinn turned to Levy. "You know the layout of the vaults better than anyone else here. Once you guys are through, stay close to each other." His eyes slid to Kael. "Trust each other's instincts."

Levy nodded, his gaze steady. "We'll get it done. Whatever Zeus is after, it won't leave those vaults without a fight."

Quinn's expression darkened for a moment, the weight of their own task pressing in on him. "Good. Ashe and I will handle Olympus. I can get you guys to the vault, but you'll have to make your own way back. If we return first, I can try to find you, but be prepared should the worst happen."

He didn't add what they were all thinking; that Olympus was a place of treachery, of gods who wanted them dead for merely existing. But he didn't need to. They all knew the risk and knew what was at stake.

Quinn extended his hand, focusing as essence coalesced around him. The air shimmered, bending and twisting as two portals began to form. Light crackled around them, a steady hum that vibrated in the very core of Ashe's bones. She felt her heart rate spike, the anticipation settling into a constant thrum of readiness.

"Go," Quinn said, watching their friends step through and disappear.

And then, just as the second portal solidified, Ashe felt the weight of Quinn's hand on her shoulder, grounding her. She looked up, meeting his gaze, and he offered her a brief, reassuring smile.

"We'll get through this," he breathed, so low only she could hear. As if he was saying it more for himself than for her.

She nodded, a flicker of warmth settling in her chest. "I'm counting on it."

With that, she stepped through the portal alongside him, feeling the strange pull of the world shifting, dragging her away from the familiar comforts of Stormhaven and into the uncertainty of Olympus.

For a moment, there was only darkness, a void in which she could feel nothing but Quinn's steady presence behind her. Then, with a jolt, they emerged into a cold room of marble. The only sign of purpose was a solitary obsidian gateway, standing empty and foreboding. The hall was vast, echoing with a silence that felt almost sentient, aware of the intruders within its sacred walls.

Ashe knew that somewhere, just out of reach, was Clotho, their last hope of understanding what this item of power was and how Zeus intended to use it.

The enormity of their task settled over her like a shroud, but Ashe pushed the thought away, focusing only on the steps before her, on Quinn's silent, reassuring presence at her side. They would succeed. They had to. For if they failed…She shuddered, not allowing herself to follow that thought to its fiery end.

As they pressed deeper into Olympus, Ashe drew her cloak closer, steeling herself for what lay ahead.

Chapter 16
Levy

The cold hit Levy like a thousand tiny needles the moment they stepped out of Quinn's portal, a frigid atmosphere sweeping over him with the kind of bite only the far north could offer. Levy pulled his jacket around him tightly, the fur lining tickling the skin beneath his chin.

The crystalline morning air filled his lungs, and with each exhale, his breath puffed out in thick, silver clouds, fading and vanishing into the stark whiteness surrounding them. Snow blanketed the land as far as the eye could see, a world washed clean by winter's hand, all framed beneath a sky tinged with the pink and golden hues of a land just waking up.

Flakes drifted softly from above, catching the morning light in such a way that each one seemed to glow, tiny stars drifting from heaven down to earth.

Before them stretched a vast expanse of frozen wilderness, untouched and pure. Here and there, silvery trees dotted the landscape; Mageia trees, branches bare yet flowing faintly with an otherworldly luminescence.

Their trunks were veined with shimmering lines of essence,

glowing faintly against the soft snowfall, a gentle reminder that the very land beneath them held ancient, untapped power.

"Isn't this a sight?" Andra gasped, drawing her scaled cloak tighter against the chill, her eyes scanning the horizon with a look of awe.

Horacio pranced around her, chasing snowflakes as they fluttered down from the grey sky above. The snow beneath their feet crunched softly as they moved forward, their steps slow, almost reverent in this breathtaking quiet.

Beside Levy, Mallory let out a low chuckle. She jabbed an elbow playfully into his ribs, her breath puffing out in misty clouds as she grinned at him.

"You know, somewhere out there is the spot where I first had to fight off your undead horde like some glorified side character while you and Quinn were off having your little 'main character blast from the past' showdown. You two really knew how to make an entrance."

Levy shot her a sidelong glance, feeling the familiar warmth of guilt settle into his chest. A small, sad grin tugged at his lips. "You're right; I never did apologize for that, did I?"

Mallory's expression softened, her usual sharp wit tempered with understanding. She halted, putting a gloved hand on his arm and forcing him to stop and look at her.

"Stop holding so much of that over yourself, Levy." Her tone was gentle, a rare break from her usual jibes. "Bring back the guy who used to have a comeback for every smart-ass comment. The one who didn't take himself so seriously. I think we all miss him."

Her eyes searched his, and Levy felt an ache in his chest that was both comforting and painful. There was a truth to her words he couldn't deny, something he'd let himself forget as the weight of his choices had buried him deeper and deeper over time.

With Quinn, the council, and their endless quest for freedom and peace, he'd somehow lost that version of himself, trading it for the armor of remorse and grim duty.

He forced a glint of mischief into his eye, tentative but genuine. "You mean the guy who could best you in a fight with his eyes closed?"

"There he is," Mallory laughed, the sound carrying through the quiet morning. She nudged him playfully again. "Keep dreaming. I'll remind you who held their own back then-"

"Enough," Kael's deep voice cut through their exchange as he trudged past them, his steady gaze locked forward, unmoved by the landscape around them. "We don't know what is waiting out here for us. Take this seriously."

He had a way of breaking through their lighthearted moments without even trying, and Levy wasn't entirely sure if it was intentional or not. He couldn't blame him if it was, though. Mallory was beautiful. But that was Kael, a rock amidst the chaos.

Andra, too, remained focused, though Levy caught the faint smile she tried to suppress, her gaze flickering toward him and Mallory as if their playful banter offered some small measure of reassurance. He supposed they all needed it.

This place—the endless snow, the silence so deep it felt like a living thing—was a stark reminder of what lay ahead. The land itself carried memories, power, and secrets long buried beneath its frozen expanse. And within it lay their destination: a vault hidden in the heart of this unforgiving terrain, a stronghold of the Masters, guarded by far more than mere walls.

Levy took a deep breath, the frigid air biting into his lungs, and let it out slowly, his breath mixing with the faint glow of the Mageia trees. Beneath this snow, beneath the quiet, lay a place of purpose. And as he walked, Levy found that a small part of him hoped that maybe, just maybe, he could begin to leave some of that weight behind.

The silence hung around them like a shroud as they walked, the only sound their own footsteps crunching through the snow. The world was still, each step somehow feeling intrusive in the vast, endless quiet of the northern lands.

Levy's eye scanned the distant horizon, where the faint outline of the vault was beginning to come into view; a hulking structure, half-buried in the snow and shadow, its towering silhouette rising starkly against the pale morning light.

Yet something nagged at him, a feeling he couldn't shake. On his last visit, he remembered hearing the calls of distant birds, the scurrying of creatures moving beneath the underbrush. But now, there was nothing.

No flutter of wings, no hint of movement, just silence that deepened with every step they took. It felt wrong, unnatural, as though the land itself was holding its breath.

Andra walked beside him, casting a wary glance around. "Does anyone else feel like something's off?" she asked, her voice low. "It's too quiet. Even the trees aren't moving, and it feels like there should be a breeze. The air is too still."

Levy nodded, brow furrowing. It was as if the cold had stripped more than just warmth from this place. Even the Mageia trees, usually pulsing with faint life and light, seemed subdued, their glowing veins dimmer than usual. The land felt as though it was holding secrets just below the surface, waiting for them to discover something they might rather not find.

Ahead of them, Kael stopped abruptly, holding up a hand to halt the group. His brows scrunched as he surveyed the path ahead, his stance rigid with focus. He closed his eyes for a moment, and Levy sensed the shift in his energy.

Kael was calling upon his Abyssillian blood, his gift allowing him brief glimpses beyond illusions and deceptions layered within the physical world.

"The path isn't as untouched as it looks," Kael said finally, his voice edged with a wary tension. He opened his eyes, and they held a dark glint, sharper than usual. "There's an illusion here, and beneath it, dozens of footprints all leading to the vault."

Levy felt his heart tighten as he looked where Kael pointed, though his own eyes saw only undisturbed snow. It was troubling enough that they had been beaten to this forsaken place, but it was more troubling still that they had cloaked themselves so thoroughly.

"That's not all," Kael continued, his gaze scanning the clearing ahead. "There are forms hidden under a veil right outside the vault entrance. I can't make out what they are from here, but they're stationed there, waiting."

They barely had a moment to absorb his words when a sudden, thunderous crack shattered the silence. Levy's instincts kicked in at once, stepping forward and shoving Kael down as two massive logs, sharpened to deadly points and strung on a thick rope, swung down from either side, aiming to skewer Kael. The logs whistled through the air, their force enough to shatter bone and tear through steel alike.

In an instant, Levy felt the brutal impact as both logs slammed into him instead, the force sending a shockwave through his frame. Wood splintered against his body, shards exploding outward as the pointed logs shattered on contact.

Mallory's scream rang out, filled with horror, but it cut off abruptly as she realized Levy was still standing, entirely unharmed, amid the wreckage of wooden fragments scattered across the snow. He was untouched, thanks to the power of Achilles surging through his veins, though his jacket was shredded, torn to ribbons where the sharpened ends had hit.

He met her eyes with a slight smile, an all too familiar pain in his expression, though he seemed to be trying to brush it off as an inconvenience. Reaching down, he extended a hand to Kael, who had fallen to the ground thanks to Levy's shove. Kael took it, and Levy hauled him to his feet.

For a moment, Kael's normally sour expression betrayed a flash of emotion, begrudging gratitude, mingled with the weight of understanding that without Levy's speed and strength, he would have been skewered and crushed on the pointed logs. His grip tightened on Levy's hand before releasing it, nodding once in silent thanks.

"Appreciate it," Kael grumbled, his voice rough but laced with genuine sincerity.

Levy merely shrugged, his expression slipping back into its usual calm. "You'd have done the same."

They continued forward, moving through the snow in a tense, silent line, the tree's shadows casting long fingers across their path. By the time they reached the edge of the clearing, Levy had saved them from three more traps, each one more cleverly concealed than the last, each one demanding him to act with near-immortal speed to protect his friends.

The first had been a series of rusted iron spikes hidden beneath a layer of snow that sprung up when triggered, meant to impale Andra as she walked over them. Levy had thrown himself forward, taking the brunt of the trap, the sharp metal tearing another large gash in his clothing but otherwise bouncing harmlessly against his skin.

The second was a rain of poisoned darts meant for Mallory, their tips coated with a dark, oily substance, arcing down from above. Once more, Levy had positioned himself as a shield, his eyes narrowing as the darts shattered on impact.

The third, more deadly still, had been a fire trap hidden among the snow, spouting a plume of flames that would have incinerated Kael had Levy not once again shoved him clear. By the time it was over, Levy was basically shirtless, his clothes no more than shredded rags clinging to him.

With each trap, Mallory had cast him uneasy glances, her eyes laced with anxiety and a dawning accusation. He could feel her gaze lingering on him, those moments when she seemed caught somewhere between awe and frustration.

But every time, Levy would offer her a small, placating smile as if to reassure her he was fine, thanks to the gift Styx had given him. Yet he knew the weight that came with those glances. He could feel her worry, her unspoken question.

How much more would he be able to endure trying to protect everyone?

At last, they reached the edge of the forest. The vault loomed closer now, its dark stone walls veiled in frost, framed by snow-laden branches. It seemed as if they had finally reached their goal, but Levy knew better than to relax. Something still felt wrong, a tension thrumming through the silence.

Kael halted, his eyes narrowing as he sharpened his Abyssillian senses once more.

"The forms beneath the veil," he murmured, keeping his voice low so it wouldn't carry beyond their group. "They're humanoid. There are many of them—stationed in the clearing surrounding the vault's entrance."

"Humanoid?" Mallory asked, her voice barely above a whisper. "Then, what are they? Are they hostile?"

"Probably about as hostile as those traps," Andra replied, peering at the gaping tears in Levy's clothing.

Kael gave a short, grim nod. "Hard to say for certain, but it's difficult to imagine they belong to anyone other than Aphrodite. If they're stationed outside, then she's likely already inside."

They exchanged glances, each pondering their next move.

Oath Breaker

Andra's line of sight shifted from the vault to the clearing, her jaw set in determination. "We'll need a way to break through the veil first," she said, frowning. "If they're shrouded, we won't be able to gauge their strength or prepare for their attack."

Mallory gripped the hilt of her weapon, her expression resolute. "If we can lure a few of them out, I can-"

"No," Levy interrupted. He looked at each of them in turn, his eyes calm, certain. "They can't touch me. There's only one way forward."

Before they could protest, he stepped into the clearing, and the world around them stirred—charged with anticipation, as if the very air recognized the shift in fate.

Chapter 17
Quinn

The once-grand palace loomed like a corpse of its former splendor, every detail of Olympus etched with decay as if it was eroding with time, despite this realm being untouched by it. Fragments of marble cracked and chipping lined the grand halls, and they slinked rough.

The walls, once gleaming in divine splendor, now held only ghostly shadows of faded beauty. Veins of gold threaded through the pale stone, casting an eerie glow, but even this was tarnished. The gold dimmed as if Olympus itself was festering from within.

Quinn drew a steady breath, forcing down the shiver that traced its way down his arms. The air here was thick and cold, dense with something unseen—something ancient, a wrath slumbering just beneath the surface. It coiled in the atmosphere, volatile, as if the very air might fracture and ignite with the slightest disturbance. Every breath felt heavy, every shifting shadow a potential threat.

Even Ashe, who was rarely rattled by anything, wore a deep furrow in her brow. She moved with uncharacteristic caution, her usual confidence edged with something dangerously close to fear.

They crept forward in sync, hand in hand, slipping between the shadows, their cloaks drawn tight around them. Their footfalls were muffled by layers of fine dust carpeting the once-immaculate floors. Marble busts lined the corridors, lifelike depictions of Zeus in all his immortal glory, seemingly watching them as they passed. Some of them had been shattered, faces chipped away, while others were decimated completely, as if someone had taken a sledgehammer and turned them into rubble.

Ahead, a low hum reached their ears, almost a whisper, and Quinn stilled, reaching a hand back to halt Ashe. They dare not speak in the quiet darkness, worried that their voices might carry to ears they did not want alerted to their presence. They pressed themselves against the wall, tightly against each other, watching as two figures drifted down the corridor.

Their forms flickered in and out of view, gliding rather than walking. Their skin held an unnatural luminescence, and though they were silent, Quinn felt a cold weight settle over him as they passed. Their presence was enough to make his heartbeat thunder in his chest.

He exchanged a glance with Ashe, who quickly pecked his nose, calming him, and they waited until the beings rounded a corner before they slipped forward once more.

Olympus sprawled before them like an intricate labyrinth, its twisting corridors leading them ever deeper into the mountain's heart. With each step, the halls grew narrower, the walls pressing in as though the mountain itself sought to consume them. The deeper they ventured, the more oppressive the space became, the air thick with something unseen yet undeniably present.

Shadows pooled in every crevice, lurking at the edges of their vision. Yet, despite the darkness, a faint golden mist clung to the air, casting an eerie glow. It distorted their surroundings, warping the shadows on the walls, making them stretch and shift unnaturally with every flicker of light.

They took another corner, only to find themselves ducking back immediately as yet another group of patrolling figures moved past. These ones were different, not as fluid but unnervingly alert, their eyes gleaming a pale blue that cut through the darkness.

Quinn held his breath, pressing into the alcove, Ashe a tense shadow beside him, her hand resting on a dagger at her waist. The beings passed within inches, but they moved with a sort of lazy authority, and after an eternity, they continued down the hall, oblivious to their presence.

Levy's instructions guided them, his carefully drawn sketches of Olympus' layout seared into Quinn's mind. The passage they sought lay at the very base of the palace, winding downward into depths that, save for Levy himself, had likely never felt the presence of a mortal.

They moved faster now, staying close to the walls, watching for every flicker of movement in the golden air. Every hall seemed identical, each stretch a surreal distortion of reality, as though Olympus itself were trying to disorient them.

Quinn nearly stumbled as the floor shifted beneath him, a piece of tile disintegrating to dust under his boot. Ashe caught him just in time, her hand warm and steady against Quinn's arm, her eyes alert with urgency.

As they moved on, the corridor began to slope, a subtle decline that hinted they were nearing the descent. They were getting closer to the passage. He could feel it, could sense the heaviness of the mountain shifting and pressing down on them. With each step, the volatile charge in the air intensified, seeping into his skin, into his bones, so that his breaths felt laced with the acetic taste of something ancient and powerful.

A faint sound, like banging metal, followed by a low rumbling, reached his ears, echoing from somewhere deep below. It was distant but unmistakable, and it sent a jolt through him. He glanced at Ashe questioningly, who looked back at him with a furrowed brow of her own.

According to Levy's notes, there was supposed to be a single passageway leading down to the cells deep beneath Olympus, but nothing he mentioned could explain the sounds they heard now. Had they made a wrong turn?

Quinn was certain they'd followed Levy's map precisely. Ashe only shrugged at his silent question. Retracing their steps wasn't an option with sentries floating through the halls, so they pressed onward.

A few more turns and the corridor ended in a massive doorway, half-crumbled and veined with fractures, leading into a yawning darkness beyond the passageway into the heart of the mountain. The air around it pulsed with an almost magnetic energy, and a flicker of movement caught Quinn's eye; a shifting shadow, indistinct but undeniably there, running down into the darkness below.

Quinn moved cautiously, one hand braced against the cold stone wall as he and Ashe began their descent. The air shifted as they left the main corridors of the palace, growing more humid the deeper they delved.

He felt Ashe's presence beside him, her steps barely audible, but the tension in her posture mirrored his own. Whatever movement they'd seen lurking below had vanished, swallowed by the darkness, yet the feeling of being watched lingered, pressing against his thoughts like an itch he couldn't scratch.

After a few flights down, Ashe leaned in closer, her voice barely a whisper. "That shadow—did you see where it went?"

Quinn shook his head, scanning the darkened stairwell. "No, just that it was there. But there shouldn't be anyone in these parts of the palace if Levy's intel holds up."

She nodded, glancing back up the stairs. "Feels like we're being followed, though. It's strange and empty, as this place is. I keep feeling like something is breathing down my neck. Where are all the immortals?"

"Same," Quinn murmured, flexing his fingers as he tried to shake off the sensation. Here, in the depths of Olympus, the volatile atmosphere of the upper halls felt sharper, as though each step was drawing them closer to some hidden doom. "Stay close. I'll try to pick up anything unusual."

They descended a few more steps in silence, Ashe's breaths measured beside him. But he felt her attention on him, her gaze searching his face for any indication of what might lie ahead. Finally, she asked, "Anything?"

He hesitated, reaching out with his senses, strengthened by his Abyssillian blood, tracing the ebb and flow of the strange energies pulsing through the stone around them. He closed his eyes for a heartbeat, letting himself attune to the essences that permeated this place. It was old—achingly old—and powerful, twisted as if bound and constrained, seeping into the very foundation of Olympus.

"There's a lot of essence below us," he whispered, opening his eyes. "It's massive, concentrated, almost like it's coiled up, waiting.

It could be Clotho," he added, though doubt colored his words. There was something off about it. He was used to Ashe's essence, the feel of Fate. What he felt did not feel like a Weaver.

Ashe's face was tense in the gloom, her hand shifting toward the hilt of her daggers instinctively. "What if it's not?"

He glanced at her, gauging the steady determination in her eyes. "Then we tread carefully, and worst-case scenario, we portal out without Clotho. Whatever it is, we're about to find out. Be on your guard."

The descent seemed never-ending, and they moved in silence again, senses heightened, steps careful. Yet, somehow, they found themselves at the bottom sooner than expected, as if the stairs had shifted beneath them, shortening their path. Quinn frowned as they stepped off the final step, his eyes adjusting to the room they found themselves in.

It was vast, the stone walls stretching upward and disappearing into darkness. Dust hung in the air, disturbed by their arrival, and the silence was heavy, as though any sound was swallowed by the very walls themselves. To the left, a crude hallway was cut into the rock, cloaked in shadows, but for a faint, orange glow that bled into the edges of the darkness, illuminating nothing but hinting at something further along.

Further ahead, another stairway descended deeper still, continuing into the depths of Olympus, where the dungeons were meant to be. Quinn stared at the hallway, brow furrowed. There had been no mention of a room and corridor cutting off their descent and certainly no mention of a split path. He'd memorized every twist, every turn, but this layout was different.

Ashe shifted beside him, her golden eyes captured in the faint orange glow. "This wasn't on Levy's map."

"No, it wasn't," Quinn replied, his voice steady as he drew his sword. His gaze shifted to the corridor, where a young woman now stood.

Before he could react, Ashe let out a cry, collapsing to the ground as golden light poured from her eyes.

Oath Breaker

Chapter 18
Talius

Talius lay suspended in a timeless void, shackled to the stone pillar, the ancient walls drawing his essence with an insatiable hunger. Darkness ebbed and flowed around him, an unrelenting companion that blurred the boundaries of reality.

The passage of time had long since dissolved into obscurity, swallowed by the eternal ache in his body and the searing pain that wracked his soul. He had chosen this—willingly subjected himself to this torment—a final service for humanity. Yet, the reasons felt distant, almost faint, buried under a mountain of suffering and exhaustion.

Was it morning? Was it night? He couldn't tell. Sometimes, he wasn't even sure if he was truly awake or if he was slipping into another vision, drifting between past and present like a leaf on a river.

Today— or was it yesterday?—a familiar scene replayed before him, vivid and merciless in its detail.

Two figures stood before him in his old office, their faces sharp and alert. The woman, with long black hair and striking red eyes, was pretty but not beautiful in the conventional sense. Her face held a severe elegance, the kind that commanded respect rather than admiration.

Beside her, the man was tall, his short black hair framing an intense, brooding expression, red eyes a fierce mirror to her own. These Abyssillian leaders had journeyed from the Wastes to meet with him, braving the hostile world of humanity to negotiate food for their people.

Their names, though; he couldn't remember their names. Time and torment had robbed him of details that once felt so clear. Even now, in the surreal haze of memory and delirium, their voices echoed with all-too-familiar emotions: shock, outrage, disbelief. They watched him, wide-eyed, as he proposed his deal, his words cool and calculated, knowing full well the weight of his offer.

"I can provide food and supplies," he had said, his voice a calm veil over cold resolve. "Enough to sustain your people for ten years."

The woman's eyes narrowed in suspicion. "And what would you ask in return?"

Talius hesitated, only a beat, but it was enough to set off a spark of foreboding in their expressions.

"Your child," he replied. "Leave him with me, and your people will want for nothing."

The response had been immediate, visceral. The woman clutched the baby to her chest, her red eyes blazing. "Our son is not a bargaining chip!"

The man's face twisted in anger. "You would ask this of us? Do you truly believe our child's life is worth mere food?"

The words cut through him even now, the accusation and fury in their voices ringing in his ears as he slumped in his chains, seething against his helplessness. He knew what was about to come next and understood the horror that he could neither prevent nor escape from.

Even within the torment of his penance, he felt the faint sting of resentment mingling with guilt, his hands curling reflexively as he watched the memory unfold.

With a heavy heart, he forced the words. "Then I regret that it must come to this."

With a flick of his wrist, two figures emerged from the shadows behind the Abyssillians. Masters, silent and deadly, trained to take life without hesitation.

Before the couple had a chance to react, the Masters struck, plunging their blades with ruthless efficiency. The woman let out a strangled cry, her arms wrapping protectively around the child, even as she crumpled to the floor. The man fought, his face a mask of rage and sorrow, but he, too, fell to the unforgiving steel.

Talius moved forward, almost mechanically, the baby now alone and wailing. Guilt gnawed at him as he bent down, lifting the child, Quinn, into his arms, his cries muffled against his chest. He whispered softly, his voice hollow. "Forgive me."

He ordered the Masters to take the bodies, to stage them in the town square. The scene would be made to look like an act of human hatred, a message designed to rally the Abyssillians, to spark the anger he needed them to feel. For the prophecy to come to pass, there had to be three heroes, and he had ensured Quinn would become one of them.

The memory faded, the faces of the couple vanishing, replaced by the jagged stone of what may as well have been his cell. But Quinn's cries lingered, haunting and piercing through the darkness.

Chapter 19
Levy

Levy stepped into the clearing, his breath hanging in the cold air before dissipating into the quiet. He expected the figures Kael had warned about to remain hidden beneath their magical veil, continuing to lurk as an unseen threat.

But he wasn't concerned. He had faced worse than these supposed guardians, and as the traps had demonstrated earlier, they wouldn't be able to harm him, no matter what they tried.

He took another step, and to his surprise, the figures did appear, materializing in the snow-covered clearing one by one, emerging from the faint shimmer of an illusion. They were…men.

Massive, muscled men, their physiques bordering on statuesque, with chiseled features and flawless skin, warriors crafted by some indulgent god.

Goddess, in this case, he supposed.

Not a single one wore a shirt, and their bare skin gleamed under the morning sun, each marked with numbers upon their powerful chests in sparkling black ink. Against the snowy landscape, their attire was absurd: they all wore tight, bright pink briefs that clung to them like a second skin.

Levy's instincts, however, flared with a sense of danger that belied their bizarre appearance. None of them carried weapons, yet there was something in their stance; a predatory, waiting energy. His eyes flicked from one face to the next, noting the identical blank expressions on each. They stood still as statues, muscular arms hanging at their sides, eyes forward and entirely unfocused as if they were staring straight through him.

The sound of snow crunching behind him signaled the arrival of the others. Mallory came up beside him, followed by Andra and Kael, each casting uncertain glances at the strange assembly of guardians. Even Horacio padded into the clearing, his scaled body tense, growling softly as his tail flicked in agitation.

Mallory took one look at the figures and arched a brow, her lips curling into a smirk.

"Well, I didn't expect to walk into a clearing full of beefcakes when I woke up this morning. Do they come with a warning label?"

She paused, cocking her head as she inspected them. "Looks like they're missing something up top…if their mouths were open, I'd almost expect them to start drooling."

Levy snorted though he kept his gaze firmly on the strange guardians. "They're not reacting to us," he muttered, more to himself than anyone else.

Their eyes held that same blank stare, so unseeing it was almost unsettling. They gave no indication they even recognized the four of them standing in the clearing.

Mallory, ever the bold one, stepped closer to the nearest figure, leaning up on her toes to wave a gloved hand in front of his eyes. There was no reaction. His head didn't tilt, his eyes didn't focus or follow, and there was not even a blink.

"Yep, definitely brawn over brains. Maybe you should try Kael. They seem like more your speed."

Kael picked up a snowball, flinging it at Mallory, who ducked and then jumped back with a gasp as it broke upon the nearest 'beefcake,' as she had called them. To Levy's surprise, there still was no reaction.

Everything about these guardians, from their absurd appearance to their unnervingly blank stares, set his instincts on edge. Whatever essence bound them, it was unlike any he had encountered before. They continued to stand there, unmoving, as though waiting.

He clenched his jaw, trying to shrug off the prickle of dread that nagged at him. His eyes shifted back to the vault ahead, the structure looming at the far end of the clearing. It was so close now, practically within reach.

"Let me go first," he told them, taking a slow, deliberate step forward, his focus fixed on the vault.

He wanted to see how the guardians would react once he made it near the structure. To his surprise, he made it without any trouble. He looked back at his friends, nodding for them to join him.

But as they advanced, the figures shifted. It was slight, almost unnoticeable at first, but then each of them raised a muscled arm, their movements eerily synchronized, and barred the path ahead with an outstretched hand.

One of them finally moved, his head tilting down to look at Levy, and for the first time, Levy saw life flicker in his eyes. The guardian's gaze settled on him with chilling focus, and in a voice as cold and deep as the frozen landscape around them, he spoke.

"Only him."

"Like hell, only him," Mallory snapped, stepping forward with a defiant glare at the guardians.

The one who had spoken slowly turned his head to look at her, his blank stare narrowing into something sharper, more present. Levy tensed, his body coiled and ready to strike, feeling the air thicken with tension as the guardian seemed to consider Mallory's defiance.

For a moment, his eyes went blank again as if waiting on some unseen authority. Then, in the same flat, unfeeling tone, he announced, "The Mistress has agreed to allow the concubine to join you."

Mallory seethed, her voice a pitch higher than usual. "CONCUBINE?!" she shrieked, her fists clenched tightly. "I've slapped men for less than that."

"If you touch me with your unclean hands," the guardian replied, his tone unchanged but chillingly final. "You will die."

Levy's expression darkened, a dangerous gleam flickering in his eyes. He stepped between Mallory and her beefcake, his voice low and edged with barely restrained anger.

"Threaten her safety again," he warned, each word laced with lethal promise. "And *you* will die."

Oath Breaker

The guardian tilted his head, regarding Levy, with an almost curious expression. Neither moved, each locked in an icy standoff, while the rest of the guardians remained as still as statues, their blank stares unwavering. The tension felt like it might snap the air itself, the silence pressing in on them with an almost physical weight.

But the standoff was broken by a distant, resounding noise from below; a deep, rumbling groan, like a massive door sliding open within the vault.

"Uh, guys?" Andra's voice cut into their heated exchange, her tone tense and urgent. "Sounds like we're running out of time."

The panic in her voice was enough to snap Levy back into focus. He cast a quick glance back at her, noting the worry etched across her face as she looked from the guardians to the vault's entrance.

Her eyes shifted meaningfully to him and Mallory. "If they're willing to let you two through, then go," she said firmly. "Kael and I will join you when we can."

Levy felt a surge of unease at the words, knowing full well that *join you when we can* was code for, "We'll handle this threat, even if it means fighting them."

Leaving Andra and Kael alone with these strange guardians didn't sit right with him, especially given the unreadable malice he sensed beneath their blank stares. His instincts screamed that these were no ordinary threat and that whatever essence bound them was powerful and likely brutal. He opened his mouth to argue, to find a way to insist they stay together.

But Kael interrupted his deliberation with a sharp, snarled, "Go!"

The command was fierce, brooking no argument. Kael's eyes bored into him, unyielding as iron, and Levy realized he would not let him hesitate. He cast one last look at Andra, whose determined nod seemed to assure him she was ready for whatever lay ahead, then gave a reluctant nod of his own.

He turned to Mallory, the two of them exchanging a brief glance, a shared understanding that if anything went wrong, they would find their way back. She took a steadying breath, drawing her own resolve, and then together, they moved forward, stepping past the guardians as they descended toward the dark entrance of the vault.

The vault's interior was a stark contrast to the open snow-covered landscape. Its narrow stone corridor was lined with ancient, flickering torches that barely managed to cast warmth or light against the rough-hewn walls.

Levy inhaled, remembering the tepid smell of petrichor from his previous visit. As they walked further in, a coldness seeped into the air, deeper and more unsettling than the chill outside. An oppressive, almost malevolent, force that weighed down on them with every step.

Mallory glanced back over her shoulder; her lips pressed into a tight line. "They better be okay up there."

Though she was putting on a brave face, Levy caught the edge of worry in her tone.

"They will be," he replied, more to reassure her than himself. But in truth, he worried about Andra and Kael as well. Those guardians were more than they seemed, and it gnawed at him that he'd left them behind.

"Let's focus on what we came here for," he added, keeping his voice steady as he reached out, wrapping an arm around her shoulder. "They'll find a way to follow."

To his surprise, she leaned further into his warmth, nodding in agreement, though her expression remained tight.

The tunnel continued to slope steeply downward, leading them deeper into the depths of the vault. Ancient runes were carved into the walls and upon individual doors, their symbols barely visible beneath layers of grime.

Some were familiar sigils, marks of more recent make, while others Levy couldn't immediately recognize. Yet each symbol seemed to pulse faintly, as though infused with watchful, lingering essence.

A flicker of movement up ahead caught his attention, and Levy halted, motioning for Mallory to stop as well. They stilled, listening to the silence, waiting for any sign of danger.

Mallory exhaled, her voice soft but laced with a hint of impatience. "If we don't walk away with something worth all this trouble down here…"

A woman's voice interrupted her, carrying a tone that was

somehow both melodic and husky, stirring an unsettling mix of emotions in Levy, none of them appropriate for the moment. "Come along now, my sweetlings. I'm freezing down here, and this vault isn't going to open itself."

"I have a feeling we will."

Chapter 20
Ashe

The last thing Ashe remembered was the oppressive, stale air of Olympus pressing in around her, her eyes on Quinn as he scanned the room. Then, in an instant, she was no longer in the depths of the mountain.

The cold hit her first, biting, bone-deep, cutting through her as if it sought to consume her from the inside out. She stood at the edge of a cliff, overlooking a vast void of blackness, as though the very ground had been swallowed by darkness.

Snowflakes drifted around her, their delicate patterns shimmering faintly, only to dissolve the moment they touched her skin. The silence was dense, laced with a deep, foreboding sense of dread that settled over her like a heavy shroud, squeezing the breath from her chest. A harsh wind picked up, slicing through the air with a chill that seemed to carry whispers from below, hissing secrets too faint to decipher.

And then, from deep within the abyss, a voice rose up to her, a cold, rasping whisper that wound its way into her mind, each word dripping with malice and taunting familiarity.

"Look who has come to visit me," it drawled, echoing up from the pit below with a mocking edge. The voice was slick with amusement, though it held a venomous undercurrent that made her

stomach twist.

Ashe's fists clenched at her sides, every instinct screaming at her to recoil from the sound, but she forced herself to hold steady. She knew this voice- knew it too well, a reminder of past battles and wounds barely healed. A shadow from her past she thought she'd left fractured in ruin.

"The last time I was graced by your presence, you shattered my vessel," the voice continued, its tone curdling with anger. "My consciousness splintered—fractured. And yet, here we are again. But look at you now... brimming with Fate's power, unraveling piece by piece."

The laughter that followed was like nails scraping against her skull. She wanted to shout back, to defy him, but her voice was trapped, locked inside her throat. The voice, as though sensing her silent resistance, slithered closer, more vicious with each word.

"Stand aside and watch, little pawn of Fate. This is the future that will unfold before you. You may have grown powerful, yes, but you will be powerless to stop it. Your mortal body cannot contain Fate's essence much longer."

The words twisted like a knife in her gut, and though she fought to ignore them, she knew, deep down, that there was truth in what he said. Even now, she felt the strain of the power within her, pulsing just beneath her skin, a force too great for any one person to bear.

A cold smile lingered in the silence.

"Watch."

The voice whispered with twisted delight. "Watch as your beloved once again makes a dangerous deal. Watch as you are powerless to stop it."

Ashe's heart lurched, her pulse pounding in her ears. She whirled, a sense of panic tightening in her chest, and saw Quinn standing at the edge of the cliff beside her. But he didn't see her. His gaze was fixed on the darkness below, oblivious to her presence as though she were nothing more than a ghost watching from a distance.

"Quinn!" She called his name, her voice desperate, but no sound emerged. She couldn't reach him. Couldn't warn him.

He looked whole, untouched- but there was something wrong. As he shifted, a jagged scar peeked out from beneath the collar of his shirt, a mark she didn't remember seeing before. And then, with a grim determination, he took a breath and spoke a name that chilled her blood.

"Chaos."

The word rippled through the air, and Ashe's stomach twisted as a faint, keening laughter answered him, filling the frozen silence. The darkness below them stirred, shifting with an almost gleeful energy, and slowly, a massive, ghastly form began to rise from the pit.

Chaos—a warped, shadowy figure, shifting between shapes and forms, but always terrible, ancient, and overwhelming. Its eyes gleamed with cruel delight as it extended a taloned hand, wrapping it around Quinn, though he remained oblivious to its presence.

"No, Quinn, don't!" Ashe reached out, but her fingers met only the biting cold of empty air. Her voice, her touch, they couldn't reach him.

She could only watch in helpless horror as Quinn spoke to Chaos, his words lost to her, swallowed by a void so dark even Fate's light could not pierce it. Whatever bargain he was making, whatever promise or oath he was binding himself to, it was costing him.

She saw his essence begin to drain, a shimmer of light pulling from him and vanishing into Chaos's grasp as if he were pouring his very soul into the creature.

"Stop! Please, don't do this!" Ashe pleaded, tears stinging her eyes, but her words faded into the silence, lost before they even reached him. She tried to step forward, to throw herself between Quinn and the terrible shadow, but her feet were rooted to the ground as if the cold itself had wrapped around her ankles, holding her in place.

"Ah, ah, ah," Chaos chided her. "The dead don't talk."

And then, as suddenly as it began, the vision shattered. The world around her fractured, the dark cliffs now dissolving into light until there was nothing left but a blinding golden glow flooding her vision.

She blinked, gasping as the light faded, and found herself back in Olympus. The cold dread of her vision clung to her like frost. Her eyes snapped open, her breaths shallow and fast, and Quinn's face swam into view, his expression alarmed as he knelt beside her. She felt the frantic beat of her heart pounding against her ribs. Her hands trembled, her skin tingling with heat as she burned.

"Ashe?" Quinn's voice was strained. His brow was creased with worry as he searched her eyes for any clue she might be injured. "What happened? One second, you were fine, and then…" Ashe struggled to find her voice, swallowing hard as she tried to shake the lingering feeling of that ghastly hand reaching for Quinn.

"You can't do it!" she shouted hoarsely. "Whatever you do, whatever happens to me, you absolutely cannot make a deal with Chaos!"

Quinn's expression softened, though worry still etched his face. He reached out, steadying her with a firm hand on her shoulder.

"Ashe, listen to me. Chaos is gone. Whatever you saw…it wasn't real. He doesn't have any hold on me anymore."

As Ashe's breathing slowly steadied, the frantic beat of her heart began to calm as well. Quinn's unwavering gaze was an anchor, pulling her back from the edge of the panic her vision had left in its wake. She clung to the certainty in his eyes, letting it ground her against the torrent of fear and confusion.

"…telling you she will not last much longer if you do not allow me to take her to him." A voice filtered into focus from behind Quinn. Ashe blinked, looking past his shoulder, and her eyes settled on the figure standing a few paces behind him.

She wore a flowing, pure-white toga that draped gracefully across her shoulders and down to her feet, embroidered with intricate golden patterns that shimmered faintly in the low light. Her dark hair framed a face that was both strong and serene, crowned with a circlet of golden leaves resting delicately upon her brow. Around her, an aura of gold radiated softly, casting her in an ethereal light that illuminated her elegance, her immortality.

Quinn tensed under Ashe's gaze, sensing her focus shift. He moved subtly, stepping protectively between Ashe and the woman. His sword remained steady in his hand, raised just slightly, a silent warning to the stranger. But Ashe noticed the telltale crease of uncertainty in his brow, an indication that he was wary but not entirely surprised by her presence.

"Who are you?" Ashe's voice was hoarse, her throat raw and in desperate need of some water.

The woman's gaze flicked to her, her expression softening with genuine concern. "I am Charis," she replied, her voice confident yet rich with urgency. "Wife of Hephaestus."

Ashe processed the name, her thoughts racing as the vision's grip continued to fade. Quinn's jaw tightened at the introduction, and his suspicion flared again.

Charis continued, her words directed at Quinn now. "Your friend is not immortal, and her body cannot bear the strain of Fate's power much longer. She will need help—his help——if you would only allow me to take her to him."

Quinn's grip on his sword remained tight, his voice edged with distrust. "Hephaestus."

His words were clipped, his tone a mix of skepticism and frustration. "We have no reason to trust him. Or you, for that matter. Last I checked, the Olympians wanted us dead."

Something stirred within Ashe as she stared at the immortal; a pulse of warmth, of comfort. She reached out, placing a hand on Quinn's arm.

"Quinn…" she said softly, though her words were still strained. "I think we can trust her."

She glanced back at Charis, feeling the unmistakable pull of something deeper, something beyond her understanding. "Fate smiles upon her."

Quinn looked back at her, his expression caught between concern for her and his instinctive distrust of the immortals. "Ashe," his tone carried an edge of warning, "you've just come out of a vision. This could be…"

Charis raised a hand, her voice urgent. "If we had any intention of betraying you, we could have called Zeus down upon you the moment you stepped into Olympus."

She held his gaze, her tone unwavering. "We both know the risks you took coming here. Hephaestus and I have been watching you since the moment you entered these halls, and if we wanted to turn you over or harm you in any way, we would have done so already."

Quinn continued to stare at Charis for a moment longer, a flicker of uncertainty crossing his face. But Ashe's hand on his arm kept him from pushing further, and the conviction in her eyes seemed to ease some of the tension in his shoulders. After a long, silent moment, he exhaled, glancing back down at Ashe, his own reluctance still clear.

"Why are you and Hephaestus hiding down in the depths of Olympus?" she asked, remembering that there was no mention of this chamber in Levy's notes.

Charis glanced up the darkened stairs, her expression shadowed with something unreadable. "Hephaestus can tell you more, but I will tell you this," she replied, her voice quiet, scared. "We do not believe ourselves safe so long as Zeus remains seated upon the throne."

Ashe felt a surge of opportunity at her words, a faint stirring of hope tempered by caution. She exchanged a glance with Quinn, who had caught the same implication. It was startling, the idea of an Olympian questioning Zeus' reign. But then Hestia came to mind, and it was her initial betrayal of Zeus that had started this all. She was a reminder that gods weren't always the enemy, that some held motives and loyalties beyond Olympus.

The glimmer of possibility nudged Ashe forward. "Do you know where Clotho is being kept?"

Charis nodded, pointing down the stairway that descended into darkness. "The dungeons are just a little further below," she answered. "But if you plan to free her, you should be quick. Zeus has been visiting her more and more frequently. You may not have long."

Ashe's eyes flicked to Quinn, a faint tremor of fear threading through the resolve in her next words. "Go. Find Clotho. I'll be fine."

Quinn's face shifted from suspicion to pure reluctance, and she felt his arm tense once more beneath her grip. "Ashe," he began, a note of barely veiled protest in his voice.

"You can't ask me to leave you here alone. You're in no condition to be left behind with immortals we don't know that we can trust."

She squeezed his arm, managing a reassuring smile despite the weakness spreading through her body. "I'll be fine. Charis and Hephaestus are not our enemies. I believe that. And I believe in you.

Go. Clotho needs us, and we need her."

For a moment, he said nothing, watching her with an intensity that sent a thrill through her heart. Then, after a heavy pause, he took her hand in his, his thumb tracing a gentle circle against her palm.

His voice dropped to a near-whisper, deep and resonant. "Stay safe. I'll tear down Olympus itself to get back to you if I have to."

He leaned forward, his lips brushing hers in a brief, tender kiss that left her dizzy. When he pulled back, his gaze lingered, an unspoken promise between them. Then, reluctantly, he turned, disappearing down the stone steps into the depths below.

Charis stepped closer; her eyes softened with understanding. "He loves you fiercely."

Ashe felt a soft smile touch her lips, but the moment was cut short as her body throbbed with renewed weakness, a low hum of heat simmering beneath her skin. Charis moved quickly, slipping her arms underneath Ashe and lifting her with a strength that belied her thin frame.

Ashe's vision swam, her skin flushed, and she knew that whatever was happening, it was worse than she had let on to Quinn.

She leaned her head against Charis' shoulder, no longer able to keep it up, as the immortal carried her deeper into the orange-lit corridor. The warmth from the hall mingled with the heat in her own body, and a wave of fear ran through her.

She had never felt so weak, so vulnerable, and now she was placing her trust in an Olympian. But she held on to the belief that she had made the right choice, even as her strength continued to slip away.

The steady, rhythmic sound of hammering echoed faintly from somewhere further down the hall, an oddly comforting beat against the hollow silence of Olympus. It grew louder as they moved forward, each strike reverberating through the stone walls.

Ashe let her eyes flutter shut, holding on to the sound as her mind drifted, the warmth of the orange glow and the distant hammering lulling her as Charis carried her deeper into the unknown.

Oath Breaker

Chapter 21
Andra

Andra watched as Levy and Mallory disappeared into the vault's shadowed entrance, his discomfort growing with every second. The guardians—the statuesque, shirtless men with their absurdly muscular builds and strange, blank stares—settled back into their stillness the moment the two had passed, their eyes losing whatever glimmer of life had briefly appeared.

Now, they simply stood in silence, barring the way.

She exchanged a glance with Kael, each of them communicating in a familiar, wordless way they had developed in their years together in Petram. They had to find a way through; leaving Levy and Mallory alone in that ominous vault was not an option.

But they had seen the guardians' swift, intimidating response, and Andra could feel Kael's mind working just as fast as her own, searching for an approach that might let them slip past without a fight.

A low snuffling sound broke her focus. Horacio was inspecting the nearest guardian, his scaled snout pressed against the man's leg. He sniffed, his nostrils flaring, golden eyes narrowed in intense scrutiny. Andra held her breath, hoping the Drakon's bold curiosity wouldn't trigger an attack.

After a final huff, Horacio did something that made Andra bite back a laugh. With an air of utter disdain, he lifted his leg and sprayed a quick stream of urine as if it were nothing more than an unimpressive tree in the wild.

The Drakon lowered his leg and stalked back to her side, looking entirely unbothered. Andra glanced at the guardian's blank face, her hand ready upon her weapon, bracing for an angry response. But the guardian did nothing.

He didn't even blink. The fact that Horacio's display of disrespect had gone unnoticed made Andra snicker, and beside her, Kael let out a howl of laughter as well.

"Good boy," she murmured, scratching Horacio's scaled neck. Kael shook his head, looking amused.

Their revelry was cut short as a sudden, piercing scream echoed deep from within the vault. Mallory.

Andra's heart lurched, and she looked at Kael, her eyes hardening. Whatever was happening down there, they could no longer afford to wait. Without a word, she stepped forward, determined to push through the wall of meat standing between them and their friends.

But as soon as she moved, the guardians shifted again, their muscled bodies snapping to attention and forming an unbreakable wall between her and the entrance. Andra gritted her teeth, frustration roiling beneath her calm surface, and she felt adrenaline course through her. Just as she was about to act, Kale moved, his own face mirroring her frustration.

"Enough of this," he growled, his hand reaching for his weapon.

Kael's khopesh gleamed in the early light as he drew it, an elegant yet deadly weapon that he wielded with expert precision. Its curved blade shimmered with a faint, dark sheen that spoke to the rare metals from which it was forged.

The hilt was carved with intricate designs, the metal etched with delicate symbols of power, while the blade itself had a beautiful, cruel curve, honed to a razor's edge and stained black. It was a blade meant for breaking armor and bodies, designed to slice through anything, mortal, monster, or otherwise.

Without hesitation, Kael swung the khopesh with a savage,

sweeping arc. The blade cut through the air with a whisper before meeting its target, slicing cleanly through the neck of the nearest guardian. The muscular figure crumpled instantly, the severed head hitting the ground and rolling to a stop at Andra's feet, its blank eyes staring unseeing up at her.

For a second, everything was silent again, then all hell broke loose.

The remaining guardians snapped to attention, their once empty eyes suddenly alive with purpose and menace, moving together as if one giant hivemind. Every head turned to look at Kael, and Andra's heart sank as a wave of unease washed over her. The silence felt dangerous now, weighted with a threat far more intense than before.

Kael glanced at her, a grim smirk tugging at his lips. "Uh-oh."

Before he could raise his khopesh again, one of the guardians lashed out, his bare, muscular leg swinging with unnatural speed and slamming directly into Kael's side. Andra watched, stunned, as the blow sent Kael flying, his body hurtling through the air and landing ten feet back in the snow with a dull thud.

"Kael!" she shouted, rushing toward him. But her path was immediately blocked by another enemy, his hulking frame standing solidly in her way. She could see Kael slowly rising to his feet, wincing as he clutched his side, his face twisted with pain.

Andra's hand tightened around the hilt of her own sword, her knuckles white. She fought the urge to unleash it from its sheathe, adrenaline and anger coursing through her, but she held herself in check, waiting to see if the guardians struck again or if that had been a simple retaliation.

These were not ordinary opponents; each movement they made was precise, controlled.

One of the guardians stepped closer to her, his blank stare focusing ever so slightly on her face. Andra met his gaze, unflinching, as her mind raced. She had to think of something, anything, that could get them past these obstacles and into the vault to help their friends. But the guardians moved with synchronized intent, forcing her back toward Kael, who was finally on his feet again.

His jaw was clenched, his breath coming in quick, shallow gasps. "Looks like this might take a bit more...persuasion," he grunted, readying his blade to strike again.

Andra nodded, drawing her sword, an elegant blade of silver that shone even in the muted light of the clearing. Its length was perfectly balanced, long, and deadly, its blade honed to a fine edge that could slice through flesh like butter.

The hilt was bound in dark leather, comfortable and secure in her grip. She took a steadying breath, grounding herself as she prepared to face the wall of muscle bearing down on them.

Beside her, Horacio released a low, menacing growl, his lips curling back to reveal rows of gleaming, dagger-sharp teeth. His scales shimmered over taut, coiled muscles—his entire form wound like a spring on the verge of release. As the guardians closed in, they struck as one—seamless, relentless, a brutal force of instinct and precision.

Andra's blade flashed as she swung it in a deadly arc, slicing through the nearest guardian's shoulder, cutting deep into muscle and sinew. The man staggered back, his expression unchanging even as blood darkened his skin. He moved to attack again, but before he could react, Horacio was on him, his powerful jaws snapping shut around the man's arm with a sickening crunch.

The guardian tried to retaliate, but Horacio puffed out a thick cloud of smoke, blinding him just long enough for Andra to step in and drive her blade clean through his chest. The man fell, finally still, but there were dozens more closing in, and they barely had a moment to regroup.

Around them, the clearing had erupted into chaos. Kael had been forced several paces away from her, surrounded by at least a dozen of the guardians. His weapon was a blur in his hands, a black arc slicing through the air in a graceful dance.

Each swing of the curved blade found its mark, tearing through flesh and leaving deep wounds that would have killed an ordinary man. But the guardians shrugged it off as though they didn't feel it at all. Even when mortally wounded, they kept coming, moving with an unnatural resilience that defied logic.

One lunged at Kael from behind, his muscled arm swinging down to deliver a crushing blow. Kael twisted, ducking just in time, his blade slicing across the man's chest in a vicious, shallow cut before he spun to intercept another oncoming attacker. The blade flew through the air, as fluid as water but as deadly as flame, yet no matter how deeply he cut, his opponents barely faltered.

Andra felt a sudden impact against her back as one of the guardians barreled into her, forcing her to stagger forward. She gritted her teeth, twisting around to drive her blade into his thigh, then sidestepped his brutal fist as he swung at her head.

Her arm burned from the effort, the force behind the strikes enough to shatter bone if she mistimed a dodge, but she pushed through, her focus narrowing to the blade in her hand and the enemies before her.

Horacio let out a roar, launching himself at a nearby threat with his claws outstretched. His talons tore into the man's bare torso, ripping through muscle, his weight alone enough to knock the guardian off his feet.

The man tried to recover, but Horacio was faster, puffing another cloud of thick, acrid smoke into his eyes, rendering him momentarily blind. As the guardian flailed, Horacio's tail whipped around, striking with the force of a battering ram and sending him crashing into another nearby.

But the rest were relentless, their sheer numbers overwhelming. Three of them moved on Andra at once, their bare fists swinging with crushing strength, and she barely had time to raise her sword in defense.

One caught her arm, a brutal impact that sent a jolt of pain down to her fingertips. She bit down hard, ignoring the sting, and swept her blade in a low arc, slicing into a thigh here, a knee there, anything to weaken their movements and keep herself upright within the press of bodies.

One grabbed her from behind, pinning her arms, and Andra cursed, thrashing against his iron grip. But Horacio was there in an instant, his jaws closing over the man's shoulder, tearing him back and freeing Andra to swing her sword upward, driving the blade through the attacker's chest in a swift, clean strike.

Despite the relentless onslaught, Horacio moved through the chaos untouched, his strikes swift and deliberate. He was a storm of claws, teeth, and smoke, lashing out at any guardian that dared venture too close. His instincts, honed for battle and bound to his duty to protect Andra, guided him as he carved through their ranks with ruthless efficiency.

But even his ferocity could only hold back so many. As the fight wore on, Andra felt the strain seep into her limbs, each swing of her weapon growing heavier, each breath harder to draw.

Her gaze flicked to Kael. His pace had slowed, his breaths sharp and ragged. His khopesh, slick with blood, gleamed darkly through his increasingly wild swings. His strikes turned brutal, desperate, yet for every foe he wounded, only a few fell.

The guardians' unnatural resilience made them nearly impenetrable, their bodies absorbing punishment with eerie endurance as they continued to press in around him.

Another guardian flung himself at Andra, his fists swinging for her head, and she ducked, pivoting to drive her sword into his side, twisting the blade for maximum damage before wrenching it free. But the force of the pull unbalanced her, and before she could regain her footing, a massive hand closed around her arm, yanking her back and sending a flair of pain through her shoulder.

Horacio snarled, lunging for the guardian's neck. With a powerful bite, he forced the man to release her, his lifeless body falling to the ground and staining the snow crimson. Andra stumbled, but she regained her balance quickly.

She raised her sword once more, bracing herself for the next wave of attacks. A chill ran through her as the truth dawned on her; they were going to need a miracle to get out of this.

Oath Breaker

Chapter 22
Quinn

The deeper Quinn moved into the dungeons, the thicker the air seemed to grow. Moisture clung to the walls, slick and cold, and the faint drip of water echoed down the stone corridor, giving the place a spooky, rhythmic cadence.

The scent of mildew and rot saturated every breath, making it almost painful to inhale. Shadows pooled in the corners of the hall, and the further he descended, the more the volatile tang of ozone built around him, sharp and bitter, pressing against his senses like a warning.

He pushed forward, every nerve taut as he passed row upon row of cells. They were all empty now, but the remnants of past occupants lingered, haunting in their silence. In one cell, a single chain lay in the center of the room, its links coated in rust, with a stain beside it that looked suspiciously like blood.

In another, a tiny wooden figurine sat abandoned on a small ledge; a crude, hand-carved likeness of a bird, its wings chipped away by time. The cell beyond held a scrap of cloth, blue once, but now so faded it was nearly colorless, fraying at the edges.

One cell, its bars slightly bent, caught his eye as he passed, and he hesitated. On the floor inside lay a collection of bones, old and brittle, scattered as though thrown down in frustration. The skull sat in the far corner, tilted as if it were still watching the world with empty, accusing eyes.

Quinn felt a chill run through him, but he pressed on, quickening his pace. The urge to reach the end of the corridor grew, as did the sense of power that prickled along his skin. It was foreign, yet faintly familiar as if it resonated with something he knew, and his mind instinctively turned to Ashe.

The faint pulse of energy felt like a thread of her essence, woven, ancient, and resilient, like the threads she held in her hands each time she dared to wield Fate. He quickened his pace, following that barely-there presence, until he reached the final cell.

The iron bars hung slightly open as though beckoning him forward. Quinn paused, unsettled. Why was the door unlocked? He strained his senses, listening, but the only sound was the steady drip of water and the faint hum of energy saturating the air, pressing against him. Cautiously, he stepped closer and peered inside.

Clotho was chained to the wall, though to call the figure before him "Clotho" felt almost incorrect. This was a woman who had been reduced to a shell of herself. Her wrists and ankles were shackled, the heavy iron biting deep into her skin.

She was unclothed, her skin marred by wounds both fresh and old, ichor and sweat mingling in streaks and patches across her bruised flesh. Her limbs bore deep burns that traced jagged paths over her body, not the marks of fire, but something sharper, harsher, with an unnatural pattern that reminded him of a sharp crack of lightning.

The smell of ozone was strongest here, thick and metallic, filling his lungs with each breath. Her hair was patchy, bald spots marring her scalp where it looked as if chunks had been torn away. Her mouth gaped as she grinned up at him, her lips cracked and bloody, her gums empty where teeth should have been.

Yet, despite her gruesome state, she looked up at him with an expression of strange delight. Her eyes, though bloodshot and clouded, shone with something almost like amusement. She let out a hoarse, rasping laugh, one that seemed to fill the dank cell with an eerie echo.

"I was wondering when I would see you again, my champion,"

she crooned, her voice scratchy, raw, yet filled with something disturbingly close to mirth.

Quinn's breath caught. This was not the reaction he had anticipated. He'd expected despair, agony, perhaps even anger. But not this. Not this strange, unhinged joy amid such suffering.

The sight of her alone was enough to unsettle him, and her words were even worse. She couldn't possibly know him…could she? He took a cautious step forward, choosing his words carefully.

"You must be mistaking me for someone else," he said softly, forcing a calm he didn't entirely feel. "We've never met."

Clotho's laughter bubbled up again, a hoarse, scraping sound that cut through the silence. She leaned her head back against the cold stone wall, her chains rattling with the movement, her eyes gleaming with a disturbing clarity as she looked at him. Her smile stretched wider; her face almost alight with amusement.

"Oh, but I have seen you," she rasped, her voice both weary and triumphant. "By the time you brought your beloved to the throne of my tower, you were right on the edge of consciousness, passing out moments after placing her upon my seat. But I saw you then," she spoke softly, her tone softening to something almost reverent. "

And I knew. I knew right then that you were one of the heroes of my prophecy. One of those foretold to be bound to Fate's threads.

Quinn felt the weight of her words settle over him, and his stomach twisted. The humid air felt thicker, more oppressive. She watched him with eyes that seemed too bright for her battered face, gleaming with a strange certainty that he didn't understand but could feel pulsing in the space between them.

For a moment, he stood there, his mind whirling, processing the implications of her words and the haunted truth reflected in her gaze.

Quinn stiffened as a new, overwhelming essence filled the doorway behind him, his hand instinctively dropping to the hilt of his sword as he turned. His eyes fell upon the figure of a young girl, though the aura that radiated from her was anything but youthful. She was in her mid to late teens by appearance, yet her presence filled the dungeon cell with a frigid authority that rivaled the chill of Olympus itself.

Her eyes were piercing, an unnatural, gleaming silver that seemed to see right through him. She regarded him with a look of cool disdain, her gaze flicking over him as if he were a speck of dirt that had dared to mar her path. Her hair, a rich, dark brown, curled around her shoulders, held back by a headband marked with a crescent moon, an unmistakable symbol of her identity. She wore dark, weathered leathers accented with fur, a hickory bow slung across her back, and two long knives glinting at her hips.

Artemis, goddess of the hunt.

Quinn met her eyes, refusing to let his expression betray the unease roiling beneath his surface. The goddess' lip curled slightly as she examined him as if the very sight of him was an insult.

"My, my," she said, her voice cool and sharp as winter's wind. "It appears the rats of Olympus have grown far bigger than I had imagined."

She took a step forward, her gaze flitting briefly to Clotho, who watched everything play out with a wide smile on her face. "Father sent me to check on our honored guest," she continued, her tone dripping with scorn.

"Though why he would think this traitorous hag could possibly be going anywhere is beyond me. But perhaps the trip has proven worthwhile after all."

Quinn kept his grip on his sword, watching her warily. Her eyes settled back on him, narrowing even further yet. He wondered if she could even still see him at this point.

"So, you are the wannabe Primordial who murdered my brother, are you?" Her voice carried a sneer, assessing him as though he were a mangy animal she had just found scavenging in her domain. "I must admit, with how much of a tizzy you have Father in these days, I expected something more…impressive. But mortals never do live up to the hype, do they?"

Quinn kept his expression neutral, the muscles in his jaw tight, forcing himself to hold her stare with a calm he didn't entirely feel. "And you're the goddess slinking through the dungeons to run errands for Daddy."

He channeled his inner Levy, allowing a faint, defiant smile to curl his lips. "Seems like neither of us got the very impressive assignment."

A glint of anger flashed in Artemis' eyes, but her expression remained cold. "I don't expect you to understand the responsibilities of a goddess, but it would be wise to watch your tone." She took another step forward, unslinging the bow from her back and nocking an arrow. "You may have ended Ares, but I assure you, any fool can strike down a meat head like him. Let us see how well you fare against the hunt."

Chapter 23
Mallory

The voice echoed through the winding stone corridors, clear, feminine, and edged with the impatience of someone used to being obeyed. "Hurry up, this vault isn't going to open by itself."

Mallory stopped in her tracks, exchanging a quick, wide-eyed glance with Levy. The strange voice was both alluring and unsettling, like velvet wrapped around iron. Her pulse quickened, but there was no turning back. She gave him a small nod, and together, they moved forward deeper into the heart of the vault.

As they made their way, the shadows seemed to shift, stretching long and thin against the stone walls. Mallory's eyes trailed over the remnants of broken traps littering their path—a net slashed to ribbons, iron-spiked jaws twisted beyond use, and arrows embedded haphazardly in the walls.

The traps had been dismantled with ruthless efficiency, a task that would have taken formidable essence or strength. The scent in the air changed from that of damp petrichor to something sweet, not quite floral, but not food either. She couldn't shake the feeling of walking into a snare that had already closed around them, though her sense of duty drove her forward.

The passage sloped downward, leveling out into a narrow corridor where a crude doorway had been carved into the wall, roughly hewn and ominous. Around its jagged frame, glowing runes pulsed with warm, reddish light, casting a frightening glow over the stone floor. From inside, the woman's voice sounded again, her words carrying a sharper edge this time.

"Well? Are you going to keep me waiting?"

Mallory took a step toward the door, but Levy's arm shot out, stopping her with a firm grip. His expression was tense, though his eyes seemed as though they were slightly fogged.

"Be careful," he spoke softly, his words slightly slurred.

Mallory was about to ask if he was feeling ok, but he continued, cutting her off. "I know that voice. It's definitely Aphrodite."

The name struck her like a splash of icy water. Though Cyrus' warning had prepared them for her presence, the reality of standing on the verge of confronting an actual Olympian sent an involuntary shiver down Mallory's spine.

She'd heard tales of Aphrodite's charm, her allure capable of beguiling even the strongest warriors, but the stories also warned of her cruelty, the sharp and ruthless edges beneath that beauty.

Taking a steadying breath, Mallory nodded. Together, they stepped through the doorway and entered a dimly lit chamber. The shadows parted as they walked in, revealing the figure of the goddess herself.

Aphrodite stood tall, the air around her humming with power. A faint, pink sheen misted the air, and the aroma Mallory had smelled earlier strengthened in her nose tenfold. Her beauty was breathtaking and almost painful to behold, each feature impossibly perfect, from her bright, perfectly curled hair to her stunning golden eyes, glinting with faint cruelty. She seemed amused, though there was an edge to her smile that made Mallory uneasy.

Mallory barely had time to react before a movement flickered at the edge of her vision. She turned, and her blood ran cold.

A massive spider lurked in the shadows, its sleek black body as large as a bull, its spindly legs splayed wide like a grotesque crown. Multitudes of gleaming eyes reflected the dim light, unblinking and alien. From its mouth, two enormous fangs curved downward, glistening with a dark, viscous fluid that dripped slowly to the ground, each drop promising something far worse than mere venom.

A scream tore from Mallory's throat before she could stop

herself, the high-pitched sound echoing back up the stairway, loud and sharp.

Aphrodite sighed, rolling her eyes with a dramatic air of exasperation. "Must you be so rude to my pet?" she chided, her voice lilting with a strange mixture of sultry and disdain.

"How would you feel if someone screamed at *your* raggedy appearance?"

Mallory swallowed hard, heat rising in her cheeks, but she couldn't tear her gaze away from the spider, which was now eyeing her with unsettling calm as though sizing her up. There was a slight sneer in Aphrodite's tone, and Mallory could sense the familiar undercurrent of contempt that gods so often held for mortals.

"Raka, come," the goddess said smoothly, gesturing with a graceful hand.

The spider obeyed instantly, moving toward her side with a horrible scuttling, its legs clicking softly on the stone floor. Mallory barely resisted the urge to retreat a step, fighting the chill in her veins as Raka settled beside the goddess, its many eyes never leaving Mallory's.

"I suppose you two are here for the box as well." Mallory and Levy shared a look; it was the first time they'd heard exactly what they were searching for. "And thank Zeus for it. These tiresome Masters, despite all their faults, somehow made it impossible for any Olympian to break into this vault to retrieve it. They must have truly feared its power, short-sighted fools."

Her grin spread wider, showing perfect, shining teeth. "But they never considered that mortals might uncover their secret. Open this vault for me, and I will agree to not have Raka tear off your head and drink your insides."

Mallory felt a surge of nausea at the thought, and a cold sweat broke over her skin. A warm hand touched her lower back, a calming presence. She could feel the color drain from her face, but she forced herself to keep her composure, her eyes fixed on the goddess even as her pulse pounded in her ears.

Beside her, Levy's low growl cut through the silence, his gaze hardening. He took a step forward, glaring at Aphrodite with open defiance, his body tense and ready.

The goddess' smile deepened, amusement flickering in her

eyes. "Oh?" she drawled, her tone thick with mockery. "Is she your little lover, Levy? And here I thought it was the blonde you pined over. No matter, soon I think you will find red much more to your liking."

She winked, tossing her auburn hair over her shoulder.

Levy's jaw clenched, but he ignored the taunt. His voice was clipped as he spoke. "Here's another idea: you leave, and we don't kill you."

Aphrodite's laugh was cold, echoing through the chamber like a melody tinged with malice. She tilted her head, watching him with a predatory gleam.

"If that is how you would like to play it. I do have the most fun with the more spirited ones."

She extended a jeweled hand toward the spider, her fingers making a simple, dismissive gesture. "Raka, go play with the girl."

Before Mallory could react, the spider shifted, its enormous body twisting with terrifying fluidity. Raka's legs unfurled, its eyes gleaming with insatiable hunger as it turned toward her. Mallory felt her heart stop, a cold shock jolting through her as the monster lunged forward, fangs foaming, ready to strike.

She yanked her sword from its sheath, raising it just as the spider's monstrous fangs snapped down toward her. The blade caught the creature's fangs with a ringing clash, the force vibrating through her arms. Raka's mandibles scraped against the flat of her sword, pressing down hard enough that Mallory feared the steel might crack under the weight.

Before she could regain her footing, one of the spider's massive, hairy legs lashed out, crashing into her side with a brutal, bone-jarring impact. She flew backward, her body slamming into the rough stone floor with a hard thud.

Pain shot through her ribs, and her vision blurred as she rolled away, instinct and years of training urging her to keep moving even as her body protested.

Just as she regained her bearings, Raka's leg came slamming down again, the sharp, needle-like end stabbing into the stone where she had just been lying. Shards of rock exploded from the impact, scattering across the chamber, and Mallory scrambled to her feet, breathing hard. She threw a glance over her shoulder, desperate to see where Levy was, but the spider charged again, forcing her attention to snap back to the fight.

Raka moved faster than anything that size had a right to, and Mallory barely had time to ready her stance before it was on her once more. Its mandibles clicked in anticipation, the horrid, glistening fangs oozing with venom.

Mallory ducked to the side, her body moving by pure instinct, and swung her blade in a wide arc, aiming for one of the spider's exposed legs. The sword struck true, slicing through the bristly hairs and biting into the joint before cutting cleanly through with another extra push.

The creature hissed, a high-pitched, furious sound, and reared back from her, the stump of its injured leg twitching. Mallory allowed herself a flicker of satisfaction, but it was short-lived. Raka's massive body twisted as it opened its jaws wide, spewing a jet of greenish, steaming venom.

Her eyes widened, and she threw herself to the side just in time, the venom splattering onto the stone where she had just been standing.

The acid sizzled and smoked, eating into the rock with a horrid hiss, filling the air with a stinging, sulfuric stench. Mallory's stomach turned, but she forced herself to keep moving, her muscles tensing as Raka charged once more, even more enraged than a moment ago.

She dodged another strike, this time twisting her blade upward in a slicing motion that scraped along the bottom of the creature's jaw, releasing a light stream of acid upon herself. She caught the scent of singed hair mixing with the now overpowering sweet smell in the air, but the injury did little to slow the monster's relentless assault.

Raka's movements became more frenzied, each lunge more aggressive, and Mallory knew if she got trapped against a wall, it was all over. She circled, trying to keep her footing steady as she avoided the spider's relentless legs, each one striking with crushing speed.

She ducked and weaved, feeling her strength wane the longer the fight went on and knew she needed to find an opening for a decisive blow soon, or she would be overwhelmed.

As if reading her thoughts, Raka lunged, forcing her to swing her blade up and block once more, the impact jarring her arms and sending a numbness through her bones. Before she could act, another leg swept out and clipped her knees, sweeping her off her feet and slamming her back down.

Mallory's vision exploded into stars as her head struck the floor, her sword clattering from her already weakened grip, skittering just out of reach. She fought to stay conscious, her lungs heaving, her hand scrambling desperately for her weapon.

With a triumphant screech, the spider lowered itself, its legs inching forward as it prepared to finish her. Mallory's fingers finally managed to close around the hilt of her sword, and she gritted her teeth, pulling herself up with the last dregs of her strength. But before she could move, Raka reared back, pointing its rear abdomen at her and spraying a thick web, sticky and shimmering.

The webbing hit her with a sickening squelch, tangling around her shoulder and arms, binding her sword arm tightly to her side. Mallory struggled, pulling at the silken strands, but they clung to her, unyielding as though they were woven with steel. She fought to keep calm, panic overtaking her mind as Raka closed in, each step one thud closer to her demise.

"Not like this," she hissed through gritted teeth, twisting and pulling, feeling the web's sticky bonds strain but hold fast.

Raka's fangs glistened in the dim light, the monster's eyes reflecting her struggle with cruel, patient enjoyment. As it leaned down to strike, Mallory angled her sword, managing to edge it free enough to slice into the sticky silk. With a fierce cry, she slashed through the binding, tearing herself free, and as the spider lunged, she drove her blade upward with all her strength.

Her sword pierced the soft flesh under Raka's jaw where her earlier gouge had taken hold, sliding deep into the creature's head. Raka froze, its many legs twitching, her eyes blinking rapidly. A wet choking sound chittered from its maw as it struggled against death.

Mallory didn't stop. She twisted the blade viciously, sinking it even deeper, and with one final, shuddering twitch, Raka went limp, collapsing onto the floor in a lifeless heap.

Panting, her body aching and coated in sticky spider ichor, Mallory staggered back and pulled her sword from Raka's limp form. As she straightened, the sound of slow, deliberate clapping echoed through the chamber. She turned, muscles still tense, and saw Aphrodite standing at the edge of the room, a cold smile playing on her lips. Beside her was Levy, clapping along, though his expression held no warmth.

Chapter 24
Ashe

Ashe's eyes fluttered open, her vision sharpening slowly, taking in the space around her. The air was heavy, almost suffocating with heat, as Charis carried her into a cavernous room carved from the very rock of Mount Olympus.

It was vast, the ceiling stretching high above, lost in the shadows. Walls of rough stone loomed around her, the ancient markings of chisel and hammer still visible on their surfaces.

The orange glow that filled the space originated from molten lava flowing in deep trenches along the room's perimeter, the heat radiating from it in waves that made the air shimmer. A thick, earthy scent mixed with the metallic tang of iron and smoldering embers.

Charis stepped carefully across the stone platform in the center, a vast expanse raised above the magma's hungry depths, each step reverberating with the distant echoes of a hammer striking metal. Ashe blinked, her senses adjusting, and it struck her just how familiar this place felt.

The memory of the volcano where she and Quinn had clashed with Levy resurfaced, a scene of fire and molten rock that had set the stage for her claim to the Tower of Fate.

Tools of every kind lay strewn across the platform's surface, arranged meticulously along the edge of an anvil, ready to be used. Forged hammers, tongs, chisels, and files, some enormous in size, lined the workspaces surrounding several anvils, each glowing faintly from recent use. The entire platform seemed alive, a place of creation and innovation. It dawned on her that this wasn't just any cavern.

It was a forge.

In the center of the platform, his massive form bent over a long piece of glowing iron, was Hephaestus, hammering away with rhythmic precision. The god was mountainous in size. Every inch of him was seemingly carved from raw strength.

His skin was bronzed, burnished by the relentless heat of his forge. Thick muscles coiled beneath his flesh, their shape honed from centuries of relentless labor. His hair was a deep red, wild and unkempt, flowing down his back in fiery waves, and a thick beard framed his face, flecked with streaks of dark auburn.

His forearms, dusted with dark hair, bulged with muscle as he brought his hammer down in practiced, deliberate strikes that sent sparks flying into the thick, sweltering air.

Despite the gritty setting, Hephaestus was dressed in intricately forged armor, pieces of metal artfully fitted to his powerful frame. His chest plate gleamed, adorned with intricate patterns and symbols that caught the glow from the lava surrounding them.

Straps and buckles secured the metal in place, and every edge was beveled, every rivet polished. His arms and legs bore similar plating, accented with ornate patterns. His very armor was a testament to his skill as a smith.

Charis set Ashe down gently, and for a moment, only the sound of Hephaestus' hammer filled the silence. Each strike seemed to vibrate through her, reverberating with a force that felt ancient, as though the gods will and power infused every blow. He paused, lifting his head to glance their way, his fiery brows drawing together in an assessing gaze.

Hephaestus straightened, setting down his hammer with a solid clang. Without a word, he rose from the forge and strode over to where Ashe sat, his heavy footfalls echoing across the platform. He was even more imposing up close, towering over her with a presence that radiated raw strength and intensity.

Oath Breaker

But despite the weakness in her limbs, Ashe squared her shoulders, meeting his eyes with a steady pride that refused to betray even a flicker of uncertainty.

The god's eyes glinted with something unreadable as he extended a calloused hand toward her, offering a small vial filled with an amber liquid that shimmered faintly in the forge's light.

"Drink it," he said, his voice a rough, gravelly command. "Ye'll need yer strength if you are to save the world."

Ashe stared at the vial in Hephaestus' hand, her gaze flicking uncertainly between the amber liquid and the god's expectant look. Hesitance crept over her, and she wished she hadn't sent Quinn away, desperate for his calming presence now.

"What is it?" she asked warily, her fingers lingering just short of the vial.

Hephaestus let out a low, irritated rumble. "I'm not trying to poison ye, girl," he replied with a note of exasperation. "Though any other mortal who drank it likely would be." He conceded. He fixed her with a pointed look. "It's nectar."

The word hung in the air between them, and Ashe's hesitation deepened. Nectar, the drink of the immortals—a liquid said to heal their wounds, satiate their thirst, and fuel their strength. It was power in its purest form, and though its reputation for godly effects was well-known, so was its danger to mortals.

"Nectar will kill me," she replied, her voice tight. Her fingers remained hesitant, tracing the vial's edge without fully taking it.

Hephaestus sighed, scratching his fiery beard, his patience clearly fraying. "It will kill mortals, aye. But you're not quite mortal anymore, are ye?"

He gave her a knowing look, his eyes tracing the threads of power barely contained beneath her pallid skin. "And not quite immortal either. It'll likely taste like shit and hurt going down, but it'll soothe your body and stitch ye back together. I swear it on my essence."

His words gave her pause, and she looked into his eyes, searching for any sign of deception. All she found was unyielding, gruff patience. She grabbed the vial, though a sliver of doubt remained.

Slowly, she pulled the stopper, and the scent that rose from the vial made her gag. It was rank, a combination of bitter herbs and something faintly metallic, like blood left too long in the sun. She winced, holding it away from her nose.

Hephaestus grunted, folding his arms. "If ye don't drink it, that power inside ye will shred ye apart before ye even make it home. This'll keep ye alive long enough to do what must be done, though I warn ye…drink too much of it, and ye'll still die."

Ashe glanced back up at him, curiosity softening the edge of her hesitance. "Why are you helping me?"

The god's face was unyielding as stone, his expression unreadable. "Drink first, then we'll talk." His tone was firm, brooking no argument. "Then, I'll make ye my offer, and we'll see if ye like what I have to give."

The weight of his words pressed her to action, and she steeled herself, lifting the vial to her lips. The smell alone was enough to make her hesitate, but she forced the thought aside and tipped the vial back, letting the nectar hit her tongue.

The taste was worse than she had imagined. It was rancid, a bitter taste that burned the back of her throat like bile, mixed with something else entirely foul, something thick and oily that clung to her tongue and refused to let go. It took every ounce of control not to retch, her stomach twisting in protest as the nectar slid down her throat, leaving a scorching trail in its wake.

As the last drop hit her stomach, Ashe felt a strange transformation. The rancid taste faded, replaced by an unexpected, overpowering sweetness that made her breath catch in her throat. A comforting warmth blossomed in her core, spreading outward like fire, a surge of life that ignited her muscles, her bones, and even her spirit.

It was intoxicating, filling her with a strength she hadn't felt in months, erasing the constant ache and fatigue that had clung to her like a second skin. Her mind cleared, her vision sharpened, and a weight she hadn't even realized was bearing down on her finally lifted, leaving her feeling buoyant and free. She closed her eyes, savoring the feeling, and had to shake her head to make sure she wasn't dreaming.

A genuine smile broke across her face, and as she opened her eyes, she found Hephaestus grinning back at her, his rugged face creasing with satisfaction. He reached down, offering a calloused hand, and helped her to her feet with a strength that made her feel as if she were lighter than air.

"There now, Weaver," he rumbled, a hint of smug satisfaction in his tone. "Isn't that better?"

Ashe gave a breathless laugh and nodded. "Much better." She caught sight of Charis at the edge of the room, a gentle smile on her face as she watched them. "Thank you," Ashe said, her gaze moving between them both, gratitude genuine in her eyes.

Hephaestus waved a meaty hand, dismissing her thanks with a wry chuckle. "Now then," he began, moving back toward his forge, "let's discuss why I brought ye here."

Ashe tilted her head, unable to resist a playful quip. "You mean you didn't just want to save my life?"

Hephaestus snorted, a dry laugh rumbling from him. "When has an Olympian ever given a favor for free?" His tone held a glint of humor, and she couldn't help but chuckle as well, following him to the forge where he settled himself, motioning for her to come closer.

Ashe's eyes drifted over his workspace, taking in the intricately forged weapons and armor spread around. Each piece was unique, showing quality and craftsmanship that she had never seen before. The metalwork was flawless, with careful engravings etched into the surfaces, symbols, and patterns that pulsed with a faint glow under the forge's light. She reached out, her fingers brushing lightly over a gleaming chest plate, enchanted by the artistry.

"Ye like them?" the Olympian's voice held a note of pride, and she glanced up to see him watching her with satisfaction in his eyes. "Because I am willing to make more for ye and yer army."

Ashe whipped around, shock flashing across her face. "You...you'd forge weapons and armor for us?" Her mind raced, barely able to process the enormity of what he was offering. "Why? Why would you do that? Zeus will come after you for helping us. Surely, you must know that. It won't go unnoticed when he sees us outfitted in Olympian craft."

Hephaestus' expression darkened. "I'm already in danger, girl. That's why I'm down here, hiding away like some common thief." His voice dropped lower, a hint of bitterness creeping in.

"Something is wrong on Olympus. Those wretched immortal

sentries ye and yer boyfriend nearly bumped into on your way down here is proof enough of that. All of them have gone mindless, like zombies. On top of that, Zeus grows more unhinged by the day, paranoid and quick to lash out at any perceived threat to his rule."

Ashe's brows drew together as she listened, the intensity in his tone prickling her skin. "What's happening?" she asked, sensing there was more he hadn't yet revealed.

The god's face grew haunted. "Zeus killed Hera, spilling her ichor upon the gateway, after she dared speak out against him."

His lips twisted in something like disgust, but there was also a deeper anger simmering beneath the words. "Now, I had no great love for the mother who tossed me down a mountain for being born 'wrong,' but even I didn't expect him to kill her in cold blood."

A heavy silence settled between them as Ashe grappled with the revelation. Hera was dead. She had braced herself for Olympus' cruelty, for its endless power plays and betrayals—but this? This was beyond anything she could have imagined.

Hephaestus shook his head, as if he could brush off the weight of it. "And it doesn't end there. Other Olympians have gone missing," he continued, his voice hardening. "Killed, but their bodies never recovered. There is something foul running through Olympus, something beyond even Zeus' paranoia."

He paused, fixing her with a grim look. "I heard that Hades was killed by yer friends Quinn and that other fool, Levy." He waited, watching her reaction as though testing her.

"They didn't actually kill him," Ashe said. "They wounded him gravely, but they couldn't strike the final blow before he managed to escape."

The god gave a knowing nod, a hint of grim satisfaction crossing his face. "Then ye know what I am saying is true. Something is going on in Olympus that isn't natural, and my wife and I...we don't feel safe here anymore, pitiable as it is for a god to say. Not under Zeus' rule."

Ashe nodded slowly, understanding the gravity of his situation. "And you want to help us because...?"

Hephaestus held her gaze, his dark eyes unwavering. "Because it's time for a change. I want to see my father fall—just as his father did before him. And I want Olympus freed from his tyranny."

Oath Breaker

His voice was steady, resolute. "If you and your allies can make that happen, then I'm in. I'll forge your army weapons and armor, built to withstand Olympian power." He tapped a thick finger against the edge of a glinting chest plate. "They'll give your soldiers a fighting chance against the wrath of Olympus. Don't expect miracles—but it'll be more than anyone has ever had."

Ashe's heart raced, the weight of his offer sinking in. If Hephaestus outfitted their army with Olympian-grade arms, they would have a fighting chance, however slim, against Zeus.

"Once the war is over," he continued, "if ye win, I ask that Charis and I be allowed to return to Olympus. We'd take the throne and rule in peace, letting ye and the rest of the mortal realm grow and change without us meddling. I'd give ye my word never to interfere with mortals again if ye grant us that."

Ashe blinked, taken aback by the simplicity of his demand. "You'd stay here? Rule over Olympus but leave the mortal world untouched?"

"Aye," Hephaestus said, his expression firm. "Olympus doesn't belong in the mortal world anymore. We've all lived too long, grown too comfortable in our own power. It's time to leave ye mortals to carve yer own paths."

His words settled over her, a strange mix of hope and unease. There was no denying the lure of his offer, the power he could bring to them. Not to mention the potential to finally, truly challenge Zeus. But she knew there were still risks, still a thousand ways this could go wrong. Allowing an Olympian into the heart of Stormhaven could be catastrophic and exactly what Zeus wanted.

Still, as she looked at the glint of steel and the unyielding resolve in Hephaestus' eyes, she felt a surge of conviction. This was the edge they needed.

"You have convinced me. Now, we must convince Quinn."

Chapter 25
Quinn

Pain detonated in Quinn's shoulder as the arrow struck, burying itself deep and sending a searing jolt through his nerves. He staggered back, teeth clenched against the agony, his fingers instinctively reaching for the shaft. His hand came away slick with his own blood, warmth spreading beneath his grip as the throbbing pain threatened to drown out everything else.

From the shadows at the edge of the cell, Artemis' voice sliced through the darkness, sharp with scorn.

"Is that all it takes to bring down the mighty Quinn—the one my father fears so much?"

Her silver eyes gleamed like cold moonlight, her lips curling into a smirk. "Perhaps I overestimated you, mortal."

Quinn let out a low, humorless laugh, yanking the arrow from his shoulder with a sharp hiss of pain. He tossed it aside, rolling his shoulder despite the fresh sting, embracing the side of himself he once reserved for sparring with Levy.

Artemis was brimming with bravado and barely contained fury—something Quinn had learned long ago could be turned against an opponent. Push the right buttons, and sooner or later, they'd slip.

"Trust me," he growled, forcing his voice steady despite the burning in his shoulder, "it'll take a lot more than a toothpick to put me down." He met her gaze, a smirk tugging at the corner of his lips. "Besides, I'm the wrong mortal to fear."

Artemis' smirk deepened, and she reached for another arrow, but Quinn was already moving, his power surging as he melded into the shadows around them. The dungeon cell was cloaked in darkness, and he used it to his advantage, his essence bleeding into the void, his form flickering as he advanced toward her.

In an instant, he reappeared in front of her, close enough to see the surprise flash across her face. Before she could react, his hand shot out, grabbing her bow and snapping it in half with a swift twist. The weapon splintered in his grasp, the crack of breaking wood echoing off the stone walls. He tossed the pieces to the ground at her feet. "Oops."

Her expression twisted into a snarl, eyes blazing with unbridled fury. "You filthy little worm!" she spat, her hand darting to her belt where the two long daggers rested.

In one fluid motion, she unsheathed them and lunged, slicing a swift, deadly X across his chest.

Quinn barely managed to spin away, shifting into the shadows just in time. Her blades sliced only through his leather armor, but he felt the bite of her immortal strength even through the protective layers. He reappeared a few steps back, throwing her a smirk to further rile up her anger.

"That's a shame," he taunted, brushing a hand over the shallow cuts in his armor. "I really liked this tunic."

Her lips curled back in a feral grin. "Oh, don't worry, I'll carve you up just fine," she hissed, stalking toward him with a lethal grace, her blades held at the ready.

Quinn waited, letting her close the distance, watching the way her muscles coiled. As she moved, he tapped into the Chaos within him, letting it swirl and pulse through his veins, fueling his movements.

When she lunged again, he met her halfway, his own blade drawn, catching the first strike on his own blade. Her strength was staggering, but he held his ground, meeting her attacks head-on, his powers lending him speed and fluidity.

Each strike resonated through his bones, her power undeniable, yet he matched her blow for blow, his blade ringing against hers in a brutal bash of steel. He couldn't activate his cloak in such a confined space, as he didn't want Clotho to be caught up within its wrath.

"Not bad for a mortal *man*, I suppose," her eyes narrowed as their blades locked, her strength pressing down on him with Olympian force.

"Not bad for a spoiled goddess who stalks dungeons," Quinn shot back, his voice tight as he shoved her back with a grunt. She stumbled, her eyes narrowing, and he saw his opening. He surged forward, slipping into the shadows once more and reappearing behind her, his blade slicing down toward her exposed back.

But she was faster than he'd expected. She twisted, her dagger flashing as it deflected his strike, and countered with a vicious slash that forced him back. Blood trickled from a shallow cut on his arm, but he ignored it, keeping his gaze locked on her.

"You think skulking in the shadows makes you powerful?" Artemis hissed out, circling him with a predator's gleam in her eyes. "You're nothing but a coward pretending to be something greater than you are."

"Tell me," Quinn smiled, knowing this would tip her over the edge. She would be dangerous, but logic would be thrown out for blind fury, and mistakes would be sure to follow. "Does it sting, knowing it was a 'coward' like me that killed your brother?"

Her eyes flared, and she lunged with renewed venom, her blades flashing wildly. Quinn dodged, ducking low and sweeping his leg out to knock her off balance. She stumbled but recovered quickly, her anger giving her strength as she struck back with a flurry of rapid blows.

Their blades clashed once more, each strike a test of willpower and resilience. Artemis fought with the lethal grace of a hunter, but Quinn matched her, the Chaos within him lending his movements an unpredictable edge that kept her off-balance.

"You Olympians are all the same," he grunted, sidestepping a particularly nasty strike. "Arrogant, entitled, taking from those weaker than you because you can. You haven't earned a damn thing in your immortal life."

Her jaw clenched with indignation. "And what would a mortal

like you know of the gods?"

"Oh, I know plenty," he countered, twisting his blade to catch her in a narrow opening, forcing her back. "I've seen your 'divine wrath' firsthand, and frankly, it's just a lot of noise. Face it, Artemis, you're all-powerful until someone actually challenges you who can hold their own."

With a roar, she drove forward, her strength almost overwhelming as she brought her blades down in a crosscut. Quinn made himself skinny just in time, feeling the heat of her anger radiating off her, and he raised his own blade, slashing in a wide arc.

"You talk too much for a dead man," she hissed, her voice dripping with venom.

"You'd think you'd be grateful for the conversation," he replied with a grin, even as sweat dripped down his face. "After all, doesn't seem like you have too many friends down here."

She snarled a wordless cry of fury and lunged at him again. But he was ready this time, tapping into the chaos once more, letting it flow through his tired muscles. He slipped past her guard, his blade slicing toward her ribs. She deflected it at the last second, but a few drops of ichor sprayed through the air, and he could see the flicker of doubt in her eyes.

"Getting tired?"

"Hardly," she spat. "But I can tell you are."

Their blades met in another wild clash, sparks flying as metal bit against metal. Quinn twisted, leveraging the darkness around him, flickering in and out of sight as he dodged her strikes. Artemis matched him perfectly, her eyes blazing now in the dim light, her movements relentless, but he could sense the edges of her nerves fraying.

Quinn gritted his teeth, struggling to keep up with the relentless assault as his own strength began to flag. Levy would have cracked by this point, a fatal mistake having planted him on his ass. Despite a few missteps here and there, Artemis had yet to truly break.

Olympian endurance consistently proved to be unmatched. He felt her blade slice through his shoulder, a hot streak of pain, but he held his ground, refusing to give her the satisfaction of seeing him falter.

"You are nothing but a speck of dust in the eyes of Olympus."

She seethed as if unaware of the hit she just scored.

"If I'm nothing, then what does that make you? Fighting a 'speck of dust' and still struggling to win?"

Their blades locked yet again, her strength pressing down on him. He gave a step, his strength waning as the multitude of cuts began to take their toll. He knew he had to end this quickly, or it would be his skull staring up at future prisoners.

With a roar, he broke the lock, launching into a series of strikes, every ounce of his power and skill focused on the fight, pushing her back. His defiance fueled him even as exhaustion gnawed at his edges. And in her eyes, he saw the flicker of frustration, the dawning realization that he was more than she had bargained for.

Both Quinn and Artemis were breathing hard, circling each other with blades raised, each one battered but unwilling to yield. They shared a single, silent understanding: this clash could not go on. The next strike would have to be decisive, an all-or-nothing blow to end the fight. Their eyes locked, hatred and resolve mirrored between them, and they lunged forward for the final time, each ready to deliver the killing blow.

But just as their weapons neared each other, a familiar, measured voice sliced through the tension, smooth and unhurried, freezing them both mid-motion.

"My, what have we here?"

Oath Breaker

Chapter 26
Mallory

Mallory's breath hitched as the dying sound of their applause settled over her like a suffocating veil. The goddess' smile remained, a soft, chilling curve of her lips as if Mallory were an insect caught in one of Raka's webs, and she was savoring the struggle before the kill.

Levy was still there beside Aphrodite, but he was no longer the Levy she had come to know. He stood unnaturally still, each line of his body rigid, his expression as blank as the guardians they'd seen outside the vault.

His gaze remained vacant, not focusing on anything, lost and unreachable. It was as if every flicker of his personality had been snuffed out, leaving him a puppet tethered by the goddess' invisible strings.

"Levy?" she called, her voice soft and unsure, desperation slipping into her tone despite herself. She took a half-step forward, searching his face for any flicker of recognition, some indication that he was fighting the hold Aphrodite seemingly had on him. But Levy's blank stare remained fixed in the same distant direction, his eyes fogged over, devoid of their usual spark.

Her heart tightened, anger mixing with fear as she glared at Aphrodite. "What have you done to him?"

Aphrodite laughed, her amusement deepening as she watched Mallory struggle with the reality of the situation. "What have I done?" she echoed, her tone mockingly innocent.

"Oh, dear, I have simply…enhanced his natural inclinations. It is incredible how subservient men can be under the right influence."

She reached up, running a possessive hand over Levy's shoulder, her hand lingering in a way that made Mallory's stomach churn.

The air was thick with that sweet, cloying scent, the strange perfume Mallory now realized was Aphrodite's doing. It filled every breath she took, growing stronger with each passing moment, wrapping around her senses in a stifling cloud.

It was too sweet, too inviting, and beneath its surface, there was a sickly, rotting undercurrent that left her both entranced and repulsed.

"You!" Mallory gasped, her voice sharp with realization. "That smell is you. Some kind of pheromone?"

Aphrodite's expression brightened, her smile deepening with what almost looked like pride. "Very perceptive. Yes, little mortal, it is me."

She tilted her head, her expression turning almost pitying. "I have been gifted with a certain…influence… over the weaker sex."

Her fingers trailed down Levy's face, tracing his jawline in a way that brought heat to Mallory's cheeks. "And men are such helpless creatures in the face of true beauty, are they not?"

Mallory's stomach twisted, her fists clenching at her sides. The sight of Levy, who had always been so steady, so infuriatingly stubborn, now standing there as docile as a statue while some harlot ran her hands all over him was more than she could bear.

She had really started coming around on him, seeing him as Ashe and Quinn did, as an ally, a friend…and potentially more. Seeing him twisted into a puppet for a goddess' amusement was too much.

Aphrodite's laughter was a soft, mocking sound, and she snapped her fingers. Levy's head turned instantly, his blank eyes finding hers, his body straightening in obedient attention as he focused entirely on the goddess. Aphrodite's arms slipped around him, draping herself across his shoulders in a way that made her claim over him unmistakable.

"See?" she purred, running her fingers through his hair with an almost fond possessiveness. "Isn't he such a good little pet?"

Mallory felt a stab of hurt mingled with the anger coursing through her veins. Of course, it wasn't Levy's fault that Aphrodite's power was designed specifically to ensnare him, but to become her mindless dog after sniffing her scent?

"Ugh, men." She muttered.

"Oh, I know," Aphrodite said, smirking, her nails tracing down Levy's chest. "Simple creatures, aren't they? Little more than toys if you know how to play with them."

Her gaze returned to Mallory, a sadistic glint sparking in her eyes. "But there is something poetic about watching you suffer like this. After all, you did kill my pet. And for that, I will savor every moment of what is to come."

Mallory's hand tightened around the hilt of her blade, her knuckles white. She took a deep breath, determined to keep her composure despite facing down an Olympian.

"So that's it then?" she shot back, fighting to keep a quiver from her voice. "You're going to hide behind your power and let someone else fight your battles for you?"

"You think yourself brave," Aphrodite countered, maintaining her graceful poise. "But that spark will be gone soon enough." Her smile was venomous, and she glanced at Levy, her face smug with satisfaction.

"I can tell he cares for you. Goddess of love and all that, you know the spiel." She leaned closer to Levy, her lips brushing his ear. "So, imagine how it will feel when he is the one to end your life. And when I allow him to remember every detail, the memory will haunt him for the rest of his days."

A shiver ran down Mallory's spine, but she forced herself to stand tall, her eyes narrowing. Levy stood still, unseeing, as Aphrodite's grip on him tightened, her fingers curling around his shoulders like a cage. Mallory knew that deep down, somewhere beneath that blank stare, he was still in there. She had to believe that.

"You won't get away with this," Mallory said, promise filling her voice. "Levy's stronger than you think."

Aphrodite scoffed, rolling her eyes as if her words were nothing more than a child's foolish hope. "Stronger? I think not. He is exactly where he is meant to be; at my side, my little weapon to point at whomever I please. And you, girl? You are who I please."

The goddess' eyes hardened, her smile turning cold and cruel. She looked at Levy and then back at Mallory, savoring every moment of Mallory's silent desperation. "This is the end for you, girl. And I am going to enjoy every second of it."

Aphrodite leaned into Levy, her lips tickling his ear as she whispered a command loud enough for her to hear. "Kill her."

Oath Breaker

Chapter 27
Quinn

Quinn's attention snapped to the cell doorway where a familiar figure stood, bathed in the dim light. Cyrus leaned casually against the frame, his scythe held loosely in one hand, the curved blade gleaming faintly.

His expression was calm, almost amused, though Quinn caught the hardness in his eyes, a spark of something dangerous lurking beneath his nonchalant façade.

Artemis whipped around, her face twisting into that familiar sneer. "And here comes Zeus' obedient hound," she spat, her voice dripping with disdain. "Run along, Cyrus. This fight is mine to handle. Go back to my father's lap."

Quinn watched Cyrus carefully, noting the slight shift in his eyes, a flash of cold irritation that betrayed his cool demeanor. But his smile remained steady, polite, even deferential as he responded, his tone silky.

"As you wish, Lady Artemis," he gestured with a flourish. "By all means, continue. I wouldn't dream of interfering."

Satisfied, Artemis nodded as if the matter had been neatly settled as she turned back to Quinn. "I almost pity you." she taunted, her words preening and cocky. "Fighting a futile battle. A worthless mortal, clinging to…"

Before she could finish, the curved blade of Cyrus' scythe arced forward, swift yet silent, wrapping around her neck in a deadly loop. Artemis froze.

Her eyes widened in stunned silence as she registered the cold edge against her throat. She barely dared to move, her breath shallow as the razor-sharp blade held her in place. Any sudden shift threatening to sever her head on the spot.

Quinn watched in silent shock, transfixed, as Cyrus took a step forward, his grip on the scythe's handle loose, his expression calm.

"Ahh, apologies Lady Artemis, but I did just remember why I came down to see you." His voice was smooth, though it held its signature hint of mockery.

"It seems Lord Zeus is rather displeased with you. Publicly questioning him in the throne room was, shall we say, a bit of a misstep." His tone remained light, conversational, yet Quinn sensed the lethal intent behind every word.

Artemis' confidence faltered, her eyes darting between Cyrus and the cold blade at her throat. Her defiance wavered, replaced by a flash of terror that Quinn hadn't expected to see in her eyes.

"Wait…Cyrus, please," she stammered, frantic with the realization that the predator had become the prey. "Let me speak with my father. He will…"

Her plea was cut off as Cyrus, with a practiced flick of his wrist, pulled the scythe back toward him, the blade slicing cleanly through her neck with a sickening finality. Time seemed to slow as her head separated from her body, ichor spurting in a gruesome arc, splattering both Quinn and Cyrus. Artemis' body crumpled to the ground, lifeless, as her head rolled to a stop nearby, her silver eyes dull and vacant.

Quinn stared, shock seizing his throat at the absurdity of what had just happened, unable to tear his gaze away as Cyrus stood over the fallen goddess, unfazed. His face was flecked with glistening drops of liquid gold.

With a casual swipe of his thumb, Cyrus wiped some of the ichor from his cheek, examining it with a faint smile before bringing it to his lips. He tasted it, closing his eyes as if savoring a fine wine, and a wolfish grin spread across his face.

Oath Breaker

"Ahhhhh, the essence of an Olympian truly does taste wonderful," he murmured, his grin flashing with satisfaction.

Quinn watched in silent horror. He could feel Artemis' essence siphoning from her corpse into the scythe and then into Cyrus himself, her power flowing into him like a dark, consuming current.

Finally, he lifted his eyes to meet Quinn, the barest trace of amusement flickering in his otherwise unreadable expression. He tilted his head, seeming to enjoy the horror on Quinn's face.

"Oh, don't look so appalled," he drawled, his voice smooth and casual, as though they were discussing the weather. "I'm not here to keep you from extracting that shell of a woman."

He flicked the ichor from his scythe with a single, sharp motion, barely glancing at Artemis' form sprawled on the ground. "If I had wanted you to be found, I'd have alerted Zeus the moment you set foot on Olympus."

Quinn shifted his stance, allowing for a swifter defense should the former Master decide to strike. "How did you know we were here?" he asked, his voice laced with suspicion.

Cyrus' mouth curved into a sly, unsettling smile. "Nothing happens on Olympus these days without me knowing. It is my business to know."

Quinn scowled, keeping his sword between them, his essence simmering just below the surface in response to the wrongness Cyrus was giving off.

"Then what's your game, Cyrus?" he asked, his eyes narrowing. "Whose side are you really on? Zeus doesn't take kindly to traitors, and I'd imagine he will have you flayed alive if he suspects you're crossing him."

The Master chuckled, a dry, humorless sound that seemed to echo through the dungeon. "Oh, I am well aware of Zeus' attitude toward betrayal," he replied with a casual wave of his hand.

"As young, Levy will soon discover if he is not strong enough to keep his wits about him." His eyes flicked to Quinn as if testing his reaction.

Quinn's expression hardened at the mention of his friend, but he knew not to give Cyrus the satisfaction of seeing him squirm. Levy had already betrayed Zeus once, and if Cyrus' vague threat was anything to go by, he might be in more trouble than they had realized.

Cyrus continued, his tone almost bored. "If you are asking whether I stand with the Olympians, then the answer is no. I'm afraid that particular allegiance is just a means to an end."

A bitter laugh escaped Quinn's lips, unbidden but not unwarranted. "That's a pretty story," he said, his voice dripping with sarcasm.

"But your actions don't exactly make a convincing case. You killed Nes for that scythe you wave around, and you just referred to Zeus as 'Lord' not too long ago. That doesn't exactly inspire confidence."

Cyrus arched an eyebrow, casting a pointed glance at the lifeless body of Artemis sprawled at their feet. "Really, Quinn," he said, feigning a look of disappointment.

"If I were so loyal to Zeus, do you think I would have bothered to tell your merry band of rebels about the little trinket he is after in my vaults?"

Quinn opened his mouth to reply but found himself at a loss. Cyrus had a point; he had been the one to warn them about Zeus' intentions, about the powerful item he was pursuing. Why would he have done that if he held Zeus' loyalty?

Cyrus' lips lifted into a condescending smile as he watched Quinn struggle for words. "And you're supposed to be the clever one." His voice filled with mock disappointment, and he let out a soft, almost pitying laugh.

"No matter, I suppose you'll figure it out eventually. When the time comes, you will see my scythe sever Zeus' thread, just as it did Artemis and Hades before her."

Quinn's eyebrows shot into the air at the mention of Hades, though he didn't give him the satisfaction of asking about it further. Every instinct screamed to fight, to try and put an end to whatever game Cyrus was playing, but something in the man's expression gave him pause. His confidence, the way it almost seemed as if he was goading Quinn into striking, made Quinn hesitate, as if a deeper game was being played that he didn't yet understand.

Cyrus straightened, casting one last glance at Artemis as though her death were nothing more than a minor inconvenience.

"As much as I would love to stay and trade insults, we both have more pressing matters to attend to. We may yet find time to cross blades, but today is not that day. Gather your Weavers and be gone before Zeus catches wind of this little excursion, which ruins all my hard work."

With that, Cyrus took a step back into the passageway, his presence fading into the shadows as if he had never been there at all.

Quinn exhaled, forcing down the turmoil that roiled within him and turned back toward Clotho. The light in her eyes had vanished, leaving behind a vacant, distant gaze.

She rocked back and forth against the cold stone wall, her chains clinking softly with the motion as though she were caught in some endless cycle of torment. Her lips moved silently, words forming without sound, and it sent a chill down Quinn's spine to see the woman who had once held the threads of Fate reduced to this.

Kneeling beside her, Quinn carefully slipped the edge of his blade between the heavy iron chains and the wall. With a strong twist, he snapped the bonds, each link breaking with a dull clang. As the last of the chains fell away, he sheathed his sword, moving to lift Clotho into his arms.

She was lighter than he'd expected, her body frail and trembling. Quinn cradled her against his chest, trying to shield her from the cold that seeped through the stone walls. Pity twisted within him, but he pushed it aside.

There would be time to worry about her condition later after they were safely out of this cursed place. For now, he focused on the steady rhythm of his own breathing, willing his heart to calm and his mind to stay sharp.

He glanced down at her, offering a thin, grim smile, though whether he was trying to reassure her or himself, he was not sure.

"Come on, Clotho," he spoke softly. "Let's go find Ashe, shall we?"

At the mention of Ashe, the old woman's body went rigid, bright, golden light shining in her wide eyes.

"THE OATH BREAKER!" she wailed. "BEWARE THE OATH BREAKER. HE WILL STEAL THE THAT WHICH DOES NOT BELONG TO HIM!"

Startled, Quinn clamped a hand over the former Weaver's mouth, worried that her screams would make their way to unwelcome ears. Though just as quickly as she had started, the yelling stopped, and Clotho went limp within his arms once more.

When it was clear there would be no more outbursts from her, he tightened his grip, shifting her weight as he moved toward the doorway. With each step, he reminded himself of the promise he had made to Ashe and the desperate need to return to her side before anything else could go wrong.

He carried Clotho up the narrow stone stairway, each step feeling heavier than the last as he pushed his way back up to the landing where he and Ashe had separated.

As he reached the top, heart pounding at the thought of reuniting with her, he noticed that the hallway that had once been glowing orange was now gone, replaced by a dark stretch of stone.

A brief surge of panic shot through him. Had something gone wrong? He looked at the wall, preparing to start breaking it down, when without warning, the orange glow returned, the wall parting to create a doorway.

Relief washed over him as he saw Ashe emerge, looking healthier than he'd dared hope. She was followed by Charis and an imposing figure, a man whose broad shoulders and powerful frame radiated a strength that could only belong to a god. He wore forged armor that gleamed in the orange light, muscles cut from marble beneath it, and a mane of wild, red hair fell across his shoulders.

Quinn tensed, gripping Clotho a bit tighter as he took in the unmistakable Olympian essence radiating from the man. The intensity of it was nearly overwhelming, as if every ounce of power contained in this god's forge had seeped into his veins.

Then his eyes fell on Ashe, standing unharmed and steady, a bright smile lighting her face. She looked whole, stronger than before, with a glimmer of hope shining in her eyes that he hadn't seen in too long.

She looked radiant, and Quinn couldn't help but feel renewed resolve to keep that spark alive, to never let the world or its burdens dim her light again.

"Ashe," he said, stepping forward, his voice a mixture of relief and concern. "You're all right?" His question was genuine, though he couldn't fully hide the unspoken one beneath it: *Did they harm you?*

Oath Breaker

Ashe's smile softened, and she shook her head. "I'm fine," she assured him, though her eyes flicked to the blood staining his arm and chest. "What happened to you?"

Quinn shifted Clotho in his arms, feeling the tension in his muscles ease slightly as he explained. "Ran into a bit of Olympian trouble myself. Artemis, specifically. Seemed she didn't appreciate me poking around the dungeons."

His tone was light, almost dismissive, but the memories of that brutal fight still pulsed in his wounds. "And then our good pal Cyrus decided to drop in and clean up the mess."

As he spoke, Clotho's frail form stirred in his arms. Her fingers tightened around his cloak, and her eyes, though still clouded and distant, widened as she took in Ashe's face. With a sudden burst of energy, she reached out, clutching Ashe's shoulders, her voice cracked and desperate.

"The Oath Breaker," she whispered, her tone urgent, her nails digging into Ashe's armor. "You must beware the Oath Breaker."

Ashe glanced up at him, startled. Quinn offered a small nod, trying to make sense of it himself. "She's been muttering that since I found her. Over and over."

Before they could ponder Clotho's words further, the deep, steady voice of the god cut through the moment.

"Right, let's be off then, shall we?" Hephaestus rumbled, his voice gruff, like boulders tumbling down a hill. "The last thing ye want is to stay here long enough for Zeus to notice."

Quinn raised an eyebrow, shifting his gaze from Ashe to Hephaestus. "We?" His skepticism was clear, his grip instinctively tightening around his blade.

Ashe drew in a steadying breath. "It's a long story, but the short version is that Hephaestus and Charis are on our side now. He's agreed to forge weapons and armor for our people—giving us a real chance against Zeus."

Hephaestus offered Quinn a slight nod, his expression firm but not unfriendly. Still, the Olympian's presence and power unsettled him. Quinn narrowed his eyes, his distrust clear. "Forgive me if I don't start cheering. Olympians aren't exactly known for their charity."

Ashe's smile held a note of reassurance, her voice calming as she continued. "Hephaestus has his own reasons, and I trust him." Her eyes met his, silently asking him to do the same.

Quinn exhaled, a wry grin tugging at his lips as he nodded, accepting her decision. "Well," he muttered, casting a glance at the god, "I can't wait to hear how you explain this to the council. Left for an old woman, came back with a big, burly Olympian."

Ashe laughed, rolling her eyes at him, and Quinn swore it was the most beautiful noise he had ever heard. He allowed himself a moment of levity before reaching out and pulling the chaos from within him to open a swirling portal.

He gestured for Ashe, Charis, and Hephaestus to step through, the vortex rippling with dark energy as they prepared to leave Olympus behind.

Oath Breaker

Chapter 28
Mallory

Mallory's breath was ragged in her ears, the sound amplified by the heavy silence of the chamber as Levy began his slow, halting approach toward her. Each step was rigid, his body moving with a mechanical, puppet-like stiffness as if he were waging a silent war with his own limbs.

His eyes, once vibrant with that spark of life she'd come to know, were now dull, a prisoner within his own body.

She forced down the surge of panic rising in her chest. This wasn't Levy. He was in there somewhere, fighting against Aphrodite's influence, and she was sure of it. She took a step back, never taking her eyes off him, even as the goddess' shrill laughter rang through the air.

"Levy," Mallory called, her voice trembling despite her best efforts to sound calm, to reach him. "This isn't you. You don't want to do this."

But her words seemed to float through him without a hint of response. His hand lifted, moving in that slow, jerking manner, fingers grasping for her with an unnatural lack of grace. His face was expressionless.

She sidestepped him, evading his reach by inches. Levy's

movements were slow, almost tentative, like he was struggling to stop himself from moving forward, and she clung to that hope that somewhere within, he was still fighting to break free.

"Pathetic," Aphrodite jeered from her vantage point at the far end of the room. Her arms were crossed; her eyes lit with dark amusement. "Pleading with him will not work. He belongs to me now."

Mallory's heart hammered painfully as she darted to the side, barely avoiding Levy's hand as he lunged for her again. "Levy, I know you're in there," she continued, refusing to let herself waver. "Fight her. You're stronger than this!"

Aphrodite's smile twisted, her amusement clearly deepening as she desperately tried to reach him. Mallory's anger flared, her grip tightening on her sword. She couldn't let this twisted version of Levy destroy him and everything he had worked toward. And she certainly would not stand there and allow Aphrodite to use him like this.

Focusing her rage on its true target, Mallory let out a cry, spinning around Levy, her sword raised as she sprinted for Aphrodite. The goddess only watched, her expression that of boredom, as Mallory closed the distance.

She was within striking range when, out of nowhere, Levy moved. His body transformed into a blur of motion, intercepting her with a speed that took her breath away.

She barely had time to raise her sword as his arm came crashing down, blocking her strike and deflecting her blade with such force that it reverberated through her bones. The impact sent her stumbling back, the sword momentarily loosening in her grip as she regained her composure.

Aphrodite laughed, the sound echoing loudly around them. "I told you, he is completely under my control, you foolish girl. Do you really think you can overpower my influence?"

Mallory swallowed, panic creeping up her spine as she looked at Levy. That sudden speed, that flash of intent; it was like he had been unleashed when it came to defending Aphrodite. The moment he turned his attention back to her, he slowed, his movements once again sluggish and halting.

She could see it now, the subtle tremor in his hands as he

reached for her, the barely perceptible tension in his frame. He was fighting it; she was certain of it.

She sidestepped him, heart pounding as she searched for some way to break him free. Her mind raced, grasping for something, anything that might reach him. She couldn't let Aphrodite win. She wouldn't let her have him.

"Levy, please," she whispered, her voice raw, pleading. But again, there came no response, his hand still reaching for her with that terrible, mechanical determination.

Mallory's heart wrenched. Her anger spiked, and without further thought, she swung around Levy once more, lunging toward Aphrodite with all of the determination she could muster. If she was going down, she was taking that bitch with her.

Her blade cut through the air with deadly intent, her aim precise as she thrust the point toward the goddess' heart. But once again, Levy moved faster than she could react, his hand wrapping around her wrist before she could even finish her swing. His grip was like iron, unbreakable, and her sword clattered to the ground as he held her arm in place.

She twisted in his grasp, trying to break free, but he held her firmly, his fingers pressing into her wrist with bruising force. She searched his face, looking for any sign of the man she knew, but his gaze was ever distant, lost in some unreachable depth.

"Levy," she gasped, her voice choked with frustration and pain.

He stared at her, his face blank, his fingers still wrapped around her wrist. But for a fleeting moment, she thought she saw something; a flicker of recognition, a brief glimmer that sparkled in his eyes before it vanished. His grip loosened just enough for her to pull her arm free, and she stumbled back, hope mingling with fear as she clutched her wrist.

"You think he's coming back to you?" Aphrodite sneered, watching her with sadistic joy. A faint blush had made its way onto her face as if she was getting pleasure from this. "You are more foolish than I thought."

Mallory's gaze shifted back to Levy, her heart racing. He was still moving slowly, still struggling with each step as he closed the distance between them. She was certain now he was fighting it. She could see the subtle resistance in his movements, the tension in his body as he tried to break free from Aphrodite's hold.

Desperation surged within her, and she did the only thing she thought might reach him. She began to speak.

"Levy, do you remember? When we first met, you were nothing but a threat on the battlefield, commanding an army of the dead against us." Her voice shook, but she forced herself to keep going, to push through the fear and pain.

"I hated you for it. I thought you were a monster, someone who would do anything for power, no matter the cost."

She dodged to the side as he reached for her again, her voice growing louder, more passionate. "And when you betrayed Ares and joined us once more, I didn't trust you.

"I kept waiting for the other shoe to drop, for you to turn on us and prove my suspicions correct. But you didn't." Her breath came fast, her words pouring out as she circled around him, avoiding his slow, halting advances.

"You kept working, training our troops, putting everything you had into helping us as if you had some unreachable penance driving you. I saw how hard you were trying, how much you were fighting to redeem yourself."

The fog in his eyes wavered for just a moment, and she pressed on, her voice trembling with emotion. "I remember watching you at night, looking up at the stars with that small, almost hopeful smile you wear on your face when you think nobody is looking. And I thought…maybe there was more to you than I'd seen. Maybe you weren't just doing this for our benefit but for yourself. To be better."

He reached for her again, his movements slower than ever before, as if her words were breaking through, tugging him closer to consciousness.

She slipped from his grasp once more, her back brushing against the cold stone wall as she continued to speak, her voice growing softer, more vulnerable.

"I discovered that I wanted to be around you, Levy. And the more I followed you, the more I watched you…the more vulnerable I saw you, I couldn't help it. I started to fall for you despite everything in me screaming at me not to."

The words hung in the air between them, raw and exposed. Never in her life had Mallory dropped her walls like this and allowed herself to be so open. Not even with Ashe. Her confession echoed in the silence, wrapping around them like a lifeline. For a brief moment, she thought she saw something in his face, a spark that hadn't been there before. A glimmer of emotion that made her heart stutter.

She realized too late that she'd backed herself against the wall, trapped with nowhere to go. Levy's hand shot out faster than she could react, his fingers wrapping around her throat, lifting her off the ground with effortless strength. Her breath caught, her pulse racing as she felt his grip tighten, cutting off her air. She clawed at his hand, panic flooding her as the edges of her vision darkened.

"Please, Levy," she choked out, her eyes locked onto his face. "I know you're in there. Come back to us. Come back to me.

Her vision blurred, and she held onto that last thread of hope, praying that her words would reach him, that he'd break free before it was too late.

For a moment, his grip faltered, a flicker of something deep within his eyes breaking through the fog. And in that fragile instant, she saw the man she knew, the Levy who had fought beside her.

She heard the soft, measured patter of feet approaching, each step echoing through the chamber like a death knell. Aphrodite appeared beside Levy, her face lit in twisted delight as she looked at Mallory's fading struggle.

"Oh, you poor thing," the goddess cooed, trailing a finger down Levy's arm. "Well, you know what they say, better to have loved and lost than never to have…blah, blah, blah."

She rolled her eyes. "I have grown bored of this. Levy, darling, rip out her throat."

Chapter 29
Levy

Levy stumbled through the thick, cloying fog, each step heavy, as though he were wading through quicksand. The air around him was sweet, unbearably so, the sickly scent flooding his lungs, clouding his mind until every thought became a blurred echo of itself.

Voices drifted around him, distant and distorted, like they were underwater. He tried to focus, straining to make sense of the sounds, but each word slipped away before he could grasp it, leaving only fragments in its wake.

Somewhere in the haze, he heard Mallory's voice, soft and urgent, as if she were calling out to him from across an impossible distance. He turned toward the sound, trying to follow it, but his legs felt leaden, his body bound by an invisible weight.

A word drifted through the fog, faint but distinct—*Levy*—and his heart twisted, recognizing the warmth in her voice, the desperate edge that tugged at him. But just as he tried to move toward it, the fog thickened, closing in around him like a cage.

A flicker in the fog caught his eye, and he turned, his breath hitching as a scene played out before him: Mallory, sword raised, facing down a monstrous creature with too many legs to count. She fought with a wild ferocity, her movements precise and unyielding.

Oath Breaker

Every ounce of her strength poured into each strike. He tried to call out to her, to warn her, but the words died on his lips, swallowed by the fog.

The image dissolved as quickly as it had come, fading back into the swirling mist. Another voice drifted in, low and mocking, filled with a dark amusement that made his skin crawl. It was familiar, achingly so, but he couldn't place it, couldn't quite reach the memory that lingered just out of grasp.

"Oh my, are you going to go back on your word to me so soon?" the voice taunted, a lilting mockery woven through every syllable.

Levy's heart pounded, the fog around him thickening with each passing second, smothering his thoughts. "Who's there?" he called out, his voice echoing strangely in the void. But the voice only laughed, deep and unsettling, as though he were a child lost in a twisted game.

"I do not give my gift to those who are weak, boy," the voice continued, sharper now, laced with disdain.

A shadow materialized in the mist, its form tall and regal, cloaked in a darkness that seemed to pulse with ancient power. Levy's chest tightened as he recognized her—the goddess Styx, her gaze as sharp as her judgment, cutting through him like a blade.

"You swore you would not harm your friends," she said, her tone cold, her eyes like molten metal.

"I haven't!" Levy's voice trembled, a swell of indignation rising in his chest, though he wasn't even sure what he was defending himself against. "I haven't hurt them. I would never..."

"Haven't you?" Styx's voice cut him off, her tone icy and implacable.

At that moment, voices and images flooded through his mind in a torrent, battering him from all sides. Mallory's words drifted through the fog, her voice carrying that edge of vulnerability that both warmed and haunted him.

He heard her calling out to him, her voice trembling as she spoke of watching him train their troops, of her growing admiration, the way she had come to care for him, to trust him. Her words felt raw and real, each one chipping away at the darkness that clouded his thoughts.

"I thought you were a monster...I thought you were selfish...

but then I saw you, night after night, looking up at the stars. And I started to trust you, to respect you, to want to be around you."

Her voice wove through his mind, fierce and soft all at once, unyielding in her honesty, in her confession. And then, like a hammer shattering glass, it broke through, and the fog began to lift.

He blinked, clarity washing over him, and the sickly sweetness in the air receded like he was breathing freely for the first time. Slowly, with a mounting sense of dread, he looked down, and his stomach dropped.

His hands were wrapped around Mallory's throat, his fingers pressing into her skin, his grip too tight, too unyielding. She was barely conscious, her eyes glassy with pain and a silent plea he could feel twisting in his chest.

Tears ran down her cheeks, glistening as they caught the dim light, and he realized with a sickening horror that she was looking straight at him, seeing him and only him.

"No," he choked out, horror clawing through him. "No, Mallory…"

But his hands wouldn't release her. They were locked in place, moving of their own volition as if they belonged to someone else. He fought against it, every muscle in his body tensing as he tried to pull away, his heart pounding with a desperation that burned like fire.

Mallory's voice, her words, filled his mind, each one a tether to the person he was, the person he was fighting to be.

"Styx," he gasped, forcing himself to look up, his voice cracking. "Please. Please help me."

The goddess' image appeared before him, watching with a cold detachment, her face impassive as she took in the scene.

"This is your one freebie, Levy," she said, her voice ringing through the fog. *"Because I cannot stand that atrocious love goddess. Next time, you lose it all."*

Her words lingered, and then she faded, vanishing as if she had never been there, leaving him alone once more, grappling with the fog and the weight of her warning.

He was left wondering if he had truly seen her or if she had been nothing more than a flicker of hope in the midst of his nightmare. But his hands, by some miracle, had loosened their grip, and Mallory slumped against him, gasping for breath, her eyes dazed but alive.

The relief was short-lived. A command rang out, laced with honeyed cruelty that slithered into his mind like poison. "Rip her throat out," Aphrodite ordered, her voice a velvet whisper filled with malice.

The fog rolled in again, thicker and denser than before, smothering him, pulling at his mind like a weight dragging him into a chasm. But this time, he was ready.

He could feel Mallory's pulse beneath his fingers, the fragile beat of her heart calling him back to himself, grounding him. He wasn't about to lose her—not to Aphrodite's twisted pleasure, not to his own weakness.

"No," he whispered, forcing the word through the fog, planting himself firmly in the memory of her voice, her confession, the hope she had given him.

The fog clawed at his mind, thick and choking, but he anchored himself in every detail of her, every word she'd said, clinging to it like a lifeline. With a strength he hadn't known he possessed, he fought back, feeling his will pulse against the haze, pushing back against Aphrodite's influence, inch by inch.

He would not let this goddess make him into a weapon against the woman he cared for. He would fight, no matter the cost, because for once in his life, he knew exactly where he stood and who he needed to be. For once in his life, he felt as though someone truly saw him, knew him.

And he would be damned if he let Aphrodite steal that away.

Chapter 30
Ashe

The soft flickering of candlelight cast a warm glow over the infirmary's stone walls, the room filled with a quiet stillness broken only by the occasional crackle of the hearth as the wood inside shifted. The air was cool and tinged with the scent of dried herbs hanging from the rafters, lavender, rosemary, and sage mixed with a faint hint of clean linen.

The bed linens were heavy and dark, embroidered with simple patterns, and neatly folded cloths lay stacked on a nearby table beside bowls of cooling water and a collection of poultices and salves.

Ashe sat beside the small bed, a warm washcloth in hand, dabbing gently at Clotho's forehead. The old immortal's breathing was steady, her eyes closed, her features softened in sleep.

Her gaunt, bruised face held no trace of her former energy, only frailty and exhaustion. Even if she couldn't help them learn about the item Zeus sought, Ashe was glad they had rescued her.

Dried cuts and deep burns marked her skin, with patches of scalp showing where her hair had been pulled away. Ashe's hand slowed, her heart heavy as she looked over Clotho's battered frame, bitterness simmering beneath her compassion. She couldn't fathom how Zeus could have inflicted such cruelty, even on his own kin.

Oath Breaker

The door to the infirmary opened quietly, and Lend entered, his footsteps soft against the cobbled floor. Lend, tall and lean, wore a simple leather tunic and trousers, his dark green hair tied back from his face. His eyes were keen and warm, the glint of experience held on his brow.

Ashe remembered when she'd first met him, a young leader, brash and eager, stumbling under the weight of his new responsibilities as he tried to prove himself. He'd made mistakes then, often charging ahead without caution.

Now, he bore himself with a confidence and steadiness that had blossomed over time. Stormhaven had found its leader, and Ashe couldn't help but feel proud of the way he had grown.

Lend gave a faint nod as he took in the scene, his voice soft. "Quinn just portaled to the vaults," he reported, his tone reassuring. "He is reconnecting with the others and bringing them back here. With any luck, the item as well."

Ashe let out a sigh, fighting the tension in her shoulders. He was wounded, even if the wounds were superficial, and he needed rest as well. She knew his talents were necessary, and there would be no arguing with him so long as there was even a chance the others were in danger.

"Good," she lied, setting the cloth aside and glancing up at him. "It'll be a relief to have them back."

"Relief, indeed," he agreed. "How are you holding up here?"

Ashe looked back at Clotho's sleeping face, her expression somber. "She's holding on, which is more than I could have hoped for when I first laid eyes upon her. But she's been through so much."

She paused. "How are things here? Are we ready with the defenses?"

Lend chuckled softly, a hint of nostalgia in his expression. "More ready than they ever were when we were on the front lines together. It's amazing how much more secure they can be when you aren't trekking endlessly into monster territory, having to be ready to move at a moment's notice."

He shook his head. "Stormhaven is as prepared with those as we are going to get."

Ashe smiled, the memory of those chaotic days flooding her mind, a time when everything had felt like survival against the odds, every choice made on instinct, each moment a gamble. She looked at Lend, thankful for the effort he had put into this new Stormhaven and the strength that now surrounded them. "Thank the gods for that."

Lend snorted, folding his arms as he leaned against the doorframe, a smirk on his lips. "Thank *us* for that."

Ashe laughed, shaking her head. "Yes, I suppose the time of thanking the gods has come to an end."

"Well," Lend replied, his tone laced with caution and curiosity. "Most of them anyway. Tell me about the one you returned from Olympus with."

Ashe glanced over at Clotho, making sure she was still resting peacefully before she settled back in her chair, leaning forward as she recounted the tale of their venture into Olympus.

She described the dark halls, the faint but oppressive aura of Zeus' presence that seemed to haunt every step, and how she and Quinn had maneuvered through the depths to reach Clotho.

Ashe spoke of Cyrus' strange intervention and of Hephaestus' unexpected offer, the god's quiet rebellion against his father, and the promise to forge arms for their people.

When he finished, Lend's expression was unreadable, though a slight frown tugged at his brow. "Do you think Cyrus could potentially be an ally after all?"

Ashe shook her head, clearly perplexed. "I don't know what his deal is, but he disturbs me. And please do not ask that question around Andra."

Lend's expression was unreadable, though a slight frown tugged at his brow. "What is it with you three," he said, shaking his head, "always making huge decisions without the council's input?"

Ashe laughed, giving him a light, apologetic shrug. "Sorry, Lend, but I wasn't exactly in a position to come back and ask first."

Lend sighed, though a faint, reluctant smile softened his expression. "No, you aren't sorry," he replied with a wry shake of his head. "But you have a point."

His eyes shifted to the window of the infirmary, looking out over the Citadel. "Besides, if it weren't for you, Quinn, and Levy, we wouldn't even have the chance we have now. It's not like I have any right to question you."

Oath Breaker

Ashe raised an eyebrow, her smile turning teasing. "That's a far cry from the man who once challenged me over what to serve for dinner in the mess hall."

Lend's cheeks flushed, and he gave a sheepish grin, scratching at the stubble under his chin. "Yes, well, I had plenty of sense beaten into me over the years…mostly by Bart."

At the mention of Bartimaeus, Ashe's smile faded, replaced by a bittersweet, distant look. Memories of the old general surfaced; Bart, whose steady hand had guided her in the chaos of war, who had held his ground against Ares to give Quinn's people a chance to escape. His sacrifice had been a final, selfless act. One that had saved countless lives but left a void that could never be filled.

"He would be proud of what you have accomplished here," Ashe said quietly, her voice tinged with sorrow.

Lend's expression softened, his head dropping as he nodded slowly. "I hope so. I still hear his voice sometimes, scolding me when I'm about to do something reckless. It has kept me from a few disasters, believe me."

Ashe chuckled, picturing Bart's gruff demeanor and no-nonsense approach, as well as his stern yet compassionate words of advice. "He'd have kept you in line well enough, that's for sure."

Lend's smile widened, his voice growing a little lighter. "And I'd have given him plenty of reasons to."

He paused, giving Ashe a sidelong glance. "Though between you, Quinn, and Levy, I don't know if he'd have ever kept up. The three of you are a whole storm unto yourselves."

Ashe shook her head, a touch of warmth filling her as she thought of all the times the Masters had told them something similar growing up. "He and I had our fair share of disagreements, but he always trusted me when it mattered."

"Seems like something the rest of us have to learn, too," Lend replied. He turned serious again, his posture holding a mixture of resolve and respect.

"And I'll admit, I wouldn't be half of who I am without having watched you three. Stormhaven's defenses, our people's strength…it has all grown because of what you started."

The weight of his words filled the quiet room, and for a moment, Ashe felt a renewed sense of purpose.

"I'll leave you be for now. When the others return, we'll meet and see where we stand with everything." He gave her a small bow as he exited the room, closing the door behind him with a muted thud.

"What a nice young man."

Ashe blinked in surprise and looked down to see Clotho peeking up at her, one eye cracked open, clear and surprisingly sharp. Though the golden sheen that had marked her powers earlier was gone, that one open eye seemed more vibrant and alive than it had been since they had brought her from Olympus.

"Clotho!" Ashe's tone was both relieved and shocked. "How long have you been awake?"

Clotho's eye crinkled with a hint of mischief. "Long enough to know that young man would march to the Underworld if you asked him to." She let out a dry cackle. "And you just might at that!"

Ashe felt her cheeks pale at the comment, thinking of the visions Fate had shown her. She knew there was truth in Clotho's words but chose to instead steer the conversation away from the notion.

"You should be resting," she said gently, laying a hand on Clotho's shoulder as if that might convince her to stay still.

"Nonsense," Clotho replied, brushing off the suggestion. "I've rested plenty." She squinted up at Ashe, studying her. "You, though—you have done what no other Weaver has done before, returning from the Fate's Tower before your time.

"But it seems you've taken more than just memories with you, haven't you? How are you holding up, dear? It's a miracle you haven't burned up already. The power you carry would be too much for one, not fully immortal. And a frail one at that. Have you eaten today?"

Ashe let out a soft sigh, almost confessing the strain that had gnawed at her bones since her return. "I wouldn't still be here had Hephaestus not given me nectar," she admitted quietly.

Clotho's eyebrows climbed her head at an alarming pace, her expression turning both impressed and incredulous.

"Nectar, is it?" she mused, clearly surprised. "That would explain it. Dangerous stuff, that, for one such as you. You had best finish what you've started before it leaves your system."

Ashe frowned, confusion knitting her brow. "Finish the job? What do you mean?"

But Clotho waved off the question, her focus seeming to wander. She pushed the blankets off and swung her bony legs out from beneath the covers, planting her feet on the floor with surprising strength.

"What did you mean earlier?" Ashe pressed, her curiosity flaring despite Clotho's evasion.

Clotho's brow wrinkled as though she were trying to puzzle out what Ashe was talking about. "Earlier?"

"You told me to beware the Oath Breaker," Ashe said, waiting for a sign that Clotho remembered.

Clotho narrowed her eyes, considering the words with a faint frown. "Did I, now?" She tilted her head thoughtfully, a few long moments passing before her lips quirked into a mischievous grin.

"Couldn't tell ya! Since leaving the Tower, I get these little fits of foresight- though none of them make much sense, nor do I remember them afterward. But if I were you, I'd be wary of anyone you catch in a lie."

Her answer left Ashe with more questions, and Clotho, as if sensing Ashe's lingering concern, reached for her hand with an impatient huff.

"Now, are you going to help an old woman up, or have I got to totter about on my own?"

Ashe bit back a chuckle, both amused and exasperated. "You really should be sleeping, Clotho." She said, though she gently helped the old woman rise, slipping an arm under her for support.

"Sleep? I'll get plenty of that when I'm dead. And based on the creak of these bones, that day will be rather soon, I'd reckon."

She said it with a cheer that made Ashe laugh, but her laughter caught as a strange, almost electric sensation rippled through her, brushing against the power of Fate simmering within.

For a moment, Ashe felt as if the room darkened, the shadows deepening. The feeling left as quickly as it had come, but her mind continued to race with thoughts she couldn't quite place.

Clotho gave her a knowing look as if she knew what Ashe had just felt, though she did not elaborate further. "I'll find you when the others return," she said, her tone oddly gentle, before turning to make her way toward the door with surprising steadiness. "In the meantime, I can feel an old friend in the air, and I'd like to pay him a visit."

Ashe watched her shuffle to the door, the echoes of her footsteps fading into the dark hallway beyond.

Oath Breaker

Chapter 31
Kael

Kael's breath rasped harshly through his mouth as he blocked another punch from one of the muscular guardians. His body ached, pain shooting through his side with each movement, his lip and nose stinging and wet with blood from the blows he'd already taken.

His knuckles were raw, each punch and slash on his blade sending another sharp jolt through his arms. The air around him was thick with the metallic scent of blood, his own mingling with the blood of the fallen, and the ground beneath him was damp and slick, treacherous with the bodies of guardians he and Andra had already taken down.

Even so, more guardians circled him, their muscles rippling in the faint light filtering down from the grey sky above. Kael's every sense was heightened; he could hear Andra's labored breathing just a few meters away, the faint rumble of Horacio's growl vibrating through the air as the Drakon readied himself to strike. Andra's footsteps were careful, each placement precise, even as exhaustion weighed them down.

Another guardian lunged for him, its bare, sinewy arm extending with brutal force, and Kael barely managed to twist out of the way, his ribs flaring in protest. He retaliated with a sweep of his khopesh, the curved blade slicing through the air with deadly grace. The blade met the guardian's throat, slicing cleanly through, and the body crumpled to the ground. Yet even as it fell, more closed in, circling him like vultures sensing prey.

A flash of movement from the corner of his eye told him that Andra was still fighting, that she was surrounded too, her shoulders heaving with the effort of every strike, every dodge. The distant crack of a branch overhead brought his attention up, and he felt something shift in the atmosphere—a dark energy threading through the clearing. He barely had a moment to register it when a voice broke through the din, smooth, calm, and unmistakably familiar.

"Need some help?"

The words were followed by a sudden surge of essence as thick, black tendrils of Chaos erupted from the ground, spiraling upward with deadly precision. They shot through the air like spears, ripping into a large group of guardians, impaling them before dissipating back into shadow. The guardians' bodies fell in unison, opening a path through the throng.

Kael let out a breath he hadn't realized he'd been holding as the way cleared, allowing him to regroup with Andra. Together, they moved quickly, stepping over the fallen as they made their way to the edge of the tree line, where Quinn emerged from the shadows, a faint smirk playing on his lips.

"Show-off," Andra said, her voice tight with exertion, but a grin tugged at her lips nonetheless.

Quinn gave a small shrug, his expression lighting with the playful affection that marked their friendship. His face was streaked with dirt, but the glint of satisfaction in his expression was impossible to miss. "You can talk to Drakons," he replied, with a trace of a smirk. "And I'm the show-off?"

Kael rolled his eyes, a faint flicker of relief mingling with the adrenaline still coursing through his veins. The unexpected support was a welcome sight, though he couldn't help but note the new gashes on Quinn's armor. The faint scent of scorched metal drifted toward him, mixed with the earthiness of the forest floor, and he felt the silent promise in Quinn's expression—a look that told him they'd talk about it later.

"Levy and Mallory are inside," Kael said, his voice rough, each word an effort through his heavy breathing, "but we haven't been able to join them. Think you can lend a hand?"

Quinn's smile widened. "Gladly."

Without another word, the three of them dove back into the fray. The ground vibrated beneath their feet as they charged forward, the chaos energy crackling faintly around Quinn as he moved, his every step leaving a whisper of darkness in its wake. Kael felt a renewed surge of strength as he pushed forward, the familiar weight of his khopesh in his grip grounding him as he swung it with deadly intent.

Another guardian lunged at him, its fists swinging, and Kael brought his blade up just in time, the curved edge deflecting the blow. The guardian's raw strength was staggering, each impact reverberating through Kael's bones, but he gritted his teeth and held his ground. He slashed upward, his sword cutting deep into the guardian's chest, and the creature let out a low, guttural sound as it fell.

Beside him, Quinn fought with a fluid grace that was almost mesmerizing. Tendrils of darkness unfurled from his fingertips, wrapping around a guardian's torso before twisting violently, snapping bone and muscle alike. The guardian dropped to the ground, its body crumpling, but Quinn was already moving to the next, his movements efficient. There was a fierce joy in his expression, a spark that told Kael he was more than ready to unleash his power.

Kael felt a sudden impact against his side as another guardian charged into him, its massive shoulder slamming into his ribs with enough force to send him stumbling. Pain flared through his side, sharp and hot, but he regained his footing quickly, using the momentum to drive his khopesh upward in a swift, brutal arc.

The blade bit into the guardian's abdomen, slicing cleanly through, and Kael twisted the weapon as he pulled it free, watching as the creature collapsed, its body joining the growing pile at his feet.

Andra was only a few paces away, Horacio at her side, the Drakon's scales gleaming dully in the dim light. She fought with a fierce determination, her every movement swift, her blade flashing as she struck down another guardian. Her breaths were heavy, her face streaked with sweat and dirt, but she didn't falter, her stance solid even as she was surrounded.

Horacio let out a low, rumbling growl, his claws digging into the ground as he launched himself at a nearby enemy. The creature stumbled under the Drakon's weight, its arms flailing as Horacio's jaws closed around its shoulder, a sickening crunch echoing through the clearing.

Andra took advantage of the distraction, her blade finding its mark as she drove it into the guardian's side, and the creature fell, limp and lifeless.

They were making headway, but the guardians kept coming, their numbers seemingly endless. Kael could feel his strength waning, his limbs growing heavier with each swing, but he pushed through, his focus narrowing to the next target, the next strike.

Another guardian lunged at him, and he sidestepped, bringing his weapon down in a brutal strike that severed the creature's arm. It let out a bellow of pain, but before it could retaliate, Quinn's chaos energy surged forward, wrapping around its head and snapping its neck with a sickening twist.

Kael shot Quinn a nod of thanks, though he was too winded to speak, and the three of them continued their deadly rhythm, moving in sync as they took down guardian after guardian. The scent of blood and sweat filled the air, mingling with the earthy tang of crushed leaves and disturbed soil.

They were beginning to gain the upper hand, the bodies of the guardians forming a macabre carpet in the now pink, slushy snow, when a final wave of the creatures broke through the trees, barreling toward them with relentless force. Kael felt a surge of determination as he braced himself for the onslaught.

"Ready?" Andra called, her voice a fierce rallying cry as she positioned herself at his side, her blade dripping crimson tears.

"Always," Kael replied, his voice low and steady, the pain in his ribs now nothing more than a dull hum. And as Quinn unleashed another wave of dark energy, spearing through the charging guardians like bolts of shadow, Kael knew they would reach their friends, no matter what.

Oath Breaker

Chapter 32
Mallory

Levy's grip loosened, and Mallory collapsed against his chest, gasping as air rushed back into her lungs. Her throat burned, each breath labored and raw, and her head spun with the rush of oxygen. There was a sudden clarity in his eyes.

A flicker of the Levy she knew pierced through the fog as he looked down at her. She saw him fighting against the poison that clouded his senses, the man breaking free.

"What are you doing, you mindless brute?" Aphrodite's voice cut through the chamber, shrill and furious, a grating sound that shattered the brief silence. "I told you to kill her!"

Levy's eye stayed clear for a beat longer, and he gently lowered her to the ground, his face pained, his breath uneven. Tears prickled at Mallory's eyes, and she clung to that flicker of awareness, to the man he was underneath the goddess' hold.

As quickly as it had come, she saw the fog creeping back over him, clouding his gaze, dulling the light that had momentarily shone through.

"No," he choked out, his voice strained, as he stumbled back from her, clutching his head with both hands. The word seemed to tremble in the air between them, a fragile defiance that trembled like glass on the edge of breaking.

Aphrodite's eyes widened, a look of outrage twisting her beautiful features. "What do you mean, *no*? I own you!" Her voice was a snarl, her command dripping with entitlement.

Levy's hands tightened against his temples, his fingers digging into his scalp as though he could tear the goddess' influence from his mind by sheer force. His body was shaking, his breaths coming in desperate, ragged gasps as he fought the invisible chains binding him.

"No," he repeated, louder this time, the word escaping in a hoarse grunt that seemed to linger in the air.

"KILL HER NOW!" Aphrodite screeched, her voice rising to a piercing pitch, a command laced with malice.

With a guttural roar, Levy spun, lashing out in a wild strike. His hand whipped through the air, contacting Aphrodite with such solid force that she went flying, her body crashing to the ground several feet away.

She lay there for a moment, stunned. Her chest heaved with indignant rage as she scrambled to her feet, her expression twisted with fear for the first time.

Mallory could feel her pulse racing, relief flooding her that Levy was no longer trying to grab her. But as she looked at him, she could see that something was still wrong.

His shoulders were tense, his muscles bunched, his entire body trembling as though he were holding back a force that threatened to consume him from within. The fog lingered, and Mallory could practically imagine it coiling around him like a shadow that refused to release its hold.

"Get… out…of…my…head," Levy growled, his voice low, straining, as though each word cost him every ounce of his strength.

His body lurched forward, and before Mallory could process what was happening, he was on Aphrodite, his hands wrapping around her head and lifting her from the ground as though she weighed nothing.

Aphrodite's face twisted in terror; her usual grace shattered by the raw panic that flickered across her features.

"Let go of me!" she wailed, her voice high and squealing, an unfamiliar sound from the normally composed goddess. She clawed at his arms, her nails raking over his skin, though the power of Achilles made sure no wounds were left.

But Levy's hands held her steady, his fingers tightening around her head, his teeth bared, jaw clenched so tightly that the veins stood out stark against his skin. "Free…me…" he ground out, his voice choked with rage and agony.

Aphrodite struggled, her hands scrabbling desperately to no avail. She twisted and writhed, her face contorted in fear and pain as she tried to escape his grip, but Levy's strength held her in place. Ichor began to trickle from her nose, her mouth, her ears, and her eyes, staining her perfect skin gold, and her body began to slacken.

Mallory watched in sick horror, frozen, as Aphrodite's struggles slowed, her limbs going limp, her eyes rolling back until only the whites showed.

Levy's hands trembled, his grip still unyielding, his breaths coming in harsh gasps as he fought against the grip of his own mind. She realized, with a sudden jolt of fear, that he was squeezing too tightly, that he was on the brink of losing himself to that fog.

"Levy!" she called out, her voice urgent, cutting through the thick silence. She took a step forward, her heart pounding, mind racing.

He didn't respond, didn't even seem to hear her, his focus entirely on the dying goddess in his grasp, as though all his rage, all his pain, were pouring out through his fingertips.

"Levy, she's gone!" Mallory cried, her voice strong, hoping to reach him, to pull him back from the edge. She stepped closer, her hand outstretched, her own fingers trembling. "Let her go. She can't hurt us anymore."

But he was lost in the haze, his face twisted in a grimace of confused pain and anger, his eyes squeezed tightly shut as though he couldn't bear the world around him. She saw a faint shimmer of tears slipping from the corners of his eyes, streaking down his cheeks in silent agony.

"Levy, stop!" she commanded, her tone firm, though it softened as she moved closer, her heart aching at the sight of him so utterly broken. "Let her go."

Slowly, his eyes opened, the fog lifting fully, and his gaze focused on the scene before him. His chest rose and fell in ragged breaths, his body trembling as he looked down at Aphrodite's limp form, her head lolling, her once-bright eyes rolled back into her skull, her body lifeless in his grasp. He released her, letting her body drop heavily to the ground, where she lay in a crumpled heap.

Levy took a step back, his body shaking as he looked around. His breaths came wild and uneven, his expression one of horror. The reality of what had happened dawned on him, and he seemed to shrink, his posture collapsing under the weight of his actions.

Mallory reached out, her hand resting gently on his back. She hoped to steady him, to bring him some sense of calm. But at her touch, he flinched, recoiling as though her hand had burned him. He stumbled back, his expression one of a cornered animal, eyes wide and panicked, his body trembling uncontrollably.

"It's ok, Levy," she said softly, keeping her voice gentle, though her heart ached at the distance he was putting between them. "We're safe now. You saved us."

His eyes found hers, his face pale, stricken with an uncertainty she'd never seen in him before. He took another step back as though he couldn't bear to be near her, his voice barely a whisper as he spoke, the words raw and broken.

"I hurt you," he said, looking at the finger-shaped bruises fading into view around her neck. "Mallory I… I didn't mean to. I would never…" He choked on the words, his expression one of pure agony.

Mallory moved slowly toward him, her own heart twisting at the pain in his voice. She kept her tone steady, soothing, each word a careful balm as she reached for him again.

"I know you didn't mean to, Levy. You were fighting Aphrodite the whole time." She took another step closer, her movements slow and deliberate, like approaching a wounded animal she was worried would sprint away. "I'm okay, truly. You saved us."

The tension in his shoulders softened just slightly, though his face remained haunted, and he searched her expression, looking for any sign of forgiveness. Mallory's gaze stayed steady, her presence unwavering, and she offered him a small, gentle smile, hoping he'd find some reassurance in it.

She reached out, gently cupping his face, staring deeply into his eyes. They stood together, silent, the weight of what had passed settling around them like a quiet, shared understanding. As she watched him, she felt the last of her fear fade, leaving only the steadfast promise that they would face this together.

The sound of pounding footsteps thundered down the passageway, echoing off the stone walls. The moment between Mallory and Levy shattered as he jerked back, going taut like a string pulled to its breaking point.

Mallory's head whipped toward the entrance just as Kael, Andra, and Horacio barreled into the chamber, weapons drawn, eyes scanning the room for danger.

Quinn sauntered in after them, his steps measured and calm, a stark contrast to the urgency of the others. His dark hair was tousled, and there were new scuffs on his armor, but his demeanor was as composed as ever.

His gaze flicked to Mallory, a hint of apology in his eyes as though he sensed the delicate moment they'd interrupted and regretted the intrusion.

Andra's steps faltered as her eyes fell upon Aphrodite's crumpled form sprawled across the cold stone floor. "Oh," Andra beathed, the single syllable heavy with surprise and unspoken questions. She lowered her sword slightly, the tension in her shoulder easing as the immediate threat seemed to dissipate.

Kael halted beside her, his sharp eyes taking in the scene with swift efficiency. His expression remained inscrutable, but the subtle shift in his stance betrayed a measure of relief.

Mallory glanced between them and noticed Quinn and Levy standing apart, a silent current passing between the two men. Levy's posture was still rigid, his hands clenched at his sides, his knuckles white.

His eyes held a haunted look, shadows flickering in their depths like ghosts he couldn't quite banish. Quinn met his gaze steadily, a wordless exchange unfolding in the span of a heartbeat. Concern etched itself into Quinn's features, but Levy gave a slight, almost imperceptible shake of his head, a silent plea to let it be.

After a moment, Quinn offered a small nod, accepting Levy's unspoken request. He turned his attention to the far wall, where a solitary rune pulsed with faint rhythmic light, a heartbeat cast in stone and essence.

The rune's glow bathed the rough surface in shades of deep

indigo and silver, casting intricate pattern that danced against the ancient rock.

"Looks like you guys handled our Olympian problem," Quinn remarked. "Care to see what all the fuss was about?"

Without waiting for a response, he reached out and placed his palm flat against the rune. A subtle hum vibrated through the air, a resonance that thrummed through Mallory's body. The light intensified, flashing three times in quick succession before settling into a steady glow.

With a deep rumble, a section of the wall began to shift, the grinding of stone against stone filling the chamber as it receded to reveal a hidden alcove. Dust and small fragments of rock tumbled to the floor, and when the movement ceased, a crude pedestal stood revealed. A simple column of dark granite, unadorned except for the natural grooves that marked its surface.

Atop the pedestal rested a box unlike Mallory had ever seen. Crafted from a material that seemed to drink in the surrounding light, it was as black as the deepest night, the surface smooth and without blemish.

Intricate filigree of pure gold traced the elaborate patterns across its surface, the delicate lines forming symbols and glyphs that seemed to shift when viewed from different angles. Mallory's pulse quickened, her breath catching as she looked at it.

It seemed to pull at them, a subtle magnetic draw that was both exhilarating and terrifying, as though it was beckoning them closer with a silent promise of secrets and strength. It was as though the box was alive, aware, waiting for someone to reach out and claim it.

Kael's eyes were fixed on it, his hand already beginning to extend, his fingers reaching toward the box as if he couldn't help himself. Just as his fingertips were about to brush its surface, Quinn and Levy reached out in unison, their hands clamping down on his wrist and arm, stopping him before he could make contact.

Kael snapped out of his stupor, staring at them in shock. Levy and Quinn stared once more at one another, sharing an expression, the silent conversation needing no words.

"Oh, yes, you two are very much in love and can have wonderfully secret conversations by batting your eyelashes at each other," Mallory quipped, a glimmer of her usual humor slipping through the lingering tension. She raised an eyebrow, crossing her arms. "Care to share with the class?"

Quinn's mouth twitched into a faint grin, though he kept his focus on the box. "Trust me, Mallory," he said, his tone measured.

"This isn't just any box. Whatever's in there, there is a reason it has been locked away." His grip remained firm on Kael's arm, the subtle warning in his touch unmistakable.

Kael huffed, clearly not entirely broken from its spell, though he pulled his hand back reluctantly.

"Fine," he muttered, his eyes lingering on the box. "But I don't see why the rest of us can't at least know what's so damned dangerous about it."

Levy took a slow, steady breath, his eyes still distant, his face drawn with a heaviness that Mallory hadn't seen before.

"There are relics made by gods," he said quietly, his voice soft. "And then, there are those made by something beyond even them."

His words hung in the air, settling over them like a blanket of cold. Mallory felt a chill prickling up her spine as she looked at him, trying to gauge the depth of what he'd just said. She knew, instinctively, that whatever was in the box was no ordinary artifact. Its very presence filled the room with an invisible weight, pressing down on them, a silent power that was both alluring and deeply unsettling.

Andra took a tentative step closer, her voice cautious. "Are we sure we should even touch it?" she asked, her eyes flicking between Quinn, Levy, and the box. "After everything we've been through just to reach this point..."

Quinn gave a slight nod, his expression serious. "Wise? Probably not. But necessary? Absolutely."

His hand lingered near the box, hesitating for a moment as he seemed to consider something. Mallory could feel the intensity of his presence, the silent struggle he waged between caution and curiosity.

Levy's hand remained on Kael's arm, holding him back, his fingers digging into her friend's sleeve with a tension that hadn't yet abated. Mallory could see that his body was still taut, his expression troubled, as though he were fighting against a lingering shadow that had not yet fully receded.

Brian Tripp

The haunted look in his eyes hadn't faded, even as he stared down at the object that had drawn them all here, each of them captivated, caught between the urge to reach out and the instinct to flee.

Mallory's heart thudded, her own hand inching toward her weapon out of habit. Whatever was inside the box felt... alive, as though it were watching them, waiting to see who would be bold enough to release it.

She watched as Quinn reached out slowly, his fingers brushing the cool, polished surface of the black box. The power it radiated pulsed faintly beneath his touch, and for a moment, he held his breath, half-expecting something to go horribly wrong.

As his hand closed around the box, lifting it from the pedestal, nothing happened—the chamber remained silent, the air still. He let out a quiet sigh of relief, the tension easing from his shoulders as he turned back to the group.

"Let's get out of here," he murmured, giving her a small, reassuring nod. She followed as he led them out of the vault and into the open air, the weight of what they'd seen and done settling into a strange kind of calm.

Once outside, Quinn extended his hand, summoning a portal that shimmered before them, a swirling gateway home. With one last look at the dark stone walls fading into memory, Mallory stepped through, leaving the vault and all its secrets behind.

Oath Breaker

Chapter 33
Talius

The memory gripped Talius, wrapping around him and dragging him back to that day, one that had been etched into his mind with the sharpness of a blade. He remembered the air that evening, thick with the scents of the slums—a heady blend of wood smoke, stale bread, and the faint, earthy smell of wet clay from the nearby riverbanks.

The light was dim, a fading twilight casting Stormhaven's poorer quarter in shades of grey and shadow, as if it were already preparing for the dark stain he would leave upon it.

From his concealed perch, Talius watched her. Even from a distance, Ashe's presence was a small beacon in the gloom. She was young, perhaps no more than seven or eight, with a thin frame and wild, platinum hair that looked as though it rarely saw a comb.

She wasn't the fastest or the strongest of her peers, her limbs often seeming a little too long for her frame, but she moved with an assuredness, a confidence that belied her youth.

Ashe was kneeling by a wounded animal—another stray dog from the looks of it—her small hands working with a gentle care, wrapping a torn scrap of fabric around its injured paw. The dog whimpered but did not resist, as if sensing that this child's touch, for all its fumbling, was meant to heal.

She spoke softly to the creature, words Talius couldn't quite make out, but her tone was soothing, the kind of voice that had comforted other children of the slums, friends and strangers alike. She had a strange effect on them, calming their fears with her gentle strength and offering what little she had with an open hand.

Talius had been watching her for some time, keeping his distance as he studied her, weighing her merits with an eye sharpened by experience. And he had found her worthy.

In the dim light, she looked like any other child of the slums— her clothes were patched in places, the fabric thin and worn from too many washings.

And yet, there was something that set her apart, a kind of inner light that defied the shadows around her. Ashe was compassionate, selfless to a fault, and possessed a quiet strength that made her invaluable. She was perfect.

Stormhaven's poorer district, where Ashe lived, was a place neglected by the city's ruling Masters, left to fend for itself in the hopes that those with ambition would claw their way up and out, showing their mettle. It was built mostly from wood, houses leaning against each other for support like weary neighbors sharing a burden.

Smoke from cooking fires hung over the rooftops, mingling with the scent of unwashed bodies and the faint tang of rotting food. For Talius, who had walked the halls of the Citadel for centuries, it was a place of squalor and desperation, but he understood it as a crucible—one that forged the strong and discarded the weak.

Ashe, he had decided, was one of the strong. She had a heart unlike anyone he'd seen in generations. She would complement Levy's raw, untamed power and Quinn's strategic brilliance perfectly. She was the missing piece of Clotho's prophecy, the third hero who would rise from the ashes to stand against the gods. All she needed was guidance.

Her parents were less than obstacles, barely present in her life except when they required something from her. Drug-addled and irresponsible, they had no use for their daughter beyond the occasional chore she performed to earn her keep.

They were gamblers, drunks, dragging their family further into *poverty with each passing month. Talius had watched her mother beg coins from strangers only to vanish into the nearest den, and her father seldom returned home at all. To them, Ashe was a commodity, an afterthought.*

He knew what needed to be done.

"Forgive me, child," he murmured, his voice barely audible over the soft crackle of the lantern he carried. "Though I think you might find a better home this way, anyhow."

Talius crouched beside the nearest building, one of the small wooden structures where so many of the district's families lived crammed together in cramped quarters. His hands moved with practiced efficiency, striking flint to steel until a spark caught, igniting a small flame that flickered hungrily in the dusk.

He leaned down, feeding the fire with bits of tinder until it grew strong enough to spread on its own. He could smell the sharp, stinging scent of smoke as it took hold, wafting upward in thin tendrils that curled and danced in the evening breeze.

One building after another, he moved with calculated precision, his movements careful, deliberate. Each spark, each flicker of flame that caught, was another link in the chain that would bring Ashe to him, another step in the plan he had spent centuries orchestrating.

Soon, the air grew thick with smoke, the orange glow of fire casting dancing shadows against the worn wooden walls as it spread, consuming each building with ravenous hunger. The flames licked upward, climbing like fingers reaching for the sky, filling the night with a sickly warmth.

The cries of alarm were faint at first, distant shouts as the residents of the slums began noticing the encroaching fire. Panic rippled through the streets, the shouts growing louder, frantic voices rising into screams as people fled their homes, carrying what few possessions they could.

The thick, greasy smoke filled the air, burning Talius's nostrils, a familiar, unpleasant sensation that clawed at his senses. He welcomed the discomfort; it anchored him in the moment, a reminder of the cost of his mission.

He heard Ashe before he saw her, that young voice breaking through the din as she shouted for help. Her words carried on the wind. Talius watched as she ran toward the heart of the fire, her small figure darting through the chaos, searching for anyone who might be trapped. She was fearless, reckless, diving into danger without a second thought. And for a brief moment, he felt a pang of something that might have been regret. But he pushed it aside. This was necessary. This was for the greater good.

A courier had already been sent to her parents, a sealed message bearing the Citadel's crest and an offer too tempting for them to refuse. The message offered them a sum of money large enough to erase their debts and start fresh, a fortune by their standards, and all they needed to do was relinquish their daughter's guardianship. The fire would be the excuse, the incident that drove them to make the decision, the catalyst that would set everything into motion.

Talius stood in the shadows, watching as the flames spread, consuming the wooden structures with a speed that was both mesmerizing and terrifying. The heat was palpable, a heavy, suffocating force that pressed against his skin, filling the air with an almost unbearable warmth. He could feel the prickling sensation of sweat on his brow, the acrid taste of smoke coating his tongue as he breathed it in.

Through the thick haze, he caught glimpses of Ashe, her small figure darting between buildings as she tried to help those around her. Even in the midst of the chaos, she moved with purpose, her face set in a determined expression as she aided an elderly woman, helping her escape the flames. She was relentless, undeterred by the heat, by the suffocating smoke, her focus unwavering as she worked to protect those weaker than herself.

Talius watched her, his heart heavy with the weight of what he had set into motion. The fire spread, growing stronger with each passing second, until the entire district was engulfed in flames, a seething inferno that illuminated the night sky with a hellish glow.

He could hear the panicked cries of the residents, the desperate pleas for help as they fled, leaving everything they owned behind. But he remained still, his gaze fixed on Ashe, his mind focused on the future he had carefully constructed for her.

The courier would reach her parents soon, delivering the offer that would change everything. And when they came to him, bringing her with them, he would be waiting.

Oath Breaker

~~~

"My, what a state you are in."

The voice, though aged by the passing of centuries, was unmistakably familiar. It stirred something deep within Talius' weary, battered heart—memory, sharp and clear as sunlight cutting through the darkness. He couldn't believe it, wouldn't dare to. But the voice was hers, a sound that belonged to his past, one he thought lost forever to time and consequence.

Those chains were never meant for you, my friend," she said, her tone soft.

Confusion stirred within him. It couldn't be her. Clotho couldn't be here. These chains—they often warped his senses, twisting his memories, conjuring figures that weren't there, voices from shadows that vanished when he reached for them.

This was different; there was a warmth to her words, a touch of familiarity that felt real, solid. He had been imprisoned in this hell of stone and iron for what felt like so long that it seemed impossible, a cruel trick of his mind, another torment born of his guilt.

Warm fingers brushed his jaw, lifting his head with a tenderness that made him want to crumble. His heart raced as he looked up, meeting the clear, striking yellow of her irises, her gaze steady and unwavering. It was actually her.

"Clotho," he breathed, the word escaping like a prayer, a fragile whisper.

She smiled at him, her face a blend of warmth and quiet pride, and he felt the years melt away, the centuries falling back in time to when he was no more than a gangly teen and she the beautiful future Weaver.

"You have done well, Talius," she said, her words soft but filled with a depth of gratitude that caught in his chest. "Everything I asked of you and more. All of our plans are in motion now, and soon, we shall watch our curtains fall on a brand-new dawn."

Tears gathered in his eyes, blurring his vision, but he couldn't wipe them away. His body felt numb; each muscle was too drained, too broken to respond. The weight of those chains had taken more from him than he had thought possible.

He could barely feel his own limbs, the once-iron strength in his arms reduced to frail shudders of exertion. His throat was parched, every breath scraping painfully as if sand had settled there long ago, rough and unforgiving. He wanted to speak, to tell her all that he had endured, to confess the doubts and fears that had plagued him, but the words were lost, buried beneath the weight of his exhaustion.

"Come," she whispered, a gentleness in her voice that sent a fresh wave of tears spilling over his grime-stained cheeks. "Let us remove you from these chains. You have given enough. With your efforts, the walls are ready. They will hold."

With a practiced ease, she reached for the chains, her fingers working quickly despite their age and damage, the sharp clink of iron echoing in the silence as she unbound him. One by one, the links fell away, and warmth spread through him, seeping into his battered muscles like sunlight through frozen stone.

It was as though he had been submerged in water all this time, the oppressive weight now lifting, letting him breathe fully, deeply, for the first time in longer than he could remember. The sensation washed over him in waves, a warm balm that soothed the wounds, both seen and unseen, and he shuddered, overwhelmed by the relief.

His muscles, once taut and strained, relaxed, a faint tremor rippling through his limbs as the pain that had become his constant companion finally eased.

The last chain fell away, clattering against the earthen floor, and his body sagged, the last remnants of his strength ebbing in a final wave of relief. But before he could collapse, Clotho caught him, her arms wrapping around him with the gentle familiarity of an old friend.

She eased him down, cradling his head in her lap, her presence soothing against the jagged edges of his exhaustion. Her touch was familiar, a reassurance that, for now, he was safe.

"That wily goddess," she muttered, a hint of amusement in her voice as she brushed dirt from his face. Her fingers were warm, and he could feel her hands steadying him, her touch anchoring him as he lay there, utterly spent. "I can feel the dregs of her essence here. She must have left some of herself with you, too. The three of us will be enough."

Her words were strange, a riddle that he would have puzzled

over if his mind weren't already so fractured. He couldn't make sense of it, but her voice, her presence, was enough to lull him. She would be there to make sense of the chaos he had endured, to bring him back to himself.

She tilted his head slightly, her fingers brushing his temple, and his eyelids fluttered, the weight of his exhaustion pulling him toward the dark, the silence a welcoming embrace that promised respite. He wanted to stay awake, to look up at her, to hold on to the reassurance she offered. He wanted to ask her what came next, to assure himself that this was real, that he wasn't lost in some fevered dream conjured by his suffering.

But he had nothing left. The years of isolation, the relentless pain that had chipped away at his will, the guilt that had dug its claws into his heart—they had left him hollow, a shadow of the man he once was. His body was broken, his energy drained, and though he tried to fight it, his eyes drifted shut, his mind slipping into the soft, comforting darkness.

Somewhere in the edges of his awareness, he felt her fingers tracing gentle circles on his temple, a touch that carried the echoes of a memory, a time when he had been strong, whole, a time before the weight of his choices had pulled him down.

She began to hum a quiet, familiar melody, a song from their past, one that spoke of courage and resolve. The tune was soft, weaving through his mind like a warm thread, binding him to the world even as he drifted further into the void.

"Rest now, old friend," she murmured, her voice a soft lullaby, each word a gentle tug that drew him deeper into a place of calm. "You have given enough. And I shall fetch you when the time comes." Her words lingered in his mind, settling over him like a protective shield, a promise that she would be there when he awoke, that he would not be alone. He clung to that, to the warmth of her lap beneath his head, to the faint scent of herbs and earth that clung to her, grounding him even as he drifted.

Talius let himself sink into that comforting darkness, his body finally surrendering to the pull of sleep, and the last thing he heard was the soft hum of Clotho's voice, her song fading into the silence as he slipped away, leaving behind the chains, the pain, and the weight of his past.

Chapter 34
Aphrodite

Aphrodite lay sprawled on the freezing stone floor, her body aching as she fought to claw her way back from the brink of unconsciousness. The vault was silent save for the relentless plunk of water dripping from above, echoing in the cavernous space.

Each drop seemed to reverberate through her skull like a drumbeat, each one a reminder of her failure, of that brute's hands wrapped around her, nearly crushing her skull like a piece of fruit. To think that he, a mortal, could have resisted her was laughable.

Unbelievable.

And that twitchy, meddling brat with the scraggly brown hair had somehow broken her hold over him. She would relish finding new ways to make them suffer for this affront. They had stolen from her, had humiliated her, and she would make them pay dearly—just as soon as she gathered enough strength to move.

A slow, smoldering rage simmered within her, the anger as hot and searing as her body was cold and numb. She could feel the damage Levy's hands had inflicted.

Her essence was fractured, her power dimmed. She was still working to restore her vision, her eyes crushed under the weight of his fury, now healing in fits and starts. Blurred, colorless shapes danced before her in the dark, as useless as shadows against stone.

Playing dead.

She let out a twisted smile at her own cunning, ignoring the spasms that wracked her body each time she moved. It had been brilliant, really. Had she fought him any longer, the brute would have finished the job. The moment she'd stopped struggling, letting herself go limp, he'd dropped her like a discarded rag. And now, she would rise and...

A scraping sound echoed through the vault, the subtle shuffling of footsteps on stone. Aphrodite froze, her senses sharp, raw, attuned to the presence now looming above her.

She couldn't see who it was—her vision was still nothing but dark, formless shapes—but she could feel it, a presence that twisted and contorted, an energy unlike any she had ever encountered before. It was an essence knotted and corrupted, a terrible cocktail of souls and powers that did not belong together.

"Still playing dead, Aphrodite?" The voice was jagged, a raspy hiss that scraped against her ears like bone grating on stone. It sent a shiver of revulsion through her, though she forced herself to keep her expression neutral. She knew that voice, knew it well.

"Cyrus." She exhaled, the relief of recognizing an ally washing over her like a balm.

Good, she thought.

She wouldn't have to waste precious time fighting him.

"Help me up, would you?" Her voice was weak, more than she wanted to admit, and she raised a hand, expecting his support.

But instead of a hand, something sharp and cruel plunged into her shoulder. She gasped, a high-pitched, raw sound that slipped out before she could stop it, pain flaring in every nerve, shooting through her like fire.

The weapon pinned her to the ground, its edge twisting deeper into her flesh, and she could feel it—her essence was slipping away, draining as though she were a tree tapped for sap. Her power was bleeding out, burning as it seeped into the cold stone beneath her.

A scream ripped from her throat, a sound filled with agony and helpless rage. She writhed, her body bucking against the pressure, but the blade twisted again, and another wave of torment rolled through her, stealing her breath and locking her muscles in place.

Brian Tripp

It was as if her body was being peeled away from her soul, stripped of everything that made her the goddess of love, the goddess of desire and beauty.

A low chuckle drifted through the air, cruel and delighted. "Hmm, not quite the kind of screams you enjoy hearing, are they?" Cyrus's voice was laced with sadistic pleasure, each word spoken slowly, savored. "But they're the kind I like."

He twisted the weapon again, and her limited vision burst with sparks of pain, her body arching against the stone as her essence spilled out faster, her lifeblood pouring away in waves. She could feel herself growing weaker, her power dimming as it left her in sickening pulses.

Her breath came in shallow gasps, her mind reeling, and all she could think of was making it stop, ending this horrid agony. This wasn't how it was supposed to go; she was a goddess, a being of eternal beauty, of power.

She was *Aphrodite.* No one had the right to take this from her.

But her protests were locked within her, her voice strangled by the pain, the breath stolen from her lungs. Her vision was all but gone, nothing but darkness and fleeting flashes of her dimming essence, and she could feel her hold slipping. She opened her mouth, the words tumbling out in a cracked, desperate plea.

"Please, Cyrus. Enough."

But he only laughed, a loud, hollow sound that echoed through the vault, louder than her wails, drowning them out with cruelty. It was a laugh with no warmth, no trace of empathy, only a cold, detached malice that made her stomach twist with fear.

Suddenly, the pressure eased, the weapon withdrawn from her shoulder with a sickening squelch, and she collapsed against the stone, her body convulsing as her essence continued to bleed out, slower now but no less painful. She could barely breathe, her chest heaving with shallow, desperate gasps as her fingers twitched weakly against the ground.

Cyrus crouched beside her, his tone softening, but there was a new edge to it, a mockery that sank into her bones like frost.

"And so," he murmured, his voice lilting, almost tender, as he leaned closer, "Love has crumbled. Aphrodite, the goddess of beauty, of lust and power—now nothing more than a broken whisper."

Aphrodite's mind swirled with panic, the reality sinking in as she lay helpless, her body unresponsive, her power slipping through her grasp like sand. This couldn't be happening.

She was a goddess, an eternal force of love and beauty, an entity whose name alone could bring empires to their knees. And yet here she was, brought down by a man once mortal and betrayed by the one she thought an ally.

"Cyrus…" she choked out, the name barely escaping her lips, her voice a strangled whisper.

But he only leaned closer, his smile a cold sliver in the darkness, a smirk that was more sinister than anything she had ever encountered. He raised a hand, letting it hover above her, his fingers twisting in a mock caress.

"Goodbye, Aphrodite," he whispered, his voice soft, almost reverent. "May your beauty fade; may your love be forgotten. It was only ever a farce anyway."

A wave of blinding pain erupted within her, and she screamed, a raw, guttural sound that echoed through the vault as her essence was torn from her in one final, agonizing surge. Her vision exploded in white-hot agony, and her body seized, her consciousness shattering as the world around her faded to black.

And then, there was nothing. No pain, no fear, no beauty to cling to.

The goddess of love was no more.

Chapter 35
Ashe

The council chamber glowed with a rare, lighthearted energy—one that had been absent for far too long. Ashe leaned back, letting the warmth of joy and camaraderie settle around her. Soft laughter rippled through the room, weaving between quiet conversations and the gentle clink of goblets raised in celebration.

It was a night of triumph, of small victories that whispered of greater ones to come. She breathed it in, allowing herself—for just this moment—to sink into the rare swell of high spirits, savoring every fleeting second of it.

Across the table, Mallory's voice rose with playful indignation as she teased Avery about some recent misstep with a girl. Avery, with his perpetually youthful face and dark, tousled hair, was blushing furiously, his cheeks nearly the color of a ripe apple.

He fumbled over his words, stammering a defense that Mallory deftly countered with a raised eyebrow and a knowing grin, clearly enjoying the spectacle. Lend, ever the quiet observer, chuckled softly into his drink, amusement dancing in his eyes as he watched over the rim of his cup, Avery squirming under Mallory's teasing.

To Ashe's left, Andra, Kael, and Levy were huddled over a map spread across the table. They conversed in low voices, their heads close together as they examined the rough outlines of the land that had once been known as the Wastes. But the Wastes were no more, transformed by recent events into something green and teeming with life.

Lush forests, verdant plains, and surging rivers had replaced the barren, scarred landscape, and they were left with the unexpected but hopeful task of naming the territory anew. Ashe couldn't help but marvel at the scene; the three of them, once at odds, were now sharing ideas and discussing names for a land that only existed in dreams before now.

She felt an odd warmth settle in her chest, a quiet pride at seeing Levy included in the conversation. Kael had once looked upon him with hatred and distrust, his words sharp with doubt and suspicion.

Andra had been wary, too, her skepticism deeply rooted. But here they were, voices lowered in earnest debate, Kael pointing out a river on the map while Levy nodded, offering an idea for a name.

It was subtle, but Ashe could see that Kael's posture had relaxed, and the usual tension in his face had softened. She felt happiness seeing her friend, once so isolated, now finding his place among them.

Her thoughts drifted for a moment, and when she looked up, she saw Quinn watching her, his expression thoughtful. Their eyes met, and she was surprised to see genuine happiness there, a silent acknowledgment of all that they had achieved together, of the family they had built from scattered pieces and broken alliances.

The hope in his face mirrored the quiet optimism blossoming within her, and for a brief, weightless moment, Ashe let herself believe that maybe, just maybe, they could finally know peace.

Quinn's attention was drawn back by Mallory's voice, who called his name with the familiar, easy tone that pulled him into their conversation. He joined her, Avery, and Lend, adding his own dry wit to their exchange.

Ashe watched as Mallory laughed at something he said, her head thrown back in raucous amusement. It was so rare to see them all like this, unwound, unconcerned, and she let herself smile softly at the sight.

With Quinn occupied, Ashe's gaze drifted to the center of the table, to the object that lay there, once wrapped in a dark cloth that barely seemed to contain its intensity. She felt it before she saw it, a subtle tug, a quiet hum at the edge of her awareness, like a whisper calling her name.

The box from the vaults sat at the heart of the table, its ornate black surface gleaming with hints of gold filigree that seemed to pulse faintly in the dim candlelight. It had been carefully unwrapped, the cloth folded neatly beneath it as if to soften the ominous presence it carried. But nothing could contain the energy radiating from it.

While the others seemed aware of its power, casting the occasional glance toward it, Ashe felt something far deeper, a resonance that throbbed in time with her heartbeat. The air around it was heavy, charged with a potent force that felt ancient and familiar as if it shared a piece of her own essence. She leaned forward slightly, drawn closer, her senses sharpening as she focused on it.

The longer she looked, the more it felt as though the box were alive, aware of her attention, its presence reaching out to her. She could feel a faint vibration in her chest, an echo of power that seemed to seep through the room, binding them all to it, but the pull grew stronger, sharper, and as she concentrated, she thought she heard something.

A voice, faint and distant, whispering words she couldn't quite make out.

Ashe closed her eyes, focusing on the hum of energy that resonated within her, reaching out toward the box, letting herself drift closer to its strange siren call. The world around her faded slightly, the sounds of laughter and conversation dimming until all she could feel was that powerful, insistent draw.

It was as if Fate itself was whispering, a sound that wove through her mind, quiet and elusive but undeniably present. The box was more than an artifact, more than a mere tool. It was a piece of something greater, something that pulsed with the same force she felt within herself, the same connection to the tapestry of destiny that guided her from the beginning.

The whisper grew louder, and for a moment, she thought she could understand it. A string of words threaded through her consciousness, brushing against her senses with the delicate touch of silk. Slowly, she reached out for the box as if entranced.

"I wouldn't if I were you," the crisp voice of Clotho broke

through, pulling her back to the present.

Ashe blinked, the trance-like pull of the box fading as she returned to the warmth and light of the room. Everyone was watching her, a curious tilt to their heads, brows raised in mild concern. Ashe managed a reassuring smile, though her heart was still racing, the memory of that strange, magnetic pull lingering in her thoughts.

No one had seen Clotho enter, but now she stood by the table, eyes narrowed beneath her bushy brows, her gaze fixed on the box with a reverent and wary expression. She looked stronger than she had in weeks as if the fresh air and sunlight of Stormhaven had breathed new life into her.

Her eyes, once dulled by her time in the dungeons of Olympus, were clearer, though they carried the shadow of wisdom that saw far beyond the moment.

"This is an item I never thought I'd see in person," Clotho murmured, her voice low and weighted with awe and dread.

Her lips pressed into a thin line as she stared at the box, as though even looking at it was a danger. "Why in Hades' name is it not locked away?"

The tension in the room sharpened, her words cutting through the last remnants of the council's jovial mood.

"What is it?" someone asked, their voice barely above a whisper.

Clotho's eyes snapped to them, incredulity flashing across her face. "You went after an item of immense power without even knowing what it was you were bringing into the world?"

Her voice was laced with disdain, and she shook her head, her expression one of disappointment and disbelief. "Foolish, foolish mortals."

Levy bristled, shifting in his chair. "Zeus was after it," he countered. "We didn't have much of a choice."

"There is *always* a choice, Levy." Clotho's voice was a low, dangerous murmur, her eyes gleaming gold as she spoke.

The room seemed to darken, the light dimming as if something ancient and powerful stirred at the edge of her words.

"This is not just any box," she continued, her voice rising as her gaze swept across each member of the council. "This is Pandora's

Box. And if you have any sense, you'll throw it into the deepest pit and pray it never sees the light of day again."

Quinn's eyes widened as the realization hit. "Pandora's Box? As in the one Zeus had Hephaestus forge to punish a mortal woman?"

"No." Clotho's voice was calm, almost resigned. "Your myths are incorrect."

Clotho reached forward, her hand hovering over the box, drawing every gaze in the room. Her fingers brushed over the filigree, her touch reverent and cautious, as if even this contact with the box was sacred. The box seemed to respond, its golden edges glowing faintly, pulsing in time with some hidden power.

"This box is older than any of the gods," Clotho said, her voice quiet and solemn.

"Older than even the Titans and the forces that came before them. This is a box forged by the Primordials. From this box came every evil found in every world, every realm, every being. By the time the gods obtained it, only Pandora herself was trapped inside."

The council sat in stunned silence, each of them absorbing the weight of her words. Ashe felt a cold chill settle over her, the legend taking on new meaning, something far darker and more profound than any tale they had heard.

Clotho's gaze shifted to a point just beyond them, as if she were seeing into the past, into the hidden depths of history itself.

"Pandora was not a mere mortal that the gods chose to torment. She was a woman of unmatched beauty, one who caught the eye of Zeus himself. He hounded her for years, coveting her as though she were a treasure made for his pleasure alone. But she wanted nothing to do with him."

Clotho's words hung in the air, each one carrying the weight of ages, of stories long forgotten and buried beneath the sands of time.

"When she denied him, slipping through his grasp one too many times, Zeus grew enraged. His pride would not allow him to be refused by a mortal woman."

Clotho's voice grew softer, her tone one of sadness and anger mingling. "In his fury, he slaughtered her village, burned her lands, and left nothing but ashes in his wake. He thought she would be broken, desperate, and that she would run to him, seeking

Oath Breaker

protection."

Clotho's expression hardened a fire sparking in her eyes. "But she didn't run to him. Instead, she chose to defy him in a way he had never anticipated."

Ashe could almost see it—the aftermath of Zeus's destruction, Pandora standing amid the charred ruins of her home, her heart hardened by grief and rage. She felt a deep sympathy for the woman, a mortal caught in the wrath of the gods, forced to seek justice on her own.

"In her despair," Clotho continued, "Pandora journeyed beyond the known world. She found a void—an endless, black chasm that existed outside of time and space, where nothing lived, where no god could reach.

"There, in the depths of that void, she felt something stirring— a presence ancient beyond comprehension, older than the earth, older even than the gods. It was Chaos, the primordial being that existed before all things."

A hush fell over the room, the only sound the soft crackling of the torches lining the walls.

"Pandora called to Chaos," Clotho said, her voice low, almost reverent. "Her voice filled with grief, with fury, her desire for vengeance roused a fragment of his consciousness. And Chaos answered.

"He offered her power beyond anything the gods had ever known, power to destroy everything Zeus cherished, everything he had built. But there was a price."

Clotho's gaze shifted to Quinn, and Ashe saw him pale, his expression ashen as he held Clotho's gaze. She didn't look away, a knowing look passing between them.

"The price," Clotho continued, her voice soft, "was that when her revenge was complete, Chaos would claim her body as his own. He would use her form to walk among the world once more."

The silence was absolute, every eye fixed on Clotho, the gravity of her tale weighing on them all.

"Pandora agreed," Clotho murmured. "Her rage and grief greater than any fear of the price. And so, Chaos gifted her this box, the very one you see before you. When she opened it, all the horrors of Chaos spilled forth—disease, famine, pestilence—poisoning the world Zeus had so carefully crafted, tainting his cherished mortals with suffering."

Ashe's heart hammered in her chest. She could almost see it—Pandora opening the box, the darkness spilling out like smoke, corrupting everything it touched. It was a twisted justice, the evils of Chaos unleashed upon a world undeserving of the gods' whims.

"But Pandora soon saw that her vengeance had consequences beyond Zeus," Clotho continued, her voice heavy with sorrow.

"She watched as innocent mortals suffered, as disease spread, as famine claimed the lives of children, as death and despair seeped into every corner of the earth. She saw the cost of her rage and felt a deep, consuming guilt."

Clotho's eyes softened, a flicker of empathy in her gaze. "In her anguish, she made one final choice. She offered her life to the box, her soul, her very being, hoping to undo the suffering she had unleashed.

"And the box accepted her, consuming her spirit and transforming it into the only force strong enough to counter the darkness within. Pandora's essence became hope—a single, fragile light buried within the box meant to balance the evil she had unleashed."

Ashe felt her chest tighten, the weight of Pandora's sacrifice filling her with a strange, aching sadness. She could almost feel it—the spirit of hope, locked away, waiting for a chance to right the wrongs of the past.

"But Chaos was not so easily defeated," Clotho whispered, her voice trembling slightly. "Enraged by her betrayal, he cursed the box, binding it so that anyone who dared open it again would suffer her fate, trapped within its depths, their essence sacrificed to its insatiable hunger."

Clotho's words lingered in the air, a warning that echoed through the room, each member of the council feeling the cold reality of the box's power.

"This is no mere artifact," Clotho murmured, her gaze sweeping over them all. "It is a prison, a doorway to everything dark and vile that lies beyond our world. And if any of you have sense, you'll lock it away, bury it so deep that no one will ever find it."

The silence that followed was absolute, the weight of her

warning settling over them all like a shroud.

Clotho's voice lingered like a chill as she finished her tale, her gaze drifting over each council member with a look that seemed to see their every secret, their every fear. She took a step toward the doorway but then stopped, turning slightly to look over her shoulder, her face half-shrouded in shadow.

"Do not believe this to be your miracle for defeating Zeus," she warned, her voice low and sharp. "Opening the box will lead to nothing but an eternity of suffering. Opening it is a sacrifice and not a pleasant one."

Her gaze settled on Ashe, her stare both piercing and grave. "Keep it from Zeus, for now, that you have it. It is your responsibility. But hide it away so that none are tempted to open it."

Ashe felt a chill creep over her as Clotho's eyes bore into her, unblinking. "Especially you, girl. It will call to your power, and your power will answer. You must be kept away from it more than anyone else."

Then, without another word, Clotho turned and walked through the doorway, her steps echoing softly down the hall until they faded into silence. The air seemed to thicken in her absence, the shadows in the room stretching long and deep as if her warning had left an enduring mark on the walls.

For a long moment, no one spoke. The chamber seemed frozen in that dark knowledge, each council member staring at the place where Clotho had been or the box wrapped in cloth, lying like an innocuous bundle at the center of the table.

Ashe felt a chill settle in her, one that started at the base of her spine and coiled its way up, leaving her with the sense that her very soul had been touched by the box's ancient power.

Mallory broke the silence first, her voice a soft murmur cutting through the stillness. "So. We all agree that we cannot use the box, right?" Her usual lightness was muted, her gaze flickering warily to each of them as though seeking affirmation. Around the table, heads nodded, voices echoing in quiet agreement.

Yet Ashe's focus remained fixed on the box, its shape barely hidden beneath the cloth that Quinn had thrown over it. She knew the others had felt its pull, but for her, it was different. The box seemed to pulse with life, each heartbeat in her chest matched by a subtle thrum of power beneath the cloth, as though it were reaching out to her specifically.

A whisper echoed faintly in her mind, coaxing her, like a gentle touch on her skin, a current of warmth and knowing that wrapped around her senses and drew her closer.

She stared, her hand twitching at her side as the urge to touch it grew, a physical ache in her fingertips that she could barely ignore. She wasn't even aware of the others anymore, of their voices or their conversation; she only felt the box, the call of something inside it that seemed to recognize her, a piece of itself that mirrored the depths of her own power.

The cloth moved abruptly, and Ashe blinked, jolted out of her trance. Quinn had crossed the table, wrapping the fabric tightly around the box once more. His face was composed, but a flicker of worry softened the edges of his gaze as he reached for her hand.

His fingers closed around hers with a warmth that steadied her and pulled her back to reality. She offered him a silent, grateful look, the words of thanks catching in her throat, too tangled with everything else she felt.

They left the chamber together, Quinn's hand still clasped around hers, guiding her through the dim, torch-lit halls of Stormhaven. With each step, Ashe felt the presence of the box fade, its pull softening as they distanced themselves, the trance-like fog that had clouded her senses slowly dissipating.

For a few moments, they walked in silence, their footsteps echoing against the stone walls, the familiar weight of Stormhaven's halls wrapping around them like a comforting blanket. She allowed herself to breathe, to focus on the rhythm of their footsteps, the faint warmth of Quinn's hand holding her steady.

She marveled at how well he seemed to sense her every thought and every feeling. He truly understood her better than anyone else.

After a moment, Ashe let out a shaky breath, and the quiet between them deepened, thickened by the weight of everything Clotho had told them.

The story, the myth, the warning—all of it pulsed at the edges of her thoughts, intertwining with the lingering tug of the box. She glanced over at Quinn, his face softened in the torchlight, his gaze steady as he watched her, as though waiting for her to find her

Oath Breaker

words.

"Thank you," she murmured, her voice barely more than a whisper. She hesitated, feeling the unspoken emotions knotting in her throat. "For stopping me back there."

Quinn's mouth quirked into a small, knowing smile, and he gave her hand a gentle squeeze. "You don't need to thank me," he replied, his voice calm, grounding. "I could feel it, too."

He squeezed her hand gently, his thumb brushing against her knuckles in a small, comforting gesture. "So long as I am here, you will never have to face anything alone."

They continued walking, each step echoing through the long, dimly lit corridor, the Citadel's ancient stones absorbing the sounds. The torches flickered as they passed, casting shifting patterns of light and shadow that danced along the walls, giving the hall a quiet, almost haunting quality.

Ashe found herself leaning into the silence, letting the calm stretch between them, a quiet reprieve from the storm of thoughts and emotions swirling in her mind.

As they neared the side hall that led toward Hephaestus' forge, Quinn's hand slowly released hers. His face grew serious, a line creasing his brow as he turned to her, a faint worry flickering in his crimson eyes.

"Promise me," he said, his voice low but resolute. "Promise me that you won't use it, Ashe. No matter what happens. No matter how dire things get. Swear to me you will not open that box."

Ashe looked at him, studying the details of his face—the crease of worry etched deep into his brow, the way his eyes softened with warmth and concern that made her heartache.

She took in the slight tension in his jaw, the way he bit the corner of his lip as he held her gaze, searching her face for reassurance. The care, the fear she saw there—it struck something deep within her, something that broke a little under the weight of it.

She wanted to promise him, wanted to say the words and mean them. But the prophecy played on a quiet loop in her mind.

A sacrifice for all to see, embodies hope, forever free.

And there was no question in her heart that the box would have to be opened, that the sacrifice it called for was inevitable. With the way, it drew her in, as if it were a part of her—how could she deny it?

"Promise me, Ashe," Quinn's voice broke through her thoughts, soft and raw. "Please."

The word barely escaped his lips, trembling at the edges, and she could hear the unspoken plea within it, the desperation that tugged at her soul.

Her heart clenched, the pain of it tightening her throat as she reached up, brushing a few stray strands of his dark hair from his eyes. She wanted to make him a promise, a vow he could hold on to, something that would ease the fear in his gaze. But all she could offer him was the truth.

"I will try, Quinn," she whispered, her voice heavy with emotion. "I'll try to keep away from it. But you know I will do whatever it takes to ensure humanity survives.

"To see us all walk away from this." She fought back the sting of tears, the words catching in her throat as she met his eyes, her heart aching with the weight of her own resolve.

Quinn's expression softened, but the desperation remained in his gaze, a vulnerability that cut into her like a blade. His hands clenched into fists at his sides, and she saw the slightest tremor there, a sign of the struggle he hid so well.

"Then—if the time comes and it's our only hope..." His voice wavered, the anguish plain in his face as he spoke. "If it comes to that, then I will open it. Not you, Ashe. Let me carry that burden."

Her heart splintered at his words, the quiet strength and sadness behind them filling her with a fierce, unrelenting love. She swallowed, her throat tight as she shook her head, a faint, sorrowful smile touching her lips.

"Absolutely not," she murmured, her voice trembling slightly. She brushed her fingers gently against his cheek, feeling the warmth of his skin beneath her touch. "But let us hope and pray, Quinn, that it never comes to that."

They lingered, their breaths mingling in the stillness of the corridor, each heartbeat echoing in the quiet space between them. Ashe's fingers curled against the fabric of his shirt, settling herself in his solid warmth in the momentary escape they'd carved out of the uncertainty that loomed around them.

His forehead, pressed to hers, steady and unwavering, was the only anchor she needed, the only solace against the maelstrom within her. She could feel his heartbeat, steady and strong, a rhythm that grounded her.

For a single, fleeting moment, she allowed herself to exist solely within that heartbeat, forgetting everything but the quiet sanctuary they'd created in the silence.

Quinn's hands lifted to cup her face, his thumb brushing over her cheek with a tenderness that both soothed and broke her heart. She could feel the weight of his unspoken words, the promises and fears lingering in his gaze, words too heavy to voice.

Her hands found their way to his shoulders, holding him close as if, by sheer will, she could protect them both from what lay ahead.

He pulled back just enough to meet her eyes, his look intense, searching her face as though committing every line to memory. And then, with a softness that was at odds with the hunger in his eyes, his lips captured hers, a breath-stealing warmth that left her spinning.

It was a kiss that held both tenderness and a fierce need, an unspoken vow woven into every touch. His hand slid to the small of her back, guiding her, and she felt the cool wood of a door press against her as he nudged her backward.

The door opened, and she stumbled lightly inside, Quinn following, his presence filling the small space as he kicked the door shut behind them. She barely registered the sound, her focus entirely on him, on the fervent way his lips found hers again, the world outside slipping further away with each heartbeat.

Chapter 36
Quinn

The room was dark, save for the soft glow of a single candle casting a gentle halo of light over Ashe's face as she lay beside him, her breathing steady. Quinn watched her, her face soft in sleep, her lips parted slightly, and he could almost see the flicker of dreams behind her eyelids as they moved.

A part of him wondered what she dreamed about. Did she have a reprieve, moments of calm in her sleep where she could find peace? Or did Fate hound her even there, weaving visions through her mind as she rested?

He hoped, for once, that it was the former, that she was in some warm, untroubled place where she was untouched by the pull of the box, by the weight of the prophecy that had shaped their lives.

He reached out, brushing a stray lock of hair from her cheek, letting his fingers trace through the strands, and she sighed softly, her face turning instinctively into his touch.

A faint smile tugged at his lips as he watched her, the rise and fall of her breath calming him in a way he couldn't put into words. It was moments like these that reminded him of everything they had fought for, of everything they'd survived. They were here together, and for now, that was enough.

But the thought of that cursed box intruded, its dark allure echoing in his mind. He couldn't forget the way it had drawn her in, as if something in her soul resonated with it, something ancient and inevitable. The idea that it could take her, that it demanded a sacrifice—no, it twisted his gut with fear.

After all they'd been through, after losing her to death's edge, to the pull of the tower, he had finally gotten her back. She was here, alive, warm beside him, and he wasn't about to let anything—least of all a twisted relic from some ancient past, tainted with the touch of Chaos—take her from him again.

If the box needed a sacrifice, it wouldn't be her. It would be someone else. Or better yet, he thought, remembering Clotho's words, they'd take it, throw it into the deepest pit they could find, and pray it never reemerged. Anything to keep its curse, its pull, far from Ashe.

His resolve burned with a fierce protectiveness. They'd all sworn themselves to protect humanity, to stop Zeus at any cost, but he couldn't stop the selfish thought that maybe, just once, he could choose her over everything else. He'd fight Fate itself if it meant keeping her safe, keeping this precious thing they'd built between them.

Carefully, he reached over to the chair beside the bed where he'd flung his clothes in the throes of passion, his fingers searching the pocket of his trousers until he found it. He brought the ring up to the light, the faint glow catching on the smooth, cool metal band, and the small diamond at the top glinted, reflecting tiny shards of light in the darkness.

He'd scrimped and saved every coin he could, forgoing comforts to make it possible, to give her something that symbolized the depth of what he felt, the commitment he wanted to make, not just in words but in action.

For him, this ring represented everything he'd longed for, fought for. And it represented a promise he was determined to keep. He was done fighting solely for others, giving up every piece of himself, of his own happiness. In this, he would allow himself to be selfish. In this, he would claim something for himself—for both of them.

He watched the diamond glint in the dim light, his mind weaving through memories of all they had endured together, the battles they'd fought, the moments they'd stolen, and the pain they'd shared. She had always been there, through the turmoil, through his doubts, his anger, and his fear. And every time he thought he'd lost her, Fate had brought her back to him as if some invisible thread bound them together.

Quietly, he slid the ring back into his pocket, feeling its reassuring weight there, a promise yet to be made. Soon. He would wait for the right moment, a moment when the world would feel a little less dark, a little less haunted by ancient curses and prophecies.

And when that moment came, he'd make sure she understood just how deeply he loved her, how unwavering his devotion was.

As he leaned back, Ashe shifted slightly in her sleep, her brow furrowing as though some shadow had crossed her mind. Gently, he stroked her cheek, his thumb brushing against her skin in soft, soothing circles.

Her features relaxed again, the frown fading, and he felt his own tension ease as he watched her settle. His hand lingered against her cheek, and he closed his eyes, letting himself be consumed by the depth of his emotions by the silent vows he made to her in the quiet of that room.

Quinn leaned down, pressing a feather-light kiss to her forehead. "No one's taking you from me," he whispered, the words more of a vow than anything else. "Not Fate, not Zeus, not anyone."

She sighed again, almost as if she'd heard him, her face softening, a gentle peace washing over her expression. His fingers lingered against her skin, a silent testament to everything he held within his heart for her.

There would be battles ahead, hardships they couldn't yet imagine, but for now, in this quiet moment, he let himself believe in a future for them, one that went beyond prophecies and curses.

This was their life, their chance to shape something beautiful from the turmoil. And he would fight, against gods and Fate alike, to see that it remained theirs.

Chapter 37
Andra

The night air outside Stormhaven was crisp, laced with the faint scents of pine and the lingering embers of the city's fires. Stars glittered above like scattered shards of glass, sharp against the inky black sky, casting a silvery glow over the high stone walls and the vast, open landscape that lay beyond. A thin mist clung to the ground, swirling gently as Andra stepped forward, her boots crunching softly against the gravel path.

Mallory watched her friend closely, arms crossed, her eyes a mix of worry and frustration.

"How long will you be gone?" she asked, her voice almost swallowed by the quiet of the night.

Her gaze flicked toward Horacio, who stood by Andra's side like a silent, protective shadow, his sleek, scaled body rippling under the faint moonlight.

Andra adjusted her pack, the leather straps biting into her shoulders in a familiar way. "Hopefully not long enough to miss anything important," she replied, trying to keep her tone light.

The path before her was calling, and every instinct told her that this journey wasn't just necessary but urgent. If Clotho's warning about the box was even partially true, Stormhaven needed something else to rely on—and she knew just the thing. She had no intention of letting them end up in a position where they might have to use Pandora's Box.

Mallory's frown deepened, her arms pulling tighter across her chest. "The mountains, huh?" she said, her skepticism clear as her gaze drifted to the dark, craggy peaks looming in the distance, dusted with early snow and bathed in the ghostly light of the moon. "And you're sure you don't want company?"

Andra met her gaze, seeing the concern etched there, the worry her friend tried to hide behind her usual dry humor. "It's just a quick trip up into the mountains," she replied, her voice softening. "I've been up there a hundred times, you know that. If there's any danger, Horacio will be there."

She reached down to scratch Horacio's chin, and the drakon tilted his head, his molten gold eyes blinking up at her with an intelligence that reassured her. "I won't be alone."

Mallory's mouth twisted in a doubtful frown. "A drakon's company is good and all, but it's still not another human, Andra. You don't know what's waiting up there. A trip like this—now, of all times—seems a little…" She trailed off, her voice carrying both frustration and care.

"A little what?" Andra challenged, a playful smile tugging at her lips.

"A little dangerous," Mallory finished, her voice dropping to a low, firm tone. Her gaze didn't waver, her worry clear. "You shouldn't be out there on your own."

Andra sighed, placing a hand on her friend's shoulder, squeezing gently. "I'll be fine, Mallory," she said, her voice filled with quiet reassurance.

"I know you're worried, but I need to do this. Everyone else gave me their blessing for the trip. And besides, Quinn and Ashe will understand once they're done with whatever they're doing."

She raised her eyebrows with a mischievous glint, and Mallory's face immediately flushed.

Andra chuckled, the sound soft and warm against the cold night air. She tilted her head toward the top of the walls, where the faint outline of a familiar figure sat, his gaze lifted to the sky, lost in thought.

Oath Breaker

"Seems like you have a bit of business yourself, don't you?" Andra teased, her grin widening as Mallory's blush deepened.

Mallory followed her gaze, her expression softening for a brief, unguarded moment. She quickly caught herself, glancing back at Andra with a look of exasperation.

"Fine," she muttered, though a smile tugged at the corners of her mouth. "But I'm holding you to that promise. Be careful, alright?"

"I will." Andra's hand slipped from her shoulder, and she offered her friend a final smile. "Besides, if I don't come back as my second in command, you have my permission to rename the Wastes whatever you want."

Mallory chuckled, though her worry remained evident. "You better believe I'll hold you to that."

She glanced down at Horacio, who huffed and nudged her shoulder with his snout.

"And Horacio, keep her safe, alright?" she added, running a hand over his smooth scales. The Drakon let out a low, approving rumble, his sharp gaze locked on the path ahead.

Andra gave a final wave, then turned, feeling a surge of anticipation fill her chest as she faced the open road, the mountains looming in the distance like ancient sentinels. The cold air bit at her cheeks, the scent of pine and frost sharpening her senses as she walked. The vast wilderness beyond Stormhaven stretched before her, cloaked in shadows and silvered by moonlight.

She didn't look back as she passed through the gates, Horacio's silent footsteps falling in sync with her own.

Chapter 38
Olympus

The throne room of Olympus, once the shining beacon of divine power and perfection, had become a hollow shell of its former glory, a decaying monument to Zeus' unraveling. The cracks in the marble floors, which once whispered of subtle neglect, now gaped like jagged wounds, revealing the blackened underbelly of the ancient structure.

Chunks of golden sculptures depicting the gods' victories lay scattered like forgotten relics, their gleam dulled under layers of dust and soot. Once-pristine columns, carved with images of heroics and grandeur, were fractured, leaning precariously, as though even they could no longer bear the weight of the throne room's tensions.

The air itself was oppressive, thick with the stench of ozone and damp stone as if the very breath of Olympus had soured. Lightning flickered erratically through the gaping holes in the ceiling, illuminating the chamber in flashes of eerie, pale light.

The storm clouds above churned violently, a constant reminder of Zeus' presence and his inner tempest. Rain slipped through the cracks, splattering onto the cold marble below, the rhythmic patter interrupted only by the occasional hiss of steam when a drop dared to strike the arcs of stray lightning coursing through the room.

Zeus sat upon his throne at the heart of the chaos, his once-imposing figure now marred by the cracks in his composure. His robes hung from his broad shoulders in disarray, scorched in places by the sparks that leaped from his restless hands.

His face, though still commanding, was a portrait of unchecked rage, veins bulging at his temples and neck as he ground his teeth audibly. The faint froth at the corners of his mouth quivered with each labored breath he took, his body quaking like a volcano on the verge of eruption.

Before him stood Cyrus, unflinching and calm amidst the storm. His dark armor gleamed faintly under the sporadic light, the edges sharp and precise, a stark contrast to the gods' tarnished and war-worn appearances.

His hands rested casually behind his back, his posture straight and steady as though he were standing in the presence of a mere mortal king rather than the ruler of Olympus himself. A faint smile tugged at the corners of his lips, the expression both infuriatingly composed and subtly mocking.

"The mortals have taken the box," Cyrus reported, his voice smooth, almost dispassionate. "And when I arrived at the vaults, Aphrodite was already gone."

For a moment, silence filled the throne room, the weight of his words pressing down on the remaining Olympians like a suffocating shroud. Then Zeus erupted. His bellow shook the very foundations of the room, his voice a thunderclap that sent tremors racing through the already fractured floor.

"WHAT?!"

His hand slammed down on the arm of his throne with the force of an earthquake, a deafening crack splitting the air as chunks of stone broke free from the ceiling above. Debris rained down in jagged shards, some shattering upon impact with the floor, others skittering dangerously close to the gods seated around the room.

Poseidon flinched, his trident clattering against the side of his throne as he leaned back, as though trying to escape Zeus' wrath. Demeter recoiled as well, clutching at her robes with trembling hands.

Hermes, ever the restless one, stilled completely, his sharp features pulled tight with tension. Even Dionysus, who usually exuded a casual indifference to Olympus' chaos, straightened in his seat, his goblet still and untouched.

Only Cyrus remained unshaken, his calm demeanor unfazed by the turmoil. The faint smile on his face lingered as if Zeus' fury were an inevitability he had anticipated and even welcomed.

Zeus' rage was palpable, a living thing that rippled through the air and sent arcs of lightning skittering along the ground. His breath came in heavy bursts, the froth at the corners of his mouth growing thicker as he struggled to contain the storm within him. His veins bulged grotesquely, standing out like twisted roots across his neck and forearms as he gripped the edges of his throne.

"They dared to take MY box?!" Zeus roared, his voice cracking with the force of his anger. "They dared to take MY prisoner? And you stand here telling me this like it is nothing?"

"Lord Zeus," Cyrus began, his tone measured, but Zeus cut him off with a sharp, almost feral snarl.

"DO NOT INTERRUPT ME!"

Lightning crashed again, striking the remnants of a once-majestic column, reducing it to rubble. The air was thick with the burning smell of charred stone and ozone, a suffocating mixture that made every breath feel labored.

Zeus rose to his feet, his towering form illuminated by the erratic flashes of lightning. His robes billowed around him as though caught in an invisible storm, and his fists clenched at his sides, trembling with barely restrained violence.

"My wife," Zeus growled, his voice lowering into a dangerous, guttural tone. "My children. My brother. One by one, they fall. And now Hephaestus, the wretched smith, throws his lot in with the mortals. MY OWN BLOOD, BETRAYING ME!"

The name fell from his lips like venom, and he spat onto the cracked marble floor as though to rid himself of its taste. The storm outside grew louder, the wind howling through the shattered ceiling and causing the flames of the torches to gutter wildly.

"Hephaestus," Zeus continued, his voice rising once more. "The ungrateful, crippled fool. After all I have done for him, all I have given him, he dares to side with those insects?"

His fists slammed down onto the armrests of his throne again, and another tremor rippled through the room. The Olympians shifted uncomfortably, their faces carefully blank, their silence a shield against Zeus' volatile wrath. None dared speak, none dared move, for fear that his rage might find a new target.

Poseidon's jaw tightened, his fingers curling around the shaft of his trident.

"Brother," he said cautiously, his voice low. "Perhaps we should focus on retrieving what has been lost rather than dwelling on..."

"DWELLING?" Zeus thundered, rounding on Poseidon with a glare that could have turned mortal men to ash. "I am not dwelling, Poseidon. I am addressing the cancer that festers among us. Do you think your seat of power will survive if we allow these mortals to continue their defiance?"

Poseidon fell silent, his eyes narrowing as he leaned back on his throne, unwilling to press further.

Zeus turned his attention back to Cyrus, his voice dropping to a dangerously quiet tone that sent a chill through the room. "And what of you, Cyrus? You stood before the vault. This was your plan. Why did you not stop it?"

Cyrus inclined his head slightly, his expression unchanged. "By the time I arrived, it was already too late, Lord Zeus. The box was gone, and Aphrodite's body was... unrecognizable."

Zeus' face twisted with rage; his teeth bared in a snarl. "Useless," he spat. "You are all USELESS. Mortals walk into our domain, steal from us, KILL US, and we stand here, DOING NOTHING."

His voice rose with each word until the final syllable erupted like a clap of thunder. Lightning arced wildly through the room, striking walls, columns, and even the floor. The Olympians flinched in unison, their collective discomfort a silent acknowledgment of their shared vulnerability.

Cyrus, however, remained still, his faint smile unwavering. He took in Zeus' fury with the detached calm of a man observing a tempest from behind the safety of glass. When he finally spoke, his voice was smooth and even, a quiet counterpoint to the chaos around him.

"With respect, Lord Zeus, the mortals are emboldened because they believe you are distracted. They see the cracks forming, and they think they can punch through them."

Zeus' nostrils flared, his breathing heavy as he stared down at Cyrus. For a moment, it seemed as though he might strike the man where he stood, but then he leaned back into his throne, his rage simmering just below the surface.

"They will learn," Zeus said, his voice low and venomous. "They will learn what it means to defy me."

The room seemed to hold its breath after Zeus' chilling declaration, his words hanging in the thick, storm-laden air. Lightning danced faintly across the walls, casting distorted shadows of the gods who sat stiff and silent, their expressions carefully blank. Zeus leaned back into his throne, his breathing heavy, his fingers twitching with restrained rage.

Then, breaking the tense silence, Apollo rose from his golden throne, his movements sharp. Though his expression carried the weight of deference to his father, his golden features were alight and fury, and his anger was barely tethered by the chain of respect. His voice, when it came, was tight with restraint but loud enough to cut through the heavy air.

"Yes," Apollo said, his words laced with accusation, directed at Cyrus like arrows aimed with precision. "It was your plan, and you were the only one of us there. How interesting that you last saw yet another Olympian moments before their death. Just like Hades."

The words struck the room like a clap of thunder, the tension thickening as every Olympian's gaze shifted toward Apollo. Hermes fidgeted uneasily, his hand darting to the edge of his throne as if he might bolt at any moment.

Dionysus let out a low whistle, an almost dismissive sound, but his grip on his goblet tightened visibly. Poseidon frowned deeply, his broad shoulders stiffening as he glanced between Zeus and Apollo.

Zeus' eyes snapped to Apollo, his expression hardening into a mask of cold fury. He didn't rise, but the shift in his posture—the sudden stillness of a predator about to strike—was enough to command the room's undivided attention. When he spoke, his voice was quiet, but it carried the weight of an impending storm.

"Apollo," Zeus said, each syllable deliberate and sharp. "Return to your seat. We are not discussing this again."

The finality of the statement was clear, a warning that should have ended the matter. But Apollo, driven by his anger and grief, pressed on, his golden skin seeming to glow faintly as his emotions flared.

"Father," he began, his voice trembling with frustration, "I saw Artemis' body. Even if it had been a mortal who cut off her head, she was practically mummified. No sword can do that."

The words reverberated through the chamber like a tremor rolling through stone. Zeus' jaw tightened, his fingers digging into the armrests of his throne with such force that faint cracks spiderwebbed beneath his grip. The other gods exchanged uneasy glances, their collective tension palpable.

Cyrus turned slowly, his calm demeanor untouched by Apollo's rising anger. A faint, irritating smirk tugged at the corners of his lips as he met Apollo's glare.

"Really, Apollo," he said, his voice laced with amusement. "If you have an accusation to make, perhaps you could say it outright instead of dancing around it with veiled words."

The smirk, so smug and unbothered, sent a fresh wave of anger coursing through Apollo. His hands clenched into fists at his sides, his golden eyes blazing as he stepped forward. "You…"

Before he could finish, a bolt of lightning erupted with a deafening crack. It struck Apollo square in the chest, launching him backward with enough force to send him crashing into his throne. The impact reverberated through the room, wisps of smoke curling from the edges of Apollo's singed robes.

Zeus rose to his feet, his colossal form towering over the room, his face a mask of wrath. His voice, when it came, was a roar that shook the very foundations of Olympus.

"I SAID ENOUGH."

The words thundered through the chamber, silencing any thought of protest. Zeus' eyes burned with fury as he scanned the room, daring anyone to defy him. Apollo dazed and slumped in his throne, smoldered but remained alive, the lightning a calculated display of dominance rather than a killing blow.

Zeus pointed a finger at Apollo, his voice dropping to a dangerous growl. "Now is not the time to turn on one another. The mortals are our enemies. Cyrus has proven his loyalty time and time again, and I will not hear any more of this."

The quiet that followed was heavy and suffocating. Apollo, though visibly furious, stayed silent, his jaw clenched as he glared daggers at Cyrus. His golden skin, now streaked with soot and ash, seemed to burn with unspoken words, but he bit them back, his anger tempered by the undeniable fact of Zeus' wrath.

Cyrus, unbothered by the accusation or the chaos that had unfolded, turned his head slightly and caught Apollo's gaze. He winked, his smirk widening into something more sinister. The gesture was small, almost imperceptible, but it radiated a smugness that sent Apollo's fists tightening once more.

The throne room was silent, but for the distant roll of thunder outside, the storm raging as a mirror to Zeus' simmering fury. Lightning flickered through the cracks in the crumbling walls, casting sharp shadows that danced with malicious intent.

At the base of the throne, Cyrus stood unmoving, his calm demeanor a striking contrast to the restless tension that permeated the room. Even the gods themselves, seated in fractured splendor, seemed cowed by the suffocating weight of Zeus' wrath.

Zeus, seemingly satisfied that the room had fallen back into order, settled into his throne. The faint crackle of lightning around his form pulsed with his uneven breaths.

His eyes swept over the chamber, taking in the shattered remnants of Olympus, the frayed remains of his pantheon, and the immortal who now stood as both ally and enigma at his feet. His chest rose and fell heavily as though the storm within him were barely contained.

"It is time," Zeus began, his voice low and resonant yet carrying the weight of a divine decree. "Time to stop groveling before a barrier that no longer holds. Time to remind the mortals why they once trembled at the mere thought of us."

Poseidon shifted slightly in his seat, his trident leaning against his throne. The god of the seas, though still powerful, looked worn, the strain of endless defeats etched into the lines of his face. He raised his voice cautiously, each word chosen with care.

"Brother, the barrier…"

"The barrier is a relic," Zeus snapped, his voice thundering like the storm outside. He gestured sharply. "Do you not see, Poseidon? It was built to keep us out—to protect their pathetic realm from OUR power.

"And yet, what has it done? Nothing! The mortals have shattered it in all but name. They walk freely between worlds, mocking us with their defiance."

Zeus stood abruptly, his towering form casting a long shadow over the chamber. His muscles bulged as his fists clenched, and the storm outside seemed to grow fiercer, the winds howling through the broken ceiling. His voice dropped into a guttural growl, each word dripping with venom.

"They stole from me. They KILLED my kin. And they have dared to weaken what once held us at bay. Do you not understand

He gestured again, this time toward the storm-lit horizon visible through the shattered walls.

"The barrier is nothing more than a dying ember, barely clinging to existence. And now, I will finish it." The room fell into a heavy silence, the weight of his words pressing down like a physical force.

Zeus took a step forward, his boots ringing against the cracked marble floor. "The mortals have used the barrier against us for too long. They thought it would keep them safe, that they could defy us without consequence. But now, their protection crumbles and I will break through what remains. I will show them what it means to stand against the gods."

Poseidon leaned forward slightly, his trident gleaming faintly in the flickering torchlight. "And what of the mortals who still worship us?" he asked, his deep voice steady but tinged with caution. "Those who remain loyal?"

"Collateral damage," Zeus growled, cutting him off. His face twisted into a sneer, his lips curling back to reveal his teeth. "They are no different from the rest. Mortals are mortals. They will fall like the insects they are."

"Lord Zeus," Hermes began, his voice hesitant but quick. "If the barrier falls completely, It will alert them."

"Silence," Zeus roared, his voice reverberating through the chamber. He turned sharply, his eyes narrowing on Hermes. "Do you fear the mortals, messenger? Do you cower before their schemes? Is that what you have become?"

Hermes dropped his gaze quickly, his hands raised in placation.

"Of course not, father. I only meant—"

"Enough. It is time for Stormhaven to fall."

"Stormhaven," Demeter murmured, her voice barely above a whisper. The name hung in the air, heavy with the weight of what was to come.

"Yes," Zeus said, his tone hardening. He stepped forward again, his movements deliberate, his fists clenching at his sides. "That wretched city. It is their stronghold, their haven, their symbol of defiance. It will be the first to crumble."

He paused, his eyes narrowing as he stared out at the storm that raged beyond Olympus. The lightning illuminated his face in sharp relief, highlighting the sky blue of his smoldering eyes.

"I will burn it to the ground," he said, his voice dropping to a chilling growl. "I will crush their walls, their hopes, their dreams. I will hear their screams rise like a symphony as their world crumbles around them."

The storm outside seemed to echo his words, the winds howling louder as if in anticipation of the destruction to come. The Olympians sat frozen, their silence a testament to the fear Zeus commanded. Even Poseidon, who had dared to question, lowered his gaze slightly, his shoulders stiff with tension.

Zeus turned back to the room, his eyes blazing with the light of a storm-given form. "Prepare yourselves," he commanded, his voice rising to a crescendo that matched the fury of the storm. "War is upon us."

As the gods began to rise from their thrones, their movements were slow and reluctant. Cyrus remained at the foot of the throne, his smirk widening ever so slightly. The storm raged on, lightning splitting the sky as thunder roared like a harbinger of destruction.

And as Zeus sat once more upon his throne, his presence towering and indomitable, the air itself seemed to tremble, carrying with it the promise of annihilation.

Chapter 39
Levy

The stars above Stormhaven stretched endlessly, a velvet canvas pierced by countless pinpricks of light. They shimmered like scattered fragments of some divine, forgotten jewel, their radiance unbothered by the turmoil of the world below.

Levy sat on the cold stone wall, his forearms resting on his knees as he gazed upward. The chill of the night didn't bother him; he barely noticed it. His mind was a mess, each thought clashing violently against the next, yet the stars brought a rare, fragile stillness.

There was something about the night sky that seemed to reach into him as if its silent expanse spoke to a part of him that words could never touch. The vastness, the quiet beauty—it made the weight in his chest a little easier to bear. Tonight, though, it felt different. As the stars blinked softly overhead, they reminded him of something. Or rather, someone.

Mallory.

Her name whispered through his mind, unbidden, and he closed his eyes tightly as if it would block out the thought. But it was impossible to stop the memories. The way her eyes lit up when she spoke of something she was passionate about, their depths twinkling like the stars themselves. That warmth, that shine—it wasn't something he deserved, not after what had happened.

The guilt clawed at him like a living thing. The bruises on her neck were fading, but they were still there, ghostly reminders of what he had almost done. The marks weren't just on her skin; they were etched into his soul, a constant reminder of his failure, of the monster he could become. How could she even stand to be near him? To smile at him?

A soft shuffle of footsteps broke through his thoughts. He tensed instinctively, but the familiar presence beside him made his heart jolt. Mallory. She eased herself onto the wall beside him, her movements uncharacteristically quiet.

Levy flinched at her nearness, a reflex born of the tangled mess of emotions inside him. She noticed, her brows drawing together with a faint frown, but she didn't mention it. Instead, she leaned back and tilted her head to the sky.

"It's beautiful tonight," she said, her voice like the faint rustle of leaves in the breeze. "The weather's mild for this time of year. And the forest smells so alive."

Levy grunted in response, unable to summon the words she deserved. He focused on the horizon, trying to will away the roiling guilt inside him, but it was no use. Her presence, so steady and unassuming, only made the weight in his chest grow heavier.

Mallory's gaze flickered toward him, lingering for a moment before she spoke again. "I'm sorry if my confession has unsettled you," she said, her voice careful, as if testing the waters. "Or caused you to feel any kind of discomfort around me, Levy."

His head jerked toward her, his dark eyes wide with surprise. She was looking at him, the soft light of the moon catching on the curve of her face, her expression as open and sincere as ever.

"I can't lie and say I was joking," she continued her words steady but carrying an edge of vulnerability. "But I understand if you don't feel the same... for the creepy girl who's been stalking your every movement."

Her self-deprecating tone stung, but Levy couldn't find the words to respond. He sat frozen, his chest tightening with emotions he didn't know how to process. Fear, guilt, shame—all of it tangled together, choking him into silence. His worst fear had been that she would see him as a monster again, as she once had when they first met. After Aphrodite's influence, after the bruises he had left on her skin... he was sure she would never be able to look at him without seeing the darkness he carried.

But here she was, sitting beside him, addressing the very thing he had dreaded most. And instead of recoiling, she was offering him understanding.

The silence stretched between them, and Mallory's shoulders sagged slightly. The light in her eyes dimmed as she pushed herself to her feet. "I'm sorry," she murmured, her voice quieter now. "I shouldn't have said anything."

She turned toward the stairs, her footsteps slow as she crossed the stone walkway. She paused at the top of the steps, her hand brushing the wall for support as she prepared to descend. Levy's chest constricted, his heart hammering painfully against his ribs. He didn't know where the words came from, but they escaped him before he could stop them.

"You have never made me feel uncomfortable."

Mallory froze, her hand still resting on the wall. Sl owly, she turned back toward him, her expression unreadable in the dim light. The air between stilled, heavy with the weight of everything left unsaid. The stars above seemed to burn brighter, as if they, too, were waiting for what would come next.

Levy stood slowly, the weight of his emotions evident in every deliberate motion. His heart pounded as he faced Mallory, her silhouette framed by the faint silver light of the moon. The quiet stillness of the night only seemed to amplify the storm raging inside him. He inhaled deeply, his hands trembling at his sides as he searched for the courage to say what had remained buried for so long.

"I don't deserve this," he began, his voice low and uneven. He forced himself to meet her eyes, even though every instinct screamed at him to look away. "I don't deserve you, or your kindness, or even the chance to sit here and talk with you. But I need you to understand."

He took a shaky step closer, the words spilling from him like a floodgate had been opened. "When I was young, before any of this... before the world turned into what it is now, I thought I had purpose.

The Masters made sure I believed that. They told me I was the one who would carry humanity.

"The one who would make it all right again. They gave me hope, and then they piled everything onto my shoulders—the weight of the world, the fate of humanity. I was just a kid, and they told me it was all up to me."

His voice cracked, and he paused, his breath catching in his throat. "But then they took it all away, just like that. They tore everything out from under me. Suddenly, I wasn't their chosen one anymore. I was nothing. Nobody. And I... I didn't know who I was without them. I didn't know what to do."

Levy's hand clenched into a fist at his side as he continued, the words coming faster now, raw and unfiltered. "I was desperate to matter. To make some kind of impact, to prove that I wasn't worthless. I latched onto the first thing I could find—power.

"I didn't care what it cost, didn't think about how it would twist me, corrupt me. I just wanted to feel like I was worth something. And every time I thought I could claw my way back out of that darkness, I ended up digging myself deeper."

He turned his gaze to the stars for a moment, as if searching for strength in their quiet beauty, before looking back into hers.

"Do you know what that feels like? To be so lost, so stuck, with no one to guide you? To not have anyone you can lean on or anyone who even looks at you like you're worth saving?"

His voice softened, trembling with a vulnerability he rarely allowed himself to show. "And then... then Ashe and Quinn came back into my life. They reached out and pulled me from that pit. And for the first time in years,

"I felt like maybe I wasn't completely alone. But even then, I couldn't escape what I'd done. The lives I'd ruined, the people I'd hurt. I was the monster they had to let back in because they had no other choice."

Levy took another step toward her, his voice gaining a fragile strength as he pushed forward. "Every day in Stormhaven, I've tried to make up for it. I've trained the troops.

"I've rebuilt homes and walls. I've thrown myself into every fight, taken every risk I could, hoping that maybe if I sacrificed enough, if I bled enough, someone might see that I'm not the monster they think I am. That I could go out knowing I'd made a difference."

His eyes searched hers, the depth of his anguish etched into every line of his face. "And then there was you."

He paused, his voice catching as he spoke the words. "You, Mallory. At first, I thought you were following me around because you didn't trust me.

"And maybe that's what it was. But... but it felt good. It felt good that someone was watching, that someone cared enough to notice what I was doing. No one had looked at me like that in so long."

A faint, bittersweet smile tugged at the corner of his lips. "And then you started to change. You weren't just watching anymore. You were seeing me. Your face softened, your eyes—they stopped looking at me like I was an enemy. They started looking at me like I was someone who mattered. Someone you trusted."

His voice cracked again, and he looked away briefly as though the intensity of his emotions was too much to bear. "And slowly, I started to believe it. I started to feel like maybe, just maybe, I wasn't alone anymore. Like someone might actually understand me."

Levy's expression darkened, the fragile hope in his voice giving way to despair. "But then I hurt you, Mallory."

His words were a whisper, trembling with the weight of his guilt. "I fell under Aphrodite's thrall, and I nearly killed you. My hands—I left bruises on your neck."

He took a step back, his hands clenching and unclenching as if trying to grasp something that wasn't there. "How could you see me as anything other than a monster after that? How can you feel safe around me after what I did?"

The night seemed to hold its breath, the silence wrapping around them like a shroud. Levy's shoulders sagged under the weight of his confession; his heart laid bare in a way it never had been before. He had caught up to her as he talked, her back against the wall. He faced her, staring down into her eyes, a silent plea.

Mallory stood frozen for a moment, staring at Levy as his words hung heavy in the cool night air. The sheer vulnerability he had shown, the raw emotion in every word—it was staggering. Slowly, she stepped toward him, her boots making soft scuffs against the stone walkway. The moonlight caught the faint remnants of the bruises on her neck, but her expression was calm, steady.

"Levy," she began softly, her voice carrying a warmth that seemed to cut through the chill of the night. "You're not a monster. You've never been a monster."

He flinched at her words as though they were too much for him to believe. She shook her head, her voice carrying both resolve and warmth.

"The past... it's the past. Yes, you've made mistakes. We all have. But what matters is who you are now. What you want, how you fight for it, how you go about making things better—not just for yourself, but for everyone."

Mallory took another step closer, her eyes never leaving his. "And I see you, Levy. I see the man who puts himself in the way of danger, who works himself to the bone, rebuilding homes, training soldiers, and trying to make life better for people who don't even know the lengths you go to for them.

"You're not doing it for recognition, or power, or anything selfish. You do it because you care."

Her voice softened, a tender smile spreading across her lips. "That's the man you are. Someone who cares so much it hurts, not just for the people closest to you, but for everyone.

"You carry this burden because you think it's yours to bear, and maybe it is. But that's not what makes you a monster. It's what makes you someone worth following, someone worth trusting."

The faint glow of the stars above reflected in her eyes, giving them an ethereal shine as she looked at him with a depth of emotion she rarely allowed herself to show. "Levy, I trust you. And I care about you more than I know how to say."

She reached up then, her fingers brushing against his jawline, her touch as light as a whisper. The starlight seemed to wrap around them, the rest of the world fading into the background. Her hands slid upward, gently clasping behind his neck as she stepped even closer.

Her lips hovered near his ear, her breath warm against his skin as she murmured, "Besides, I like your hand on my neck."

The words were low, intimate, carrying a playful edge that sent a jolt through him. The tension between them shifted, the air

Oath Breaker

growing heavier, charged with something new and unspoken. Mallory's lips lingered near his ear, her arms still wrapped around his neck as the moment stretched out between them, both fragile and electric.

The world around them seemed to dissolve, leaving only the faint hum of the stars above and the heat building between them. Levy froze for a split second, her words echoing in his ears, her warm breath brushing against his skin.

Then something inside him snapped—a dam breaking, an instinct taking over. He didn't think, didn't hesitate; his hands found her waist, pulling her closer, closing the distance between them until there was no space left at all.

Mallory gasped softly as his lips pressed to hers, the kiss anything but hesitant. It was raw, urgent, filled with everything he'd kept buried for so long. His hands gripped her firmly, one sliding to the small of her back, the other tangling in her hair as he angled her head to deepen the kiss. She responded with equal fervor, pressing herself into him as if she could melt into his very being.

The stone wall at their backs was cold, a stark contrast to the heat blooming between them. Levy backed her against it without breaking the kiss, his movements driven by a need so intense it made his chest ache.

Her arms tightened around him as if anchoring herself, her legs instinctively wrapping around his waist, pulling him closer still. The new angle brought their bodies flush against one another, and he let out a low, guttural sound that vibrated against her lips.

His mouth trailed from hers, hot and hungry, down to her jawline, then to the curve of her neck. He paused there, his breath warm against her skin, his lips brushing over the faint bruises he had left. He stilled for a moment, his chest heaving as the guilt flared up again, but Mallory tilted her head, her voice a breathy whisper that made his pulse pound.

"Don't stop."

It was all the encouragement he needed. His lips found her neck again, trailing heat down her skin as her fingers tightened in his hair. The faint scent of the forest around them—pine and damp earth— mingled with the intoxicating warmth of her skin, leaving him dizzy, consumed. He pressed closer, his hands gripping her thighs where they wrapped around him, the pressure of her body against his sending sparks racing through him.

Mallory tilted her hips, the movement deliberate, teasing, and he groaned, the sound low and full of need. His lips returned to hers, this kiss deeper, rougher, his teeth grazing her bottom lip before pulling her into him fully. She answered with equal fire, her fingers dragging down his back, through the fabric of his shirt, desperate to feel more of him.

The cool breeze of the night ghosted over them, but neither noticed. The warmth between them burned too brightly, a flame that seemed to consume everything else. Mallory pressed closer, her breath hitching as his hands roamed, mapping every curve, every line of her.

The rough texture of his calloused palms against the softness of her skin sent shivers racing through her, her pulse pounding in time with the frantic beat of her heart.

Levy's control slipped further, his body reacting to every sound she made, every shift of her hips. He pressed her harder against the wall, his lips devouring hers with a hunger that bordered on desperation. She met him with equal intensity, her legs tightening around him as her hands traced the hard lines of his shoulders, his arms, and the curve of his jaw.

Their breathing grew ragged, the world around them fading entirely. Nothing existed beyond the sensation of their bodies pressed together, the heat of his hands on her skin, and the way their lips and tongues moved in perfect rhythm. The soft sounds she made drove him to the brink, his control hanging by a thread as his name slipped from her lips in a breathless moan.

"Mallory," he murmured against her lips, his voice rough and strained, filled with everything he couldn't put into words. She pulled back just enough to meet his eyes, her gaze steady and filled with something that made his chest tighten—trust, desire, and something deeper.

"Levy," she whispered, her fingers brushing his cheek before pulling him back into a kiss that was softer, slower, but no less intense. It wasn't just hunger anymore—it was connection, a deep and undeniable bond that had been building between them all along.

The stars above shone down, bearing witness to the fire they shared as the night wrapped around them like a cocoon, holding them in a world entirely their own.

The first streak of lightning split the sky with a violent crack, illuminating the world in stark, blinding white. The deafening thunder that followed rolled through the night like the roar of some angry, ancient beast.

Mallory gasped, her eyes wide as she pulled back just enough to look up, still cradled in Levy's arms. The stars, so peaceful only moments ago, were now obscured by turbulent clouds that churned and writhed as if alive.

"Levy," her voice was barely audible over the growing roar of the storm.

A second strike of lightning lashed through the heavens, then a third, each one brighter and more violent than the last. The air felt charged, thick with energy that made the hair on the back of their necks rise.

And then it happened—a long, jagged crack appeared in the sky itself, spreading outward like fractures in glass. The unnatural fissure widened with every flash of lightning, the sharp edges glowing with an eerie, molten light.

Levy's heart pounded as he stared upward, his arms instinctively tightening around Mallory. "No..." he murmured, his voice drowned by the cacophony of the storm. The cracks multiplied, splintering and branching out across the sky, until one final, earth-shaking bolt of lightning struck with devastating force.

The sky shattered.

It broke apart like a vast pane of glass, the pieces falling in slow, shimmering fragments that caught the light and refracted it in every direction. The fragments tumbled downward like delicate snowflakes, but they were anything but harmless.

The air was immediately filled with the howling of a monstrous wind, a storm so fierce it seemed to tear at the very fabric of the world. Thunder roared, and lightning slashed at the ground, leaving deep, smoldering gouges in the earth.

Mallory clung to Levy, her breath caught in her throat as she watched in stunned horror. "Levy," she whispered again, her voice trembling. "What's happening?"

Levy tore his gaze from the fractured sky, his jaw tightening as his instincts kicked in. "The barrier," he said, his voice grim and heavy with understanding. "It's gone."

Another flash of lightning ripped across the heavens, striking a nearby tree and sending a cascade of sparks into the air. The sharp smell of burning wood filled the wind, which had whipped into a frenzy, tearing through the forest and sending debris scattering across the stone walls. Mallory flinched, her grip tightening on him.

"Go get Quinn and Ashe!" Levy shouted with a commanding urgency, his voice barely reaching her over the howling wind. His dark eyes locked on hers, filled with a mix of fear and determination.

Mallory hesitated for only a heartbeat, her instincts warring with the desire to stay by his side. But the urgency in his voice left no room for argument. She nodded, releasing him and sprinting toward the stairs that would lead her into the depths of Stormhaven, her figure disappearing into the storm-tossed night.

Levy turned away, his feet already carrying him down the steps in the opposite direction, his mind racing as he headed for the barracks. The soldiers needed to be ready. They needed to know what was coming. The howling wind tore at his clothes, the air thick with the taste of ozone and the biting cold of the unnatural storm. Lightning continued to crackle above, illuminating the night in harsh bursts.

As he reached the courtyard, his voice rang out over the growing din, sharp and commanding. "TO ARMS!" he bellowed, his voice a rallying cry that cut through the noise. "EVERYONE TO ARMS!"

The soldiers stirred, their movements sluggish at first, their expressions bewildered as they stumbled into the open, staring upward at the shattered sky. Levy didn't slow, didn't stop. He grabbed one man by the shoulder, spinning him toward the armory. "MOVE!" he barked. "GET THE OTHERS. THIS ISN'T A DRILL."

The storm raged on, unrelenting, as the fragments of the broken barrier continued to drift down like falling stars. Levy's heart pounded in his chest as he rallied the troops, his mind fixed on one thought.

They weren't ready for this. Not yet. But they would have to be.

Chapter 40
Ashe

Ashe stood in darkness. It wasn't the comforting kind of dark that came with sleep or the peaceful silence of a starless night. This was an oppressive void, vast and smothering as if the world had been swallowed whole and left her suspended in nothingness. The air was heavy and damp, clinging to her skin like mist, and the only sound was her own ragged breathing.

She reached out, her fingers trembling, but they met no resistance. There was nothing to grasp, nothing to anchor her in this emptiness. The void hummed around her, a deep, low vibration that seemed to seep into her bones, rattling her core. Each passing moment stretched endlessly, the oppressive silence pressing harder until she thought she might scream.

Then, faintly, came the sound. A dull, rhythmic pounding, distant at first but growing steadily louder. It wasn't footsteps, not yet, but something deeper, a resonant thrum that made the void itself quiver. Ashe turned, searching for its source, but the sound seemed to come from everywhere at once.

The darkness began to lift, a faint, sickly light creeping in from the edges of her vision. Slowly, the world took shape. The ground beneath her feet was cracked and dry, its surface riddled with jagged fissures that glowed faintly with molten heat. Smoke curled lazily from the cracks, carrying the sickly stench of burning earth and sulfur. The air was oppressive, every breath tasting like ash.

Ahead of her stretched a vast battlefield, its edges obscured by swirling smoke and flickering shadows. The pounding grew louder, sharper until she could distinguish the rhythmic drumbeat of footsteps. They were distant but unmistakable—hundreds of them, marching in perfect unison, their cadence shaking the ground beneath her.

Ashe's heart hammered in her chest, her pulse echoing the relentless rhythm of the footsteps. Figures began to emerge through the haze, their outlines distorted and monstrous. The air grew colder, and her breath misted in front of her, mingling with the smoke.

The immortals came into focus first. Their forms were twisted, grotesque parodies of human shapes, their bodies glowing faintly with an unnatural light. Their armor, golden and jagged, seemed to pulse like a living thing, and their weapons dripped with a viscous, dark ichor that sizzled and hissed as it hit the ground. Their eyes burned with an eerie fire, and their faces were devoid of emotion, moving as one under some terrible force.

And at their head, the gods.

The Olympians marched in radiant contrast to their monstrous army. Each step they took was deliberate, their divine auras illuminating the battlefield with a harsh brilliance. Demeter strode with vines coiling around her arms like serpents, their thorned edges dripping with venom.

Apollo walked with his golden bow drawn, flames licking at his boots and trailing sparks in his wake. Poseidon's trident glowed an icy, electric blue, water churning unnaturally around him as if the very ground was bending to his will.

Hermes darted in and out of the ranks, his movements too quick to follow, his form flickering like a shadow in firelight. Behind them came Dionysus, a goblet of wine in one hand, his other clutching a bloodied dagger, his wild eyes glinting with manic joy.

And then there was Zeus.

Ashe's breath caught in her throat as he appeared, his massive figure dominating the horizon. Lightning coiled around him,

Oath Breaker

illuminating his golden armor with every strike, casting ragged shadows across the battlefield. His face was stern, chiseled, and terrifying in its intensity—but it was his eyes that made her blood run cold. They weren't eyes at all.

Two hollow pits stared back at her, leaking golden ichor-like molten tears. The ichor dripped down his face, pooling in the crevices of his armor staining the earth beneath him. He turned his gaze toward her, and even from this distance, she felt it—a weight, a pressure that crushed her chest and made it impossible to breathe.

The army halted. The drumbeat stopped, replaced by a deafening silence that stretched out like the calm before a storm. Ashe felt the hairs on her arms rise, a chill running down her spine despite the molten heat beneath her feet.

Then they began to chant.

"Heed these words; a prophecy foretold,
Of valor, virtue, and warrior bold.
As Heavens weep, when realms collide;
Three heroes rise to stem the tide.
A sacrifice for all to see,
Embodies hope; forever free."

The voices rose as one, deep and rhythmic, the words reverberating through the air like a war drum. Each syllable struck her like a physical blow, the weight of the prophecy sinking into her bones. The chanting grew louder, echoing in her ears until it drowned out every other sound, filling the void with its terrible melody.

Zeus stepped forward, his towering form casting a long, grotesque shadow across the battlefield. His hollow eyes burned into her, their ichor dripping faster now, staining his armor with streaks of gold. He raised one massive hand, his voice cutting through the chant like a thunderclap.

"Beware the Oath Breaker."

Ashe tried to move, tried to speak, but her body was frozen. The air around her grew heavier, the smoke thicker, as if the battlefield itself was closing in. The chanting grew louder, more insistent until it seemed to come from inside her own mind.

"BEWARE THE OATH BREAKER!" Zeus roared again, his voice shaking the ground beneath her feet.

Brian Tripp

The earth cracked open, the molten fissures spreading and widening, the battlefield fracturing into chaos. Ashe screamed as the ground gave way beneath her, flames and smoke engulfing her as she fell into the void.

Then, the voice that had been haunting her visions came once more. Familiar, commanding, echoing through the chaos like a beacon.

"Rise, Ashelia, they are here. THEY ARE HERE!"

Ashe jolted upright, the sheets tangling around her legs as she struggled to catch her breath. The room was dark, the shadows heavy and oppressive, broken only by the flashes of lightning strobing through the arched windows. Each breath came in shallow, ragged gasps, her chest heaving as if she had just surfaced from deep water.

Her hands flew to her neck instinctively as though expecting to find the searing heat of Zeus' hollow gaze still burning into her skin. But it was only her own pulse she felt, hammering against her fingertips, wild and erratic.

The dream clung to her like a living thing, the prophecy's chant still echoing in her ears, that all too familiar smell of burning earth and blood still sharp in her nose.

"Ashe!" Quinn's voice broke through the fog of her panic, sharp and urgent. His hands gripped her shoulders, steadying her as he knelt beside her bed. The warmth of his touch anchored her, cutting through the lingering chill of the vision.

"They're here," he said, his tone low and urgent, his crimson eyes fixed on hers. "The Olympians are here. We need to move."

Her heart stuttered at his words, the weight of the dream crashing down on her with renewed force. "The barrier..." she whispered, her voice hoarse and trembling. "It's gone. I saw it break."

Quinn nodded, his jaw tightening. "Zeus shattered it. Their army is already moving. They're at the edge of the forest."

The room seemed to tilt around her, the enormity of his words slamming into her like a physical blow. Her hands gripped the edge of the mattress as she forced herself to steady her breathing, her mind racing. The faint rumble of thunder reached her ears, low and menacing, a warning of the storm that had been unleashed.

"What do we do?" she asked, her voice barely above a whisper.

Quinn stood, his movements sharp and deliberate as he crossed the room to her armor, which rested on a stand near the window. The moonlight glinted off the polished steel as he began gathering the pieces. "We fight," he said, his tone leaving no room for doubt. "We protect Stormhaven. We protect each other."

The distant roar of the storm grew louder, the wind picking up outside, its howling cry seeping through the cracks in the stone walls. Ashe swung her legs over the side of the bed, her feet touching the cool stone floor. Her body felt heavy, her muscles sluggish, as though the weight of the prophecy was pressing down on her, making every movement a struggle.

But she couldn't afford to falter. Not now. Not when everything was at stake.

The clink of metal echoed in the dim room as Ashe fastened the straps of her breastplate, her fingers trembling as they struggled to find purchase on the buckles. The weight of the armor settled over her shoulders, familiar yet oppressive, a reminder of the battles that lay ahead. She fumbled with the final strap, her frustration mounting as it refused to cooperate.

Quinn appeared at her side, his hands steady and sure as he took over, fastening the strap with practiced ease. His touch was gentle, his presence a calming anchor in the whirlwind of her thoughts. "You're shaking," he said quietly, his voice tinged with concern.

"I'm fine," she replied quickly, though the tremor in her voice betrayed her. She looked away, focusing on the flickering shadows cast by the torchlight on the walls. "It's just... the dream. The prophecy. Zeus."

Quinn didn't press her, instead reaching for her gauntlets and handing them to her. "You've carried us through to this point," he said, his words filled with quiet confidence. "We'll get through this too."

Ashe nodded, slipping her hands into the gauntlets and flexing her fingers to test their fit. The leather and steel felt heavy, a stark contrast to the raw vulnerability she felt inside. She forced herself to focus, to push aside the lingering fear and doubt.

The distant roar of the storm outside grew louder, the sound mingling with the faint clamor of soldiers rallying in the Citadel's halls. The air was thick with anticipation, the kind of tension that settled before a battle, sharp and electric. Ashe adjusted the belt of her daggers at her hip, the familiar weight a small comfort.

Quinn busied himself with his own armor, his movements efficient and deliberate. Ashe watched him out of the corner of her eye, the way his brow furrowed in concentration, the way his hands moved with practiced ease. He seemed calm, but she could see the tension in his shoulders, the tightness in his jaw. He was just as afraid as she was, though he would never show it.

"You felt it too, didn't you?" she asked quietly, breaking the silence. "The prophecy... the barrier shattering..."

Quinn paused, his hands stilling as he adjusted the strap of his chest plate. He turned to her, his crimson eyes meeting hers for a moment before he nodded. "I felt it," he admitted, his voice low. "It's like the storm is alive, pressing against us."

Ashe swallowed hard, the memory of Zeus' hollow eyes flashing in her mind. The words of the prophecy echoed again, relentless and haunting: *A sacrifice for all to see.*

She pushed the thought away, focusing instead on the task at hand. "We need to warn the others," she said, her voice steadying. "They'll be counting on us."

Quinn nodded, slinging his sword across his back and adjusting the straps. "They're already moving. Levy and Mallory are rallying the soldiers. Kael and Lend are gathering them all at the gates. Everyone is as ready as we can be."

Ready. The word felt like a cruel joke. How could anyone be prepared for what was coming? For Zeus and his army? For the wrath of Olympus itself? But Ashe pushed the doubt aside, clinging to the hope she held in her friends and in herself.

Quinn stepped closer, his hand resting lightly on her shoulder. "We've fought gods before," he said, his voice filled with quiet determination. "We'll fight them again. Together."

Together. The word carried a weight that settled in her chest, both comforting and terrifying. She nodded, her grip tightening on the hilt of a dagger. They would face this storm together, no matter what it brought, for their own future and that of humanity.

As they stepped into the corridor, the Citadel was alive with movement. Soldiers sprinted past, their armor clanking as they shouted orders and rallied to their posts. The flickering torchlight cast their faces in sharp relief, their expressions a mix of fear and duty. The world was alive with the sound of boots on stone and the rustle of weapons being readied.

The storm outside raged louder, the wind howling like a beast, its cries echoing through the halls. Ashe felt the chill of it seeping through the stone walls, a cold that settled in her bones, and refused to leave. Lightning flashed, illuminating the windows in jagged bursts, casting fleeting shadows that danced and twisted like specters.

Ashe glanced at Quinn, her heart pounding as they made their way toward the central courtyard. The weight of the moment pressed down on her, but she refused to let it break her. The prophecy's words lingered in her mind, a haunting reminder of what was at stake. But as she gripped her sword and stepped into the chaos, she knew one thing for certain: they would stand victorious, or they would burn so brightly the darkness itself would remember their defiance.

Chapter 41
Talius

The storm raged with a fury unlike any Talius had seen in his long, cursed existence. The winds howled like the cries of tortured souls, tearing at his robes and lashing his exposed skin with icy needles.

Each gust carried with it shards of debris—splinters of wood, pieces of stone, and the scorched remnants of trees—that struck the ancient walls of Stormhaven like relentless battering rams. The night sky above was a smothering canopy of red, the clouds swirling, pregnant with malice and anger.

Talius stood upon the wall, his frail form silhouetted against the flickering lightning that illuminated the world below. His bones ached with the weight of centuries, yet he had never felt more alive. The fragment of essence Clotho had shared with him burned within his veins, a reminder of the strength he had once wielded, the strength he now channeled for this final stand.

The air hummed with static energy that crawled across his skin like phantom fingers. Every breath was thick and metallic, tasting of static and ash, Zeus' wrath sinking into his lungs with each inhale. He tightened his grip on the edge of the parapet, feeling the rough, time-worn stone bite into his palms. Below him, the city of Stormhaven stretched out like a battlefield waiting for the first blow, its flickering torches and rushing soldiers a testament to the resilience of its people.

At the edge of the forest, the gods had gathered.

Talius' sharp eyes pierced the distance, focusing on the clearing where the Olympians stood like sentinels of destruction. Zeus was at their head. His towering form wreathed in a violent aura of power that pulsed and crackled.

Lightning coiled around him, illuminating his golden armor in blinding bursts. His face was a mask of fury, his eyes shining blue and silver, radiant and overflowing with power.

Beside him, Poseidon bled with icy malevolence, his trident glowing with a pale blue light that seemed to freeze the very air around him. Water churned at his feet, defying the scorched earth, a testament to his dominion over the seas. Demeter stood to his left, vines and thorns coiled around her arms with glistening barbs. Her hair was wild, adorned with flowers that seemed to bloom and wither in the span of a breath.

Hermes lingered at the edge of the group, his form a blur of motion even when still. His feet skimmed the ground, and the golden wings on his sandals shimmered as though ready to propel him into action.

Apollo stood apart, his golden bow in hand, flames licking at his boots as he watched the horizon with an expression of cold resolve. Even Dionysus, usually the most chaotic of their number, was subdued, his wild eyes darting across the battlefield as he sipped absently from his blood-stained goblet.

"They look ready to burn the world to cinders," Clotho spoke beside him, her eyes scanning the trees with calm resolve.

Talius turned to her, taking in the sight of his old friend. She was thinner now, her frame frail from her imprisonment in Olympus' dungeons, yet she stood with the same quiet strength she always had. Her silvered hair whipped around her face, but her sharp eyes remained fixed on the gods. Though her body bore the marks of Zeus' cruelty, her spirit was unbroken.

"They're not the only ones," Talius replied, his voice steady. He turned his gaze downward to the mortals gathered at the base of the wall. Soldiers rushed to their posts, their armor gleaming in the flickering torchlight. The air was filled with the sound of shouted orders and the clamor of steel. But what drew his attention most were the figures moving among them—the leaders, his students.

Ashe stood at the forefront, her presence commanding as she directed troops with calm precision. Power burned within her, a quiet intensity that radiated in every movement.

Quinn was nearby, his weapon drawn, his posture unyielding as they prepared to face the Olympians head-on. Levy was a flurry of motion, rallying soldiers, his expression fierce and determined.

"They're magnificent," Talius said, his voice tinged with pride. "Everything we hoped they would become."

"They've surpassed everything we dreamed of," Clotho agreed, her lips curving in a faint smile. "And they will succeed. But only if we give them a chance."

A faint shimmer appeared beside Clotho, and Talius felt a familiar warmth. He turned to see Hestia's spectral form solidifying, her presence faint but unmistakable. She glowed softly, her essence a fragile tether to the mortal plane. The sight of her brought a pang to Talius' chest, a reminder of all they had sacrificed to reach this moment.

"Hestia," Clotho greeted her, her voice soft with affection. "You've come."

"I wouldn't miss it," Hestia replied, her voice steady despite the flicker of her form. "This is what we began. I will see it through."

Talius inclined his head in silent acknowledgment. The three of them stood together, the remnants of a plan forged in secrecy, bound by millennia of sacrifice and struggle. They had endured so much, and now, at the final hour, they stood ready to make their last stand.

Below, Zeus stepped forward, his massive form rising into the air. The very ground seemed to tremble beneath him, the trees at the edge of the forest bowing under the weight of his power.

His golden armor shone with a blinding light, and the lightning that coiled around him surged violently. His voice boomed across the battlefield, but the words were lost in the cacophony of the storm.

"Are you ready, my friends?" Hestia asked, her gaze steady.

Talius and Clotho exchanged a glance before nodding. "We're ready," Talius said, his voice filled with quiet determination.

They linked hands, their resolve firm. The energy of the walls surged around them, a hum that grew to a deafening roar as they channeled the accumulated power. The walls had siphoned essence for centuries, first from Athena and then from Talius himself. Now, that power flooded into them, a torrent of energy that threatened to consume them.

The air around them crackled with raw power, the storm intensifying as their barrier began to take shape. Zeus roared, his voice a thunderclap that shook the earth, and the wave of energy he unleashed was unlike anything they had ever seen. It swept across the battlefield like a tidal wave, a wall of destruction that incinerated everything in its path.

Talius, Clotho, and Hestia cried out as one, their voices a defiant roar against the god's wrath. The barrier flared to life, its pale light clashing violently with Zeus' power. The collision sent shockwaves rippling across the battlefield, the force of which quake the walls of Stormhaven.

The energy coursing through Talius' body was unbearable, a burning flood that threatened to tear him apart. His hands tightened around Clotho's and Hestia's, their combined strength the only thing keeping him rooted. He could feel his essence unraveling, his physical form beginning to dissolve under the strain. But he held on, pouring everything he had into the barrier.

The light grew blinding, the roar deafening. The world around them was consumed in chaos, a violent, churning power that seemed to stretch on forever. And then, as suddenly as it began, it was over.

The light faded, the thunderous roar subsiding into a heavy silence. Talius blinked, his vision sharpening to reveal the battlefield below. The clearing was gone, replaced by a massive, charred crater that stretched as far as the eye could see. The forest behind it was reduced to ash, the ground scorched and lifeless.

But Stormhaven stood untouched.

The barrier shimmered once before fading, its energy expended. The city's walls were unscathed, its people unharmed. The mortals below stared in stunned silence, their disbelief giving way to a roar of triumph.

Talius staggered, his body feeling weightless and insubstantial. He looked down at his hands, watching as they began to dissolve into shimmering essence. His physical form was fading, unraveling into the energy he had channeled. He turned to Clotho and Hestia, seeing the same fate overtaking them.

"The rest is up to you," he said, finding his students with his eyes one last time. His voice was steady despite the dissolution of his form.

Talius smiled, the weight of his existence lifting as everything around him faded to white.

Oath Breaker

Chapter 42
Clotho

The world around Clotho was a blur of light and sound, fading rapidly as the last remnants of her strength left her frail body. The roar of the storm and the cries of the soldiers below had dulled to a distant hum, barely reaching her ears.

She could feel the essence unraveling within her, each strand of energy she had borrowed, saved, and sacrificed slipping away, leaving nothing but a hollow ache in its place.

Her legs gave out first, crumpling beneath her as she sank to her knees atop the ancient walls. The stone was rough and cold beneath her hands, settling her in these final moments.

She looked down at her fingers, pale and trembling, and watched as they began to dissolve into shimmering motes of gold, carried away by the wind.

Her breath hitched, but not with fear. No, there was no fear left in her—not for herself. The emotion that gripped her chest now was sorrow, deep, aching sorrow that she would not be there to see the end, to guide the ones she had come to love as her own.

Clotho lifted her head, her vision blurred and dimming, but her heart was steady. Beside her, Talius and Hestia were already fading, their forms dissolving like sand swept away by the tide. She could feel their presence, their strength woven with hers, but it was slipping, retreating into the void that awaited them all.

"I hope we've done enough," she whispered, though her voice was barely a breath against the storm.

The light grew brighter, surrounding her and filling her vision until the world was swallowed by a radiant white. And in that brilliance, her sight sharpened. Her golden eyes, glowing with the last remnants of her gift, saw it again—the vision that had haunted her for centuries, the threads of Fate weaving and tangling in patterns she had only partially understood until now.

This time, it was clear.

The tangled threads straightened, their meaning unfolding before her like a story she had always known but never fully grasped. It was all there: the beginning, the middle, and the inevitable end. Her lips parted, her voice rising with the clarity of the truth revealed.

"The Oath Breaker shall shred the loom; the Oath Breaker shall spell your doom."

Her words rang out, carried by the wind like a ghostly echo, a warning meant for ears far away. She did not know if they would hear her, if they would understand. But she had to try. This was her final gift, her final hope.

Her body was nearly gone now, the last remnants of her essence scattered like threads torn from the fabric of life. She felt no pain, only a lightness, a quiet peace that came from knowing she had given everything she could.

She thought of Ashe, of Quinn, of Levy, of all those whose lives she had touched, even in small ways. She hoped they would forgive her for the burdens she had placed on them, the trials they had faced because of her.

And then, like a thread cut from the loom, she was gone.

The walls of Stormhaven stood silent, the storm still raging overhead. The faint glow of her essence lingered in the air for a heartbeat, a soft golden shimmer that danced in the wind before vanishing entirely.

Chapter 43
Quinn

Quinn stood at the forefront of the gathered army, his dark hair snapping violently in the wind as he gripped the hilt of his sword. His eyes, burning like molten fire, were locked on the figure hovering at the edge of the battlefield—the King of the Gods, Zeus.

Zeus radiated an aura of raw, unbridled power that defied comprehension. His massive form hovered effortlessly above the ground, the golden armor adorning his body gleaming with an unnatural light.

The air around him shimmered with energy, lightning writhing across his skin. Every crackle of electricity, every flicker of that unholy light, sent vibrations coursing through Quinn's body, making his teeth chatter and his very essence recoil.

A primal fear gripped him. He was no stranger to battles, but this was not a battle—it was an execution. Zeus' power was all-encompassing, a force of nature-given will. The realization clawed at Quinn's mind, an anguished thought piercing through the haze of terror.

We are not ready for this.

Stormhaven's army stood behind him, hundreds of soldiers clad in gleaming armor forged by Hephaestus himself, their weapons infused with the divine essence of the gods. Levy's relentless training and leadership had transformed them into a force to be reckoned with, and yet, none of that seemed to matter now.

Quinn's fingers tightened around his weapon, his knuckles white. The troops around him stirred uneasily, the chorus of their voices blending into the howling wind. He could feel their fear—hell, he *shared* it. No amount of preparation could have readied them for this.

Zeus floated higher into the air, his hollow sky-blue eyes scanning the battlefield with contempt. His voice rang out, thunderous and filled with fury. The words were lost in the roar of the storm, but Quinn didn't need to hear them to understand their meaning. This wasn't a rallying cry—it was a death sentence.

And then it happened.

Zeus raised his arms, the motion slow and deliberate as though savoring the moment. The lightning around him coalesced, converging into a sphere of pure energy that pulsed with devastating power. The air grew still, heavy with anticipation, and then—he released it.

The energy burst outward in a blinding wave of light, a sheet of destruction that tore across the battlefield with impossible speed. Trees, earth, and debris were obliterated in its wake, the ground itself ripped apart as the wave surged toward Stormhaven. This would not be a war; it was annihilation.

Quinn's heart sank as he watched the wave approach, unstoppable and all-consuming. For the first time in a long while, he felt truly helpless. They had prepared to fight against the gods, but this? This was the end.

His breath caught in his throat as he turned to look at Levy and Ashe, both of whom were staring at the oncoming destruction with wide eyes. There was no time to move, no time to act. He clenched his fists, preparing himself for the inevitable. *At least we tried,* he thought bitterly. *At least we fought.*

But just as the wave of energy drew within striking distance, something shifted.

A sudden surge of essence roared to life behind him, so overwhelming that it made Quinn stumble. The air seemed to crackle with the force of it, a raw, unrefined energy unlike anything he'd ever felt before. He whirled around, his heart pounding, as a translucent green barrier erupted from the walls of Stormhaven.

The barrier shimmered with pale light, its surface rippling like water as it stretched across the city and its gathered army. The power radiating from it was immense, ancient, and fierce, and for the first time since Zeus had arrived, hope flickered in Quinn's chest.

The wave of destruction slammed into the barrier, and the world exploded into light.

Quinn shielded his eyes with his arm, the blinding radiance swallowing everything. The roar of Zeus' attack drowned out all other sounds, a deafening rumble that made his ears ring and his head pound. The ground beneath his feet shook violently, cracks splintering through the earth as if the world were breaking apart.

For what felt like an eternity, there was nothing but overwhelming light and sound.

And then, as suddenly as it had begun, it was over.

The light faded, the thunderous roar subsided, and the storm seemed to hold its breath. Quinn lowered his arm cautiously, blinking against the afterimage burned into his vision. The battlefield came into focus once more, and his breath caught in his throat.

The clearing beyond the barrier was gone, replaced by a massive, smoking crater that stretched as far as the eye could see. The forest that had once surrounded Stormhaven was obliterated, reduced to char and rubble. The ground was scorched black, steam rising from the shattered earth like the remnants of some hellish inferno.

But Stormhaven stood.

The city's walls were untouched, its buildings unscathed. The barrier had held, shielding the city and its people from Zeus' wrath. A collective murmur rose from the soldiers behind him, a sound of disbelief and tentative relief.

Quinn felt the surge of essence falter, the barrier cracking and splintering before dissipating entirely. The power that had protected them was gone, leaving behind a void that sent a shiver down his spine. He turned toward the walls, his eyes drawn upward to the source of the energy.

His breath caught at the sight before him.

Atop the walls stood Talius, his weathered figure radiating the last vestiges of essence he had siphoned for centuries. Beside him was Clotho, her frail frame barely holding together, her silver hair glowing faintly in the storm's light. And there, shimmering like a golden flame in the wind, was the spectral form of Hestia, her presence fragile.

They stood together, the three of them, their hands outstretched as the remnants of their energy faded into the air. Talius' shoulders sagged, his body trembling as he began to dissolve, his form breaking apart into warm motes of light. Clotho was little more than a shadow now, her essence unraveling as she turned her gaze toward the battlefield.

Quinn, Levy, and Ashe stood frozen, their eyes locked on the trio. None of them spoke, their minds struggling to comprehend what they were witnessing.

Clotho's lips moved, forming words that were carried away by the wind. Quinn couldn't hear her, but he saw the faint glow of gold in her eyes, a light that burned with purpose even as her body faded.

Beside him, Ashe stiffened, her eyes widening as if she had heard something they could not.

And then, with a final shimmer of light, the three figures were gone.

Quinn's heart twisted painfully in his chest, a hollow ache settling in its place. The storm surged around him, the winds howling with renewed fury, but all he could feel was the loss. Talius, Clotho, Hestia—they had given everything and spent the last of their lives to protect what mattered most. And now, they were gone.

"We have to move," he heard himself say, his voice rough. "They bought us time. We can't waste it. We have to finish this before Zeus regains his strength."

Levy nodded silently, his jaw clenched, while Ashe remained still, her gaze fixed on the spot where Clotho had stood. The weight of her final words lingered in the air, unspoken but felt by all.

Quinn turned back to the battlefield, his resolve hardening. The gods had made their move, and now it was time for humanity to respond.

"Summon them."

Quinn's voice cut through the lingering stillness like the edge of a blade. He turned his sharp gaze to Levy, nodding toward the orb that gleamed faintly in Levy's hand. "It's time."

Levy hesitated only for a heartbeat before his grip on the orb tightened. He nodded, understanding the gravity of the moment. Lifting the artifact high above his head, he let his essence flow into it. Quinn could feel it, a raw surge of power traveling down Levy's arm, twisting through his fingertips, and pouring into the orb.

The artifact drank the energy greedily, its translucent surface glowing brighter with each passing second. Pale green light suffused the orb, growing stronger, more vibrant until the artifact was almost blinding to look at.

Mist began to swirl around it, thick tendrils of green vapor coiling like serpents, wrapping themselves around Levy's arm and twisting outward. The orb pulsed once, then again, a rhythmic beat that mirrored the pounding of Quinn's heart.

A wave of energy rippled outward, the force rolling across the battlefield, vibrating through the ground beneath their feet. At first, nothing happened. Quinn scanned the area, his jaw tight. The soldiers around him, already frayed with nerves from Zeus' devastating display, looked toward the orb expectantly, their faces a mixture of hope and dread.

The storm seemed to pause once more. The lightning stilled, the thunder quieted, and the howling wind softened into an eerie, unnatural calm. The air was heavy, filled with the weight of something unseen.

Then, the ground began to glow.

Soft, green light seeped from the earth, faint at first but growing stronger with each passing moment. It spread like fire, tracing along the battlefield in intricate, ethereal patterns. Slowly, forms began to emerge, rising from the illuminated ground like specters pulled from forgotten dreams.

One by one, warriors appeared.

Each figure was clad in ghostly armor, their spectral forms shimmering faintly in the strange light. Their faces were resolute, their weapons held with the confidence of those who had already faced death and emerged on the other side.

Their numbers grew steadily, an army of the fallen assembling alongside the living soldiers of Stormhaven. Awe spread like wildfire through the ranks as mortals stared in stunned silence at the allies rising to stand beside them.

"Well, it's about gods damned time!" a familiar voice called out, breaking the reverent hush.

Quinn turned his head, a smile tugging at his lips as a small, wiry figure floated into view. Sen. The irrepressible troublemaker from his past, whose humor had been as sharp as his blade. Even in death, Quinn loved that it hadn't changed.

"I was starting to wonder if you'd lost the orb," Sen quipped, his spectral form grinning at Levy.

"Good to see you again," Quinn said, unable to stop the warmth in his tone. Sen had always been able to spread joy, even in the darkest times.

"Sen, now is the time to be serious," another voice chimed in, deeper, steadier—Nes.

"Shove off, Nes," Sen retorted, rolling his eyes and flipping a very human gesture at his brother. "It's so boring down there. I'm ready for some action."

Quinn turned to Nes, unable to hold back his smile, despite the shit they were in. "Good to see you again."

Nes nodded in return, though his attention was clearly elsewhere. His eyes scanned the field, searching for someone. Quinn followed his gaze and smiled knowingly. "She'll be here," he said softly. "Just stay alive until she returns."

"Stay alive, this guy says," Sen laughed, pushing his hand theatrically through his head and out the other side. "Good one."

"*Can* you guys actually die again?" Levy interjected, his voice cutting through the humor with practical curiosity.

Nes turned to him. "They can send our souls back to the underworld with their essence and their godly weapons, but they can't actually kill us. Even so, if we are defeated, you won't be able to call us back for quite some time. Once we're gone from this fight, it's in your hands."

"Noted," Levy replied with a curt nod, the weight of the statement settling heavily on his shoulders.

"Where do you want us?" Nes asked, his spectral gaze locking onto Levy with an intensity that surprised Quinn.

Quinn blinked, caught off guard by the question being directed

Oath Breaker

at Levy. He had expected Nes to defer to him, as he always had in life. But as he looked between them, it struck him how much had changed. Levy was no longer the outsider, the rogue trying to prove himself. He had earned their trust, their respect, in ways Quinn hadn't fully appreciated until now.

"Aww, did that hurt, Teach?" Sen teased, catching the look on Quinn's face. "Don't worry—you'll always be my favorite."

Quinn chuckled. "No, he's the right one to ask. It's just… surprising to see you three so friendly after all the history."

"Don't you worry, Quinn," Sen said with a wink. "You're still top of the list."

Nes shook his head in exasperation before turning his attention back to Levy. Without missing a beat, he and Sen followed as Levy began organizing the spectral warriors, their ghostly forms dispersed through the ranks of the living soldiers.

Quinn watched them go, his heart heavy with both pride and apprehension. The storm remained unnaturally quiet as if holding its breath before the next explosion of chaos. The sight of the spectral army, their forms glowing faintly in the eerie light, filled him with a strange mixture of hope and dread.

The distant horizon pulsed with an unnatural light as the gods began forming their ranks. The immortal army that had been summoned stood like statues, silent and unmoving, their forms barely human in the haze of red light that spilled from the sky. From where Quinn stood, he could see Zeus at the center of it all, his presence an unrelenting storm, a beacon of malice and power.

The weight of the moment settled heavily on his shoulders. He could feel the tension in the air, thick and almost tangible, as the soldiers around him shifted uneasily.

Ashe's hand slipped into his. He turned to see her standing beside him, her expression fierce. The sight of her steadied him, and for a brief moment, the fear threatening to overwhelm him dulled.

"You should say something to them," she said softly.

Quinn arched a brow at her, his lips quirking into a faint smirk. "I should? Seems to me like you've been the leader here of the three of us. I'm just your favorite soldier."

Ashe laughed quietly, the sound a rare comfort in the midst of the tension. Her eyes shone with determination as she looked up at him, the soft curve of her smile doing strange, wild things to his heart. "No matter what you think, you're the one they look to. Levy has earned their respect, and they look to me—and the council—for day-to-day guidance. But when it comes to battle, when it comes to the impossible odds we're about to face, you're the one they watch."

Quinn frowned, the weight of her words settling in his chest. He opened his mouth to protest, but Ashe placed her other hand gently against his cheek, silencing him.

"You have the power of Chaos at your fingertips," she continued, her voice soft. "You've shown them time and again that you will never back down, no matter how insurmountable the odds. Going into this fight, into what might be their last stand, it's your voice they'll want to hear. You're the one who will give them the courage to keep fighting."

She leaned up, brushing her lips against his with a tender kiss. Quinn closed his eyes, leaning into the moment, drawing strength from the warmth of her touch. "Go, raise their spirits. Share with them your reason to fight."

"You are my reason to fight, and they cannot have you," he growled playfully against her lips, his voice low and possessive, eliciting a small laugh from her.

Quinn exhaled deeply, a sharp pang of nervousness settling in his stomach. But he nodded, drawing himself to his full height as he stepped away from Ashe. He made his way to a large crate nearby, climbing onto it to stand above the crowd. Around him, the soldiers—both living and spectral—were still bustling about, making their final battle preparations.

He drew in a deep breath and raised his voice, letting it carry across the field. "WARRIORS OF STORMHAVEN!"

The clamor ceased in an instant, every head snapping toward him. The living soldiers halted mid-motion, their gazes sharp with attention. Even the ghostly warriors turned, their faces set with a sense of duty. The sheer weight of their collective focus bore down on him, heavy and unyielding—but he stood firm, his heart steady, his resolve unwavering.

"Look around you! Each and every one of you stand here today because you chose to fight. You chose to rise, not for yourselves, but for something greater. For your families, for your city, for the very future of humanity! You are here because you refuse to bow to tyrants who think they are better than us simply because they were born to the heavens!"

A murmur rippled through the crowd, a flicker of agreement and pride in their expressions.

"These gods think they are invincible," Quinn continued, his voice growing stronger with every word. "I can tell you firsthand they are not. They think we are nothing but ants beneath their boots, to be crushed without thought.

"But look around you. Look at what we've already accomplished. They tried to destroy us, to wipe Stormhaven from existence, and yet here we stand, unbroken. Their storm could not break us. Their wrath could not destroy us. And their arrogance will be their downfall!"

A cheer began to rise, faint at first but growing louder with each passing moment. Quinn's heart swelled as he felt the energy of the crowd shift, their fear giving way to something fiercer, something brighter.

"They look down on us, thinking we are weak because we are mortal. But that mortality is our greatest strength. They cannot understand what it means to fight for something bigger than yourself, to sacrifice for those you love.

"That is what makes us powerful. That is what makes us dangerous. They will never understand the fire that burns in our hearts, the unyielding spirit that drives us to stand and fight, no matter the odds."

The cheer grew louder, soldiers raising their weapons into the air, their voices blending into a roar of defiance.

Quinn's voice boomed over the noise, commanding their attention once more. "Today, we fight not just for Stormhaven. We fight for the future of this world, for every soul that has put their faith in us and that deserves to live free from the shadow of their tyranny. Today, we fight to prove that we are not insects. We are not lesser beings to be forgotten. We are humanity, and we Will. Not. Bow!"

The roar of the crowd was deafening now, a surge of energy that made the very air vibrate. Quinn raised his sword high, the onyx blade catching the faint light of the storm as he shouted the final rallying cry.

"FOR STORMHAVEN! FOR HUMANITY!"

"FOR HUMANITY!" the soldiers roared in return, their voices shaking the ground beneath their feet.

Quinn stepped down from the crate, his heart pounding with adrenaline and pride. He felt Ashe's presence beside him again, her hand slipping into his. He turned to look at her, a small, knowing smile on his lips.

"You were right," he admitted, his voice quieter now. "They needed that."

"They needed you," Ashe corrected gently, her smile warm. "And you gave them what they needed."

Quinn squeezed her hand briefly, his resolve hardening as he turned his gaze back toward the battlefield. The gods were waiting, their ranks vast and unyielding. But so was humanity.

And they would not bow.

Chapter 44
Cyrus

The aftermath of Zeus' wrath hung heavy in the air. Cyrus stood at the edge of the crater, surveying the devastation with a mixture of amusement and disdain. The landscape was unrecognizable, the once verdant forest reduced to ash and smoldering debris.

The red haze that veiled the sky cast an eerie glow over the scene, the occasional flicker of lightning throwing jagged shadows across the ruins.

Cyrus had expected destruction—after all, Zeus had long promised that the mortals would suffer for their defiance. But this… this wasn't the slow, meticulous torment the king of the gods had always prided himself on.

Zeus had often boasted about the symphony of despair he would compose, savoring every scream, every plea. Yet here he was, resorting to a single overwhelming strike, one meant to crush everything in its path with a single blow.

Cyrus frowned, his sharp features tightening. *How uncharacteristic,* he thought. The display was impressive, certainly, but it reeked of desperation, not the calculated cruelty Zeus had once embodied. It was another sign of how far the Olympian had unraveled.

Brian Tripp

The king of the gods had become a blunt instrument, wielding his power indiscriminately. No finesse. No subtlety. Just raw, chaotic destruction.

And yet, it had failed.

Stormhaven still stood, its walls untouched, its defenders readying for battle. Cyrus hadn't missed the telltale shimmer of the translucent barrier that had absorbed the brunt of Zeus' attack. He knew exactly what it was.

Of course, he did—he'd helped build the defenses during his time as one of the Masters, though Talius had always been the true architect. Talius had guarded his secrets jealously, and Cyrus had wondered if the mortals would even know how to trigger the barrier when the time came.

Apparently, they did.

Cyrus' lips curled into a faint smile. The amount of energy Zeus had expended on that single strike was staggering. Cyrus could feel it in the air, the residual essence crackling like static against his skin. Zeus was still terrifyingly powerful, but he was no longer untouchable. He had left himself vulnerable.

"CYRUS!"

The booming voice shattered his thoughts, laced with the kind of command that brooked no delay. Cyrus rolled his eyes, the expression hidden beneath the shadow of his hood.

Always so theatrical, he thought. Straightening his posture, he turned to face the source of the bellow.

Zeus loomed above the crater, his form larger than life, still brimming with power despite the drain of his attack. The Olympian's sky-blue eyes crackled with energy, though Cyrus didn't miss the strain in them, the faint flicker of exhaustion buried beneath the storm.

"It is time you fulfilled your role in our bargain," Zeus growled, his voice a low rumble that made the ground tremble. "Do not march with us. Slip into their ranks once the battle has begun and wipe them out from within. When this is over, I will grant you a true seat of power as an Olympian."

Cyrus inclined his head, bowing low. Lower than he ever had before.

"As you command, Lord Zeus," he said, his tone perfectly

deferential. The bow served another purpose, hiding the wide, mocking smile that spread across his face.

An Olympian? Cyrus suppressed a laugh.

The promise was as hollow as the god making it. Zeus' seat of power had become his prison, a gilded cage he couldn't escape. Why would Cyrus want to shackle himself to the same fate? But Zeus didn't need to know that. Not yet.

Straightening, Cyrus turned without another word and slipped into the shadows at the edge of the crater. The air was still thick with dust and the stench of ozone, stinging his nostrils as he moved. His steps were silent, his movements fluid as he disappeared into the surviving trees on the outskirts of the destruction.

The forest, or what remained of it, was eerily quiet. The storm above seemed to temporarily pause, the wind dying to a faint whisper. Cyrus moved like a phantom, his dark cloak blending seamlessly with the charred surroundings. The path ahead twisted and turned, but he knew exactly where he was going.

Stormhaven.

He could already see it in his mind's eye—the city's walls standing defiant against the gods, its defenders bristling with resolve. Mortals, foolishly clinging to hope, believed they could stand against the heavens themselves. Cyrus couldn't decide whether to admire their tenacity or pity their naivety.

They do not know how outmatched they are, he thought, though his amusement was tempered by a grudging respect. The mortals had accomplished more than he'd expected. Their defiance had brought them this far, but they were running out of miracles.

His steps quickened, the shadows swallowing him whole as he made his way toward the city. The storm above rumbled faintly, a promise of destruction yet to come.

Chapter 45
Ashe

Ashe stood a few steps behind Quinn, her heart swelling as his voice carried across the battlefield, firm and unwavering. His words wrapped around the soldiers like armor, steeling their resolve, binding them together beneath the storm-darkened sky. Each syllable rang with the weight of conviction, his presence a beacon amid the looming chaos.

She had always known him to be strong, but it was in moments like these—when the world was on the precipice of ruin, and yet he stood, fearless, unyielding—that she saw the true depth of who he was.

Yet, even as she listened, caught in the fervor of his speech, her fingers drifted involuntarily to the satchel at her hip.

Pandora's Box.

Her fingertips traced the ancient grooves, the intricate filigree that wound around the surface like a thousand interwoven threads of Fate. The box was warm against her skin, pulsing faintly as if alive as if the hope within it stirred at her touch. Ashe swallowed hard; the sound of Quinn's voice muffled under the hammering of her heart. She hadn't meant to bring it.

Before the battle, they had locked it away—deep within the Citadel, beneath layers of wards, spells, and stone. They had all agreed. It was too dangerous, too unpredictable. Even Clotho had warned them that opening it was a sacrifice, not a miracle. And yet, here it was. Nestled against her like it had always belonged to her.

She hadn't stolen it. Hadn't retrieved it. But when she had been preparing for the fight, strapping on her armor and lacing her boots, she had felt it—a thread of Fate snapping taut, pulling her toward something unseen. The sensation had left her breathless, a sick feeling churning in the pit of her stomach. And when she had opened her satchel, it had been there.

The box had *chosen* to come to her.

A shiver ran through her, though the air was thick with the battle's coming heat. She tightened her fingers around the artifact as if she could will it to disappear, to ignore the ominous weight of its presence. She hated how it called to her, how its essence whispered in the back of her mind like a lover's murmur.

Set me free. Let me out. Let me help.

She clenched her jaw and forced herself to focus, dragging her attention back to Quinn. He stood tall, eyes ablaze with purpose, his leather armor molded to him like a second skin. He belonged here, in this moment, rallying their people for war. The fire in his crimson eyes reflected the storm raging above, and she wondered if the soldiers before him could feel it—that same unshakable belief that had carried them this far.

If he knew I had the box...

Ashe inhaled sharply, glancing down, away from Quinn's face, away from the soldiers drinking in his words like lifeblood. He hadn't noticed. Of course, he hadn't. Not with the raw essence still crackling in the air, remnants of the cataclysmic clash between Zeus and the barrier. Even the gods would struggle to pinpoint the presence of the box amid such chaos. And yet, despite all the noise, *she* could feel it.

It *wanted* to be opened.

A cold sense of inevitability washed over her, curling like mist in her chest. She couldn't shake the feeling that before the end of this battle, she would have to make a choice.

And if it comes to that, I will be the one to pay the price.

She exhaled slowly, a quiet tremor in her breath. Quinn would hate it. He would rage; he would grieve. But he would understand.

Brian Tripp

In the end, they had all agreed—whatever it took to stop the gods, to end this once and for all, they would do it. No hesitation. No regrets.

I'll make sure of that, she promised herself.

Still, her mind drifted back to a different battle. A different time. Stormhaven's first fall.

The night Athena had torn their world apart, when fire and death had swallowed the streets, and she and Quinn had barely escaped with their lives. She had accused him then of being willing to doom the world for her. Of being blinded by love, of being willing to make reckless choices if it meant keeping her safe.

She had *feared* the depth of his devotion, the terrible, beautiful strength of his love for her. And now, here she was, doing the same. Hiding the truth from him because she was afraid of what he would do.

Her stomach twisted. She hated herself for that fear, hated the betrayal she carried in silence. But if she told him now—if she pulled the box out of her satchel and showed him—it would only distract him. It would shake his focus. And he *needed* his focus.

No, she couldn't tell him. Not yet. She would carry this weight alone. Because if the moment came—if there was no other way—he would be the one to do what had to be done.

She closed her fingers tightly around the box, her resolve like iron.

Please, let me be wrong.

Let them win without it. Let them drive Zeus into the earth, let them cut down the gods without the need for something so unpredictable, so dangerous.

Let her not have to open Pandora's Box.

But if she did—if she had to unleash whatever lay within—then she would do it with no hesitation.

For Quinn. For their people. For humanity.

And for that, she would pay the price.

She swallowed hard and lifted her eyes back to Quinn, watching as he finished his speech, as the soldiers roared their agreement, as the ground itself seemed to tremble beneath their war cries. She drank in the sight of him, of the way he carried them all with his words, and she felt the ghost of a smile touch her lips, even through her inner turmoil.

The battle was upon them. And Fate, it seemed, had already made its choice.

Chapter 46
Levy

Levy surveyed the battlefield that stretched out before him, a landscape of devastation and ruin, the very air thick with the scent of scorched earth. He could still feel the tremors beneath his boots from the force of the Olympian king's attack as if the world itself trembled in anticipation of what was to come. The uneasy silence settled over both armies, a prelude to the storm, a hush before the screaming began.

Across the crater, the gods stood like statues carved from the essence of the heavens themselves. Their golden armor gleamed unnaturally in the eerie, red-hazed sky, their bodies radiating raw, unfiltered divinity.

They were not like Ares, reckless and eager for blood, nor like Aphrodite, toying with her victims before sinking her teeth in. No, these gods had watched the mortals defy them time and time again, and now, at the edge of their patience, they were prepared to annihilate them without another word.

Levy's fingers flexed around his weapon, his heart pounding a steady rhythm against his ribs. This was it. This was everything.

The ghosts of Elysium stood silently among the living warriors, their presence unsettling yet strangely reassuring. They shimmered faintly in the growing storm, their translucent armor flickering like dying embers, their weapons glowing with an otherworldly light.

Despite their lack of physical form, they stood as proud as any soldier, their spectral faces resolute. They had come back from death itself to fight for the humanity they had lost. And they would not be the only ones.

A gust of wind whipped through the ranks, sending banners rippling like waves on a restless sea. Ash and dirt swirled into the air, the storm intensifying as though it, too, knew what was coming.

The sky had darkened to a bruised red, clouds swirling in an angry vortex above the battlefield. The wind howled, carrying with it the distant sounds of something primal, something ancient as if the world itself lamented what was about to take place.

Then—lightning.

A jagged bolt tore through the sky, illuminating the battlefield with an unholy brilliance before it struck the center of the crater. The impact sent a shockwave rippling outward, the ground quaking as fire ignited in the pit below. But there was nothing there to burn. The flames licked at the darkness, fueled by something unnatural, something divine.

Levy exhaled slowly. One breath. One last moment of peace before hell itself erupted.

His eyes found Mallory.

Even across the distance, past the rows of shields and bodies between them, she met his stare with unwavering intensity. The firelight flickered against her armor, her chest rising and falling in steady determination.

She was his anchor in this storm, the one thing keeping him from drowning in the chaos of it all. His pulse thrummed wildly at the sight of her, at the sheer certainty that no matter what happened today, he would fight with every ounce of his strength to see her through it.

He would not die. Not now. Not when he had found something worth living for.

They had both come too far, fought too hard, endured too much loss. Humanity would survive. And when the dust settled, when the war was finally over, he would stand at her side and help build the world they had fought for. A future where they were free of gods, free of war, free to simply be.

But first, they had to kill Zeus.

Movement flickered across the battlefield.

Levy's sharp eyes caught it instantly—the first shift in the Olympian forces. The time had finally come. A ripple of motion passed through the immortal army as they began their advance, gleaming golden armor spilling over the edge of the crater-like an unstoppable tidal wave.

Their spears glowed with divine light; their shields held firm in unbreakable formation. There was no sound at first, no war cries, no rallying call. Just movement. Cold. Calculated. Purposeful.

Then came the first roar.

A cry that split the silence like a knife through flesh, reverberating through the battlefield. More followed a chorus of inhuman voices, the battle cry of immortals who had never known defeat. A sound meant to shake the resolve of mortals, to remind them of their place.

Levy did not falter.

He turned back to Mallory one last time.

She nodded, a wordless promise between them, and it filled him with an unshakable resolve. He let it steady him; let it flood him with a force greater than fear. This was not the end. This was only the beginning.

He bellowed the charge.

And with a resounding roar, the warriors of Stormhaven surged forward.

The ground shook as hundreds of boots pounded into the earth, a wave of steel and flesh crashing toward the gods. Swords were drawn, shields raised, the air filled with the metallic chorus of weapons unsheathed. The ghosts moved alongside their living allies, silent but no less fearsome, their spectral blades slicing through the air with chilling precision.

On the other side of the crater, the Olympians charged to meet them.

The world erupted.

And the battle for humanity had finally begun.

Chapter 47
Mallory

Mallory had almost forgotten the sheer, all-consuming chaos of war. The past months had been filled with battles, yes, but nothing like this—nothing that could compare to the raw, deafening brutality of two forces colliding with the fury of gods and mortals alike.

She had grown accustomed to the tense peace that followed the war for the Tower, to the rebuilding, the preparation, the waiting. But this? This was something else entirely.

She'd tried to keep her eyes on Levy when the fighting began and had caught one last glimpse of him across the battlefield before everything descended into madness. And then, the world had erupted.

The deafening clash of steel against steel drowned out all other sounds as bodies crashed together in a frenzied charge, human and immortal forces tangling in the deadly waltz of combat. The tides of war swallowed all waking thought, and from that moment on, it was only a battle to survive.

Around her, the cries of agony cut through the air—sharp, raw, and unrelenting. Mortal and immortal alike fell in droves, blood and ichor thickening the churned earth beneath her feet. The once-solid ground had become a treacherous mess of slushy mud, each step a risk as it threatened to pull her down into the carnage. She knew that a single misstep could be her end. If she fell, she would not rise again.

Despite every fiber of her being screaming at her to go to him—to find Levy in the chaos, to ensure he was still standing—she forced herself to remain focused. He had his own battle, just as she had hers. If they were to make it through this, she had to trust him to do the same.

Mallory didn't stop moving. To stop moving was to die, and she planned to live a long, active life when this was all over. Her sword cut through the air, slicing through the chest of an approaching immortal, his expression still twisted in rage even as the light left his eyes.

She pivoted, raising her shield just in time to catch a blow from another, the impact rattling her bones. With a grunt, she shoved forward, throwing the attacker off balance before driving her blade through his throat. His body slumped against her shield, and she kicked him off without a second thought.

There was no room for hesitation here. No room for weakness. She had lost count of how many she had killed, her arms aching from the relentless cycle of parry, strike, kill, repeat. But still, she pressed on, hacking through the enemy forces as she pushed forward.

And then—something changed.

At first, she thought it was just exhaustion clouding her perception, the way the battle seemed to shift, the air thickening like the storm raging in the sky above was about to unleash its fury. But as she cut down another enemy and took a moment to assess her surroundings, she realized it was far worse.

The battlefield ahead of her had become something else entirely.

The ground was shifting unnaturally, thick roots coiling up from the bloodied earth like grasping fingers. They writhed and snapped forward, ensnaring human soldiers by the ankles and dragging them down, the mud swallowing them whole as if the battlefield had turned against them. And before the trapped warriors could even struggle to free themselves, golden streaks rained down from above, each arrow striking true with merciless precision.

Mallory's breath caught in her throat as her eyes flicked up.

Apollo.

The god stood at a distance, his golden armor pristine, untouched by the filth of war. His bowstring never stopped moving, the divine weapon glowing as he loosed another volley into the ensnared mortals, picking them off like they were nothing more than animals in a hunt. His expression was one of detached amusement as if this were a game he had already won.

But that wasn't all.

A ripple of unnatural energy crawled across her skin, sending icy fingers wriggling down her spine. She turned her head, her breath hitching at what she saw.

Dionysus was weaving through the chaos like a specter, his movements fluid, his dark curls bouncing as he twirled his staff with lazy precision. Where he passed, mortal warriors faltered.

Some clutched their heads, their weapons slipping from their grasp as if some unseen force had stolen their reason. Others turned, eyes wild and unfocused, and began attacking their own allies, their screams of rage blending into the cacophony of battle.

Mallory gritted her teeth, bile rising in her throat.

The madness was spreading.

"Shit," she hissed.

She had fought gods before and had seen their overwhelming power firsthand, but to see them working together, weaving their divine abilities into something so utterly devastating was something else entirely. The human soldiers barely stood a chance. If this kept up, Stormhaven's forces would be whittled down before they even got the chance to engage properly.

She needed a plan.

A sudden clash of metal against metal beside her drew her back to the immediate fight. She spun, raising her shield just in time to catch a sword meant for her ribs. With a grunt, she shoved forward, knocking the attacker off balance before driving her own blade into his side. He crumpled, and as she stepped over his body, a familiar voice called her name.

"Mallory!"

Kael.

She twisted just as he reached her, his kopesh slick with ichor, his chest rising and falling in rapid bursts. Lend and Avery followed close behind, their weapons drawn, expressions grim. Sen, his ghostly form flickering faintly in the storm's eerie light, materialized a second later, twirling his sword in his hand with practiced ease.

"I take it you see what I see?" Kael asked, nodding toward the gods wreaking havoc on the battlefield.

"Oh yeah," Mallory said darkly.

"We need to put a stop to that," Lend added, wiping a streak of blood from his brow. "Or this is going to turn into a slaughter."

"No kidding," Avery muttered. "But how? We don't exactly have divine power of our own to counteract that."

Mallory took a deep breath, assessing the battlefield. The Olympians had spaced themselves out, but their coordination was deadly. Dionysus' influence was turning their soldiers into little more than mindless berserkers, leaving them vulnerable to Demeter's vines, which ensnared them in place for Apollo to pick them off with his never-ending supply of arrows, raining death down upon them with chilling precision.

"We have to split them up," she said finally. "Dionysus is the biggest problem right now. We can't fight if our own people are turning on us."

"Agreed," Kael said, flicking ichor from his blade. "But even if we take care of him, we still have Demeter and Apollo raining hell down on us."

"Then we divide and conquer," Mallory said firmly, already mapping out their movements in her head. "Sen, you and the other spirits can handle Dionysus. His madness doesn't affect ghosts, so you'll have the best shot at negating his influence in this fight."

Sen grinned. "Oh, you're gonna let me have all the fun? You shouldn't have."

"We'll cover you," Nes said, his voice steady beside him. "We'll keep him focused on us so the rest of the field can regain control."

Even as he spoke, he was already moving, Sen right beside him, their spectral forms flickering in and out of sight as they surged toward the battlefield. "Come on, you lazy bastards!" Sen bellowed, slamming the flat of his sword against his shield with a resounding clang. "You all didn't claw your way back from the Underworld just to sit on your asses and watch!"

The spirits stirred at his call, responding like an army waking from a trance. The ghostly warriors turned as one, their glowing forms flickering against the haze of war. At Nes' sharp nod, they moved with precision, flowing into formation behind the brothers, their weapons raised high.

They disappeared into the melee, weaving between the mortal soldiers, their presence like a haunting force sweeping across the battlefield.

"Good. That leaves us with the other two." Mallory turned to Kael, Lend, and Avery. "Demeter's roots are pinning our soldiers down, making them sitting ducks for Apollo. If we can sever her connection to the battlefield, we can free up our forces to fight back properly. Kael, you're with me—we'll cut her down before she can tangle us up."

Kael nodded, adjusting his grip on his weapon. "That leaves Apollo."

"Lend, Avery, that's you two." Mallory's eyes flicked to the golden-armored god, still standing at a distance, loosing arrows without pause. "You don't have to kill him. Just keep him occupied. If he's focused on you, he's not wiping out our ranks. Draw him into close combat—he won't be able to fire as easily if he's dodging blades."

Lend exhaled sharply. "Fantastic. The archer god versus two people who fight with swords."

"Perhaps I might be of some assistance?"

Mallory narrowed her eyes.

Cyrus stood before them, calm as ever, his scythe glinting with the same unnatural glow that always made her skin crawl. His expression was relaxed, almost amused, as if none of this—the blood-drenched battlefield, the bodies littering the ground, the gods reigning destruction upon their forces—troubled him in the slightest.

"Why would you help us?" Mallory's voice was cold, sharp with distrust.

Cyrus smirked, slow and deliberate, but there was no warmth in it, no sincerity. "I have unfinished business with Apollo." His grip on his scythe shifted, his fingers tightening for just a fraction of a second before he tilted his head almost lazily. "Besides, I guided you to Pandora's Box, did I not? Just imagine the carnage had that fallen into Zeus' hands. This battle would have become a rout."

Mallory's stomach twisted. He wasn't wrong, but that didn't mean she trusted him. She flicked her gaze to the others—Kael, Lend, and Avery. Each of them wore the same wary expression, each of them uncertain.

Cyrus, of course, noticed.

"I told you, I have my own intentions," he continued, rolling his shoulders as if this conversation bored him. "I am not with the Olympians. I would just as gladly have them dead as you all, so you may as well take my help because I am going to fight them whether you accept it or not."

Mallory hesitated. Cyrus had never pretended to be an ally. He was dangerous and unpredictable, and every instinct screamed not to trust him. And yet...

She looked back at the battlefield.

The immortal army was relentless, sweeping through their forces like an unbreakable tide. Demeter's vines lashed out like living whips, ensnaring warriors and dragging them through the muck.

Apollo's golden arrows rained down without pause, feeling soldiers before they could even raise their weapons. Dionysus' madness had already spread through sections of their ranks, turning mortals against mortals and forcing them to cut down their own comrades.

They were out of their depth. Outmatched.

Lend looked at her, his jaw set, his eyes dark with frustration. "We don't have time for this," he said, his voice low. "Like it or not, he's right. We need him."

Kael didn't look thrilled about it, but he gave a slow nod. Avery exhaled sharply, clearly hating every second of this, but he, too, didn't argue.

Mallory ground her teeth. This was a mistake. But what other choice did they have?

She exhaled through her nose, leveling Cyrus with a cold look. "Fine. But if you betray us—"

Oath Breaker

"Yes, yes," Cyrus interrupted with a dramatic sigh. "You'll make me suffer, you'll kill me, you'll drag me to the depths of the Underworld yourself. Very original." His smirk deepened. "Now, are we done posturing"

Mallory scowled but turned back toward the battlefield.

"Alright," she said, voice steeled. "We stick to the plan. Kael and I will take on Demeter," Mallory continued. "We need to cut her off before she buries us all in roots and vines."

Kael adjusted his grip on his kopesh, giving her a tight nod.

Mallory's eyes flicked to Avery and Lend. "Apollo is yours. Get him in close quarters—make him fight on your terms, not his."

Avery's fingers curled around the hilt of his sword. "And if he doesn't take the bait?"

Cyrus tilted his head, his smirk widening. "Oh, I'll make sure he does."

Mallory didn't trust him. She didn't like him. But she wasn't about to waste any more time. The battle was far from over.

"Let's move."

Chapter 48
Quinn

The battlefield was a nightmare—steel on steel, bellows of rage, and the sickening crunch of bone beneath the weight of battle. Blood and ichor painted the crater, a grotesque canvas of mortality and divinity intertwined.

Through it all, Quinn moved like a shadow, slipping between the fray, his blade flashing as he cut down another immortal before vanishing into the darkness once more.

The humans were outmatched in strength and power. That much was obvious. But what they lacked in godhood, they made up for in determination, strategy, and sheer grit. They did not bow. They did not yield. And Quinn refused to let them crumble.

Around him, his makeshift unit fought like hell itself had spat them out, though he supposed with the warriors of Elysium that weren't entirely untrue, refusing to break under the weight of the battle pressing in on all sides.

What had started as a scattered band of survivors, torn apart by the first devastating clash, had been reforged into a cohesive force under his command. Every call he made, every shadow step to reinforce a faltering line, kept them holding steady.

Quinn had always been a fighter. A warrior. But this was different. He was leading. He was responsible for these lives. And though the burden of it should have weighed him down, it instead sharpened him, honed his instincts into something lethal.

A soldier to his left stumbled back, a spear grazing his side, but before the enemy could finish the job, Quinn was there, stepping from the shadows like death itself and severing the immortal's head in a clean stroke. He caught the soldier's arm, steadying him.

"Hold the line," Quinn barked, and those around him answered with a chorus of steel against shields.

They pushed forward, slowly, methodically, forcing the immortals back step by step. Every gain was paid for in blood, but Quinn could feel the tide shifting. Just a little longer, and they could push them back enough to regroup and reinforce their position.

Then, a deep, guttural roar split the sky.

The wind shifted—cold and sharp, thick with the scent of brine. Quinn barely had time to register the shift before the ground trembled beneath his feet. A monstrous wave, impossibly large, reared up from the battlefield as if the sea itself had been summoned from the depths.

The soldiers barely had time to scream.

Quinn reacted on instinct, reaching deep into the power thrumming beneath his skin, the darkness of Chaos roaring to life in response to his will. He flung his arms outward, his energy manifesting in a jagged, vertical line, cutting through the very fabric of reality. The waves split cleanly in two, crashing down on either side of the unit but leaving them untouched.

The force of it sent tremors through the battlefield, sending men and immortals alike sprawling in the mud. Quinn held his ground, his breathing ragged, eyes scanning the battlefield until they locked onto the Olympian standing just beyond the wreckage.

Poseidon was a towering figure, his form wreathed in power. His bronze breastplate gleamed with a dull sheen beneath the stormy sky, the trident in his grasp still dripping with the water he had summoned. His presence alone was like an unrelenting tide, pressure pressing against Quinn's skin as if the very air bowed to him.

A grin curled Poseidon's lips as he took a step forward, casual, unhurried, like a predator that knew its prey had no escape.

"You think you impress me, mortal?" Poseidon's voice rumbled like the distant crash of waves against a cliffside. "A mere child playing with shadows against the might of the ocean?"

Quinn clenched his jaw, gripping his sword tighter. He could feel the eyes of his soldiers on him, waiting for his command, waiting for a plan. But he knew the truth—Poseidon was too great a threat for them to handle while also holding the line.

Which meant it was up to him.

Quinn turned, scanning the warriors that had fought so fiercely under his lead. Many were injured, and all were exhausted, but their eyes held nothing but resolve. He refused to let them die here.

He took a breath, steadying himself. Then, he met the eyes of the man nearest to him—a grizzled Abyssillian with a scarred face and unwavering determination. Quinn gripped his shoulder.

"Hold them together," he ordered. "Keep pushing forward, keep the line strong."

The man hesitated for only a second before nodding. "We won't let you down."

Quinn's expression hardened. "I'll be back."

And then he was gone.

He moved through the battlefield like a phantom, weaving between bodies and shadows, until he emerged behind Poseidon. The god barely had time to turn before Quinn was there, his voice low and laced with challenge.

"Why don't we go have a chat?"

Before Poseidon could react, Quinn's power surged, tearing open a portal of seething darkness. He grabbed the god by the back of his head, his fist gripped hard around Poseidon's curly hair and pulled him through, vanishing from the battlefield in an instant as the Realm of Night swallowed them whole.

~~~

The moment they emerged on the other side of the portal, the world around them shifted, reality stretching and bending to accommodate the ancient power saturating this place.

The Realm of Night was unchanged since the last time Quinn had stepped foot here. The sky remained an endless expanse of shifting hues—deep blues, rich purples, and streaks of ethereal silver twisting like celestial ink spilled across a canvas. There was no true sun, no moon, yet the air was alight with a ghostly glow that illuminated the swirling abyss above. It was as if the very essence of Chaos breathed life into the heavens, painting a masterpiece of infinite motion.

The ground beneath Quinn's boots was solid—black stone that seemed to absorb all light yet gleamed as if slick with unseen mist. Shadowy wisps curled around his feet as he moved, flickering and dissolving into nothingness when disturbed.

There was a time when the wind had howled here, an unrelenting force that had once whispered in his ear, taunted him, and beckoned him to surrender to the vast unknown. But now, the silence was absolute, thick, and suffocating in its weight. A stark contrast to the battlefield they had just left behind.

For a moment, Quinn allowed himself to take in the eerie tranquility.

And then Poseidon roared.

The god wrenched himself free of Quinn's grip, his body surging with divine energy. The weight of his presence pressed against the realm itself as if his sheer existence rejected the chaotic nature of this place.

His once immaculate armor, gleaming bronze and etched with waves of ancient craftsmanship, was spattered with the blood of battle. His eyes burned like the deepest parts of the ocean, violent and raging.

"You insolent wretch!" Poseidon's voice was a tidal wave of fury, crashing through the stillness. "You dare lay hands upon me?"

Quinn had barely released his hold on Poseidon's hair when he sensed the strike coming. Instinct flared like a spark in his chest, and he threw himself backward just as the trident sliced through the space he had occupied a moment before.

The three gleaming prongs whistled past his face, missing by a hair's breadth, but even the displaced air was sharp enough to leave a thin sting along his cheek.

Poseidon wasted no time. He spun the trident in his grip, his movements effortless, practiced over millennia of war. The god lunged again, thrusting the weapon forward with deadly precision.

Quinn shadow-stepped.

One moment, he was in front of Poseidon—the next, he was behind him, the darkness swallowing him whole and spitting him out a dozen feet away.

Poseidon snarled, whirling around to face him once more. His anger rolled off him in crashing waves, the very fabric of the realm trembling under his godly presence.

Quinn smirked, dusting off his shoulder as if brushing away the mere idea that Poseidon could have hit him. "I thought the God of the Sea would have better aim. You must be getting old."

Poseidon's nostrils flared, and in an instant, he threw his trident with a force that could have split mountains. Quinn sidestepped at the last possible second, the weapon spearing into the obsidian ground and shaking the entire realm upon impact. Black stone shattered, jagged cracks spiderwebbing outward from the point of collision.

The trident vanished in a flash of blue light, reappearing in Poseidon's outstretched hand a moment later.

Quinn let out a low whistle, crossing his arms. "Neat trick. But I gotta say, if this is the best you've got, I'm a little underwhelmed."

Poseidon bared his teeth. "Your arrogance will be your downfall, mortal."

Quinn rolled his shoulders, shifting his weight slightly, keeping his stance loose. "You know," he mused, "I'm getting really tired of being called that. You keep throwing it around like it's supposed to be an insult. But last I checked, I'm the one who just dragged you out of the battle kicking and screaming."

Poseidon's lip curled. "You think yourself powerful because you wield stolen strength? You are nothing more than a desperate child playing with forces beyond your comprehension."

Quinn tilted his head, his smirk never faltering. "Oh, I comprehend just fine. I comprehend that I'm standing here, alone, against a god—and yet, here you are, treating me like a threat."

He let that sit for a moment before taking a slow step forward. "Tell me, Poseidon—how does it feel? Knowing that a mortal forced your hand? That despite your power, you're stuck here with me instead of out there, where your soldiers need you?"

Poseidon's eyes flickered, barely perceptible, but Quinn saw it. That tiny, minuscule hesitation.

Oath Breaker

Quinn chuckled, shaking his head. "See, that's the thing about gods. You all think you're untouchable. You love lording your divinity over us, looking down at humanity like we're insignificant."

He gestured around them. "And yet, here we are. The war you started isn't going how you wanted. Your kin are dying, your king is being challenged, and now you? You're standing here, trapped."

Poseidon straightened, his expression darkening. "You speak as if you have already won."

Quinn's grin sharpened, his crimson eyes gleaming under the eerie glow of the Realm of Night.

"I have won," he said, his voice smooth, assured. "Even if you kill me right now, you're still stuck here." He spread his arms, gesturing to the vast, endless expanse surrounding them. "Either way, your role in this war is over."

Poseidon's grip on his trident tightened, his jaw clenching. He was an ancient god, one who had ruled the seas for countless eons, one who had laid waste to civilizations without effort. And yet, he could not deny the truth in Quinn's words.

The realization infuriated him.

Power surged around the god of the sea, the very air thrumming with the force of his anger. The stillness of the Realm of Night was shattered as vast waves of water roared into existence, curling and twisting like living creatures, eager to drown Quinn where he stood.

Quinn rolled his neck, loosening his shoulders as Chaos coiled around him in turn, a living abyss that swallowed the light.

He flashed Poseidon a grin.

"Well then," he mused. "Let's see which one of us gets out of here first."

Chapter 49
Hephaestus

The walls of Stormhaven groaned beneath his weight as Hephaestus leaned against the stone, arms crossed over his massive chest as he surveyed the battle below. It was a sight he had seen countless times across the ages—war, bloodshed, the clash of steel, and the cries of the dying.

But this was different. This wasn't a war waged by mortals in their endless struggles for land or pride. No, this was the end of an era, the reckoning of gods and men alike.

The sky had turned to hellfire, thick clouds rolling in hues of crimson and black, casting their twisted light upon the battlefield. Ash and embers floated like dying stars, carried by the furious winds that howled through the broken land.

Lightning split the heavens, its angry fingers clawing at the ground, striking indiscriminately amongst friend and foe alike. The scent of ozone and charred flesh was prevalent in the air, mixed with the iron tang of blood that had turned the earth below into a bog of carnage.

He exhaled through his nose, watching as mortal and immortal clashed in the ruined crater. The mortals were holding their own, but barely. They had their weapons, their clever tricks, and their unbreakable will, but the gods were beings of pure power, and they were dwindling, one by one.

Charis stood beside him, her delicate fingers twisting strands of hair into nervous knots. Her usual grace was gone, replaced by tension coiled tight in her frame. She, too, had watched this war unfold, but where Hephaestus saw a battle to be fought, she saw an outcome to be survived.

"It's done, then," she murmured, breaking the silence between them. "We did what we promised. We gave them weapons, armor, a fighting chance." She turned to him, the flickering light of war casting shadows across her elegant features. "But this? This fight is not ours. We should go."

Hephaestus didn't answer right away. He should have expected this. Charis was wise, practical. She had always been the voice of reason when his heart burned too hot with his convictions. But she also knew him better than any god or mortal ever could.

"I can see it," she continued softly, stepping closer to him. "That look in your eyes. You want to go down there."

Hephaestus huffed, shifting his weight. "Aye," he admitted, his voice rough like crushed gravel. "I do."

Charis sighed, turning back to the battlefield. She didn't argue—not yet, anyway. But she was right to be worried. He wasn't like the others. He had never been one for war, never had a stomach for the cruelty of battle the way Ares had, the way Zeus relished in it. But he had his strength, his resilience, and more than anything, he had his stubborn will.

"If you go down there, you'll die," Charis murmured.

"Aye," he repeated.

She looked at him then, and for the first time in an eternity, she looked afraid, not for herself, but for him. And that nearly broke him more than anything.

He opened his mouth to speak, to offer her some reassurance, but the sound of soft footfalls behind them cut him off. They both turned as a figure stepped from the shadows of the high walls.

Hermes.

Even now, in the middle of this war, he moved with effortless grace, though there was a weariness to him that hadn't been there before. Hephaestus had seen him in countless battles and schemes, always with that same smirk of mischief, as if the whole existence was some game only he knew the rules to. But now, his smirk was nowhere to be seen.

Hephaestus straightened, his lips pulling into a gruff sneer. "Look who finally decided to stop runnin'."

Hermes returned the look, but there was no humor in it. "I figured it was time for a chat."

The three of them stood there for a long moment, no weapons drawn, no hostility. Just gods standing together, neither allies nor enemies.

"You regret it?" Hermes asked finally, his voice quiet. "Betraying Olympus?"

Hephaestus tilted his head, considering the question. "Nah," he said. "Regret would mean I did somethin' wrong."

Hermes let out a sharp breath, somewhere between a laugh and a sigh. "You always were the most stubborn of us."

Hephaestus snorted. "I take that as a compliment."

Silence stretched between them, heavy with sentiments unsaid.

"I should've left, too," Hermes admitted after a long pause. "When he killed Hera… that should've been it. That should've been the line." His jaw tightened, his fingers curling into fists at his sides. "But I stayed. I stayed because—because I was afraid."

It wasn't often that gods admitted their fears. And it was even rarer for Hermes, the ever-smirking trickster, to speak with such raw honesty.

Hephaestus grunted. "Aye. He made sure there was plenty to be afraid of."

Hermes exhaled heavily, nodding. "You were brave. And I wasn't. And now look at me." He laughed bitterly. "Stuck fighting a war I don't believe in. Watching Zeus tear apart everything we built. And for what? His pride? His madness?"

He shook his head. "I don't want to see a world where Zeus wins, Hephaestus. But I don't have it in me to fight for the mortals, either. I'm just tired."

There was something in his tone that made Hephaestus' chest tighten. A finality.

"You don't have to fight," Hephaestus said. "Come with us. You still got a choice."

But Hermes just smiled—small, weary, and sad.

Oath Breaker

"No, I don't," he said. "Not anymore."

And then, before Hephaestus could say another word, Hermes stepped forward, his form flickering, his godly essence humming like a heartbeat. "But I can still do something."

Hephaestus felt the shift in the air before he understood what was happening. The power radiating from Hermes was unraveling, bleeding from his very being.

"I came here to give you something," Hermes said. "A parting gift."

Hephaestus' brow furrowed. "What in Tartarus are you talkin' about?"

Hermes closed his eyes, and the wind around them stilled as if the entire world had paused for a single breath. Then, golden essence began to lift from Hermes' skin, swirling like threads of starlight.

Hephaestus realized what he was doing.

"No," Hephaestus said, shaking his head. "Don't."

But Hermes just smiled, his eyes gleaming with something Hephaestus couldn't quite name—maybe peace, maybe relief.

"You'll need this more than I will," Hermes murmured.

And then, like a breath exhaled into the night, his essence flowed into Hephaestus.

A rush of power flooded his limbs, burning hot, electric. It was Hermes—his speed, his cunning, his presence—melding with Hephaestus' own strength. He staggered back; his hands clenched into fists as the sheer force of it nearly overwhelmed him.

By the time he steadied himself, Hermes was almost gone.

Hephaestus looked up, his throat tightening.

"You fool," he muttered.

Hermes' form flickered, barely holding together. "Takes one to know one."

And then, with a final smirk—a ghost of the mischief he once was—Hermes faded into nothing.

Just like that, he was gone.

Hephaestus stood unmoving, his fists trembling at his sides. Charis stepped closer, resting a hand on his arm, but said nothing.

There was nothing to say.

Hermes, the Messenger of the Gods, the Trickster, the Swift One—was dead. And with his power now running through his veins,

Brian Tripp

Hephaestus knew one thing for certain.
He would make Zeus pay.

Chapter 50
Levy

The battlefield was an afterthought. The world around him blurred into insignificance; the clash of weapons ringing out, the war cries, and the wails of the dying all faded into the background. There was only one thing that mattered now—reaching Zeus.

Levy moved through the chaos like a force of nature, letting weapons glance harmlessly off his skin, feeling the scrape of metal against his arms and the bite of arrows that failed to pierce his flesh. He did not slow, did not pause.

He had long since learned the advantage of his invulnerability, and today, he would wield it with purpose. The mortals and immortals around him were locked in a war for their existence, but the truth was, this war would not be won or lost in the hands of soldiers.

It would be decided here, in the heart of the storm, where the King of the gods watched over the battlefield like a specter of destruction.

Zeus stood tall at the far edge of the battle, a being wreathed in power, his form glowing faintly with static charge. The storm above them roiled in answer to his presence, dark clouds churning like the fury of the cosmos itself. The golden armor that draped his form was cracked in places and blackened at the edges, but the smirk carved onto his face was one of complete, utter control.

He had been waiting for Levy.

That realization struck Levy like a fist to the gut, but it did not deter him. He kept moving forward until he was standing just feet away from the god, his hand tightening on the hilt of his sword.

Zeus exhaled a laugh, shaking his head in amusement. "I must admit, I wondered how long it would take before you came running to me. How poetic, really, that it would be you."

Levy didn't flinch. He didn't entertain the taunt with a response. He had spent too much of his life trying to prove himself with words. He had nothing left to say. His blade was already drawn.

But Zeus, ever the showman, continued.

"You truly think yourself my equal, don't you?" His voice curled around the words, thick with condescension, with something almost akin to disappointment.

"You believe that simply because you crawled from the muck of mortality and bathed in the Styx, you can stand where no man should? That because you were foolish enough to turn on me, you can slay a god?"

Levy's grip tightened. "You want to talk about foolishness? What's foolish is believing you're untouchable. That your power is eternal. But you're wrong, Zeus." He took a step forward, his voice steady, measured. "You've lost more in the last week than you have in a millennia. Your kingdom is falling, your soldiers dying, and your own children turning against you. You're not eternal. You're bleeding."

Zeus' smirk faltered. Just slightly. Just enough to show the flicker of madness behind his eyes.

Then, his hand shot out with impossible speed, catching Levy by the throat.

Or rather, trying to.

The moment his fingers made contact, the magic of the Styx recoiled, lashing out with a searing hiss of divine energy. Zeus snarled, yanking his hand back as golden ichor oozed from the fresh burn now etched into his palm.

A soft, mocking laugh echoed through the air—Styx herself, reveling in his rejection. Levy smiled. "Looks like you can bleed after all."

Thunder cracked violently above them, shaking the ground beneath their feet. Levy braced himself as the storm surged, electricity dancing along Zeus' form like living fire. The god's smirk was gone now, his lips pulling back to bare his teeth.

"I will enjoy watching you die," Zeus seethed, flexing his fingers as the burn on his hand healed instantly, the divine ichor reabsorbing into his body.

"I will break you in ways you cannot fathom. I will reduce your people to dust, your city to ruin, and I will leave your body on display for the few survivors to weep over before I erase them as well."

Levy lifted his chin, staring at him unshaken. "You really don't get it, do you?" His voice was quiet. Steady. Dangerous. "No one fears you anymore. That's why you're losing."

Zeus laughed then, the sound sharp and filled with static. "And you think they fear you?"

Levy shook his head. "No," he said. "I don't want them to."

Zeus scoffed. "Then what is it you want, boy? Power? Recognition? What purpose could possibly drive you to stand before me with such conviction?"

Levy's mind flashed to Mallory—her fire, her stubbornness, the unwavering way she looked at him as if she saw something good beneath all the wreckage. Then, to Quinn and Ashe, the closest things he had to family, who had given him a second chance when he didn't deserve one. To Stormhaven, to the people who had suffered for generations under the weight of the gods' tyranny.

He took a deep breath. "I want to live in a world where no one has to bow to you ever again."

Zeus' eyes flashed, something old and terrible stirring behind them. "Then you are a fool," he whispered.

"Maybe," Levy admitted, rolling his shoulders as he raised his blade once more. "But I'd rather die a fool than serve a coward."

The sky ignited. Lightning struck the battlefield in violent succession, each blast shaking the earth, sending power rippling through the air. The storm had reached its peak, mirroring the storm inside the god before him.

Zeus raised his hands, piercing blue light gathering in his palms, raw and merciless.

Lightning crashed down upon Levy's raised sword, the crackling bolt screaming through the air like the fury of the heavens itself. The instant it connected, a white-hot agony seared through him, his blade acting like a conduit, drawing Zeus' power directly through his body.

The explosion sent him flying backward, his body arching through the air before he crashed into the churned-up mud of the battlefield, the impact jarring his entire frame. His skin smoldered, steam rising from the burns branding his flesh despite his invulnerability. Every nerve in his body screamed, his breath rasping painfully in his chest.

Zeus stood across from him, lightning licking up his arms in wild arcs, his smirk one of absolute certainty. "What did I tell you, boy?" His voice boomed, filled with contempt, with victory. "You may have stolen power from the Styx, but you are still just a mortal. And mortals? They burn."

Levy coughed, the acrid taste of ozone thick on his tongue as he forced himself to move. His arms trembled as he pushed off the ground, his vision hazy from the shock. But even through the pain, he smirked, shaking the sweat from his face as he straightened to his full height.

"Funny," he rasped, rolling his shoulders. "For all your power, you sure do talk a lot. I thought you'd have killed me by now."

Zeus' smirk faltered, a flicker of irritation in his storm-bright eyes.

Levy exhaled as he threw his sword aside, letting it clatter into the mud.

Zeus' gaze flicked to the discarded blade, then back to Levy, a laugh bubbling up from his chest. "Have you finally accepted your fate?"

"No." Levy cracked his knuckles, the raw determination in his eyes blazing as fiercely as the lightning dancing around Zeus. "I just don't need a sword to put you in the dirt."

And then he charged.

The battlefield trembled beneath his feet as he sprinted forward, dodging the crackling lances of lightning Zeus hurled his way. Every hair on his body stood on end, the air so charged with power it felt like it was pressing in on him, trying to crush him. But he didn't falter. Didn't slow.

He had learned the rhythm of the storm.

The moment the static in the air spiked, the instant the pressure shifted—he moved. Ducking, weaving, slipping through the arcs of destruction by inches. Zeus' attacks lit up the world, but Levy kept moving. His entire life had been a battle, a fight for survival, and there was no damn way he was losing this one.

And then—he was in close.

Zeus' expression flickered with surprise, but before he could react, Levy's fist slammed into his ribs.

The effect was instant. The burning power of the Styx surged through the impact, sizzling against divine flesh, tearing through Zeus like acid.

The god roared, staggering back, but Levy didn't stop. He pressed forward, raining blows down with punishing efficiency. Every strike landed with the power of a titan, enhanced by the boiling touch of the Underworld itself.

Zeus' head snapped to the side as Levy's fist drove into his jaw. The god's lip split, golden ichor dripping onto the battlefield. His wrath ignited in an instant.

With a snarl, Zeus retaliated. He moved so fast that even with Levy's reflexes, he barely saw it coming.

A devastating backhand crashed into his chest, sending him flying. Even though it didn't hurt, the sheer force of it knocked the air from his lungs as he was blasted backward, rolling through the mud and wreckage.

Levy groaned as he pushed himself up again, barely in time to dodge the next strike—Zeus, now a blur of divine fury, drove a thunderous knee toward his gut. Levy twisted, narrowly evading the blow, and countered with a brutal uppercut to Zeus' chin, making the god's head snap back with a satisfying crack.

But it wasn't enough.

The moment of triumph lasted only a second before Zeus surged forward, grabbing Levy's face in his massive hand, ignoring the searing burn from the power of the Styx.

The pain was instant and unbearable.

Lightning poured directly into him, his entire body arching and spasming as raw, unfiltered energy seared through his skull. He screamed, the sound strangled as his muscles locked up, his vision white-hot agony.

Zeus' smirk returned, cruel and gloating. "The Styx makes you invulnerable," he mused, watching Levy convulse in his grip, fighting to stay conscious. "But I never needed brute strength to kill you."

His fingers tightened around Levy's face, another pulse of lightning lancing through his body before dropping him back into the mud. The world blurred. Blackness crowded the edges of his vision. Not yet. He couldn't go down yet.

Levy fought to stay conscious, his vision swimming as he struggled against the residual electricity still crackling through his limbs. He pushed himself up onto his elbows, his body aching, every muscle feeling like it had been seared from the inside out. Zeus loomed over him, the jagged bolt of lightning in his grasp sparking and twisting with raw, unbridled power.

"You put up a fight, I'll give you that," Zeus mused, rolling his wrist and letting the lightning twist into something sharper, deadlier. "But this is where it ends."

With a flourish, he reared back, preparing to drive the bolt straight through Levy's chest.

And then his arms jerked violently backward.

Golden threads of light wrapped around Zeus' wrists like unbreakable shackles, pulling taut as they locked his arms in place. His fingers twitched, the lightning bolt flickering wildly before sputtering out entirely. A low snarl rumbled from his throat as he struggled against the force binding him.

Levy exhaled sharply, rolling onto his hands and knees as he fought to regain his footing. He looked up just in time to see Ashe step into view behind Zeus, her fingers splayed, the golden light of Fate wrapped around them like woven fire.

She tilted her head at Levy, her lips quirking into a smirk.

"What part of 'together' is hard for you to understand?"

Despite the battlefield raging around them, despite the searing pain still coursing through his veins, Levy felt a sharp, breathless laugh leave him. He ran a hand through his scorched hair, shaking his head.

Oath Breaker

"Yeah, yeah," he muttered, pushing himself fully to his feet. "You're starting to sound like Quinn."

Ashe rolled her eyes. "That's because he's right."

Zeus let out a furious bellow, his muscles straining against the golden bindings, the storm overhead roiling with his frustration. The air crackled with his rage, pressure building like the moment before a lightning strike.

Levy's fingers flexed, the lingering burn from Zeus' lightning still humming beneath his skin. But he pushed through it, standing tall beside Ashe, his eyes locked onto the furious god before them.

For the first time since the battle began, Zeus looked *truly* enraged.

Levy clenched his fists.

"Let's end this."

Chapter 51
Andra

The wind roared past her ears, sharp and relentless, slicing across her skin like a blade. The world around her was a blur of darkened earth and shadowed peaks, the jagged outlines of the mountains shrinking behind her with every passing second. She was moving fast—faster than anything humanly possible—but it still wasn't fast enough.

Faster.

The word tore from her lips in a desperate whisper, barely audible over the howling wind, over the deafening drumbeat of her own heart slamming against her ribs. Even from this distance, she could see the monstrous storm gathered over Stormhaven, a swirling abyss of thunder and wrath that bled across the heavens, smothering the stars.

Beneath it, the battlefield stretched out like a writhing beast, a chaos of shifting bodies, flashing steel, and dying screams. The air itself seemed thick with death, a living thing that hung over the land like a vulture waiting to feast.

Faster.

Andra clenched her jaw, her fingers digging into the rough straps at her sides, knuckles white with strain. The muscles in her legs burned, her core tight with the effort of holding steady, but she refused to slow. She couldn't.

Somewhere down there, amidst the carnage and ruin, her friends were fighting for their lives. Quinn. Mallory. Levy. Ashe. Lend. Kael. Avery. The people she had bled beside, laughed beside, built a future beside.

A future that would be nothing more than a scorched ruin if she didn't make it in time.

A fresh gust of wind slammed against her, sending her hair whipping around her face, and she hissed between clenched teeth. Below, rolling hills flattened into ruined plains, the ground charred and torn apart by divine power.

The scent of smoke, of burnt flesh and blood, mingled in the air, carried up toward her by the relentless storm. It burned the inside of her nose, a grim reminder that the battle had already raged on for too long.

Too many had died.

She would not let her friends be among them.

She tilted forward, urging herself onward, feeling the rush of speed, the sheer force of her movement pressing her body downward. Her breath came in quick, shallow pants, her lungs burning as she pushed harder.

Faster.

She could make out the figures now—tiny in the distance like ants swarming over an anthill. But they weren't ants. They were soldiers, warriors, men, and women she had trained beside. Friends, family, brothers, and sisters in arms. And between them all, titanic figures stood out—beacons of power, their auras seething, burning brighter than the lightning flashing overhead.

The Olympians.

Andra swallowed hard, her throat dry. Even from here, she could feel the sheer force of their presence.

Zeus was a living storm at the center of it all, raw, unchained devastation rippling outward from him in waves. Apollo gleamed like a golden sun amidst the carnage, his arrows slicing through the darkness like streaks of fire.

Demeter's roots twisted through the battlefield, ensnaring and strangling nature itself, turning against the mortals who dared stand against the gods. Dionysus was a phantom of madness, his influence slithering through the ranks, twisting minds into a violent, rabid frenzy.

It was too much.

She knew it the moment she saw it, the moment she truly *felt* the weight of their power from so far away. The mortals were holding the line, but barely. They were breaking. And if they broke, there would be nothing left.

She gritted her teeth, shifting her grip, the muscles in her arms locking as she braced herself. The wind whipped against her, but she no longer felt the cold. No longer felt the ache of exhaustion creeping into her bones. All she could hear was the battle below.

All she could see was the storm of destruction that raged over the city she called home.

She would make it.

She had to.

Faster.

Chapter 52
Cyrus

The battlefield churned around them, an orchestra of violence played in discordant tones. The air reeked of blood and burning ichor, the ground slick with the aftermath of man. But amidst the cacophony of war, three figures cut their way toward a singular goal—Apollo.

The Sun God stood atop a mound of fallen warriors, his golden form radiant even beneath the oppressive storm overhead. His bow was already raised, a gleaming arrow of pure solar fire nocked and drawn, poised like a predator waiting to strike.

Cyrus smirked. Oh, this would be fun.

The first arrow came like a comet, splitting through the rain and ruin with terrifying speed. But Cyrus was ready. With a flick of his wrist, he spun his scythe into motion, the blade a blinding blur as it caught the projectile, redirecting it harmlessly into the mud.

Another followed, then another, each more furious than the last, until Cyrus moved like a storm himself, his scythe a violent whirlwind that sent Apollo's wrath careening into the dirt.

Apollo's eyes narrowed, and his rage darkened the battlefield. "You dare wield that power against me?" his voice boomed, shaking the very ground beneath them.

"Oh, I don't just wield it," Cyrus grinned, his scarred lips stretching into something wolfish, something primal. "I drink it. I savor it."

Apollo's hands trembled, not with fear, but with unbridled fury as recognition settled in. Cyrus saw the moment the god pieced it together—the moment his mind flashed back to that day in the ruined halls of Olympus when he had accused Cyrus of slaying his sister, Artemis.

Cyrus held out his arms, daring him to shoot. "Go on, then. You were so certain before, weren't you?" His voice was silk and poison, wrapping around the Sun God like a noose. "Say it."

The golden light of Apollo's arrows trembled upon his bowstring; his fury barely leashed.

"It *was* you." His words were venom, spat through clenched teeth.

Cyrus bared his teeth in a cruel, delighted grin. "Oh, the gurgling noise she made as my scythe pierced her and she choked on her own ichor was *music* to my ears."

Apollo loosed the arrow with a scream of pure hatred, but Cyrus was already moving. The shot seared the air where he had just stood, but he spun effortlessly, his boots skidding against the blood-slicked earth.

The Sun God prepared another arrow, but before he could fire, two mortal figures struck from his blind spot.

Avery and Lend.

They moved as one, Lend's weapon flashing like quicksilver while Avery's blade aimed for the god's ribs. Their timing was perfect, a strike Apollo hadn't been prepared for.

Except he *was*.

With infuriating ease, Apollo twisted, catching Avery's blade with his forearm while ducking under Lend's swing. With one savage strike, he sent both of them sprawling into the mud.

Cyrus sighed dramatically, tilting his head as he approached. "Tsk, tsk. Did you really think you could sneak up on an Olympian?" He clicked his tongue, stepping on Avery's groaning form. "You should know better."

Lend pushed himself up on shaking arms, his breath ragged, eyes dark with fury and something colder—understanding. "We were fools to trust you."

Cyrus chuckled, amused by the sheer audacity of these men. "Yes, little soldier," he mused, his grip tightening around his scythe. "You were."

Without further warning, he lashed out.

A wave of concentrated essence exploded from him, slamming into Lend and Avery like a hurricane, sending them tumbling across the battlefield. They landed with dull, lifeless thuds, unmoving.

Cyrus didn't bother watching them die, unconscious and trampled beneath the armies fighting around them. He had a more interesting plaything to entertain.

When he turned back, Apollo was already upon him.

The god struck with the force of a dying star, his golden bow transforming into a radiant spear, burning white-hot as he lunged. Cyrus barely ducked in time, the tip of the weapon slicing through the air just inches from his throat.

Apollo was faster than expected.

Good.

Cyrus countered with a wide, sweeping arc of his scythe, forcing Apollo back as sparks erupted where divine weapons clashed. The god's expression was twisted with fury, but there was something else beneath it—something raw.

Grief.

He was fighting like a man with nothing left to lose.

Cyrus relished every second of it. He danced through Apollo's attacks with a cruel elegance, his movements effortless as if the battle were merely another amusement for him. The Sun God's rage burned, his spear striking with divine precision, but no matter how fast, how powerful he was, he could not land a killing blow.

Cyrus was toying with him.

"Is that the best you can do?" Cyrus taunted, sidestepping another lethal thrust. "No wonder Artemis died so easily."

Apollo roared and lunged; his spear aimed for Cyrus' heart.

Cyrus twisted with divine grace, stepping behind the god in one fluid motion. And in the next breath, his scythe was looped around Apollo's throat, its wicked curve pressing into golden skin.

Apollo froze, his breath sharp.

Cyrus leaned in, whispering against his ear. "Ah, that's right.

This is how I killed your sister."

Apollo's eyes widened.

Cyrus smiled, and with one merciless pull of the blade, the Sun God's head was severed from his body.

For a moment, silence stretched across the battlefield. Then, Apollo's decapitated form collapsed to the ground, golden ichor spilling like molten sunlight into the mud.

Cyrus tilted his head, watching the ichor pool with mild interest. Then, as if taking a slow sip of fine wine, he inhaled deeply, his body shuddering as the god's essence surged into him.

Power.

Pure, raw, *divine* power.

He exhaled, his eyes flashing with something ancient, something insatiable.

Apollo was no more.

And Cyrus was just getting started.

Oath Breaker

Chapter 53
Kael

The battlefield had become an unrecognizable hellscape of twisting roots and blood-soaked mud. Kael's boots sank with every step, the earth feeling like it was trying to swallow him whole. The air was thick with the scent of damp soil and something sickly sweet—rotting vegetation, decay mingled with the sharp tang of ichor and human blood.

Screams of dying soldiers cut through the storm-laden sky, and the metallic clang of swords and shields rang like a discordant battle hymn. But above it all, weaving through the chaos like an unseen force, was the whisper of something ancient, something alive.

Nature itself had turned against them.

Kael's eyes locked onto the goddess standing amidst the carnage. Demeter.

She was eerily still. Unlike the other Olympians, who roared into battle with divine fury, she barely moved. There was no frantic energy, no flicker of emotion—just a quiet, knowing patience, as if she were watching the inevitable unfold.

Her golden-green robes billowed slightly in the unnatural wind that had swept through the crater, her hands clasped before her as she observed the chaos around her with the cool indifference of an empress surveying her domain. But it wasn't the goddess herself that terrified Kael—it was what moved beneath her feet.

Thick, gnarled roots slithered through the mud like serpents, coiling around the legs of fallen soldiers, dragging the screaming wounded beneath the surface. Vines lashed out like whips, snapping bones and cutting through armor with ease. Where her gaze lingered, the ground churned, and the earth itself seemed to pulse like a living, breathing entity.

She did not need to fight. She was nature itself, and nature was fighting for her.

A scream to his left snapped Kael back into action. A Stormhaven soldier—young, barely more than a boy—was caught in the snare of Demeter's vines, his face contorted in terror as they coiled around his throat.

Kael didn't hesitate. He spun on his heel and slashed downward, severing the tendrils in one clean stroke of his kopesh. The soldier gasped, stumbling away as Kael shoved him toward the safety of their ranks.

"MOVE!" Kael barked. There was no time to check if the boy had heeded his warning.

He turned back to the fight, locking eyes with Mallory. She was already moving.

With the kind of ruthless efficiency that had made her one of the deadliest warriors in Stormhaven, Mallory cut her way through the battlefield, her sword flashing in the dim red light. She was relentless, her movements fluid as she hacked through Demeter's immortal guards.

Each kill was precise calculated—she wasted no energy, no effort. And yet, despite her skill, despite the ichor she spilled, it was like carving through an endless tide. The immortals were too many, their numbers seemingly endless.

"We need to break through!" she shouted over the chaos, parrying a strike before driving her sword into the chest of her opponent.

Kael gritted his teeth and pushed forward, slashing through anything in his way. "Then let's make a path."

They fought their way toward Demeter, carving through her defenders in tandem, moving like two halves of a whole. The weight of the battle pressed down on them, but they didn't stop. Couldn't stop. Every second wasted was another second their people were being slaughtered.

Kael's blade met an immortal's throat, cutting clean through flesh, and as the body fell, he saw his opening—Demeter, standing at the center of the storm, still unmoving, still watching.

Mallory was already there, her sword poised to strike.

They lunged together, weapons flashing—

And then Demeter raised her hand, and the world **exploded**.

A massive tree erupted from the earth, splitting the ground apart like a wound tearing open. The force of it was a hurricane, a shockwave that sent Kael flying. His body twisted midair before he slammed hard into something unyielding—a fallen soldier, no doubt, but the impact was enough to knock the breath from his lungs.

He tumbled, skidding through the mud, branches, and debris crashing down around him. The metallic taste of blood filled his mouth as he groaned, forcing himself onto his hands and knees.

Mallory lay sprawled a few feet away, coughing, pushing herself up as splintered wood and shattered bark rained down around them.

Kael shook his head, dazed, his vision swimming. His entire body ached, but he ignored it. Through the haze of dust and debris, he could still see her—Demeter, standing amidst the destruction she had wrought, untouched, unbothered. Watching them.

Kael exhaled slowly, his fingers tightening around the hilt of his sword as he took in the horrifying sight before them. The battlefield had already been a graveyard of the fallen, but now it had become something worse—a feeding ground for Demeter's monstrous creation.

The massive tree loomed over them, its twisted trunk pulsating as though alive, roots slithering through the blood-soaked earth-like veins feeding into a hungry beast. From its gnarled branches, thick vines lashed out, wrapping around the necks of nearby soldiers and hoisting them into the air.

Screams of agony filled the air, gurgling and choking before they cut off with sickening cracks as necks snapped like brittle twigs. Others struggled in vain as the vines tightened, their faces turning shades of blue and purple, feet kicking uselessly against the empty air.

Mallory let out a slow breath beside him, her shoulders tensing.

"How do you suppose we deal with that?" Kael asked, his voice low, though he already knew there was no easy answer.

"Pray to Demeter?" Mallory replied, her lips twisting into a grim smirk.

Kael shot her a sideways glance. He knew that look. It wasn't amusement—far from it. She was holding back the same creeping despair that was crawling up his own spine, using humor as a shield against it.

He almost snorted. It was ridiculous, wasn't it? That they could stand in the middle of a battlefield, watching their people be slaughtered by a goddess and her nightmarish creations, and still find a way to joke.

Maybe they were all a little mad.

"Okay, but seriously?" he asked, the question hanging between them like the weight of inevitability.

Mallory's smirk faded. She looked at him, her expression momentarily raw, stripped of bravado. She hesitated—not out of uncertainty, but because she knew the answer and hated saying it out loud.

"The only way we know how to deal with these things," she finally admitted. "Keep attacking them head-on until they break."

"Or until we do," Kael added quietly.

Mallory gave him a curt nod.

"To the end then," Kael said, meeting her gaze.

"To the end."

They sprinted forward as one, weaving through the battlefield, blades raised and bodies braced for whatever hell awaited them.

Demeter's gaze shifted at last, her expression impassive, almost bored. She lifted a hand.

The earth trembled beneath their feet. Roots exploded upward, twisting through the air like serpents poised to strike. The battlefield around them churned and groaned, nature itself shifting to swallow them whole.

Kael didn't hesitate. He let out a battle cry, raising his kopesh.

Mallory did the same, her sword flashing in the storm light.

Together, they charged.

Chapter 54
Sen

Sen marched beside Nes, the two spectral brothers leading the warriors of Elysium toward their next fight. Their ghostly forms flickered, a sickly green sheen rolling over them as they moved in unison with the mortal army.

Ahead of them, the battlefield stretched on, vast and unrelenting. Dionysus' madness had already begun to seep into the minds of the warriors on the front line, his influence curling through the air like an intoxicating vapor.

In the distance, Sen could hear the laughter—hysterical, broken, the kind that came right before a scream. It was a sound he'd heard far too often in war. He gritted his teeth, forcing his mind away from it.

"How are you holding up?" Nes asked, his voice cutting through the storm in Sen's head.

Sen scoffed, but there was no real humor in it. "What does it matter how I'm holding up?" he said. "I'm already dead."

Nes didn't look at him right away. Instead, he kept his eyes forward, his expression unreadable.

"Just because you're dead doesn't mean you have no choice but to be okay," he finally said. "We may not be facing extermination like the living, but we still have eternity to live with our thoughts. And with our regrets."

Sen faltered for half a step before recovering. He turned his head, studying Nes through the shifting, unnatural glow of their ghostly forms. It was a familiar face, identical to his own, yet something about it looked older—weathered in a way that even death couldn't erase.

A sad smile pulled at Sen's lips. "Sometimes I forget we're twins, and you're not just my older brother."

Nes gave a quiet chuckle, though there was something heavy in it, something that clung to the air between them like an unspoken truth.

Sen exhaled, rolling his shoulders as if that could shake the weight pressing against his chest. "Look, Nes. You're right. And if we win this war, I'll have eternity to reflect on those words."

His voice softened, the sarcasm draining out of it like sand slipping through his fingers. "You want the truth? I'm bitter. I'm so fucking bitter that I died. That I left everyone to fend for themselves. That I wasn't there when you needed me."

Nes finally turned to him, his eyes searching, listening, and for once, Sen let himself speak the words he never had.

"I hate that you had to face what you did without me at your side. I hate that Quinn had to go up against a primordial bastard alone.

"I hate that our people got dragged into this gods-damned war, and I wasn't here to fight beside them." He clenched his fists, his spectral form flickering as if even his essence couldn't hold back the emotion storming inside him.

Sen huffed out a bitter laugh. "So yeah, I have the rest of eternity to wallow in my own self-pity when this is over. But right now?"

He shook his head, swallowing down the sharp, aching lump in his throat. "Right now, I've been given a second chance to make a difference. And if the only thing I can do is keep them smiling, make them laugh in the face of all this shit, then I'm going to do it. Because as happy as I am to see them again, the last thing I want is for them to join us down below before it's their time."

His voice had grown hoarse, thick with emotion he hadn't

meant to let slip. He sucked in a breath, forcing it all back down.

Silence stretched between them. Nes' expression was unreadable again, his shoulders tense, his lips slightly parted as if trying to find the right words.

Then, to Sen's absolute horror, his brother's eyes glistened.

Sen groaned, throwing up his hands. "How the hell is it possible for a ghost to have tears?"

That finally earned him a real chuckle from Nes, who wiped at his eyes in amusement despite the sorrow still lingering in them.

When he spoke again, his voice was steadier. "Then let's make sure our friends make it through this so they can live long, happy lives for all of us."

Sen stared at him for a moment before rolling his shoulders and forcing a grin. "Damn right."

And with that, they turned forward, marching onward into the chaos ahead.

~~~

The warriors of Elysium crashed onto the battlefield like a wave of pale fire, spectral blades gleaming under the blood-red storm clouds. They advanced with chilling precision, forming a barrier between the retreating mortals and the Olympian threat. Sen moved swiftly, his eyes locked onto their target—Dionysus.

The god of madness was a spectacle of chaos, his bare feet kicking up blood-soaked mud as he twirled through the carnage. His wild, unkempt curls bounced with every exaggerated movement; his painted lips stretched into a manic grin.

Mortal soldiers collapsed around him, shrieking and clutching their heads as his invisible tendrils of madness seeped into their minds, twisting their thoughts until they saw only enemies where allies once stood.

"This guy is nuttier than I am," Sen muttered under his breath, shaking his head in something close to amusement.

Beside him, Nes shot him a side glance, unimpressed. "And that's saying something."

Sen pulled a mockingly exaggerated face at his twin.

"Warriors of Elysium, get in front of the mortals and stop Dionysus from following!" Nes barked. The specters surged forward at his command, forming an immovable wall between the retreating humans and the raging god.

Dionysus let out a wail of protest, stamping his foot like a petulant child. "NO, NO, NO!"

His voice rang through the battlefield, high-pitched and eerily melodic. His arms flailed wildly as he spun in circles. "You took away my toys! Now, what am I supposed to play with?"

Dionysus, seeing his fun slipping away, suddenly dropped to his hands, tucking his knees to his chest and rolling forward in an erratic somersault, his shrieking laughter echoing over the battlefield.

Sen blinked. "He's really committing to the bit."

Nes let out a breath through his nose. "You seem to have a lot in common."

Sen grinned. "Har har."

Dionysus skidded to a halt in front of them, tilting his head so sharply it was a wonder his neck didn't snap. His eyes—wide, dilated, and shimmering with a strange violet glow—locked onto them with unfiltered glee.

"Ohhh, you're different! You are like little flickering candles, still burning even after someone tried to snuff you out." He clapped his hands together, his nails digging into his own palms hard enough to draw golden ichor. \

"Do you think you can make me feel something? I would like to see you try."

"I can make you feel dead," Sen offered helpfully, brandishing his weapon. "How's that?"

Dionysus threw his head back and howled with laughter, a sound that twisted and warbled like the echoes of a thousand voices layered over one another. Then, without warning, he lunged.

Dionysus was a blur, his form twisting unnaturally as he closed the gap between them. Sen barely had time to raise his sword before the god was in his space, a clawed hand swiping toward his throat. He twisted away at the last second, but the air where Dionysus' fingers had passed shimmered with violet energy, distorting reality for a fraction of a second.

Nes wasn't as lucky. He had gone for a downward strike, attempting to cleave Dionysus in half, but the god *wasn't there*—he had bent his body at an impossible angle, contorting out of the path of the axe, and before Nes could recover, Dionysus' fist slammed into his stomach.

Nes was sent flying backward, his ghostly form flickering as he crashed into the mud. Sen immediately leaped into action, swinging his sword in a tight arc.

Dionysus bent backward like a marionette with its strings cut, the blade whistling just above his face. His head snapped back up instantly, his grin splitting wider. "Oooh, you almost got me! That was fun!"

"Glad you're enjoying yourself." Sen flipped his grip on his sword and lunged again.

This time, Nes was back on his feet, charging from the side to catch the god off guard. They moved in sync, a twin assault of sharp steel and relentless strikes. Dionysus ducked, twisted, rolled, his movements erratic and unpredictable.

But for all his playfulness, his counters were precise. His fingers curled into claws, slashing at their ethereal bodies, raking through them with a burn of essence-draining magic.

Sen gritted his teeth as pain lanced through his ribs. Even though he was already dead, the wounds still hurt. Nes wasn't faring much better, though he was managing to keep Dionysus occupied long enough for Sen to get a better read on him.

They weren't going to win this alone.

"Nes," Sen grunted, dodging a strike aimed at his head. "We need to move him."

Nes deflected an incoming blow with his axe. "Where?"

"Toward Demeter," Sen said. "We're not taking him down alone, but Kael and Mallory are hopefully handling her. If we get him over there, we might stand a chance."

Nes hesitated for only a second before nodding. "Alright. Lead the way."

Sen turned back to Dionysus, flashing a wide grin. "Hey, Wine Boy! How about you chase me instead?"

Dionysus blinked. "Chase you?"

"Yeah, you look like you've got energy to burn. Let's make this a game. If you can catch me before I make it to my friends," Sen waggled his brows, "I'll let you keep playing with me all you want."

Brian Tripp

Dionysus clapped his hands in delight. "Ohhh, I *love* games!"

Without another word, Sen bolted.

Dionysus shrieked with laughter and bounded after him, his movements exaggerated and wild. Nes followed close behind, watching his brother's back as they weaved through the battlefield, slashing at immortals who got in their way.

Sen could feel the god's breath at his nape, could hear his delighted giggles turning to shrill excitement. "Run, run, little candle! Let's see how long you burn before I snuff you out!"

Sen clenched his teeth, his focus dead-set on one thing: Get him to Demeter.

Because this was a fight they couldn't win alone.

Oath Breaker

Chapter 55
Quinn

The storm raged in violent tandem with their battle. Waves of darkness and torrents of seawater crashed against each other in the Realm of Night as if the world itself recoiled from the clash of titanic wills. Poseidon's bellowing war cries were lost beneath the howling wind, but Quinn could see the pure rage in the god's expression as he lashed out with his trident, determined to rip him apart.

Quinn ducked beneath the prongs, shadows swirling around him as he narrowly avoided the strike. The ground beneath his feet trembled with Poseidon's might, the damp earth cracking and giving way to a churning sea of abyssal water. Quinn leaped back, his body twisting through the air as a spear of solidified water shot up where he had just been standing, sharp enough to impale.

Poseidon's ocean surged, responding to its master's fury, and Quinn had mere seconds to react as a monstrous wave rose behind the god, forming the shape of a great sea serpent. The liquid beast lunged; its jaws open wide to consume him whole.

Quinn's body flickered into shadow, melting into the darkness and reappearing high above the battlefield. The wave crashed where he had been standing, obliterating a portion of the landscape, water steaming as it licked against the unnatural essence of the Realm of

Brian Tripp

Night.

Poseidon snarled in frustration, whirling to track Quinn's movements. "You fight like a rat in the dark," he spat, his voice a rolling thunder, his torso dripping with golden ichor from the wound Quinn had already carved across his chest.

Quinn smirked despite himself. "And yet, this rat has drawn first blood."

Poseidon roared in answer, thrusting his trident forward. From its three prongs, a cascade of razor-thin water blades burst forth, cutting the space between them into deadly ribbons. Quinn twisted midair, shadows coiling around him as he bent the darkness to his will, letting it absorb the attacks before he dropped to the ground once more. The moment his boots hit solid earth, he sprinted forward, blade flashing in his hand as he aimed straight for the god's throat.

Poseidon barely dodged in time. The tip of Quinn's blade nicked his jaw, drawing another streak of golden ichor. Snarling, the god retaliated, swinging his trident in a brutal arc. Quinn raised his sword to block, but the force of the impact sent a shudder down his arms. A fraction of a second later, Poseidon twisted the weapon and drove the shaft into Quinn's side, knocking the wind from his lungs.

Before Quinn could recover, Poseidon moved with supernatural speed, spinning the trident and slashing the prongs across Quinn's shoulder.

Pain ignited in his arm. He staggered back, blood spilling down his armor in rivulets. The wound wasn't deep, but it was a warning—a reminder that he wasn't fighting some lesser god. This was Poseidon, the Earth-Shaker, the master of seas and storms.

And Quinn was still holding back.

He exhaled, his breath ragged as he clenched his sword tighter, willing the pain to become fuel. The swirling storm around them reflected the battle raging inside his mind. For so long, he had feared the full depths of Chaos' power, terrified of what it could turn him into, of the path it might drag him down. He had fought to control it, to master it, but never to truly wield it.

That hesitation had cost him before. He wouldn't let it cost him now.

Quinn lifted his head, locking eyes with Poseidon.

Oath Breaker

It was time.

A slow breath. Then another. He closed his eyes, reaching inward—past the fear, past the restraint—until he found the core of Chaos burning within him.

And then, he let go.

The effect was instant.

A pulse of energy exploded outward from his body, a shattering wave of primordial essence. The air warped around him, black tendrils of raw power seeping from his skin, his once-human form now wrapped in a violent aura of unfathomable depth. His eyes, once crimson, darkened to an abyssal void, the swirling cosmos of the Realm of Night reflecting in their depths.

The ground beneath his feet cracked and split apart, shadows pouring from the fissures as if the world itself was unraveling around him. The ever-present glow of the Realm of Night dimmed, the distant swirls of blue and violet overtaken by streaks of black and crimson.

Poseidon took a step back.

For the first time, Quinn saw something flicker across the god's face—hesitation.

But Quinn wasn't done.

The darkness around him writhed, and when he stepped forward, it moved with him. The Realm of Night bent to his will. He could feel it now—no longer an untamed force but something he could shape, command. He was no longer bound by the limitations of mortal flesh.

He was Chaos.

He lifted his hand, and with a mere thought, the very air warped, space distorting around Poseidon's frame. A crushing force struck the god, sending him stumbling backward as gravity itself shifted beneath him.

Poseidon snarled, adjusting with the instincts of an immortal warrior, but Quinn was already moving. He blurred forward, faster than even the god could track, appearing directly at his side. His blade, now wreathed in raw Chaos, cleaved toward Poseidon's chest.

The god barely managed to block, his trident intercepting the strike at the last second. But the moment their weapons clashed, a shockwave of energy erupted between them, hurling Poseidon back several feet.

Quinn didn't give him a moment to recover.

He raised his free hand and clenched his fist. The shadows at Poseidon's feet surged upward like living tendrils, grabbing onto the god's limbs, wrapping around his arms and torso like a vice.

Poseidon thrashed, his muscles bulging as he fought against the restraints, his golden ichor gleaming under the ethereal glow of the Realm of Night.

Quinn stepped forward, his voice as cold and unrelenting as the abyss itself. "You called me a rat in the dark," he said, his voice laced with the power of Chaos. "So let me show you what lurks in the darkness."

He tightened his grip.

The tendrils yanked Poseidon down, slamming him into the cracked ground with enough force to leave a small crater. The god let out a grunt, his trident knocked from his grasp, the weapon rolling away into the shadows. Quinn loomed over him, his blade glinting with dark energy.

Poseidon wiped his mouth, his fingers coming away streaked with ichor, the golden liquid glimmering even in the dim, swirling half-light of the Realm of Night.

His oceanic eyes, turbulent as a raging sea, locked onto Quinn with a mixture of wariness and something dangerously close to amusement.

"So," the god murmured, rolling his shoulders as if shaking off the sting of the wound. "The mortal finally bares his fangs."

Quinn remained silent, his grip tightening around his sword. The dark energy licking up the blade pulsed in rhythm with his heartbeat, a steady, thrumming power that vibrated through his very bones.

The part of him that had always feared Chaos' influence—the part that worried he might become something uncontrollable, something monstrous—had gone silent. He had spent so long fighting against the current, against the power that had been gifted—or cursed—upon him.

But now? Now, he let it in.

And it felt *right*.

Oath Breaker

Poseidon's lips curled in amusement, mist swirling at his feet, tendrils of seafoam rising in lazy, sinuous spirals. "You think you're stronger than me?" The humor in his voice was deceptive. A heartbeat later, the entire world around them *shifted.*

A tidal force crashed into Quinn from nowhere, slamming into him with the weight of an ocean. It sent him flying, tumbling end over end through the airless void before he managed to right himself, slamming his blade into the ground to stop his momentum. He landed in a crouch, the cracked earth beneath him trembling under the weight of Poseidon's power.

Quinn spat blood, his body aching from the force of the strike, but his grin was razor-sharp.

"You're gonna have to do better than that," he taunted, flicking his sword in a sharp, deliberate motion, sending a crackling arc of black lightning splitting toward the god.

Poseidon merely lifted his hand, water rising from the ground in a towering wall to absorb the strike. The impact sent a shockwave rolling through the realm, the force of it tearing apart the ground beneath them. But the god stood firm, lowering his hand slowly, regarding Quinn as though reevaluating him.

Quinn straightened, rolling his neck. "What's wrong, old man? Thought you were supposed to be a warrior."

Poseidon's expression darkened. "You've got a sharp tongue for a mortal."

Quinn exhaled sharply, his breath curling into the air, tinted with energy. "I've got more than that."

Without warning, he *moved.*

One second, he was standing still; the next, he was upon Poseidon, his sword a black blur as he struck. The god barely had time to react, raising his trident in a desperate block. The force of the impact sent ripples through the air, warping the space around them. Chaos crashed against divinity, neither force willing to yield.

Poseidon snarled, thrusting his hand forward. Water erupted like a geyser, an unrelenting force that sought to drown Quinn in its grasp. But Quinn was faster.

His body flickered—once, twice—like a shadow cast by a dying flame, and then he was behind Poseidon, his blade arcing toward the god's exposed back.

Brian Tripp

At the last second, Poseidon twisted, sweeping his trident upward to deflect the strike. Quinn felt the jarring impact travel up his arms, but he used the momentum to pivot, dragging his sword along the god's weapon, sending sparks of dark energy cascading through the void.

Poseidon was strong. *Too strong.*

But Quinn wasn't afraid.

He had been strong before, had fought and survived battles no mortal should have. But this—this was different. He wasn't surviving anymore.

He was *winning.*

Poseidon seemed to realize it too. His expression twisted into something like frustration, his form flickering as though he was struggling to maintain control of his own dominion. "You—" he started, but Quinn cut him off.

"No more speeches," he growled, lunging forward again, the black energy around him growing more intense.

Their weapons clashed again, ringing through the Realm of Night like a war drum.

This time, Quinn did not yield.

Oath Breaker

Chapter 56
Mallory

The air was thick with the scent of damp earth and decay. The battlefield was alive—*too alive.* Mallory swung her blade in a wide arc, slicing through the endless vines and roots grasping at her limbs.

She could hear Kael behind her, his sword cutting through the unnatural growths with sharp, precise movements, their backs pressed together. It was the only way to keep from getting separated, from being devoured by the relentless forest Demeter had summoned.

She tightened her grip on her sword, the leather of the hilt slick with sweat and ichor. The roots beneath her feet pulsed, shifting, trying to throw them off balance. Every step felt precarious as if she were walking on the back of some great beast slumbering beneath the surface.

"Kael," she gritted out, ducking under a mass of thorned branches lashing toward her face. "This is getting worse."

"Yeah, no shit," Kael responded, cleaving a root thicker than a man's arm in half, only for another to sprout in its place. "We're not getting anywhere at this rate."

"Incoming!"

Sen's voice rang out across the battlefield like a warning bell, and Mallory's stomach dropped.

Dionysus stumbled into the fray, his once-pristine robes now torn and soaked with his own ichor. Wounds crisscrossed his body—deep, jagged gashes that leaked gold, the evidence of his dance with Nes and Sen. Despite his wounds, his face was alight with a feverish grin, his wild eyes darting between them all with gleeful madness.

Behind him, Nes and Sen emerged, their ghostly forms flickering, their once-solid edges blurred and hazy. They looked... *damaged.* Ectoplasm seeped from their wounds, staining the air with a faint shimmer, proof that even in death, pain could still find them.

Dionysus staggered toward Demeter as if a petulant child running to his mother. He collapsed into her arms, his fingers curling into the fabric of her gown as he let out a miserable, theatrical sob.

"What have they done to you, my sweet boy?" Demeter's voice was gentle, almost matronly, as she cradled his head, stroking his hair as he whimpered against her.

"They *hurt* me," Dionysus sniffled, burying his face into her shoulder like a wounded child. "They *ruined* the game. They didn't *play fair.*"

His voice was thick with emotion, his sobs exaggerated, as if performing for an unseen audience.

Mallory's stomach twisted. *Gods, he's deranged.*

Demeter pressed a kiss to Dionysus' forehead, her expression unreadable. Then, her golden eyes flickered with something cold, something ancient.

"Then we will punish them together."

The moment the words left her lips, Dionysus stilled in her arms, his sobs cutting off mid-breath. Slowly, his trembling body relaxed, his fingers uncurling from where they had clutched her. Then, ever so slowly, he lifted his head from her shoulder.

His lips stretched into an impossibly wide grin, his teeth flashing in the eerie green light filtering through the cursed canopy.

"Yes," he whispered, his voice trembling with anticipation, with hunger.

His fingers curled around the bark of the great tree Demeter had summoned, and she did the same, their hands sinking into the gnarled wood up to their elbows.

Oath Breaker

And then, the world *shifted*.

The battlefield lurched beneath them, and suddenly, the ground was not just earth—it was something else. Something *alive*. It pulsed and writhed like a great, slumbering beast stirring from its ancient rest. The air around them thickened, twisting and shimmering with Dionysus' maddening energy.

The forest moved.

Not like before—not just vines and roots.

The trees *breathed*. Their trunks twisted unnaturally as though possessed by unseen hands. Faces stretched across the bark, their wooden eyes hollow, their mouths twisted open in silent, eternal screams. The ground itself groaned, shifting beneath them like a living thing, the soil heaving like the chest of someone breathing.

And suddenly, Mallory felt trapped.

She wrenched her sword upward, aiming for one of the thick, thrashing roots—but as her blade connected, the wood *screamed*. A chorus of agonized, inhuman wails filled the air, vibrating through her skull like a thousand voices crying out at once.

Her heart slammed against her ribs as she staggered back, her fingers tightening on the hilt of her sword.

"Gods above," Kael breathed, eyes wide. "They're alive."

Mallory barely had time to register his words before the ground itself lunged at them.

Roots shot up from below, not grabbing—but clawing. Long, gnarled fingers burst from the mud, skeletal hands made of bark and thorns, reaching, grasping, *hungry*.

A thick vine lashed around her wrist, yanking her forward, her feet slipping in the blood-soaked muck. Her sword was wrenched from her grasp as another root coiled around her waist, tightening like a vice, squeezing the air from her lungs.

She struggled, twisting, her vision swimming as the grip tightened.

"Mallory!" Kael shouted, but he was just as trapped, his legs wrapped in tangled vines, his body slowly being dragged toward the waiting maw of the tree's gnarled trunk.

She fought, clawing at the vines constricting her chest, but the more she struggled, the tighter they became. Her breath came in short, desperate gasps, her vision darkening at the edges.

And then, a voice, soft and smooth as silk, barely more than a whisper.

"Shhh," Demeter crooned.

The forest closed in around them.

Mallory gasped as the branches above engulfed her, the roots below dragging her down. The skeletal hands of bark and thorn dug into her skin, pulling, pulling, pulling her into the waiting, devouring dark.

She could barely see Kael anymore. The light was gone.

Dionysus' laughter rang through the air, a fractured, echoing racket—one voice, a thousand voices, an entire forest laughing at her suffering.

The weight of it was unbearable. The world was suffocating her.

This was it.

They had lost.

Oath Breaker

Chapter 57
Mallory

The battlefield trembled beneath the weight of a new force—primal, ancient, and utterly unstoppable. Mallory barely had time to process what was happening before the illusion around her snapped, shattering like fragile glass. The suffocating darkness peeled away, retreating into nothingness, and for the first time since the fight began, she could breathe deeply again.

The massive roots and vines cocooning her crumbled into nothing more than brittle husks. Their sickly green glow extinguished in an instant.

The twisted, writhing land that had threatened to swallow her whole was now illuminated by something brighter—something hotter. Fire raged across the battlefield, searing through the Olympian ranks with an intensity that made even the gods themselves falter.

A chorus of screams filled the air as the immortal soldiers burned, their divine ichor boiling away in the inferno. The scent of scorched earth and seared flesh was thick, cloying, and unmistakable. Mallory coughed, shaking the ash from her hair, and then her gaze was drawn up.

The storm-wracked sky was no longer empty.

Brian Tripp

The heavens had been set ablaze.

Towering silhouettes cut through the chaos, monstrous shapes framed against the crackling lightning. Wings spread wide, each beat of them sending waves of wind and dust sweeping across the battlefield. Drakons.

The sound of their roars sent a visceral shockwave through the Olympian ranks—pure terror.

Mallory didn't have to look to know that Demeter and Dionysus were staring up in horror. She could feel their panic, their utter disbelief, the way their divine arrogance cracked apart at the sight of the creatures descending upon them.

And there, leading the charge atop a scarlet beast whose scales shimmered like molten rubies, was Andra.

"MARILYN, BURN THAT ABOMINATION TO THE GROUND!"

The command echoed through the battlefield, cutting through the chaos like a blade.

A chorus of draconic roars responded to Andra's call, the sky erupting as streams of fire cascaded downward, scorching through the Olympian host. Mallory watched, wide-eyed, as entire swaths of immortal warriors vanished in the blaze, their screams piercing through the night before being swallowed by the inferno.

Marilyn spread her wings wide, hovering above the battlefield, her gleaming scales reflecting the hellish glow below. Then, she turned her enormous head downward, fixing her burning golden eyes upon the massive tree where Demeter and Dionysus still stood, their arms still merged with the cursed bark.

"Marilyn!" Kael and Sen shouted in unison; their voices filled with raw, unfiltered joy.

Nes, however, was silent. His eyes weren't on the Drakon. They were on her—Andra. She sat astride Marilyn's back, her iridescent hair shimmering with every color imaginable in the storm's fractured light.

Demeter's expression twisted in sheer panic; her usual mask of cold indifference shattered. "What have you done?!" she shrieked, yanking at her arms, trying desperately to tear herself free from the tree's cursed grasp.

Beside her, Dionysus had stopped laughing. His wild, unhinged glee was gone, replaced by wide-eyed horror as Marilyn opened her maw, a dull glow beginning to form deep in the back of her throat.

"No, no, no—" Dionysus stammered, scrambling against the tree's surface, trying in vain to pull himself free. His face twisted, and then his manic expression returned, though it was stretched thin with desperation.

He let out a sharp, high-pitched giggle, wild and brittle, and turned his crazed eyes toward Demeter.

A mighty WHOOMPH shook the battlefield as a torrent of fire blasted from Marilyn's mouth.

The inferno engulfed the tree, the heat so searing that even Mallory, standing a safe distance away, felt her skin prickle and sting from the sheer intensity. The fire roared like a living beast, consuming everything in its wake—bark, vines, and the two Olympians trapped within them.

Demeter let out a shrill, inhuman scream as the flames devoured her, her body writhing and twisting in the blaze. Her arms, still fused to the tree, blackened and splintered.

Dionysus let out a high-pitched, delighted cackle—not in defiance, not in fear, but in some twisted joy as if he relished the pain as much as he feared it. His laughter only grew more feverish as his flesh burned away, his form collapsing into the inferno, vanishing within the sea of flame.

Mallory stood frozen, her breath caught in her throat, staring at the firestorm.

Then, she let out a wild, exhilarated laugh, her adrenaline surging as she threw her arms wide and bellowed:

"YEAH, BABY! WE'RE DRAKON THESE FIREBALLS ACROSS YOUR FACE!"

Kael groaned. "By the gods, Mallory—"

But it was too late. The words had been spoken. Sen howled with laughter, clutching his stomach. "Oh, Mallory, I love you. That was awful."

Mallory grinned, breathless. "Yeah, yeah. But come on. That was satisfying."

As the fire finally began to die down, the battlefield fell into a temporary silence. The massive tree was nothing more than a charred husk, its twisted, blackened limbs reaching skyward like skeletal fingers. The ground was scorched, the air thick with heat and smoke.

And where Demeter and Dionysus had once stood, there were only two shriveled, half-dead husks. The two gods were barely clinging to existence, their forms little more than blackened skeletons held together by the faintest threads of divine essence.

Mallory took a deep breath, her grip tightening on her sword. "Well," she exhaled. "That was dramatic."

Kael nudged her. "Not as dramatic as your one-liner."

Sen wiped a tear from his eye. "Truly. That's going in the history books."

The silence stretched, and then— a chill swept through the battlefield.

Mallory's body went rigid. Her instincts screamed at her, every fiber of her being locking up as the air itself shifted. A presence. Something dark. Something hungry. Something waiting.

A slow, methodical clap echoed through the scorched clearing. Cyrus.

The moment the sound registered; a heavy weight settled in Mallory's gut. The others turned, their breath stilling as the figure stepped into view, his signature smirk plastered across his face. His cloak billowed behind him as he strode toward the barely alive husks of Demeter and Dionysus.

"Beautiful," he mused, tilting his head as he looked upon the charred remnants of the Olympians. "Absolutely beautiful."

Mallory's pulse pounded as she stepped forward, instinctively raising her sword. "Get away from them, Cyrus."

He didn't stop. Didn't even hesitate. And then, he grinned.

"Now, now, Mallory," he crooned. "Don't be *selfish*." His scythe gleamed. And before any of them could move—

He struck.

Mallory barely had time to breathe before the last of Demeter and Dionysus' divine essence was siphoned away. Their bodies collapsed into dust, vanishing on the wind.

Cyrus let out a low, satisfied sigh, rolling his shoulders as the new power surged through him. Then, he turned his sharp, golden eyes toward them.

"Well," he said, "this has been fun, but I have another

Oath Breaker

appointment." And in the blink of an eye, he was gone.

Chapter 58
Ashe

The world was a storm.

Lightning carved jagged lines through the sky, illuminating the battlefield in bursts of silver and violet. Thunder rolled through the air like the war drums of an unstoppable force, a deafening rhythm that set the tempo for destruction.

Wind howled, ripping through the ruins of the battlefield, scattering embers and ash-like whispers of forgotten lives. The ground itself trembled beneath the weight of divine fury.

And in the center of it all stood Zeus.

The King of Olympus radiated power, his form wreathed in arcs of searing lightning that licked at his golden armor, casting sharp reflections across the blood-soaked battlefield. His piercing sky-blue eyes burned with unchecked wrath, and the storm above answered his fury, a chaotic mirror of the god's emotions.

Ashe wiped the sweat from her brow and forced herself upright. The edges of her vision pulsed with pain, but she shoved it aside. Across from her, Levy was already moving—charging back into the fray, unrelenting. He didn't pause. Didn't falter.

Even with his invulnerability, she knew Zeus' power had to be getting to him. But Levy wasn't the kind of man to let pain slow him down. And she sure as hell wasn't about to be left behind. They had trained for this moment. They had bled for this moment.

And yet, even together, even using everything they had—they were losing.

Zeus moved with terrifying precision. Every attack was executed with the casual ease of someone who had never been beaten. Every motion—every step, every flick of his wrist—came with the weight of absolute dominion.

Levy's fist came down in a brutal arc, a blow that could have crushed a boulder into smithereens. But Zeus was faster. He caught the fist on a single finger.

A finger.

Levy's eye widened.

"Impressive," Zeus mused, his voice deep and thrumming with power.

A crackling snap of lightning coiled up his arm, and in the next instant, a blast of electricity exploded from his palm. The force sent Levy hurtling backward, his body searing as the lightning coiled around him like living chains.

Ashe didn't hesitate.

A golden thread whipped through the air, latching onto Levy mid-flight. She yanked, rerouting his trajectory just enough to let him crash into the ground rather than continue tumbling uncontrollably.

At the same time, she moved.

The threads of Fate glowed at her fingertips, weaving and shifting as she called upon her power. She reached, twisting the threads of reality itself, and suddenly, the air around Zeus snapped—dozens of thin, golden lines wrapping around his limbs, binding him in place.

Zeus tilted his head, looking down at the glowing restraints with something like mild curiosity. Then, without ceremony, he flexed his arms—and the threads shattered into nothing.

Ashe's stomach dropped.

She barely had time to react before Zeus turned his attention to her. The moment their eyes met, the air itself shifted. In a single, instantaneous motion, Zeus was in front of her. A fist slammed into her gut.

She felt everything—the impact ripping through her body,

every nerve screaming as the force sent her rocketing backward. The wind was torn from her lungs as she crashed into the earth, the crater forming around her in a splintering explosion of shattered stone.

"Ashe!"

Levy's voice.

She forced her body up, gasping for breath.

Zeus turned his head, surveying them both with the amused indifference of a father humoring his children's futile attempts to overpower him.

"Pathetic," he mused. "You dare think yourselves capable of challenging me?"

Levy, breathing hard, wiped sweat and blood from his brow. "Pathetic?" he scoffed, rolling his shoulders.

He spat onto the ground, shaking off the last remnants of the lightning that had burned its way through him. "Buddy, we're just getting started."

Ashe barely had time to register the moment before Levy launched himself forward again, unrelenting. He spun mid-air, angling himself downward, his fist surging toward Zeus' skull.

Zeus caught the punch.

The impact was jarring, the very air bending from the sheer force. But Levy did not stop.

He twisted his body, using the grip Zeus had on him to swing himself up, locking his legs around the god's neck. With a sharp twist of his core, he dragged Zeus off balance, forcing him forward—just enough to open him up.

"Ashe," Levy roared.

She was already moving.

Golden threads lashed through the air, weaving together in an intricate net—binding Zeus' arms just for a moment. That was all she needed. Ashe flicked her wrist. A column of fire erupted from beneath Zeus, the flames swallowing him whole. Heat billowed outward, the sheer intensity of it burning the rain before it could touch the ground.

The flames twisted, shaped by Ashe's will, engulfing Zeus in the vortex of a roaring inferno. She gritted her teeth, pouring everything into the blaze.

For a second, for one fleeting moment, she dared to hope—

Oath Breaker

Then lightning exploded from the fire.

The inferno was ripped apart, flames guttering into sparks as Zeus emerged, utterly unscathed.

He stepped forward through the dying embers, his form wreathed in crackling arcs of divine power. His smirk was gone.

"I tire of this." Lightning coiled around his form, building—gathering—

And then, with a deafening crack, Zeus unleashed it.

The bolt of lightning split the air so blindingly fast that Ashe barely had time to register the danger before it hit. Levy took the full force of it.

His body seized, the power of the king of the gods forcing its way through his invulnerability, tearing through flesh and bone like fire through parchment. His scream—his agony—was drowned out by the storm.

Levy wasn't moving.

His body slumped forward, steam rising from his flesh, his breaths shallow and ragged. His fingers curled weakly into the dirt, grasping at nothing as if he were trying—and failing—to will himself back into the fight.

And Zeus...

Zeus wasn't even winded.

He stood over Levy's motionless form like a judge passing final judgment, his golden-bronze skin untouched, his hands still humming with electricity. He rolled his shoulders as if shaking off an inconvenience, his face impassive and as if he was bored.

A god looking down at mortal things.

Ashe couldn't breathe. This was it. They were going to lose. She didn't know where Quinn was. Didn't know if any of the others were still standing. Didn't know if anyone was coming to help them.

But what she did know was that she wouldn't survive Zeus alone.

The nectar that had once strengthened her had worn off, her body burning from the strain of wielding a power no mortal should possess. She could feel the cracks in her bones, the tension in her veins where Fate was trying to unravel her.

And yet.

She still had one option left. Her fingers twitched.

Brian Tripp

Almost without thought, her hand drifted down—fingertips brushing against the satchel at her hip, feeling for something she knew was inside. Something she had locked away.

The Box.

The moment her fingers brushed against the cool, ancient surface, a sharp thrumming ran up her arm as if a heartbeat had synced with her own. The pull of it was instant, a siren's call whispering in the back of her mind.

It wanted to be opened. It must be opened.

She clenched her jaw, her breath shaky. This wasn't supposed to happen. They had locked it away. Had all agreed that it was too dangerous, that no matter what, they would not use it.

And yet.

It was here.

Because the moment she had left the Citadel, a string of Fate had pulled taut—an invisible tether binding her to it. And when she had reached inside her satchel, she already knew what she would find.

The box. It had chosen her. A sense of dread wrapped around her, cold and heavy. She didn't want to do this. She didn't want to pay the price. But looking at Levy's crumpled body, at Zeus standing above them, untouched, victorious.

She knew.

Her hand closed around it. A pulse of energy surged through her arm as the box began to manifest, glowing faintly in her grip, its power rising to answer her call.

Zeus' head snapped toward her instantly. His storm-lit eyes widened. For the first time since this war had begun, Ashe saw fear in the King of the Gods.

"You dare…"

She flinched as he stepped toward her, her fingers tightening around the box. She hated this. She hated that it had come to this. But if this was what it took.

If this was what it took to end him.

A roar. Not from Zeus. Not from the storm. A war cry. Then.

Impact.

A massive force slammed into Zeus from the side, a shockwave of pure, crushing power sending him hurtling through the air. He rocketed across the battlefield, crashing into the ground dozens of feet away, the very earth splitting beneath the force of his landing.

Ashe staggered back, nearly dropping the box in shock. Her head snapped to the side, and her heart nearly stopped.

Towering over her, his hammer resting against the ground, was a man built like a living mountain. Flame-red hair. A wild, soot-streaked beard.

A chest broad as a fortress, shoulders thick with the weight of centuries spent forging weapons, cities, and gods alike. His arms were still smoking from the impact of his swing, golden ichor staining his knuckles where he had struck Zeus directly across the face.

His steel-grey eyes flicked to her, and he grunted.

"Put that away, lass," he muttered, nodding at the box. "Ya shan't be needin' it now."

Hephaestus.

Her breath caught. He was here. Not watching from the sidelines. Not hiding. Not waiting. Fighting.

Zeus stirred in the distance, slowly rising from the crater his body had carved into the earth. His eyes burned with fury.

"You dare."

"Aye," Hephaestus cut him off, rolling his shoulders, his hammer dragging against the scorched earth. "I do."

Zeus' form crackled with power, lightning igniting the air around him.

"You are a fool to stand against me."

Hephaestus laughed.

"Nah," he said, lifting his hammer with a single hand, resting it against his shoulder. "Ya see, father, it's been too long since I got to swing this thing." A sharp grin cut across his face. "Thinkin' I'd best make up for lost time."

Zeus roared.

Hephaestus charged.

Ashe exhaled and let the box disappear.

Chapter 59
Nes

"Well, that was weird," Sen muttered, staring at the spot Cyrus had stood only moments ago.

Nes didn't hear him. Didn't hear anything. The world around him ceased to exist—the battle, the war, the cries of pain and victory, the scent of burning flesh and bloodied earth. Nothing mattered anymore.

Because she was here.

For the first time since he had died, Andra stood before him.

Alive.

Breathing, whole, radiant in a way that stole the breath from his nonexistent lungs.

Though it hadn't been long since he had fallen, the woman before him was not the same girl he had loved. The quiet, uncertain girl who had once hidden behind her strength, afraid of her own worth. The woman who had only just begun to step into who she was meant to be before fate had torn them apart; they were both gone.

In their place stood a queen.

A leader forged in hardship, in loss, in wars fought and battles survived.

Oath Breaker

Her iridescent hair shimmered under the storm-torn sky, a shifting cascade of violet and blue and silver, catching the flickering lightning like a beacon. Her armor gleamed despite the grime of war, regal and battle-worn, fit for the ruler she had become.

She was everything he had always known she would be.

And he.

He was dead.

A choked breath tore from Nes' throat. He didn't even know if ghosts could cry, but there was a sudden pressure behind his eyes, an aching weight in his chest as though his very soul had just cracked into a million pieces.

Andra stared at him. Her lips parted, trembling. She didn't move. Didn't breathe. Didn't even blink, as though she didn't believe he was real.

Nes could only stare back, just as frozen, just as afraid. If he moved, if he spoke, would she disappear? Would this be the moment that shattered whatever fragile dream had placed her in front of him again?

Seconds stretched into eternity.

He wanted to touch her.

Gods, he wanted nothing more than to touch her, to pull her into his arms, bury his face in her hair, feel the warmth of her skin against his own. But he couldn't. Because he was not alive. His hands were spectral, a shade of existence, and no matter how much he ached to hold her, he knew if he reached for her, his hand would pass right through.

His throat tightened.

Andra breathed in sharply. The sound shattered the spell. A broken laugh fell from Nes' lips, choked and quiet.

"You..." His voice cracked. He swallowed and tried again, softer this time. "You're here."

A single tear slipped down Andra's cheek. She took one step forward—hesitant, cautious—then another, her boots shifting in the bloodstained mud as though walking was the hardest thing she had ever done. And then, suddenly.

She moved.

Fast.

Too fast.

She lunged toward him, her hands reaching for his face.

And passed right through.

Nes felt nothing.

Andra's eyes widened, her hands snapping back as though burned. Her breath hitched, another tear spilling down her cheek. And at that moment, Nes knew this wasn't right.

He shouldn't be here. She shouldn't be seeing him like this. He wasn't supposed to exist in her world anymore. And yet.

And yet.

His hands clenched into fists. His soul screamed to touch her. To feel her fingers, to wipe her tears away, to press his forehead against hers, just once.

But he couldn't. His voice broke as he whispered, "I'm sorry."

Andra shook her head.

"Don't," she choked out. "Don't say that."

Her arms trembled. Her entire body trembled. "I…"

Her voice cracked like shattered glass. "I never got to…" She cut herself off, her hands curling into fists at her sides. Her chest rose and fell in ragged, desperate breaths. "I lost you."

Three simple words, yet they gutted him.

Nes swallowed the lump in his throat. He wanted to say something. Anything. But what words could possibly fix this? How could he tell her that he had watched her from the Underworld? That he had whispered her name into the void, wishing for one more moment?

That he would have given anything, *anything*, for this?

Instead, he just smiled. A small, soft smile. And whispered, "But you're still here."

Andra let out a choked sound, something between a laugh and a sob. Then—

She lifted her hand again. Slowly, this time. As though afraid of what would happen. As though she just needed to see for herself that he was real. Her fingers hovered just above his cheek—so close, yet not quite touching. And then, in the barest whisper, she said,

"I missed you."

Nes let out a shaking breath.

"Me too."

A lifetime passed between them. Just the two of them, staring at one another, feeling the weight of all the years, all the unspoken words, all the love that had never been given the chance to last.

A voice, distant but sharp, cut through the moment.

Mallory. She wasn't speaking to them directly but to Kael and Sen.

"Come on," she said, urgency in her voice, her sword dripping with ichor. "We need to find the others. We're running out of time."

The world came rushing back. The battlefield, the war, the screams, the storm. Everything slammed back into place. Andra's face hardened. Her hands fisted at her sides. Nes nodded.

The moment was over. But for just a second, for one perfect second, it had been just them again. Just Nes and Andra. Just love. He smiled.

"Yeah," he murmured, forcing his voice to stay light. "Wouldn't want to be dead twice."

Andra huffed a quiet laugh. Then, without another word, she turned.

And Nes followed.

Brian Tripp

Chapter 60
Levy

Levy groaned as consciousness clawed its way back to him. Every nerve in his body screamed in protest, the scent of scorched earth and the sharp tang of ozone thick in his nose. His vision blurred and pulsed with pain as he blinked against the darkness.

The last thing he remembered was the unbearable agony of Zeus' lightning searing through his body, a pain that the Styx could not fully shield him from.

He gritted his teeth and forced himself to sit up, wincing as his muscles spasmed in protest. Through the haze of smoke and dust, he caught sight of something that made his breath hitch.

They were fighting.

Not mortals against gods. Not humans scrambling to survive the onslaught of Olympus. No—this was something else entirely.

Two Olympians were battling with a fury that made the air vibrate.

Levy barely had time to process the sheer spectacle of it—of Zeus, glowing with divine power, and Hephaestus, his towering form swinging his hammer with earth-shaking force. The world seemed to bend beneath the weight of their strikes, the sky flashing with each collision of weapon against flesh.

BOOM!

Oath Breaker

A single blow from Hephaestus sent Zeus skidding backward, his boots carving gouges into the battlefield. The blackened dirt curled and smoked beneath his feet; the god's golden breastplate dented where the hammer had landed. Yet, Zeus only rolled his shoulders, his expression twisting into something both amused and enraged.

"You always did hit like a damn forge press," Zeus sneered, rubbing his chest where the dented armor had absorbed the impact. "But if brute force was all it took to win a war, you would've ruled Olympus."

Hephaestus spat onto the ground, his breath coming in measured bursts. "Aye, and if you had any sense in that thick skull of yours, you'd know how much better off Olympus would've been without you on the throne."

He lifted his hammer and braced himself, eyes smoldering with an intensity Levy had never seen before.

Then they were on each other again.

Hephaestus moved like a war machine—methodical, powerful, and unrelenting. His hammer swung in devastating arcs, each strike backed by the kind of raw, unbreakable strength that had been forged in the heart of Olympus itself.

He was no flashy warrior; he didn't summon storms, didn't wield the elements, yet he hit harder than anyone else, and when his blows landed, they landed hard.

Zeus ducked beneath a heavy swing, his movements graceful for his size. He twisted, summoning a spear of lightning in his palm, and drove it forward with all the precision of a master combatant.

Levy barely saw Hephaestus move.

With a snarl, the smith-god deflected the lightning spear with the flat of his hammer, sending sparks cascading across the battlefield. The sheer force of it rattled Levy's bones, the air ringing like a struck bell.

He had seen Hephaestus' craftsmanship in the weapons and armor he had gifted to them, but seeing the god himself in battle was another matter entirely. He didn't just forge weapons—he was one. Every movement was calculated, every counterstrike devastating.

Zeus lunged, his palm crackling as another bolt formed, but Hephaestus was faster. He twisted his grip on the hammer and brought the handle up like a battering ram, slamming it into Zeus' ribs with a sickening crack. The King of the Gods grunted, staggering back.

"Not so high and mighty without your throne beneath your arse, are you?" Hephaestus growled, advancing.

Zeus wiped ichor from his lip, his eyes narrowing. "You're making a mistake, Hephaestus."

"You think I don't know that? You think I don't know what happens to those who stand against you?" Hephaestus' voice was ragged but not with fear—with fury.

"You butchered my mother. I saw you destroy Olympus with your pride. If this is my last fight, then I'm going to make you earn it." With a roar, he swung his hammer again.

Zeus, this time, did not dodge.

Instead, his hand shot forward with the speed of a thunderclap, catching the hammer mid-swing. The impact sent a shockwave across the field, kicking up debris and sending loose stones skittering like frightened insects.

For a brief, terrible moment, they were locked in place—Hephaestus pushing forward with everything he had, Zeus holding him at bay with a single hand. The strain was visible in their bodies, in the flex of Hephaestus' powerful arms and the way Zeus' feet dug into the charred earth. And then Zeus smiled.

With a guttural snarl, he yanked Hephaestus forward, twisting him off-balance. Before the smith-god could recover, Zeus slammed his forehead into Hephaestus' nose with a resounding crack.

Levy flinched as ichor burst from Hephaestus' shattered nose, his head snapping back. Before he could stumble, Zeus capitalized, slamming his fist into Hephaestus' gut with the force of a falling mountain.

Lightning surged with the impact, illuminating the night in an electric-white explosion. The shockwave hurled Hephaestus back, his massive frame sent flying across the battlefield like a discarded toy. He crashed through the remains of a stone barricade, his body carving a deep trench into the earth before coming to a grinding halt, motionless.

Silence fell, the battlefield itself seeming to hold its breath.

Zeus exhaled, rolling his shoulders, his smirk triumphant.

"Fitting," he muttered, wiping his hands. "For all your talk, son, you were never anything more than a hammer. And a hammer is useless without someone to wield it."

Levy's fists clenched. His breath came in short bursts, the world sharpening around him in terrifying clarity. Zeus turned, his storm-filled eyes locking onto him.

"Now," the god said, flexing his fingers, lightning dancing between them. "Where were we?"

Levy got to his feet. His body ached, his skin still smoldering from Zeus' attack, but he ignored the pain. He had more pressing concerns—like the king of the gods standing before him, power rolling off him in waves.

Ashe appeared at his side; her breath labored but her stance unwavering. Their bodies screamed in protest, but neither were going to surrender. They had faced death before, and they would do it again.

Zeus exhaled sharply through his nose, his lips curling into a condescending smirk. "Such a shame my son turned against me."

He gestured vaguely in the direction Hephaestus had been blasted as if the god's unconscious body were nothing more than an afterthought. "And for what? To fall alongside mortals? To die a meaningless death before the battle is even won?"

Levy's fists tightened, his nails pushing deep into his palms, rage curling in his gut—but before he could respond, another voice rang out, cool and sharp as a blade slicing through the storm.

"Standing for what you believe in is never meaningless."

The words slithered through the battlefield, and for a moment, the world itself seemed to hold its breath. The air grew heavier, charged with something different than Zeus' thunder—a deeper, older energy.

The kind that sent shivers up the spine, warning of something inevitable.

Zeus' smirk vanished.

The voice continued, this time laced with something darker, something final. "Besides, all Hephaestus had to do was buy me enough time to finish up with this nuisance."

The space between them rippled, the very fabric of reality warping as a swirling portal of pure darkness burst open between

Zeus and Levy. The storm winds howled in protest as something came hurtling through the gateway.

Poseidon's lifeless body, his once-mighty form crumpling at Zeus' feet. The god of the sea lay sprawled in the dirt, his eyes vacant. The king of the gods—Zeus, the untouchable, the supreme ruler—stared down at the fallen Olympian, his expression frozen in something that might have been disbelief or perhaps even the faintest flicker of fear.

Levy felt the moment stretch impossibly long, the world itself seeming to quiet down around them.

And then, a step. Boots on earth. A ripple of dark energy that sent cracks splintering through the ground beneath it.

Quinn stepped through the closing portal.

The very air warped around him, his body cloaked in shifting tendrils of Chaos. The black-and-purple energy pulsed like a living thing, rolling off him in waves that bent the light and cast long, stretching shadows across the battlefield. \

His eyes—once mortal, now something beyond—burned with the weight of unleashed power. In this state, he was no longer Quinn. He was a force. A being who had stepped into the abyss, embraced it, and emerged something else entirely.

The portal behind him snapped shut with a finality that left the world trembling.

Zeus, for the first time in his long, immortal life, was silent.

Levy let the moment hang, savoring it as he rolled his shoulders and lifted his hands once more. His lips curled into a smirk as he threw Zeus' own words back at him, his voice laced with defiance and satisfaction.

"Now, where were we?"

Oath Breaker

Chapter 61
Quinn

Quinn readied his sword, Chaos energy seething along the edges of the blade, its dark energy pulsating in tandem with his own heartbeat. His body was alight with power, his essence roaring through his veins, untamed, unyielding.

He had never let himself unleash everything before. But now, standing alongside Levy and Ashe, he knew this was the moment to do so.

Before them, Zeus loomed, crackling with divine wrath. The storm above coiled and writhed in a chaotic frenzy, mirroring the rage in the god's sky-blue eyes. The carcass of Poseidon lay at his feet, a silent testament to Quinn's resolve.

Yet Zeus did not look afraid. He looked enraged.

"You dare…" Zeus' voice rumbled like distant thunder, his fingers curling into fists as arcs of lightning flickered between them. His lips curled into a snarl, his fury a tangible thing, pressing against the battlefield like an impending tidal wave.

"You dare bring my brother's corpse before me as some mockery? You think you have won some victory?"

Quinn grinned, his eyes glowing in the eerie light. "Oh, I know we have."

Zeus let out a roar that shattered the sky. Lightning lashed down from above, carving through the earth, illuminating the battlefield. Quinn, Ashe, and Levy moved as one.

Quinn was the first to strike, vanishing into the shadows like a phantom. In an instant, he reappeared on Zeus' flank, his blade a streak of obsidian light as it cut toward the god's ribs. Zeus twisted at the last second, his reflexes inhuman, and deflected the strike with the back of his arm, but the sheer force sent him stumbling.

Before Zeus could recover, Levy was upon him. The Styx-blessed warrior surged forward, his fists raised, using his indomitable strength to hammer into Zeus with a brutal haymaker to the gut.

The impact blasted forth, the ground cratering beneath them. Zeus reeled, but his expression darkened, and he lashed out with a backhanded strike that would have shattered any normal man's skull.

Levy took the hit—let it connect, let it knock his head to the side. But when he turned back, he was grinning. "That all you got?"

Zeus' answer was a bolt of lightning, but before it could strike, golden threads of Fate wove through the air, snaring Zeus' wrist and jerking his arm upward.

The lightning arced harmlessly into the sky, and Ashe appeared in a swirl of embers, her hands glowing with molten fire. With a flick of her fingers, flames erupted around Zeus, licking at his armor and burning along his skin.

The king of the gods roared, ripping against the threads binding him, but Ashe clenched her fist and twisted her power—her threads turned jagged, siphoning essence from Zeus himself. His body pulsed with resistance, but she held firm, her teeth gritted in concentration.

Zeus bellowed in fury, wrenching against the bindings, but Levy surged forward again, using the god's momentary distraction. He landed a brutal uppercut to Zeus' jaw, sending him staggering once more.

Quinn didn't waste a second.

He shadow-stepped behind Zeus, his blade humming with raw Chaos. He slashed upward in a brutal arc, aiming for Zeus' spine. At the last second, Zeus pivoted, tearing through his restraints and catching the blade with his bare hand. Energy crackled between them, divine and primordial clashing,

Chaos and Olympus locked in a deadly grapple.

Quinn pushed forward, pouring every ounce of his strength into the strike. Zeus snarled, tightening his grip, and suddenly, with sheer brute force, he crushed the edge of Quinn's sword. The blade cracked, fragments of dark energy scattering into the wind.

Quinn had barely a second to react before Zeus hurled him backward with a concussive blast of lightning. He slammed into the ground, the impact sending him skidding across the battlefield, his breath knocked from his lungs.

Levy was there in an instant, shielding him as another bolt of lightning streaked toward them. It struck Levy's chest, the impact making him grimace, but he stayed on his feet, fists clenched. "You good?"

Quinn coughed, shaking off the pain as he pulled himself up. "Peachy."

Ashe appeared at their side, fire curling around her fingers. "We're wearing him down," she said, eyes flicking to Zeus, who was breathing heavily now, his once-immaculate form marred by burns, bruises, and cracks in his armor. "We just need to keep the pressure on."

Zeus was far from finished. He lifted his hands, the storm above swirling in response. Thunder boomed. Lightning coiled in his palms like living serpents. His expression was a mask of pure wrath.

"You insignificant creatures," he seethed. "I AM *ETERNAL*! YOU ARE NOTHING BUT DUST WAITING TO BE SCATTERED!"

The sky *exploded*.

Bolts of lightning rained down in a storm of raw destruction. The battlefield was chaos. Fire and darkness clashing with divine wrath. But Quinn, Levy, and Ashe moved in tandem, dodging, striking, working in perfect unison.

Levy lunged first, taking the brunt of the assault, using his Styx-infused resilience to absorb the strikes, giving Ashe the opening she needed to send a devastating whip of golden threads across Zeus' chest, gouging armor and flesh alike. Quinn followed it with a brutal wave of Chaos, the energy latching onto Zeus like hungry shadows, siphoning his strength.

Zeus staggered. For the first time, true doubt flickered in his eyes. Quinn saw it. He felt it.

This wasn't impossible.

They were *winning*.

With a fierce grin, he surged forward, his shattered blade reforming in his grip, a jagged mass of Chaos and fury. "What's the matter, Zeus?" he taunted, his voice a low, deadly growl. "Are you starting to feel a bit...mortal?"

They had forced Zeus onto the defensive, something he never would have thought possible before today. The god who had once seemed untouchable now bled, his pristine golden armor scorched and cracked, his breath coming heavier with each passing moment.

A strangled sound reached his ears through the roar of the storm. A *cheer*?

Quinn's gaze flicked briefly past Zeus' shoulder to the edge of the fight, where the remnants of their battered but determined forces stood watching. Mallory, Kael, Andra, and the others had caught up, eyes wide with awe as they witnessed the impossible.

Three mortals standing their ground against the King of the Gods.

Mallory was the first to move. "Kael!" she barked, snapping him out of his trance. "Help drag Poseidon's body to the edge. Get it out of the way!"

Kael hesitated only a fraction of a second before he nodded and ran toward the discarded corpse of the Sea god.

Malory, however, didn't spare Poseidon another glance. She was already running, Andra following close behind her.

"Time to put this bastard down for good!" Mallory shouted, her voice fierce as she drew her blade.

Zeus barely had time to react before the two warriors joined the fray.

Oath Breaker

Chapter 62
Mallory

The moment Mallory entered the fight, she fell into rhythm with Levy. They moved as if they had been fighting together for years, a perfect balance of offense and defense. Levy surged forward, blocking a crackling strike of lightning meant for her.

The moment Zeus' focus was drawn toward him, Mallory was there, spinning low, her sword a gleaming arc of steel as she drove it into the god's exposed ribs.

Zeus let out a strangled gasp, ichor spilling from the wound. His expression twisted in disbelief.

Levy smirked. "I thought you were supposed to be untouchable."

Zeus' face contorted with rage, and a massive pulse of divine energy erupted from him, sending them all skidding backward. Before he could capitalize on the moment, Andra was there.

She stabbed out with a Drakonscale spear, striking Zeus' shoulder with a resounding *crunch*. He stumbled, barely catching himself before Ashe's golden threads snapped around his arms again, pulling tight. He roared, jerking against the binds, but she held firm, her essence burning as she siphoned away his divinity, draining him piece by piece.

Brian Tripp

"You dare…" Zeus' voice crackled with fury, but before he could free himself, Quinn surged forward.

He brought his Chaos-infused blade down in a brutal strike aimed at the god's neck. Zeus twisted at the last second, barely avoiding what would have been a killing blow, but Quinn adapted instantly, driving his elbow into Zeus' sternum instead, sending him stumbling right into Andra's spear once more.

The teamwork was relentless, seamless.

Mallory and Levy were a force of nature, weaving in and out of each other's movements like two halves of the same soul. Where one struck, the other followed. Zeus tried to land a blow on Mallory, but Levy intercepted, taking the force of it without flinching before sending a devastating counterattack into the god's injured ribs.

Quinn and Ashe fought like twin shadows, slipping through Zeus' attacks with unnatural fluidity. Ashe's threads snaked through the air like living things, ensnaring Zeus' limbs at just the right moments, creating openings for Quinn's devastating strikes.

Andra fought with an almost godlike grace. She never wasted a movement, her spear, now coated in ichor, gleaming with every thrust and strike, forcing Zeus to stay on the defensive.

Zeus, the mighty King of the Gods, was *losing*.

Chapter 63
Cyrus

"Well, well… what do we have here?"

Cyrus crouched beside Hephaestus, tilting his head as if regarding a particularly interesting piece of broken machinery. The god of the forge lay sprawled before him, his mighty frame crumpled against the stone, thick fingers twitching as the last embers of his strength smoldered within. Each breath was a ragged, wheezing rattle.

Death clung to his lungs like molten slag refusing to cool.

Cyrus let out a soft chuckle, tapping two fingers against his chin. "I must say, I expected more of a challenge. I imagined a grand forge of resistance, an inferno of defiance.

"But instead, here you are—delivered straight to me like a half-finished sword left to rust. And look at this…" He reached out, brushing his hand through the dissipating, golden embers that clung to Hephaestus' skin. "Still warm, but cooling fast. Such a pity."

Hephaestus coughed, a thick, bubbling sound. Ichor, thick and golden, seeped from his lips, but his eyes, heavy-lidded with pain, still held glimpses of defiance.

Cyrus gave a mock gasp, pressing a hand to his chest. "Oh, dear Hephaestus, I do love when your kind clings to optimism, even in the end. It's quite charming, really. But let's not pretend. We both know how this ends."

He leaned closer, his voice a hushed, conspiratorial whisper. "The truth is, you were always disposable. A hammer, nothing more. Beating metal into shape for hands greater than your own. And now, like every old tool… your time is up."

Hephaestus growled, his fingers twitching toward the handle of his hammer. But the Master slammed his heel down onto the god's hand.

Cyrus clicked his tongue. "Ah, ah—none of that. Let's not make this messy. You wouldn't want your Charis seeing you like this, would you?"

Hephaestus let out a deep, guttural snarl, his fury boiling over. But before he could lurch forward, before he could let loose any final act of defiance, Cyrus' scythe was already in motion. The curved blade plunged downward, piercing straight through Hephaestus' massive chest. For a brief, flickering moment, the god tensed—his body arching, his teeth clenched in a final act of resistance. Then, the light within him began to fade, drawn out in thick, swirling tendrils of golden energy.

The essence rushed into Cyrus, filling him with an intoxicating heat that hummed through his veins like molten gold. He let out a slow, satisfied sigh, relishing the sensation as Hephaestus' form withered beneath him.

But he wasn't done.

His gaze flickered to Hephaestus' chest, where a faint, secondary glow pulsed beneath the surface—lighter, thinner. A presence not his own.

"Oh, what's this?" he murmured, pressing a palm over the faint light. A shiver ran through him as another current of power flowed into his body, distinct yet unmistakably divine.

Hermes.

Cyrus let out a wicked chuckle. "Ah… so you carried him with you, did you? A little gift tucked away in your dying heart. How poetic."

The last of Hermes' stolen essence poured into him, mingling with the forge god's strength. The remains of Hephaestus crumbled to dust; his once-mighty body was reduced to a lifeless husk—an empty shell where a god had once stood.

Cyrus exhaled sharply, flexing his fingers as the rush of energy settled within him. "Well, that was delightful."

He straightened, stretching his shoulders as if waking from a particularly satisfying nap. A multitude of cheers rang out ahead, but his eyes weren't drawn to the onlookers. No, his focus drifted to the storm of battle at the center of it all, where the so-called champions of mortals clashed against Olympus' crumbling king.

Quinn. Levy. Ashe.

They fought like demons, their bodies moving in perfect tandem, their power clashing against Zeus in a dazzling storm of light and chaos. And despite everything, despite the sheer might of the god they faced… they were winning.

Cyrus tilted his head, watching with quiet amusement as Zeus staggered, his once-mighty form kneeling beneath the combined onslaught.

"Well, well," he murmured, stepping closer to the scene.

He lingered at the edge of the battlefield, his expression unreadable as the tide of battle shifted. The mortals were prevailing. The impossible was happening before his very eyes.

For a moment, he watched.

Then, in one smooth motion, he dipped the tip of his scythe into the lifeless remains of Poseidon at his feet. The blade sank in, greedily drawing the last remnants of the sea god's fading divinity.

The stolen power flowed through him, filling every inch of his being with something deep, dark, and ancient. He smiled, letting out a slow, satisfied breath.

No one saw him.

No one noticed.

And that was exactly how he wanted it.

Chapter 64
Levy

Zeus roared in frustration, golden ichor leaking from a dozen wounds. His once-pristine form was battered, his energy dimming. His breaths came hard and fast, labored with exhaustion and rage.

Levy could see it—the first hints of fear flickering behind Zeus' fury.

This was their moment.

Levy struck first, feinting low before launching upward, his fist slamming into Zeus' jaw with a sickening *crack*. The god reeled, head snapping back—just in time for Mallory to sweep in from the side, her blade carving another deep wound across his chest.

Zeus tried to retaliate, summoning another devastating blast of lightning, but Ashe's threads were already there, wrapping around his wrists, yanking his arms down before he could release it.

Andra lunged next, her spear a blur of silver and red as she drove it through Zeus' leg and into the earth, *pinning* him in place. His face twisted in agony, but before he could wrench himself free, Quinn stepped forward.

His sword burned with black essence, pulsing with power. He met Zeus' gaze, unrelenting.

"You're done."

Zeus' wide, golden-stained smile twisted into a mask of rage and bitter triumph as he threw his head back and laughed—a sound so broken, so raw, that it reverberated across the battlefield like a death knell. His laughter echoed louder than the cries of war, louder than the clash of steel. It was a sound that seemed to fracture reality itself, the sky trembling beneath his unhinged amusement.

Levy felt a chill creep down his spine. This was not the victorious end he had imagined, and for the first time, he wondered if they had made a terrible mistake. He tightened his grip on his weapon and cast a glance at Quinn. "End him, quickly. He's lost his mind."

But before Quinn could step forward, Zeus lifted a bloodied hand, the movement almost languid, and his laughter died into a sinister whisper of words.

"Do you think you've won?" His voice was raspy, strained, yet laced with a terrible, chilling certainty. He spat a glob of golden ichor onto the scorched earth, the thick liquid sizzling where it landed.

"You pathetic insects. I see the triumph in your eyes. You believe you've defeated the King of the Gods. You believe you've conquered Olympus. You fools."

The battlefield seemed too quiet, as if even the wind was holding its breath. Zeus' head lolled to the side, his eyes glowing with a malevolent light, staring at nothing as he continued.

"You think I didn't know what you were up to? You forsook your brethren, forsook your purpose, and forsook your oaths for power. Do you believe me so blind as to not have felt my own kin within you?"

Zeus laughed again, a strangled sound that made the hair on the back of Levy's neck stand on end. "Oh, I felt them, squirming inside your soul like vermin. Like a disease.

"But I was going to deal with you afterward. You think I didn't plan for betrayal? That I didn't see the seeds of treachery sown from the very beginning?"

Levy frowned, his brow furrowed in confusion. He glanced at Ashe and Quinn, but neither of them seemed to understand Zeus' words. Yet the way the god's voice carried across the field made the mortal soldiers nearby hesitate, shifting uneasily as they listened.

Zeus' eyes roved the battlefield, his burning gaze locking onto some of the mortal army. His lips curled back into a grin, a predatory gleam of satisfaction lighting his face.

"You mortals—such desperate, pitiful things. You ally yourselves with treachery, hoping for a future that will never come. You think that victory lies in slaughtering the gods themselves?"

Zeus spat again, more ichor streaking his chin, dripping down onto his chest. "But gods do not die like mortals. We leave behind echoes—imprints of our rage. We rot the world from within."

His words resonated with a dark truth that made the air feel thick, heavy, as if the world had grown hostile.

"Well, fine then." Zeus' tone shifted, cold and final. "I have lost. I am undone. But I will take you down with me. I will see this world burn before I allow you to live free of our shadows."

His fingers curled into claws, and the ground beneath him trembled, cracks spider-webbing outward, glowing with faint light.

"I see you, Oath Breaker. I see the treachery festering within. Even as I fall, mortals, I will make sure you fall too."

Levy shifted uncomfortably as Zeus' gaze swept over him, and for a brief, horrifying moment, it felt as if the god was speaking directly to him. He saw a few wary glances from soldiers and companions, and he could hardly blame them. The weight of Zeus' accusation seemed to hang heavily in the air as if he had named a blight on their victory.

The Olympian's eyes flashed; his teeth bared in a final, defiant grin. "Come and take it, Oath Breaker. Come and claim your victory."

Zeus' final words, heavy with venom and prophecy, were cut short by a sickening, wet crunch. A sharp, gleaming blade erupted from between his teeth, splitting his mouth open, his final sneer frozen in place. His golden eyes rolled backward, sightless, as a violent shudder wracked his massive frame.

For the first time since the dawn of Olympus, the King of the Gods was dead.

The battlefield seemed to tilt in on itself, reality recoiling from what had just transpired. Silence crashed down like a tidal wave, even the storm above stilling for a fleeting moment, as though the heavens themselves had not yet caught up with what had just occurred.

Oath Breaker

Standing behind Zeus' twitching corpse, his scythe embedded through the god's skull was Cyrus.

The Master's face was alight with manic glee, his lips stretched into an impossibly wide grin. The swirling, stolen divinity that he had hoarded throughout the battle gleamed in a violent storm around him—gold and silver, red and blue, shifting and writhing like a living thing.

But now, Zeus' essence joined the mix, crackling with pure, divine lightning as it funneled from the king's lifeless body into Cyrus.

Thunder rumbled, Olympus itself shrieking in horror at what had just transpired.

Cyrus exhaled, his entire body convulsing as he absorbed the last vestiges of Zeus' power, his fingers twitching as streaks of lightning danced up his arms, wrapping around him like spectral chains before sinking into his skin. The glow in his eyes was not just power—it was madness, a multitude of hues flashing violently within his irises, a grotesque tapestry of stolen might.

Then, he threw his head back and laughed.

It was not the crazed cackle of an unhinged man nor the triumphant howl of victory. It was deeper, richer, vibrating through the air with an unnatural resonance. It was the sound of something vast and limitless. It demanded to be heard.

As his laughter faded, the oppressive pressure of his presence settled over the battlefield like a thick fog, crushing and inescapable. The warriors of Stormhaven, who had just fought the battle of their lives, found themselves paralyzed, their breaths stolen, their exhaustion now mingled with a deeper, more primal terror.

Cyrus lowered his head, his gaze sweeping over them all, and for the first time, everyone could feel him.

Before, he had been a powerful force, a dangerous unknown. But now? Now, his essence burned against their senses, heavy and suffocating, more than Zeus, more than any god before him. He was something else entirely, a nightmare made real.

His grin sharpened as he tilted his head, golden lightning still crackling over his fingertips.

"And now," he murmured, his voice rich with amusement, with promise, with finality. "The true devastation can begin."

Chapter 65
Cyrus

Cyrus had been many things in his young life—a thief, a runaway, a survivor. He had known hunger so deep it gnawed at the bones, had felt the whip of a master who thought cruelty and discipline were the same thing. He had lived by his wits alone, scraping by in the cracks of the world that the gods had abandoned, feeding off the misery they left behind like carrion birds.

And then Talius found him.

It had been in a half-burned village, still smoldering after one of Zeus' lightning storms had turned homes into charred ruins. Cyrus had been picking through what remained, sifting through ash-covered corpses for anything worth taking. That was when he felt it—a presence, cold and watching.

Talius stepped out from the smoke like a figure carved from the ruins themselves. He had an air about him, something steady and unbreakable. His eyes were the kind that had seen too much, held too many ghosts, and yet, they burned with purpose.

"You're wasting your talents." Talius had said, his voice rough, aged beyond his shown years.

Cyrus straightened, clutching the small dagger he always carried, more out of habit than a real threat. "Funny, I don't remember asking for career advice from a stranger."

Oath Breaker

Talius smirked. "No, but you are looking for something. A purpose. A fight worth bleeding for."

Cyrus narrowed his eyes. "What makes you think I'm interested in bleeding for anything but myself?"

"Because you hate them as much as I do." Talius motioned toward the ruin around them—the wreckage of lives torn apart by gods who didn't care to look back.

"Because the world is rotting under their rule, and you've been waiting for someone to tell you there's a way to end it."

Cyrus hesitated. The words were a hook, a whisper of something he hadn't allowed himself to hope for. But hope was a dangerous thing. "What exactly are you offering?"

"A war," Talius said. "A war fought in silence, in shadow. Not with swords, but with knowledge. You and I are not warriors, not heroes. We are keepers. We find what gives the gods power in this realm, and we take it from them."

Cyrus' heart pounded. The idea alone sent a thrill through him. A war against the gods.

"I suppose you need someone like me for this little cause of yours?"

"I need someone clever," Talius said. "Someone who can slip through cracks, find things hidden where others can't. A man who understands that power isn't just in holding the blade, but in knowing where to place it."

Cyrus was silent for a long moment. Then, slowly, a grin spread across his lips.

"Alright, you've got my attention."

Talius only nodded as if he had expected nothing else.

~~~

The Citadel of Stormhaven was nothing like what Cyrus had imagined. It was no grand fortress, no towering temple built for warriors. It was a sanctuary, humming with power that had nothing to do with war. It felt alive.

Talius led him deep into the heart of the Citadel, down a spiraling staircase lined with flickering torches. The air changed the deeper they went, thick with something ancient. At last, they entered a chamber lined with worn tapestries—woven depictions of gods and mortals, history stitched into every thread.

And at the center of the room, waiting for them, was Hestia.

Cyrus knew her from temple murals—the hearth keeper, the quiet one, the goddess who never sought power but kept the flame burning for those who did. But the goddess before him was not a painted figure. She was real, and her presence sent a chill through his bones.

Talius knelt before her without hesitation. Cyrus hesitated only a moment before following suit.

"My lady," Talius said, bowing his head. "We come before you as servants of humanity to swear an oath that will bind us until the end of our days."

Hestia's eyes—warm and old—landed on Cyrus. She regarded him in silence for a moment before speaking. "Do you swear, Cyrus, to wield the knowledge and power entrusted to you not for yourself but for the good of humanity?"

Cyrus opened his mouth, then shut it. He felt something ancient wrap around his skin, a whispering heat curling at the edges of his soul. There was no way to lie here.

"I swear it," he said finally.

"Do you swear to resist the temptations of power, to safeguard these relics not as weapons, but as shields, so that humanity may know freedom?"

The words were heavy. Meaningful. Binding.

Cyrus swallowed hard, feeling their weight settle over him.

"I swear it," he said again.

Hestia nodded once. "Then rise, Keeper of the Vaults."

As Cyrus stood, something in him shifted. A thread tied to something greater than himself, something larger than his own desires. He had felt many things in his life—anger, hunger, ambition.

But now?

Now, he had a purpose.

~~~

Cyrus secured the final seal on the chamber doors, feeling the

Oath Breaker

power ripple through the runes he had carved into the stone. The Scythe of Demeter was now buried beneath ten layers of protection, hidden from even Talius' knowing.

Talius wouldn't understand.

There were some relics too powerful, too tempting, too—useful. If they were going to defeat the gods, shouldn't they use every weapon at their disposal?

Cyrus clenched his jaw, staring at the heavy stone door. His own reflection wavered in the polished surface—his face was unchanged, frozen in time by Hestia's gift of immortality.

He had once seen it as a blessing. Now, it felt like a chain.

"All this power," he muttered, pressing a hand against the door as it faded from view. "And all I do is lock it away."

There was a flicker of something in his chest. Something that felt wrong. For the first time in centuries, the words of his oath came back to him.

"To safeguard these relics not as weapons, but as shields."

His fingers curled into a fist. There was so much more he could do.

He turned away from the door and walked into the darkness, the first seed of treachery rooting itself deep within his soul.

Chapter 66
Quinn

"I WILL RAZE THIS WORLD TO THE GROUND, BURNING EVERYONE IN IT TO ASH, AND REBUILD IT IN MY OWN IMAGE!"

Cyrus' voice thundered across the battlefield, shaking the very air with its commanding power. His essence swelled, distorting the space around him, sending tremors through the shattered earth. Winds howled in protest, the sky twisting above in a vortex of swirling storm clouds, responding to the sheer presence of him.

"GONE WILL BE THE HUNGER AND STRIFE OF MAN. GONE WILL BE THE PREJUDICES OF MAN AND ABYSSILLIAN. GONE WILL BE THE POWERFUL LORDING OVER THE POWERLESS."

His voice rang with conviction, with something dangerously close to righteous fury. "I WILL RIP OUT THE ROT OF THIS WORLD AND REBUILD A UTOPIA THAT ANSWERS TO ME AND ME ALONE."

Then, the battlefield erupted.

A pulse of energy detonated outward from him, a wall of destruction that rippled across the land, obliterating the already ruined terrain, tearing through what was left of the immortal ranks, and hurling mortal warriors through the air like broken dolls.

Oath Breaker

Everyone fell.

Except Quinn.

The force of it battered against him like a tidal wave, but he stood firm. Chaos wrapped around him like a living shield, grounding him where others had crumbled. He gritted his teeth against the crushing pressure, the essence of raw devastation pressing against his skin, but he did not fall.

Quinn's sword glowed in his hand, thrumming with power, chipped and battle-worn but still as unrelenting as its wielder.

Cyrus exhaled, eyes dark with amusement. "Still standing?" he mused. "I suppose I shouldn't be surprised."

Quinn wasted no time on words. He lunged, his cloak of essence flaring from his body in a wave of black and violet.

Cyrus met him, scythe swinging upward in a vicious arc. The clash of their weapons was like a thunderstrike, sparks erupting from the impact, energy crackling between them as if the very world struggled under the weight of their power.

Quinn pushed forward, his muscles straining, his feet digging into the ruined earth as he fought against the unrelenting force of Cyrus' scythe.

Cyrus grinned. "You lasted longer than I expected."

Quinn shoved him back. "Then you clearly haven't been paying attention."

Cyrus laughed—sharp, wicked, and utterly without fear. Then he struck.

His scythe twisted in his grip, moving with the elegance of a dancer's step, the blade cutting through the air in a blur. Quinn met him blow for blow, steel clashing in a deadly rhythm, every movement honed, precise, a battle fought in seconds.

Cyrus was fast, ruthless, a predator in every sense of the word, but Quinn had long abandoned restraint. He had nothing to hold back for, nothing to fear. Chaos flowed through him, responding to his every command, bending to his will, his movements effortless, his counters perfectly timed.

Cyrus spun his scythe, swinging in a sweeping arc meant to carve through his ribs. Quinn ducked, the blade slicing through empty air above his head, and retaliated with a savage upward slash. Cyrus moved at the last second, his coat flaring as he barely avoided the strike, but Quinn was already moving, his blade a blur of black steel as he pressed the attack.

Sparks flew, steel screamed against steel, and the battlefield trembled beneath the storm of their clashing powers.

Sudden movement behind Cyrus caught his eye.

Quinn sensed it the moment before it happened—Kael.

The Abyssillian warrior rose from the dirt, his kopesh battered but still gleaming in his grip. Blood dripped from a gash at his temple, but his eyes were bright, sharp, locked onto Cyrus with unwavering determination.

Quinn saw the shift in his body. The brief flex of muscle. The telltale inhale before a warrior moves to strike, and—

Oath Breaker

Chapter 67
Kael

Kael had felt outclassed in this war for a while now.

He had grown up believing himself strong, a prodigy of the Abyssillian military. He had never been the largest or the fastest, but he was clever, tactical, his victories built on strategy and raw determination. No opponent had ever made him doubt himself—until he met Quinn and Ashe.

Then Levy.

Then the gods.

He had thought himself powerful once, a force to be reckoned with. But compared to them? Compared to these monstrous entities, these warriors wielding powers that bent the fabric of reality, he was just a man with a sword and a dream. But still, he had dreams.

Dreams for his people. For his homeland. For Abyssillians who had suffered under the weight of a world that had never been theirs to control. Nes had believed in those dreams too—had fought for them, died for them. Kael still remembered the moment he had heard of Nes' death, cut down by the very man now standing before him if Cyrus could even be called a man anymore.

Even now, with chaos breaking out across the battlefield, with power crashing like waves of a storm around him, Kael could feel

Brian Tripp

the weight of his people on his shoulders. And he would not let them down. What he lacked in divine power, he made up for in heart. What he lacked in brute strength, he made up for in courage.

And courage, Kael had learned, was what made legends.

So, when the battle between Quinn and Cyrus raged closer when the monstrous tide of their blows sent tremors through the earth itself, Kael waited.

He kept his body still, his breathing measured, his fingers clenched tight around the hilt of his blade. He ignored the ache in his muscles, the bruises that lined his ribs, the exhaustion that begged him to collapse.

He waited. Waited until Cyrus' back was turned. Waited until Quinn's strike forced the Master's weight to shift ever so slightly, exposing the perfect angle—the perfect opportunity.

Then he moved.

A single fluid motion.

He launched from the dirt, his kopesh cutting through the air like judgment itself, a direct line toward Cyrus' spine. A clean strike. A lethal strike. Victory was a breath away.

And then his world ripped apart.

A blinding, searing pain ignited across his abdomen.

Kael's momentum was halted instantly, his body locking in place, a sharp exhale tearing from his throat as something wet and hot spilled down his stomach. For a moment, he didn't even understand what had happened. One second, his blade was mere inches from Cyrus' back.

The next, his gut was open. His legs failed him.

The kopesh slipped from his grip, falling to the ashen earth with a dull thud as he crumpled forward, his forehead slamming into the dirt. His ears rang, drowning out the battle, drowning out the shouts of his allies. Darkness crept in at the edges of his vision, blurring the sky above into nothing more than a hazy swirl of color.

No.

He couldn't die here. Not before he had done something. Not before he had ensured that Nes' sacrifice wasn't for nothing. But his body was no longer listening. A bitter thought flickered through his mind as the blackness overtook him.

So this is how it ends.

Oath Breaker

Chapter 68
Andra & Mallory

Andra didn't know who was screaming, but she heard it—raw, guttural, agonized. It wasn't until her throat burned that she realized the scream had come from her. Kael's body crumpled like a discarded doll, his blood soaking into the dirt.

A friend. A brother. One of the first people to see her, to believe in her before she had even believed in herself.

And now, Cyrus had taken him away.

Rage swallowed the grief in an instant. White-hot, blistering, suffocating. She didn't think. Didn't hesitate. She launched forward, the Drakonscale spear clutched tight, the wind roaring past her ears as she charged.

Beside her, Mallory moved as well—silent, deadly, a mirror of her fury. Cyrus didn't flinch, didn't turn—but Quinn did. He knew.

His sword met Cyrus' scythe in a deadly clash, blocking what they couldn't see. The force of it was intense, but neither Andra nor Mallory faltered. She wouldn't stop.

Not until she ran her spear through the bastard's heart.

Mallory's blade sang through the air, a deadly whisper slicing toward Cyrus' hamstrings. At the same time, Andra struck from above, her spear gleaming in the storm light as it drove through

Cyrus' chest.

For the first time, Cyrus froze.Mallory's heart slammed against her ribs as a sickening hope rose. Had they done it? Had they finally...

Then his lips parted.

And he laughed.

Mallory's stomach plummeted.

Impossible.

He turned like lightning, his scythe forgotten as his hand snatched Andra by the hair, yanking her downward with brutal force.

CRACK.

Andra's body met the earth hard, and before she could react, Cyrus' boot stomped down onto her throat. A choked gasp left her lips—then nothing.

Mallory's world tilted. She lunged, desperation twisting inside her, but Cyrus moved too fast. His hand ripped the sword from her grasp—her sword—and in one fluid motion, he drove it straight through her stomach.

Pain—searing, blinding, all-consuming.

Her breath hitched, her knees buckled—then his foot struck her chest, launching her backward. She hit the ground with a sickening thud, rolling across the battlefield before coming to a shuddering stop. Everything blurred. Pain—everywhere. The sky was spinning, wrong, the sounds of war distant, as if muffled by water. She blinked, vision swimming.

And a trembling hand reached down to her.

Levy.

His face was ashen, his hand shaking as he stretched toward her. Her fingers twitched, trying to reach back. But she was so tired.

So cold.

Oath Breaker

Chapter 69
Levy

Levy reached out with trembling fingers, his breath catching in his throat as his palm brushed against Mallory's cheek. The warmth was already fading.

No. No, no, no.

He pressed his hand to the side of her face, lifting her head slightly as if just by holding her, he could anchor her here—keep her from slipping away into nothing. His fingers curled into her tangled hair, his thumb brushed against her temple, but there was no flicker of response. No intake of breath. No heartbeat.

Nothing.

The world caved in around him.

The din of battle became a distant, muted hum, drowned beneath the deafening roar of his own pulse. His chest rose and fell in uneven, ragged breaths, something breaking inside him so utterly that it left him hollow, stripped bare.

A part of him still clung to denial, to the absurd notion that this wasn't real, that in the next second, she would groan, call him an idiot for looking so wrecked, and tell him to focus because they still had a war to win.

But she didn't move.

She was gone.

Levy's shoulders shook. He let out a breathless, broken sound, something between a gasp and a sob. A raw, splintered pain clawed its way up his throat, burning like acid. His fingers curled into fists, his nails biting into his palms so hard that blood pooled in the creases of his skin.

Tears blurred his vision, streaking down his dirt-streaked face. He had thought he'd known pain before. He had been shattered, had been beaten down, had lost himself more times than he could count. But this? This was something else entirely.

Because he had let himself hope.

He had allowed himself to dream of something beyond war and bloodshed—of building a world with her, of finally having something worth living for. And now that dream lay in the dirt, cut down before it could ever truly begin.

Through the haze of grief, movement caught his eye.

Quinn. Ashe.

They stood a few feet away, watching him, their own eyes filled with the same unspoken devastation. A single moment passed between them, stretched thin with unbearable loss. They didn't need to say anything. They all felt it—the void Mallory had left behind.

Levy let out a shaky breath.

And then, he screamed.

The sound tore from his chest, raw and primal, shaking the very battlefield. The storm above raged in answer, wind and lightning swirling in a furious crescendo as though the world itself was mourning with him.

With a renewed force that sent the ground splintering beneath his feet, Levy launched himself at Cyrus.

Quinn moved at the same time, falling into rhythm beside him, their movements a perfect, practiced symphony of vengeance.

Levy struck first, his fist hurtling toward Cyrus' ribs, but the Master twisted at the last second, deflecting the blow with the handle of his scythe. Quinn capitalized on the opening, his sword swinging in a deadly arc. Sparks flew as their weapons clashed, chaos against god-forged steel.

Cyrus grinned. He was keeping up with them effortlessly.

Quinn and Levy pressed forward, relentless. Quinn's blade

blurred as he struck again and again, while Levy fought with reckless abandon, his fists landing like meteors. But no matter how hard they hit, no matter how fast they moved, Cyrus was faster. Stronger. His scythe wove through the air with deadly precision, each sweep nearly taking off a limb, each counter forcing them back.

Levy barely had time to register Cyrus' movement before a devastating blast of water erupted from his palm, slamming into Quinn and sending him skidding backward.

Cyrus turned to Levy. His grin widened.

"You know, I may not be able to harm you physically," he mused, his voice almost mockingly amused as he closed the distance between them. His fingers lashed out, seizing Levy by the throat. The grip was firm, unyielding. Levy clawed at Cyrus' wrist, but there was no breaking free.

Cyrus leaned in, his lips curling into a slow, wicked smile. "But I've learned how to deal with you regardless."

A deep, echoing boom split the air.

Lightning crashed down.

It struck Levy like a vengeful god's fury, crackling and burning through his body. His entire form seized, his muscles locking up as blinding pain surged through every nerve. The Styx's invulnerability meant nothing against this. This wasn't a blade or a fist—this was power. Pure, unrelenting essence, something that didn't just wound—it burned from the inside out.

Levy's vision swam. The air in his lungs turned to fire as strike after strike blasted through him.

The moment the energy faded, his body collapsed, hanging limply in Cyrus' grasp, his breath coming in ragged, shallow gasps.

Cyrus let out a quiet, almost disappointed sigh. "Tch. I expected you to last a bit longer."

Then, with absolute indifference, he tossed Levy's body aside. Levy hit the ground hard, sliding through the dirt. He barely felt the impact. His limbs refused to move, his body smoldering, weak. The only thing he was aware of was the shape lying just a few feet away.

Mallory.

His trembling hand reached for her—one last, desperate attempt, though he didn't even know why.

Darkness threatened to pull him under.

Brian Tripp

For the first time in his life, Levy had no strength left to fight it.

Oath Breaker

Chapter 70
Quinn

"NO!"

The scream tore from Quinn and Ashe in unison, their voices broken sobs. Quinn felt the weight of failure crash over him, dragging him under, suffocating him. Not again. Not again.

His fingers clenched around the hilt of his sword so tightly that his knuckles ached. His vision blurred—not from exhaustion, not from pain, but from the unbearable truth staring him in the face.

Levy, motionless. Mallory, still. Andra and Kael, unmoving. Avery and Lend nowhere to be found. His friends—his family—were crumpled across the battlefield, broken bodies sprawled upon the ash-streaked earth like discarded remnants of a dream.

This wasn't how it was supposed to go.

He had trained for this, prepared for this. He had fought gods and walked through the abyss, and he was supposed to be strong enough.

And yet, Cyrus stood before them, power radiating from him in waves, unshaken, untouched, drinking in the devastation like it was his due. His essence swirled, streaks of golden ichor merging with the corrupted storm of power he had stolen. His eyes—those eyes—held no trace of concern, only cruel amusement as if he were watching the pieces of a grand game fall exactly where he wanted them to.

Quinn's teeth ground together. He wanted to rip that look from his face.

"Ashe!" Quinn's voice was hoarse. He barely heard himself over the blood pounding in his ears. He turned, finding her standing a few paces behind him, her own body barely holding itself together.

Her breaths came sharp and uneven, her fingers twitching at her sides as embers of golden fire crackled from her palms. Her body swayed with the sheer effort of remaining upright, but her eyes— her blazing, determined golden eyes—locked onto him, unyielding.

"Quinn," she rasped, voice thick with exhaustion, thick with finality. "I'm going to put everything I have left into this binding."

Quinn's heart clenched.

"You put everything you have into one last strike. Everything."

It took him a moment to realize he had stopped breathing.

One last strike.

This was it. This had to be it.

Cyrus was too powerful. He wasn't fighting them; he was dismantling them. If they didn't end this now, they wouldn't get another chance. Quinn took a slow, measured inhale, locking eyes with her. A silent understanding passed between them. He nodded.

Ashe closed her eyes, and Quinn could feel the shift before he even saw it. With a cry of both agony and unrelenting determination, Ashe unleashed everything inside of her. The world broke open with golden fire.

The ground trembled beneath them as thousands—tens of thousands—of radiant threads wove themselves into existence, spilling forth from her hands in an endless tide of luminous energy. Each thread crackled with power, searing and divine, blazing against the storm-dark sky like strands of woven sunlight.

Cyrus let out a snarl, his eyes narrowing as the first strands wrapped around his limbs.

He swung his scythe. The blade sliced through dozens at once— but for each one that fell, another took its place. The threads swarmed him. They wrapped around his arms, his legs, and his torso, weaving over his body like a spider spinning an intricate, golden web. He fought, twisting and cutting, his essence flaring with every strike—but he could not keep up.

Not this time.

Not against this.

The golden threads tightened, blazing even brighter as they layered over one another, cocooning him in fire and fate itself.

Quinn braced himself, summoning everything within him, his blade darkening as Chaos roared to life at his command. He had to time this right. The cocoon pulsed, shuddering as Cyrus' struggles grew more violent. Quinn raised his sword. The cocoon bulged.

And then—a silver arc ripped through it.

Quinn's heart stopped.

Cyrus' scythe burst through the cocoon, its wicked edge slicing through the golden weave as if it were nothing more than gossamer strands.

A second later, the cocoon ruptured.

Cyrus stepped free, his scythe dripping with molten gold, his lips curling into something between amusement and mockery.

Ashe let out a broken, disbelieving sound, staggering backward as the remnants of her binding spell collapsed into flickering embers around them. Quinn's grip tightened around his sword. His stomach twisted into knots. That was everything she had left.

Everything.

And it wasn't enough.

Quinn felt the weight of that failure settle like a stone in his chest. Cyrus had stolen every advantage they thought they had. Every ounce of strength they poured into this fight, he met with terrifying ease.

Cyrus straightened, shaking off the remaining golden threads as if they were nothing more than dust. He locked his piercing gaze onto Ashe, something dark and predatory gleaming in his eyes. His lips curled into that ever-infuriating smirk, the one that promised he was always three steps ahead.

"I have absorbed the essence of every Olympian," he said, his voice rich with the power surging through him. "My ascent is nearly complete. But do not think I have forgotten, Ashelia."

Ashe tensed at the sound of her full name on his tongue. He took a slow step forward, twirling his scythe idly as if he had all the time in the world.

"I remember how it felt when you held me at your whim. Your threads, your will, bending me like some wretched puppet." His smirk widened.

"I will take your essence from you as well. I will steal Fate and make it my own. And when I do, my ascent to primordial will be complete."

Quinn stepped in front of her before he could take another step, his sword raised, his stance unyielding. "I won't let you have her!"

Cyrus laughed—a full, delighted sound as if Quinn had just said the most amusing thing in the world.

"Strong as you are," he said, "you are but a shell of Chaos. And he…" he gestured around them as if addressing the world itself, "Will be a shell of what I am to become. When I am complete, there will be no gods, no monsters, no primordial beings but myself."

His voice dropped, a growl of promise. "Now come and end this futile battle. I will take Fate from Ashelia, even if I must rip it from her." His eyes burned with hunger. "In fact, I would prefer it that way."

Quinn felt Ashe stiffen behind him. His own grip tightened around his sword, his knuckles white.

"So long as I breathe," he growled, his voice low and steady, "you may not have her."

Cyrus smiled. "I can take care of that."

Lightning cracked overhead as they lunged at each other, weapons colliding with deadly force. Darkness and energy flared, the impact shaking the very earth beneath them.

And this time, Quinn knew—this was the endgame.

Chapter 71
Ashe

The world blurred around her, fading into nothing but the ringing in her ears and the searing pain that crawled through her body like wildfire. It hurt—gods, it hurt so much that her very bones felt as if they would splinter apart from the inside. But it was nothing compared to the agony of watching Quinn fight alone.

Cyrus and Quinn clashed again and again, the impact of their blows deafening. The ground beneath them cracked and trembled, unable to withstand the raw power being thrown between them.

Quinn fought like a man possessed, his sword a blur of obsidian light, Chaos itself bending to his will. But it wasn't enough. Cyrus wasn't fighting with desperation nor with the rage of someone trying to win.

He was testing Quinn, treating the battle as nothing more than an experiment—an amusement.

Ashe stood frozen, gasping for breath, her body trembling violently from the strain of holding onto Fate's power. She knew it was killing her.

She had been at her limit long before now, yet she had pushed through, again and again, because she had no choice. Because the moment she let go, it would devour her completely. But even if she did hold on, even if she somehow clawed her way through the unbearable weight pressing down on her, what could she do? She could barely stand.

She was useless.

Quinn knew it, too.

And still, he fought.

Quinn, who had every reason to abandon this world to its doom, who had been betrayed, used, hunted, and cast aside—he was fighting with every last ounce of strength in his body for people who would never even know the weight of the burden he carried. His control over Chaos had become something terrifying, something magnificent.

He should have been standing atop the world with the power that pulsed in his veins. But instead, he was standing against the greatest threat the world had ever known, not for power, not for glory, but because it was the right thing to do.

Because that's who Quinn had always been.

Tears burned tracks down Ashe's face as she watched him move, his body twisting and pivoting, intercepting every strike, every blast of energy meant for her. She felt his presence like a shield, unwavering, indomitable, pushing himself to the very brink of his mortality to keep her safe.

She wanted to scream at him to stop.

She wanted to throw herself between them and tell him to let go, to stop bearing the weight of everything alone, to stop breaking himself for a world that had never deserved him.

But she couldn't.

She could do nothing.

And that was what truly shattered her.

She loved him—gods, she loved him more than words could ever convey. And she was going to lose him. Not now, not at this exact moment, but she could see it as clearly as the golden light flickering on her skin.

The moment he let go of that Chaos, his mortal body would collapse under the strain. He was holding himself together through sheer force of will, through the essence he wielded, but as soon as the battle ended, assuming he somehow managed to come out on top, there would be nothing of him left.

And he knew it.

She could see it in his eyes, could see the quiet acceptance in the way he fought.

Quinn wasn't fighting to survive.

He was fighting to make sure *she* did.

Ashe clutched her chest, her entire being trembling under the weight of helplessness. The power of Fate burned inside her, but it wasn't enough. Not against Cyrus. Not against the monster he had become.

And as Quinn fought, as he took hit after brutal hit, bleeding from wounds that should have killed him a dozen times over, she realized the truth.

This was the last fight they would ever have together.

And she couldn't do a damn thing to help.

The battlefield burned.

Ashe stood in the center of a living nightmare, her legs shaking beneath her, the taste of blood thick on her tongue. Every breath felt like it was ripping her apart from the inside, but none of it compared to the agony of watching her friends—her family—broken around her.

Mallory's unmoving form lay sprawled near Levy's limp body. The once-unbreakable warrior collapsed beside the woman he loved. Andra had yet to rise, her spear buried in the dirt where Cyrus had struck her down. Kael wasn't moving.

And Quinn—Quinn was still fighting.

Even now, his sword clashed with Cyrus' scythe in a deadly dance, his movements sharp, precise, filled with the desperation of a man who refused to break even as the world crumbled around him. But Ashe knew the truth. She saw it. The end was near now.

The visions that Fate had forced upon her—visions that had haunted her dreams and left her waking in cold sweats—were no longer just possibilities. They were reality. This was the moment she had been warned about.

The Oath Breaker had come to end her. Fire raged behind Cyrus, embers swirling in the violent winds, turning the battlefield into a twisted mockery of Tartarus itself. And in the midst of it all, Cyrus stood like an unholy god, his body brimming with the power of every Olympian he had consumed.

He had become something beyond divine—beyond monstrous. How could they ever hope to stop him?

Ashe closed her eyes, her chest rising and falling in sharp, ragged bursts. Clotho's words drifted back to her, spoken so long ago, yet echoing as though they had been whispered into her ear just now.

"Sometimes the world is going in a direction you cannot control, and you must choose the best of the worst, in the hopes that from the ashes, new hope will rise."

This was the worst Clotho had been warning her of. Clotho had been willing to let Quinn—possessed by Chaos, out of control, lost in his own darkness—claim the Throne of Fate rather than allow *this* to happen. She had seen what would come if Cyrus succeeded.

"There is always something worse, dear."

If that was true... If there was always something worse for *her*... then there had to be something worse for Cyrus.

Ashe's eyes opened. She *knew* what had to be done. Quinn would be upset. He would rage against the very heavens. But he would understand.

Because he would have done the same if their places were reversed. Because of how things stood now, they were not going to win.

It was as simple as that. The fight had become *truly* hopeless. There were no more branching paths. No more endless strands of possibility. Just a single, unavoidable fork in the road. One path led to certain doom. The other... well, she wouldn't be around to see where it led. But she knew it was the only chance at salvation.

Ashe took a slow step forward. Agony ripped through her, her body screaming in protest, her very cells unraveling beneath the weight of Fate's power. But she did not stop. Step after step, she walked.

The battle raged around her. Quinn shouted her name, his voice raw and desperate, but she did not turn. Cyrus saw her now, his eerie, multicolored eyes gleaming with amusement. But it didn't matter.

She reached out, her fingers trembling.

And she *pulled.*

Their salvation was coming.

The world would be saved.

Oath Breaker

Chapter 72
Ashe

Ashe did not look at Quinn when he called out her name. She couldn't. Because if she looked at him—if she saw the desperate plea in his eyes, the sheer, unrelenting agony that she knew would be there—she would break. She would falter. And she could not afford to falter now.

So she kept walking.

She did not turn when he called her again, his voice hoarse with urgency, nor when she heard the telltale shift of energy that meant he was trying to reach her. He had figured it out. Of course, he had. Quinn always knew her better than anyone. But she could not allow him to stop her.

A sudden gust of power, sharp and precise, split the air. The sickening sound of impact followed—metal through flesh.

Quinn let out a strangled gasp, and though it nearly shattered her resolve, she did not turn to look. She did not allow herself to see how Andra's spear had found its mark, impaling him through the chest, pinning him to the ashen battlefield.

His voice, broken and breathless, called her name one last time.

Her hands clenched into fists at her sides as she forced herself to keep walking.

Across from her, Cyrus stood in a sea of destruction, watching her with undisguised amusement, his expression split into a wide, gleeful grin.

"Now, now, Quinn," he murmured, licking his lips in anticipation, "it seems Ashelia has made her decision. It wouldn't do for you to undermine her."

Every step Ashe took forward caused the glow beneath her skin to intensify. The threads of Fate, the very power that had been eating away at her body, were rising to the surface, shimmering with golden fire, an offering to the abomination standing before her.

"Have you come to realize that fighting me is futile?" Cyrus purred, tilting his head with mock curiosity. "Or perhaps the pain has become just so unbearable that you can no longer stand to hold it within?"

Ashe exhaled softly, closing her eyes for the briefest moment. Then, she answered, her voice steady despite the war raging within her. "You're right. Fighting you in this state is futile."

With that, she turned her back to him, finally facing Quinn. And for the first time since making this decision, she allowed herself to meet his gaze.

The devastation in his eyes nearly undid her.

No longer was he snarling in defiance. No longer was he fighting against his bonds. He was staring at her, his chest rising and falling with labored breath, the anguish so deep, so raw, that it felt like the world itself might collapse under its weight.

Her fingers trembled as she lifted her hands slightly, positioning them just out of Cyrus' sight.

She mouthed one single word. A name.

Quinn's entire body tensed. He sucked in a sharp breath. But Ashe only gave him a sad, knowing smile before addressing Cyrus.

"I offer you the power of Fate," she said, her voice clear, unwavering. "May it burn you to cinders."

Cyrus chuckled, amused by her theatrics. "Unlikely," he said smoothly, his scythe twirling effortlessly in his grip. "I have absorbed the essence of every Olympian. Fate cannot harm me as it did you. I am beyond simple immortality."

Ashe tilted her head, studying him. "Are you?" she murmured.

There was a flicker of something in Cyrus' eyes—something

just beneath his arrogance. A sliver of hesitation. Of doubt. But it was gone in an instant, swallowed by his endless hunger for power.

A slow, predatory smile spread across his lips. "Thank you for your sacrifice," he said, his voice dripping with satisfaction. "Because of that, I will make this quick."

He surged forward, thrusting his scythe into her, but Ashe did not feel the cold bite of metal sink into her flesh. For the first time since wielding Fate, she felt nothing.

No pain, no burning, no exhaustion. Only light.

Golden threads exploded outward, wrapping around Cyrus in brilliant tendrils, sinking into him, filling him with the power of Fate itself. He threw his head back, letting out a triumphant, exultant laugh, his body glowing with divine energy as the last remnants of Fate were pulled from Ashe's body.

He had forgotten. In his thirst for power, he had forgotten one simple fact. And that would be his undoing.

Ashe's hand closed around the object tucked within the folds of her armor, her fingers curling around the ancient, engraved surface. And then, with the last ounce of strength left in her, she looked back to Quinn.

Tears fell from his eyes, leaving clean streaks in the dirt upon his cheeks.

His face was twisted in pure agony, his mouth open in a soundless plea, his body straining against the spear holding him in place. He was watching her slip away from him, just as she had known he would.

Her heart ached.

"I am grateful for every moment I had with you, and I will love you always—now and forever," she whispered.

And she opened the lid to Pandora's Box.

Chapter 73
Quinn

The world held its breath.

A blinding, pure white light erupted from the box in Ashe's hands, swallowing everything in its radiance. The storm overhead stilled, the wind silenced, and the clash of battle faded into nothingness. In that endless moment, there was no war, no death, no suffering—only light.

Only *her*.

Quinn's vision burned with it. His lungs seized, his limbs locked in place. His heart screamed out in denial, even before his mind could process what was happening. He *felt* her—felt Ashe being unraveled before him. The very threads of her existence unwinding, dissolving into the cascading light as if she had never been.

"Ashe!" His voice was broken. He lurched forward, arms straining to reach her, to stop this, *to save her*. But he could do nothing as the love of his life—the woman who had walked beside him through war, through loss, through fate itself—shattered into a million pieces of radiant essence.

One by one, the particles of light swirled and lifted, drawn toward the obsidian box. They danced like golden fireflies, drifting through the air before vanishing into the artifact's dark surface. The last shimmering fragment of Ashe hesitated, wavering as though reluctant to leave. And then it, too, disappeared.

The lid of Pandora's Box snapped shut with a sound like the sealing of fate itself. For a heartbeat, the battlefield remained suspended in eerie silence. And then, in Ashe's place, the light reformed.

A spirit of white energy stood where she had been, humanoid in shape but ethereal, shifting as though woven from mist and sunlight. It had no distinct face, and yet Quinn *knew*—felt deep in his bones—that it was *her*. Not Ashe, not exactly. But *what she had become.*

Hope.

Warmth radiated from the spirit in waves, washing over him, soaking into his very essence. It was *infectious*—an overwhelming, boundless *hope* that curled around his grief and soothed its sharp edges, that reached into the wounds of his soul and whispered that all was not lost. That it *could* be better.

That they could *still* fight.

The spirit stepped toward him, soundless, weightless. Quinn trembled as it reached out, ghostly fingers trailing along his cheek. The moment it touched him, *power* rushed through his veins, flooding every corner of his body.

His pain evaporated, every wound closing, every ache soothed. His strength surged beyond anything he had ever known—even greater than the power of Chaos he had once feared to unleash.

He gasped, shaking, overwhelmed. He had never *felt* this before. *Never*.

Hope—pure and untainted—wrapped itself around him, bolstering him in a way Chaos never had.

The spirit turned, gliding away from him as it moved across the battlefield, passing over his fallen friends.

Levy, his body still seared from Zeus' lightning, twitched as warmth flowed into him. The burns faded, strength returning to his limbs, his breath coming easier as the spirit's light wrapped around him.

Mallory, limp and unmoving in the dirt, suddenly inhaled sharply as white radiance engulfed her. Her wounds sealed, her fingers twitched, life returning to her veins.

Brian Tripp

Andra, bloodied and battered, stirred as the light cascaded over her, erasing the pain, the exhaustion, and the endless struggle that had worn her down.

Kael, whose broken form had been crumpled against the ruined earth, let out a groan as his bones knit together, his wounds vanishing beneath the spirit's touch.

One by one, they were restored.

And yet, the spirit was *fading*—its once blinding light now dimming, the last of its strength leaving its form as it completed its purpose. It turned back to Quinn, its body now barely more than wisps of soft, white light.

Its voice, when it came, was not Ashe's—but it carried *her*.

"A sacrifice for all to see, embodies hope, forever free."

The last words of Clotho's prophecy.

The spirit gave him one final lingering look—though it had no eyes, Quinn felt it watching him, waiting. And then, just as it had come into being, it vanished, dissolving into the air, its essence lingering in the battlefield, in *them*.

Hope was gone.

But she had left them behind to finish what she started.

Quinn clenched his fists. His tears fell freely now, but there was no time to mourn. Not yet.

His eyes lifted to the battlefield.

Cyrus was still standing.

And he *was next*.

Chapter 74
Levy

Levy felt warmth against his skin. Soft, like sunlight after a storm. His mind drifted in that warmth, hovering between nothingness and wakefulness, until something touched his face—a gentle hand, light as air.

His breath hitched. His body, which had been numb and empty, suddenly hummed with life. Strength poured into his limbs, invigorating, powerful.

His eyes fluttered open, adjusting to the radiance surrounding him. A figure of pure white light stood above him, shifting, flickering like a candle caught in an unseen breeze. It wasn't just light—it was presence. It exuded something he had almost forgotten in the madness of this war.

Hope.

As quickly as it had come, the presence left him, gliding away without a sound, its luminous glow trailing through the battlefield like mist. Levy sat up, his heart pounding, his breath coming quick. He had expected pain, fatigue, something to remind him that he had just been at death's door. But there was nothing. No aches, no exhaustion. Only power. Energy thrummed through his veins, coiling beneath his skin, waiting to be unleashed.

Brian Tripp

His gaze darted to his surroundings. Time itself seemed to stand still. Cyrus was frozen mid-motion, his face twisted into a look of triumphant glee, his body crackling with stolen divinity. Nearby, Quinn stood tall, his expression stricken with grief and anger. Chaos still cloaked him, but it no longer swirled in its usual black tempest. Now, it burned brilliant white, radiant, something more than it had ever been before.

A stirring caught his attention, pulling him away from Quinn's grief-stricken form. Levy turned his head just in time to see Mallory's chest rise in a deep inhale, her body shuddering back to life. His heart slammed against his ribs. His vision blurred. He didn't think—he just moved.

Mallory's eyes fluttered open, locking onto his, confusion and then clarity flashing through them in rapid succession. She barely had a moment to breathe before he grabbed her, pulling her into his arms and crushing his lips against hers.

Relief, joy, desperation—it all poured into that kiss, into the way his hands held her face as if she might disappear if he let go.

Mallory melted into him, her fingers tangling into his hair, matching his urgency, his hunger. She was alive. She was here. He felt her smile against his lips before she pulled back just slightly, her forehead resting against his. He could feel her heart hammering just as wildly as his own.

A gasp pulled them apart, and Levy turned to see Andra and Kael rising to their feet, looking down at themselves in shock. Their fingers flexed, their bodies stretching with strength that had not been there before.

"How is this possible?" Andra murmured, her gaze flickering over the battlefield before settling on Quinn.

Quinn turned to her and then to each of them, his eyes finally resting on Levy's. And in the deep sorrow within them, Levy knew. His stomach twisted, and the strength in his limbs suddenly felt too heavy and unnatural.

"Ashe opened the box," he said, the words barely above a whisper.

Quinn didn't answer. He didn't need to. His silence, the grief carved into every line of his face, was confirmation enough.

The battlefield remained frozen. The air hung thick with

something unspoken, something neither alive nor dead. And in that silence, in that moment of unbearable stillness, the weight of what had happened settled deep into their bones.

And then, the stillness shattered.

The world came crashing back in an explosion of sound and fury. The howling wind surged around them, the battlefield trembling beneath their feet as time lurched into motion once more.

A deafening roar split the heavens, raw and exultant. Cyrus stood at the epicenter of it all, his body thrumming with untamed power, his form no longer entirely human. His eyes, devoid of pupils, burned with a golden-orange radiance, the embodiment of Fate itself.

His hair had transformed into something unnatural—white, not like Quinn's blazing Chaos, but as if woven from an infinite number of Fate's own threads, snapping and writhing like living strands of destiny bound to his will.

A storm of essence spiraled around him, and his lips parted in a wide, manic grin.

"FINALLY, I AM COMPLETE."

The words resonated across the battlefield, thunderous and triumphant, as if the very world acknowledged his ascension.

His gaze swept over them, drinking in the sight before him.

Quinn stood at the forefront, shrouded in an incandescent glow, the brilliance of Hope and Chaos merging into something breathtaking. His crimson eyes burned, twin stars of fury and purpose, an unshakable conviction solidifying in his expression.

To his right, Levy stood, his body outlined in the same radiant glow that pulsed from within him. He could feel it surging in his veins like molten fire, but instead of burning, it was invigorating.

It was a force unlike anything he had ever known—one that did not demand, did not consume, but gave. Beside him, Mallory's fingers intertwined with his, her presence grounding him, her own power thrumming in perfect harmony with his own.

To Quinn's left, Andra and Kael stood side by side, their newfound strength radiating from them like a beacon. The five of them formed a line, their glowing figures illuminating the battlefield, cutting through the despair Cyrus had sought to drown them in.

Cyrus' triumphant grin faltered.

His eyes widened, flicking between them, his mind struggling to process what he was seeing. His lips parted, a breathless whisper escaping like a curse. "How is this possible? You were dead."

Levy stepped forward. Strength coursed through him, not just from Hope's gift but from something deeper. Something unshakable. His voice rang clear, cutting through the howling storm, steady and unyielding.

"As long as we stand, we fight. As long as we fight, we endure. And as long as we endure—you will never win."

Cyrus' expression twisted into something ugly, something furious. He clenched his fists, his entire form pulsing with barely contained power.

Quinn stepped beside Levy, his presence like a wildfire contained only by sheer force of will. His voice was quiet but resolute, spoken for them alone. "He isn't as complete as he believes. Ashe remembered before she opened the box."

Levy's jaw tightened. Ashe. The weight of her sacrifice settled over them like a heavy mantle, and yet—it had not been in vain.

He turned to Quinn, meeting his eyes. "Then let's break him."

Quinn nodded.

Oath Breaker

Chapter 75
The Heroes

Cyrus lunged forward, his entire form ablaze with essence, but before he could take even three steps, Kael and Andra were there.

They moved faster than they had ever moved before—faster than they had ever thought possible. Before this moment, Cyrus had been untouchable, a force too quick for the mortal eye to follow. But now, they saw him. With every shift of his weight and every flicker of tension in his muscles before a strike, they could read him.

Kael's kopesh sliced through the air, intercepting Cyrus' path and forcing him to pivot. Andra followed immediately, her spear a blur of silver and red, forcing him to change direction again. But Mallory was already waiting.

It was instinct, it was precision, it was something more—a force inside her, inside all of them, igniting their every movement. Cyrus barely had time to react before her blade carved across his face.

For a fraction of a second, the battlefield seemed to still. Cyrus staggered a single drop of gold splattering onto the ground. Mallory's breath caught, the realization hitting her all at once. He wasn't untouchable.

He wasn't invincible. For all his stolen power, he still bled. Her heart pounded, disbelief and determination flooding through her veins. He was still flesh and ichor, no matter how much divinity he had stolen. He was not a Primordial, not yet. And she wasn't the only one who realized it.

Levy took a slow step forward, watching as Cyrus wiped the mess from his face. His fingers came away stained gold. His expression flickered, something unreadable passing over his features before twisting into sheer rage.

Levy exhaled sharply, rolling his shoulders. "Would you look at that."

Cyrus' hand clenched into a fist, his golden eyes burning with fury. "You—insignificant—"

He didn't get to finish.

Quinn was already there.

With a burst of speed, he collided with Cyrus, his sword flashing with light so brilliant it could have been a star falling from the heavens. The impact sent a shockwave over the battlefield, the sheer force of it splitting the earth beneath them. Their weapons clashed—sword against a scythe.

Hope against stolen divinity. Sparks flew as their blows rained down, Chaos and Hope intertwining around Quinn in tandem.

Cyrus grinned, wild and feral. "You think this changes anything?"

Quinn pushed harder, his crimson eyes flaring. "I think it already has."

Their battle erupted with violent intensity, each strike sending tremors through the air. Sword carving, scythe slashing, neither willing to yield. But they were not alone in this fight. Mallory, Andra, and Kael flanked from every angle, attacking in seamless unison.

Kael struck low, his sword slicing toward Cyrus' knees, forcing him to jump back. Andra followed, her spear flashing upward, catching him just before he could fully regain his footing. Mallory surged in, her blade cutting an arc through the air.

Then Levy moved. A blur of motion, unstoppable, unrelenting. Cyrus lashed out at him, but Levy didn't even flinch. Cyrus' fist connected with his ribs, but Levy drove forward, unaffected, his own fists colliding with the Master's jaw with devastating impact. Hit after hit, punch after punch, Levy forced Cyrus back.

Oath Breaker

Cyrus faltered.

For the first time since his so-called ascension, he was losing the fight.

Cyrus roared, the air around him bending and warping as he tore into the very fabric of reality itself. Essence exploded from his core, the power of stolen gods and shattered oaths surging outward like an unstoppable tide.

The battlefield trembled beneath the sheer weight of it— lightning split the heavens, golden threads of Fate coiled and lashed like the tendrils of some eldritch horror, and the very earth convulsed under his rage.

The heroes staggered under its force. Mallory was wrenched backward by unseen hands, roots curling around her ankles, dragging her down. Kael's blade was ripped from his grasp as a blast of wind sent him tumbling across the charred battlefield.

Andra barely had time to raise her spear before the air concussed around her, throwing her into Levy, who grunted as the impact sent them both sprawling.

But Quinn did not falter.

He did not tremble in the face of this power. He did not feel fear as threads of Fate lashed at him, only to unravel before they could touch his skin. He did not bow beneath the storm, nor the lightning, nor the wrath of a man who had deluded himself into thinking he was untouchable.

This battle had already been decided.

The moment Ashe sacrificed herself, the moment her essence bled into Pandora's Box and left them with this final, impossible chance, Quinn swore that he would not let it be in vain. He had no right to falter.

So he didn't.

He stepped forward, unyielding. The roots that slithered toward him crumbled into dust before they reached his feet. The lightning that rained down split harmlessly against the white-hot energy surrounding him, scattering across the field like shattered stars.

The threads of Fate twisted wildly, writhing, searching for something to cling to—but they did not touch him. They refused to touch him. Ashe had seen to that.

His friends were still fighting, still struggling against the onslaught of destruction Cyrus was hurling at them, and Quinn would not risk losing another one of them. He clenched his fists, reaching deep into the core of himself—into the chaos, into the hope, into the power that had been given to him—and he pulled.

And from the heavens, the sky answered.

A torrent of white and black energy erupted from above, a pillar of raw power cascading down like the wrath of the universe itself. It struck Cyrus with an earth-shattering force, obliterating the storm, drowning out the thunder, devouring everything in its wake.

The battlefield was bathed in its brilliance, a light so blinding that even the gods themselves would have looked away.

Cyrus screamed, his golden aura flickering, splintering, breaking apart beneath the crushing weight of Quinn's attack. He dropped to one knee, his breath ragged, his once-radiant form flickering like a dying flame. The divine armor he had woven for himself cracked. The threads of Fate that had bound him frayed. The scythe that had stolen so many lives weakened.

And within the storm of energy, where once had stood a being who proclaimed himself a god, a primordial, there now knelt a man.

Not a king. Not an all-powerful deity. Just a man.

The light faded, and for the first time since his ascension, Cyrus looked up at Quinn—and there was fear in his eyes.

He was not invincible.

He was not untouchable.

And now, he knew it.

Oath Breaker

Chapter 76
Cyrus

Talius was furious.

Cyrus wasn't sure how the Master had found out about his hidden stockpile of divine artifacts, but he had. And now, standing in Talius' chambers, surrounded by ancient tomes and the flickering glow of warded lanterns, Cyrus was paying the price.

"You betrayed your oaths," Talius seethed, pacing the room like a caged beast. His hands were clenched into fists, trembling with restrained fury.

"We have yet to even find the heroes of prophecy, and you've taken it upon yourself to squirrel away power for your own selfish desires!"

Cyrus stiffened. "My selfish desires?" His voice was sharp, venomous.

"I simply fail to see the point in hiding away every valuable asset we have against the gods. Are we supposed to just kneel? To pray that these so-called heroes appear before Zeus rains fire upon us?"

Talius slammed a fist against the table. "THESE ARE NOT OUR WEAPONS TO USE!"

The words cracked through the air like a whip. "The prophecy must be fulfilled, or everything we have worked for—everything Clotho sacrificed—will have been in vain!"

Cyrus sneered. "Oh, excuse me if I don't want to put my life in the hands of ghosts and shadows, waiting for your mystical warriors to show up while Zeus hunts us down like dogs. Your faith in prophecy is quaint, Talius. Naïve, even. But me? I make my own destiny."

"Enough!" Talius' voice carried finality, cold and unwavering.

Hestia had been silent the entire time, seated in the corner, her expression unreadable. She did not speak often—but when she did, the world listened.

Talius exhaled sharply, his jaw tight as he turned back to Cyrus. "You have forsaken your oaths. Your immortality is now void, and you will be exiled from the Citadel."

A slow, ugly grin spread across Cyrus' face. "Forsaken my oaths? Oh, I think not." He let out a low chuckle, shaking his head.

"I have never broken my promise to protect mankind. Unlike you, I have merely prepared for the inevitable. I have not used these artifacts for personal gain. I have left room for an alternative—for the moment, your precious prophecy fails. And it will fail."

Talius opened his mouth to argue, but Hestia finally spoke.

"He is right."

The room fell into absolute silence.

Talius turned to her, disbelief written in every line of his face. "Lady Hestiai…"

"I do not approve of his methods," she interrupted, her voice calm yet firm. "And I fear what his intentions may become. But he has not yet forsaken his oaths. Exile him so that he may not interfere further. But his immortality remains."

Talius' shoulders sank. He exhaled through his nose, then nodded, his voice hollow when he finally spoke.

"Very well." He turned back to Cyrus. "From this day forth, you are no longer a Master. Your access to the Citadel is revoked. Should you ever step foot in Stormhaven again…" His eyes hardened. "You will be executed."

Cyrus laughed—a hollow, bitter sound, mocking even as it dripped with promise.

"Very well, Talius," he murmured. "But know this—there will

Oath Breaker

come a day when you fail. And when you do…" His grin widened, but his eyes were like steel.

"I will be there to pick up the pieces."

~~~

Cyrus could not believe he had been brought so low. His body trembled, battered and weak, yet his mind refused to accept the truth. This was not how it was supposed to end. He had clawed his way to power, had seized control of Fate itself, had consumed the very essence of the gods—he was supposed to be untouchable.

Talius and Hestia had always been fools. There was no way they could control Fate to the point of manufacturing heroes. The gods would always have had their day, their revenge.

Cyrus had beaten them to it. And he deserved to. He had outplayed them all. He deserved this power. He deserved the world handed to him on a silver platter, shaped by his will alone.

And he was close. So damn close.

His gaze lifted, locking onto the man standing before him. Was he still even Quinn? The way Hope and Chaos clung to him, enshrouding him like a second skin, made him look more god than man. No, not even god—something more than that. Something eternal.

Fear clawed its way up Cyrus' spine.

And anger.

So much anger.

To be brought low was bad enough, but to be brought low by Talius' so-called *heroes of prophecy*? To be undone by mortals who should never have stood a chance against him? He could not stomach it.

He still had power within him. He could feel it, like an ember waiting to be reignited. He would force it to obey him. He was stronger than any of them. He had claimed the power of the gods—he *was* power.

Cyrus gritted his teeth, reaching deep inside himself, pulling at the well of stolen divinity within. He could feel it surge through him once more. His veins filled with fire; his skin hummed with raw essence. His eyes burned, filled with golden light, and for a moment, the sheer magnitude of it threatened to overtake him.

Yes. YES.

He would not fall.

He would not lose.

And then, the pain began.

First, a sharp, searing sensation in his chest. Then, an unbearable, scorching agony spread through every fiber of his being, setting him ablaze from the inside out. It clawed through his bones, boiled his blood, and shredded his essence. He tried to release it, to stop it, but the power would not obey.

It was burning him alive.

The gods' essence, the power of Fate—it was consuming him.

Like a wildfire in a dry forest, it spread, devouring everything in its path, raging and roaring, turning his very being to cinders.

Cyrus threw his head back and screamed.

Oath Breaker

Chapter 77
Quinn

Cyrus' screams filled the battlefield, raw and broken. He clawed at his own chest, fingers digging into his skin as if he could rip the power out of himself. His body pulsed, the essences of the gods he had stolen surging beneath his flesh, fighting for dominance.

Sparks of lightning cracked across his limbs, golden ichor and red mortal blood both spilling from his nose and mouth in sickly rivulets. The fabric of Fate itself wove and unwove around him in a chaotic frenzy, betraying the very being who had sought to claim it.

His breath rattled, half a sob, half a shriek. "HOW?!" His voice was hoarse, ragged, a man undone by his own hubris.

"I WAS READY FOR THIS POWER! I TOOK THE DIVINITY OF EVERY OLYMPIAN! MY BODY WAS COMPLETE! WHY DOES FATE TURN ON ME NOW?!"

Quinn stepped forward, Chaos and Hope clinging to him, the white light of Ashe's final gift rippling through his aura. His allies—his family—moved with him, circling Cyrus like wolves around a dying beast.

"No, you didn't." Quinn's voice was quiet, cutting through the agony like a blade.

Cyrus' wild, pain-maddened eyes snapped to him, trembling.

He gasped, sweat and ichor dripping from his chin as he struggled to stand. His body jerked, convulsing under the strain of the power eating him alive.

Quinn tilted his head, his voice steady and grim. "In your greed, in your desperation to ascend, you forgot something important."

The others watched in silence, listening, waiting.

"The night Levy and Janus unleashed Athena upon Stormhaven, she burned herself out, destroying the city. But even then, her essence remained within the walls. A piece of the gods left behind. But that, too, was spent when Talius, Clotho, and Hestia released it to counter Zeus' initial attack."

Cyrus' body shuddered violently, his golden-glowing fingers twitching, the weight of Quinn's words sinking in. "No...NO!"

His voice cracked, his lips peeling back over bloodied teeth in panic.

Quinn took another step forward. "Yes."

Cyrus shook his head wildly, his entire being trembling. "I...I can fix this, I..."

"You can't." Quinn cut him off, his voice like stone. "You never finished the collection, Cyrus. You never took Athena's power. And do you know what that means?" He let the words settle, watching as realization dawned, terror widening the fallen Master's eyes.

Levy smirked, stepping beside Quinn, his arms folded as he regarded Cyrus. "It means you're not Primordial. Your body was not truly prepared to handle so much essence at once."

Mallory joined them, blade in hand, her voice flat. "You're not immortal. Not truly."

Andra, standing tall despite the lingering pain of battle, nodded. "You can still die, just like us. Just like the Olympians."

Quinn's gaze was sharp, unwavering. "And do you know what happens to an incomplete being that tries to contain the power of Fate?"

He let the silence hang for a heartbeat. "They break down."

Cyrus took a shaky step back, but his legs buckled beneath him. The glow around him flickered wildly, fluctuating between gold and a deep, rotting crimson. His essence was turning against him, eating him alive from the inside.

Quinn's voice softened, but there was no kindness in it. "You don't have days, Cyrus. You have hours at best."

Levy cracked his knuckles, rolling his shoulders before stepping forward, grinning like a wolf who had cornered his prey. "Actually," he mused, "why don't we make that seconds?"

Cyrus' eyes shot wide with horror. He opened his mouth—to beg, to plead, to curse them all—but Levy was already moving.

"Curious what a dip in the Styx feels like?" Levy sneered, pressing his palm against Cyrus' forehead. Without hesitation, he surrendered its essence to him.

The effect was immediate.

Cyrus' body arched, a strangled scream tearing from his throat as his glow intensified, blindingly bright. The stolen essences within him reacted violently, hunger clawing at the strands of Fate still clinging to his flesh.

They devoured each other, a feeding frenzy of divine energy with nowhere left to go. The ground cracked beneath his feet, blood and ichor spilling in equal measure as his body convulsed. His own stolen power was consuming him like a fire starved of oxygen and suddenly given too much.

From across the battlefield, warriors—both mortal and immortal—turned, drawn by the sheer magnitude of energy pouring from him. The remaining Olympian forces had already begun their retreat, scattering into the shadows of a dying war. Those that remained watched in silence, their gazes filled with awe and horror.

Among them, the warriors of Elysium stood tall. Nes walked up beside Andra, their eyes locking for a moment. No words were exchanged. None were needed. A small, knowing smile passed between them.

Sen stood next to Mallory, his grin wild, his sword resting against his shoulder. "Well, look at that. The universe finally saw fit to hand out some karma."

Levy turned back to Cyrus, watching as the last embers of defiance flickered in the former Master's eyes.

"If you have any last words," Sen called out, arms wide, "I'd say them now, glowstick."

Cyrus choked on his own breath, his body shaking violently as the last remnants of his essence burned away. His hands clawed at his chest, his fingers curling uselessly as if he could physically hold himself together.

As if he could stop what was coming. His once-golden eyes flickered wildly, no longer glowing with power but consumed with panic. He tried to speak, to fight—to do *something*—but there was nothing left.

The glow around him became unbearable, his entire form pulsating as though he were a dying star, seconds from collapse. His limbs twitched erratically, jerking and spasming.

Then, his body convulsed hard enough that his knees buckled beneath him. His breath hitched, a strangled, desperate sound, and suddenly, his limbs began to inflate—uneven and grotesque, bulging in unnatural ways as if something inside him was struggling to escape.

Quinn, Levy, and the others stood in a wide arc, watching in silence, their weapons still raised. No one dared to move, their expressions shifting from grim satisfaction to something between wariness and growing horror.

Cyrus' face twisted, swelling at the cheeks, his skin stretching until it looked like it might split apart. His entire body quivered, his outline warping, distorting—like a balloon filled beyond its limits.

Then Kael's voice broke the tension. "Uh… guys?" His tone was cautious, uneasy.

But it was too late.

With a sickening *POP*, Cyrus *exploded.*

Not metaphorically.

Literally.

One second, he was there. The next, a burst of gore and energy ripped through the battlefield, sending chunks of flesh, blood, and ichor spraying in every direction. The sheer force of it knocked back the closest warriors, covering them in what used to be the most powerful man in existence. The battlefield, which had been filled with the sounds of battle and war cries not long ago, was now frozen in stunned, deafening silence.

A thick, wet *plop* echoed as something unidentifiable slid off Quinn's shoulder and splattered onto the ground at his feet. He didn't move. He didn't even blink.

Mallory's strangled noise of revulsion was the first to break the silence. "*EWWWWWWWWW!*" she shrieked, flinging her arms out and staring at her hands in absolute disgust. "THERE'S MASTER IN MY HAIR!"

"You're complaining about your hair?" Sen shouted, coughing violently. "I got some in my mouth."

"You don't even have a mouth," Andra quipped dryly, holding out her arm in pure horror as a gelatinous mass—something she prayed wasn't an eyeball—slid off her armor with a sickening squelch.

Kael wiped a hand down his face, his fingers coming away stained red. He exhaled slowly, shaking his head. "I feel like I should say something profound... but honestly, I'm just so disgusted."

For a moment, they just stood there, the sheer absurdity of it sinking in. Then, one by one, laughter started bubbling up among them, hesitant at first, then uncontrollable.

Sen doubled over, wheezing. "We just spent this entire war fighting a power-hungry lunatic who thought he was invincible, and in the end... he *popped*."

He lifted a hand, wiping at his spectral face even though nothing stuck to it. "I mean... how do you even come back from that?"

Mallory groaned, shaking out her arms. "I *swear* if this stuff doesn't wash out."

Levy wiped his own face with the back of his arm, sighing deeply. "You know what? Fine. This is how it ends. The all-powerful Cyrus was reduced to battlefield chunky salsa. I can live with that."

Quinn was still silent, staring at the ground where Cyrus had once stood. He exhaled slowly through his nose, shaking his head. "I had a whole speech planned." He looked up, expression blank. "But honestly? Nothing I could've said would've been better than that."

That did it.

The battlefield, which moments ago had been a war-torn land of blood and tragedy, erupted into cheers. Not just from Quinn's group but also from the warriors of Stormhaven and even the ghosts who had fought alongside them. It was relief, pure and unfiltered.

The sound of victory.

The war was over.

For the first time in what felt like an eternity, *they had won.*

Brian Tripp

And as Mallory struggled to wring Cyrus out of her hair and Sen continued to fake-gag, Quinn let his head tip back to the sky, exhaling a slow breath.

It's over, Ashe. It's finally over.

Oath Breaker

Chapter 78
Mallory

The fields of Stormhaven stretched before them in silent ruin, a graveyard of gods and men alike. Days had passed since the final blow had been struck, yet the air still carried the bitter tang of scorched earth and spilled blood. Smoke from smoldering wreckage curled into the sky, mixing with the remnants of dissipating storm clouds. The war was won, but victory felt hollow.

Stormhaven's warriors, the survivors, worked tirelessly. In the days following the battle, they combed through the wreckage, searching for the fallen—identifying the dead and laying them to rest.

Some were lost beneath the churned-up dirt, their bodies swallowed whole by the chaos of war. Others lay where they had fallen, frozen in final moments of bravery or terror.

Mallory had thought herself numb to death after everything they had been through, but everybody they uncovered hit her like a blade to the gut. Every familiar face—soldiers who had fought beside them, who had laughed in the barracks and raised drinks in Stormhaven's halls—was a fresh wound upon her soul.

Then came the worst discovery of all.

She heard Levy's sharp intake of breath before she turned and saw it. Lend's tall, lean form lay sprawled in the dirt, his dark green hair matted with blood and dust, his once-bright eyes empty and staring.

Beside him, Avery—always composed, always in control—lay eerily still, his usually pristine armor battered and dented beyond repair. His head was tilted slightly toward Lend as if, even in death, they had found each other.

Mallory couldn't move. A weight heavier than any blade she had ever wielded settled over her chest, crushing the air from her lungs.

Someone whispered a curse. Another let out a strangled sob.

No one spoke for a long time. What was there to say? The two men before them had been giants, not in size but in will, in the sheer force of their leadership. And now they were gone.

Avery—tactical, razor-sharp Avery—who had seen every move before it was played, who had been the backbone of Stormhaven's strategies, ensuring that every plan they had forged in the war was executed to perfection. Without him, the war might have been lost before it even began.

And Lend. Gods, Lend.

He hadn't just been a warrior. He had been a builder. A mender of things, a leader of men, the very heart of them. When Stormhaven had been razed to the ground all those years ago, it had been Lend who had refused to let it be the end.

He had helped rebuild, stone by stone, training a new generation of warriors, instilling in them the belief that they could fight back, that they could survive.

Without them, there would have been no Stormhaven. Without them, none of them would have made it this far.

Mallory's hands curled into fists at her sides, nails biting into her palms. They had survived against gods. They had brought down the king of the heavens and defied Fate itself. And yet, they had not been able to save everyone.

Levy dropped to his knees beside Lend, his fingers trembling as he reached out, brushing the dust from the man's face. His voice, when it came, was barely a whisper.

"They should have been here to see this."

Mallory swallowed, but the lump in her throat refused to budge.

Oath Breaker

She felt tears sting at the corners of her eyes, but she refused to let them fall. Not here. Not yet.

She looked up at Quinn, who stood motionless, his crimson eyes darker than she had ever seen them. His energy was dimmer now, no longer burning so brightly with the powers of greater beings, but it was still there, simmering beneath the surface. There was no triumph in him. Only grief.

Kael knelt beside Avery, silent. Andra stood nearby, her knuckles white as she gripped her spear, her face unreadable.

For all their strength, for all their power, they had been unable to stop this.

Mallory took a slow, steadying breath.

They had work to do.

Chapter 79
Andra

Andra was sick of funerals. For the last few days, it seemed like it was funeral after funeral, each one a fresh wound on her heart. Every face she recognized, every name she knew, every friend or Abyssillian she had to bury dragged at her spirit.

She knew she was not alone either. The drawn faces of her friends told her that they were feeling it, too. But they endured because they had to. These people had followed them unquestioningly into war—a war against forces they could not have hoped to survive against.

And yet, they did. So, Andra owed it to those who had paid the ultimate price to see them celebrated one final time.

Yet as the last of the funerals wrapped up, she wished she could have gone back and done them all again, just so that she had a little bit more time.

~~~

She met him outside the gates of Stormhaven. The sun had just started its descent below the horizon, bathing the world in hues of crimson and gold. The gentle breeze carried the scent of fresh earth and rain from the battlefield, mingled with the faint, metallic tang of blood that still lingered in the air—a reminder that even victory came with an unbearable cost. The sky was streaked with colors, vivid reds and purples, like a masterpiece painted in mourning.

Horacio quietly plodded along beside her, sensing the heaviness in her heart. The Drakon's gentle presence was comforting, even as her chest tightened with grief that she wasn't yet ready to let free.

Nes stood at the edge of the crater left by Zeus' wall of destruction that had signaled the start of the war. His ghostly arms were crossed as he stared across its vast expanse, his form slightly translucent in the fading light, like a memory caught between worlds.

"Have you seen it yet?" he asked, not yet turning to face her.

"No, not yet," she replied softly. "Now that the war is over, once we get everything figured out, I plan to lead however many of our people wish to return back home. The reports from the scouts I sent before this all started, though…"

She swallowed hard, pushing back the ache in her throat. "They report a land greener than they've ever seen. Teeming with wildlife and vegetation."

Nes finally turned to look at her, and she nearly broke under the weight of that gaze. The sight of him standing there, so achingly familiar yet untouchable, carved a jagged line of grief through her heart.

"Good," he said, his voice soft. "That's good."

A silence stretched between them, not awkward by any means but unbearably sad. They both knew what was about to come, yet neither was willing to initiate it. The rest of the ghosts had returned to the underworld soon after the war had ended.

Nes had stayed for her. They had all agreed that it would be best for the world to destroy the godly artifacts so that they could never again be used by those who grasped for power.

But Levy had lent the orb to Andra so that she might say one final goodbye to the man she had loved so fiercely.

She drew a shaky breath, holding the orb close, feeling its weight pressing into her palm, holding her in the moment that she desperately wished she could delay.

Andra clenched the orb in her hand as she stared at Nes, willing herself to stay strong. But how could she? How could she possibly prepare herself to say goodbye, truly, for the last time? The ache in her chest was unbearable, an open wound that no amount of time or distance could ever hope to heal.

Nes smiled at her, that same soft, knowing smile that she had fallen in love with so long ago. It was steady, reassuring, but beneath it, she could see the sorrow that mirrored her own.

"You don't have to say anything," he said gently, his voice low, steady. "I already know."

Her breath hitched. "That's not fair," she whispered, shaking her head. "You don't get to try and make it easier for me."

He exhaled, a quiet laugh escaping him, though there was no humor in it. "I never wanted this to be easy," he admitted. "But, Andra, it has to happen. I've been holding on for too long for you. And I don't regret a second of it. But I can't stay."

Andra shook her head again, fiercely this time, even as tears began slipping down her cheeks. "Then stay a little longer," she pleaded. "Just a little longer."

Nes took a slow step forward, his translucence flickering faintly in the twilight. "And what would that change?" His voice was so achingly tender that it broke her even more.

"You know this isn't something we can fight. You still have a life ahead of you, Andra. A full, brilliant, beautiful life. That's what I want for you."

She let out a shaky breath, forcing herself to meet his eyes, memorizing every line of his face, every fleck of warmth in his gaze. "I don't know how to do that without you." Her voice barely above a whisper.

"You already have been," he said. "I've watched you, Andra. You became everything I always knew you would. I'm so damn proud of you."

Her throat tightened, and she bit her lip hard enough to taste blood. "I don't want you to go," she choked out.

He smiled again, but this time, it was laced with something heavier, something final. "I know," he murmured. "But I need you to do something for me, okay?"

She nodded, even though she wasn't sure she could promise him anything.

"I want you to live," he said, stepping even closer, so close that she could almost pretend she could feel his warmth. "Not just exist. Not just survive. I want you to love, to lead, to be happy. And I don't want you to hold yourself back because of me. Promise me that."

A sob tore from her throat before she could stop it, her fingers clenching uselessly at the empty air where she so desperately wished she could touch him.

"I don't want to love anyone else," she admitted, raw and broken.

"You will," he said softly. "And that's okay. That's good. Because you deserve to be loved. And I want you to find that. But no matter where life takes you, Andra, no matter who you love, I will always love you. That won't change. Not in a thousand lifetimes."

She sucked in a shuddering breath, trying to hold herself together. "You promise?"

He nodded. "I swear it."

Her legs felt weak, and she let herself fall forward, passing straight through his ghostly form, her body wracking with sobs. "I love you," she whispered into the cold air where he had stood.

"I love you, too," Nes murmured.

And then, just as the sun dipped below the horizon, his form grew lighter, his edges softening, his presence fading like mist in the breeze.

Andra lifted her head, her tear-streaked face illuminated by the last golden rays of daylight. For a moment, she swore she could feel a warm hand ghost over her cheek, like the memory of a touch, before the wind carried it away.

Then, he was gone.

The world around her felt impossibly empty, unbearably quiet.

Horacio let out a low, mournful sound beside her, his large head lowering until his snout nudged gently against her back. Andra let herself lean into him, closing her eyes against the flood of emotions threatening to consume her.

The last remnants of Nes' presence faded into the air, and she breathed in deeply, tasting the salt of her own tears. And then, with the weight of grief sitting heavy in her chest, Andra stood and smashed the orb against the earth. The world had not ended. The stars had not ceased to shine. Life would go on. And so would she.

Chapter 80
Quinn

Quinn felt broken like something inside of him had shattered and could never be made whole again. His body had mended—every bruise and wound erased by the Spirit of Hope—but his soul had not. The ache inside of him was raw and unrelenting, a gaping void that no amount of time or celebration could fill.

Pandora's Box sat on the shelf in his quarters, untouched yet ever-present. No matter where he was in Stormhaven, no matter what he was doing, it was there, lurking at the edges of his thoughts, an obsession he could not shake.

He had picked it up from the battlefield with trembling hands, unable to leave it behind. Now, every waking moment orbited that single, solid block of obsidian.

The box had no hinges, no lid, no seam. It was perfect, seamless. Unbreakable. An object that should not exist. And yet, it did. Sitting there, watching him. Mocking him.

He owed it to his friends and to the people of Stormhaven to help rebuild. He had walked the streets, picking through the remnants of war, offering a hand in rebuilding walls, homes, and lives. He had stood before the pyres, watching flames carry away the fallen, standing as a symbol of victory, of survival, of hope.

He sat at tables of honor, smiled when the people cheered for him, and let them pat him on the back for the role he had played in securing their future. And for their sake, he played his part. He wore his most convincing smile, laughed in the right places, let them believe that he was proud, that he was whole.

But inside, he felt nothing.

No—he did feel something.

Sorrow. Anger.

A fury so deep it roiled like a storm beneath the surface, lashing against his ribs, demanding release. Anger at himself for not being strong enough to win without the box. Anger at the gods and their endless hunger for power. Anger at Cyrus, for taking so much from them. For forcing her hand.

The masses were fooled by his masks, the ones he had learned to wear long ago. (A mask of power, of control. The irony of it was not lost on him.) But his friends—his true family—they were not fooled.

Levy and Mallory, the two who had always known him best, saw through the illusion. They didn't push, didn't pry, but they stayed close. Levy dragged him to the training grounds, where their sparring sessions stretched longer than they should, each strike laced with something unsaid.

Mallory sat with him in quiet companionship, swapping stories about Ashe, making him talk about her. About who she was before she was Fate, before she was sacrifice. And in those moments, he almost felt like he could breathe again.

Almost.

But his mind always wandered back. Back to the obsidian box. Back to what had been lost inside of it.

And no matter how tightly he clenched his fists, no matter how many times he told himself to let it go.

He couldn't.

~~~

The night had stretched long, the weight of war finally giving way to the warmth of celebration. It was the first true night of peace since the gods had fallen. The main hall of the Citadel was alive with light and laughter, the air thick with the scent of roasted meat and spiced ale.

The echoes of music and the clatter of raised mugs filled the vast chamber, a stark contrast to the days of silence and mourning that had preceded it.

For the first time in weeks, Stormhaven was not weighed down by grief. Tonight, they allowed themselves to rejoice.

At the head of the hall, on a raised dais, sat the ones they called the heroes of the war. Quinn, at the center, nursed a goblet of untouched wine, his fingers curled loosely around the stem. To his right, Levy lounged comfortably, Mallory draped across his lap, her arms looped lazily around his neck.

She whispered something into his ear, and whatever it was sent them both into a fit of quiet laughter, their foreheads resting against each other's for just a moment.

Further down the table, Andra and Kael were deep in conversation, their voices low but excited. They were set to leave soon, bound for the Wastes—no, *Nesrithil*, the name they had chosen in honor of the man who had given everything for their people. A land that would no longer be barren, but full of life and magic once more.

The mead had flowed freely all night, the tension of months—years—finally lifting. It was the first time in a long time that any of them had seen their people truly happy.

And then, as if the moment had been waiting for itself, the hall fell to a hush.

A single voice cut through the quiet.

"Speech! Speech! Speech!"

It started as a lone chant, but quickly, it was taken up by the crowd, rising into a thunderous demand. Stormhaven's people turned toward the table, their eyes alight with admiration, with gratitude, and with hope.

Levy groaned, already shaking his head, but before he could object, Quinn was rising to his feet. A sudden wave of emotion surged through him, a tightness forming in his chest. He had spent so long speaking through masks, through half-truths, through walls built to keep others at bay.

Not tonight.

He exhaled slowly and raised a hand to quiet the room.

Oath Breaker

"Instead of a speech," he said, his voice steady but carrying something deeper, something weighty. "Allow me to tell you a story instead. A story of a girl, who gave everything to save the world, and the people, that she loved dearly."

The hall fell utterly silent. Waiting. Listening.

Quinn let the silence stretch, let the weight of the moment settle deep into the bones of the hall. He looked out over the faces turned toward him—people who had fought, who had bled, who had lost, but who had survived. Because of her.

His fingers curled into fists at his sides, nails pressing crescents into his palms. He swallowed hard, blinking against the sting in his eyes before lifting his chin, his voice quiet at first, but steadily growing louder.

"There once was a girl," he began.

The hall seemed to hold its breath.

"She was not born to greatness. She did not wear a crown or wield a sword larger than herself. She was not blessed by a god, nor did she come from a long line of warriors. But she was fierce.

"She was brilliant. And she was kind in a way that was effortless, as natural to her as breathing." His lips twitched, but it was not a smile—it was something more fragile, more painful. "And gods, was she stubborn."

A ripple of soft laughter passed through the room, brief but warm.

"She was the kind of person who, if the weight of the world rested on her shoulders, would carry it not because she wanted to, but because she believed no one else should have to. She never considered herself special.

"She never thought she was stronger, braver, or wiser than anyone else. She just *was*—and that was enough to change the course of Fate itself."

Quinn's throat tightened. He exhaled, forcing himself to continue.

"When I met her, she was *small*—not in presence, not in spirit, but in stature. She fit neatly beside me, barely coming to my shoulder, and yet somehow, she always felt *bigger* than me. Brighter.

"The kind of light you don't notice right away because it

doesn't blind you—it just *is*, comforting and warm, something you don't realize you're moving toward until you've already been caught in its gravity."

He took a slow breath, rolling his shoulders back. His voice didn't waver.

"I have not always made the right decisions," he admitted. "I have done things I regret. Things I have paid for, and will continue to pay for, in ways that no one will ever see. And she—she knew that. She knew what I was, the weight I carried, the things I had done. And she still chose to believe in me."

His gaze flickered across the hall, his words resonating deep, pulling at every heart that listened. "She forgave endlessly. Not blindly, not foolishly, but with purpose. She understood people in a way that made them want to be better."

His hands trembled. He curled them into fists to still them.

"She was relentless," he continued, his voice softer now. "When she loved, she did so fiercely. She would burn for the people she cared for. She would bleed for them. And she did."

A muscle feathered in his jaw. "And she forgave them, too. Even when they betrayed her. Even when they broke her heart. Even when it killed her."

The room was deadly silent. Quinn swallowed hard, his breath shaking as he pressed on.

"She should have been selfish. Should have clung to her own life with everything she had. Should have let us fight for her like she had fought for all of us. But that wasn't who she was." He closed his eyes briefly before looking up again.

"I begged her once—pleaded with her, to stop sacrificing herself for people who wouldn't do the same for her. And she looked me in the eye and told me, '*That's the difference between you and me, Quinn. You think of sacrifice as something given only to those who deserve it. But to me, everyone does. Every person deserves a chance at peace, no matter how broken they are.*'"

His voice hitched on the last words. He let the silence stretch, raw and aching, before he continued.

"She never stopped believing that. Even when she stood before the man who wanted to unmake the world. Even when she held the last hope of mankind in her hands. She made the choice no one else could make. And because of that—because of *her*—we are here."

His vision blurred. He blinked it away, lifting his chin higher.

"I could tell you how much I loved her," he said, voice thick. "How she was my world. My light. But that would be selfish. Because she wasn't just mine. She was *all* of ours. And I will not make her sacrifice about what I lost."

His fingers loosened at his sides. "I will make it about what she gave."

He let his gaze sweep the room, his heart hammering against his ribs.

"She gave us the world," he said, the words ringing clear. "So let us make it one worth the price she paid."

The silence stretched, heavy and thick, pressing down on every soul present.

Then, slowly—one by one—their people began to rise.

Not with words. Not with cheers.

But with quiet reverence.

With hands pressed over their hearts.

With bowed heads.

With gratitude.

And in the hush of the great hall, Quinn let himself grieve.

Let himself feel every ounce of love he still carried.

And when he finally sat back down, swallowing against the ache in his throat, he felt lighter. Not healed. Not whole.

But maybe, just maybe, on the path to being so.

Chapter 81
Levy

The gates of Stormhaven stood open, the road stretching out before them, leading back to a land no longer known as the Wastes. The land of their people—Nesrithil. It was a name born from sorrow, but one that would foster new life, new hope.

Andra and Kael stood at the forefront of the Abyssillian ranks, their people gathered behind them, packs slung over their shoulders, weapons strapped to their backs, ready for the long journey home.

Levy stood with Quinn and Mallory, watching as the moment they had been dreading finally arrived.

With a dramatic flourish, Mallory produced the Second's badge and tossed it to Kael, who caught it effortlessly. He raised an amused brow, glancing at Andra, who snorted.

"Oh, stop it, Mallory," Andra chided, her grin teasing. "I would never dream of being upset with you for giving up your position. Especially not when it means separating you from your man."

Levy smirked and threw an arm around Mallory's shoulders. "And her man thanks you for that."

Laughter bubbled among them, but it was tinged with the melancholy of farewell.

Mallory sighed, running a hand through her hair. "I know, but I still feel bad. I told you I would help you rebuild your home as your

Oath Breaker

Second."

Andra smiled, shaking her head. "Don't you worry about that. Kael and I have got it covered. And with the amount of resources we have at our disposal now, it won't be long before business is thriving between our peoples. Especially with how we just saved all of their lives." She winked.

Levy chuckled, but there was truth in her words. The bonds between their people had never been stronger.

"And with Horacio reaching adulthood soon," Andra continued, "and Marilyn and her brood taking residence in the lands around Nesrithil, the Drakon business will be booming.

"We'll be able to supply Drakonscale armor, medicines, resources—everything to ensure our people flourish. All of that is to say..." she spread her arms wide with a flourish, "we will be just fine."

Kael stepped forward, offering a confident nod. "And it goes without saying that you are all welcome to come and stay with us anytime."

Levy clapped him on the shoulder, grinning. "Careful, Kael. You might not be able to get rid of us."

Kael huffed a laugh, but then his eyes flickered toward Quinn. They all did.

Andra took a step closer, unable to hide all the concern she felt—though she tried.

"Are you sure you don't want to come with us?" she asked softly. "You will always have a home with your people."

Levy held his breath. Quinn had never belonged to one place, but with them—with the people who understood him, who had bled and suffered beside him—he had been home. And yet, he was choosing to stay behind.

Quinn simply smiled, small and knowing. "I appreciate the offer, Andra. And hopefully, I'll be able to come see it soon. But I have something I want to take care of first."

Levy couldn't help the feeling of apprehension that lodged itself in his gut.

He had discussed this with Quinn at length. Had argued against it, repeatedly. It felt too close to a path he himself had already walked—a path that had nearly destroyed him.

But Quinn had conviction in his eyes. And so, Levy had promised to keep it between them, after making Quinn swear he wouldn't do anything rash.

"Well," Andra said after a pause, her gaze searching Quinn's, "if you change your mind, you know where to find us."

She pulled him into a fierce embrace, and Quinn held on, his arms tightening just a fraction more than necessary.

One by one, she hugged each of them—Mallory, Levy—before stepping back to Kael's side. The two of them turned, and their people followed. Abyssillians, no longer lost. No longer wanderers, but builders of a home that would thrive.

Levy, Mallory, and Quinn stood at the gates of Stormhaven, watching as their friends walked off into the distance.

"Think they'll be alright?" Mallory murmured.

Levy exhaled. "They'll be better than alright. They're finally going home."

The wind carried their laughter as they disappeared into the horizon.

And for the first time since the war ended.

Levy felt peace.

~~~

They stood on the opposite side of the vast crater that had scarred the land, the remnants of Zeus' wrath now serving as the dividing line between the old world and the new. The air was still thick with the scent of scorched earth and lingering embers, though the fires had long since been extinguished.

Beyond them, Stormhaven stood, its battered walls rising defiantly against the horizon. Behind Charis, a gathering of immortal warriors remained poised, their expressions unreadable, yet their presence alone spoke volumes.

Levy exhaled, steadying himself as he addressed her. "We still hold true to our promise."

Charis inclined her head, her hair catching the fading sunlight. Despite the regality she carried, grief was etched into every line of her face. She was a widow now.

A goddess without a husband, a leader without a pantheon. But she had stepped into the role Hephaestus had left behind, taking command of the survivors of Olympus—the remnants of a shattered divine empire.

Quinn stood beside Levy, his voice calm, measured. "Olympus is your home, and we would not dream of taking it from you."

His crimson gaze flickered to the warriors behind her, silent and observing. A pointed glance, a reminder of the history between their sides. The war had torn their people apart, and while Charis and Hephaestus had stood against Zeus in the end, it had not erased the centuries of conflict that preceded it.

Charis took the words in stride, nodding in quiet acceptance. "Perhaps sometime in the future, we might come together and discuss a more long-term allyship? When the dust settles, when our people have found their footing again."

She exhaled slowly, her fingers curling at her sides. "We stand on the brink of extinction, both of us. Our numbers have been decimated. Zeus' madness left no victor."

Her voice trembled, just slightly. Red still ringed her eyes; a widow mourning the god she had loved. "It's what my husband would have wanted. What he intended to offer when this was all said and done."

A heavy silence stretched between them, broken only by the faint, intermittent calls of birds echoing through the distant trees.

Levy nodded. "I can't make that decision on my own, but I think it's worth trying."

For too long, their peoples had known nothing but war. Perhaps now that they had found peace, there could be something else.

Charis studied them for a long moment before nodding. "Then we will be in touch."

Quinn raised his hand, summoning a portal with effortless ease, the power flowing naturally through him now. It shimmered before them, a gateway carved through the fabric of existence, leading back to the shattered halls of Olympus.

The immortals stepped through first, silent as wraiths, vanishing one by one into the light. Charis lingered at the threshold, her gaze sweeping over them—over the mortals who had defied the gods and won.

"Goodbye, Quinn. Levy. Mallory." Her voice was quiet,

solemn. Then, with a final nod, she stepped into the portal.

The silence stretched between them as the portal vanished, the gods leaving the world of mortals behind. The battle was over. The war was over. And for the first time in what felt like a lifetime, there was no looming threat, no divine wrath waiting just over the horizon.

There was only the gentle breeze rolling in from the mountains, the faint hum of voices carrying from the city, and the warmth of the sun settling over them like a long-forgotten embrace.

Mallory shifted, breaking the quiet. "So, what now?"

Levy turned toward her, then to Quinn, throwing his arms around their shoulders as they started toward Stormhaven. Toward home. The city bustled ahead of them, alive with the sounds of people rebuilding, of laughter, of children running through the streets that had once been littered with bodies. The people of Stormhaven had survived. And now, they would live.

Everything felt... good. Better than Levy could ever remember. Lighter.

There was a crater in his heart, a wound so deep he doubted it would ever fully heal. Ashe should have been here with them, walking at Quinn's side, teasing him for taking everything too seriously, smiling at them as they stepped into their future together. He would have given anything to change what had happened. Anything to bring her back.

But still, he felt hope.

It burned within him, quiet and steady, as if the spirit that had touched them had never truly left—or had left a piece of itself behind to light their way.

He exhaled, the weight of war finally lifting from his shoulders.

"Now," Levy said, his voice steady, full of quiet certainty. "We embrace the future."

And together, they walked forward, toward the dawn of something new.

Oath Breaker

Epilogue
Stormhaven

The summer air carried the scent of wildflowers and fresh-cut grass, mingling with the distant scent of pine drifting down from the mountains. The sun hung high above Stormhaven, casting golden light over the sprawling city.

Its stone walls no longer blackened by war, but alive with ivy and banners of deep blue and gold, the colors of unity. Laughter echoed from the training courtyard below, where a group of young warriors sparred under the watchful eyes of their instructors.

Levy stood on the balcony of the Citadel tower, watching the scene unfold beneath him. The courtyard had changed since the war, once a place of strategy and council, now a space filled with hopeful energy.

The clinking of wooden training swords and the soft grunts of effort from the young recruits, mixed with the rustling of the leaves, the whisper of the wind through the tall trees that had been planted along the pathways.

The warm breeze tugged at the fabric of his brown and orange Master's robes, sending them fluttering against his legs. His hair was slightly longer than usual, tousled by the wind, and a small amount of stubble dusted his jaw.

"They're coming along well," Mallory's voice carried over the soft hum of the city, warm and affectionate.

Levy turned as she approached, her hand resting over the swell of her belly, her smile full and cheerful. She glowed in the summer light, the deep crimson of her tunic setting off the warmth of her skin. Without hesitation, Levy bent down, pressing a kiss to the top of her head before resting his own hand atop hers, feeling the steady rise and fall of life beneath it.

"They are," he murmured, his gaze flicking back to the young warriors in training. Stormhaven's future. Strong, disciplined, free. "They'll be in top shape for when the immortals from Olympus visit."

The road to peace had been long, but here they stood, five years later, and humanity had found its footing. It had taken time—convincing, rebuilding, healing—but with his and Quinn's word, the people of Stormhaven had chosen to look forward. The Olympians, under Charis' leadership, were no longer seen as overlords, but allies. A hesitant friendship, but a friendship nonetheless.

Mallory nudged him playfully. "Come on," she said, slipping her fingers between his and tugging him away from the view. "He's leaving soon. We need to see him off."

Levy hesitated for only a moment longer, stealing one last glance at the courtyard before letting himself be pulled inside, toward the tower's exit.

They met Quinn at the edge of town, where the cobbled streets gave way to open fields, golden with the glow of the setting sun. The air was warm, filled with the scent of summer earth. Quinn stood tall, dressed in pristine black leather armor, the dark material absorbing the waning light. His travel pack sat high on his shoulders; the straps secured tightly across his chest.

Levy's eye flickered toward the pack, toward what rested inside, before meeting his friend's gaze. "Are you absolutely sure about this?"

Quinn exhaled slowly, the conviction in his expression unwavering—but behind it, just beneath the surface, grief still lingered. "I am."

Levy nodded, stepping forward and gripping Quinn's forearm in a firm clasp. A warrior's farewell. "Then I wish you luck," he said, his voice heavy with the weight of years, of memories. "I wish I could come with you. It'd be like old times."

A small, genuine smile pulled at the corner of Quinn's lips, a rare warmth in the sharp planes of his face. "I would never dream of taking you away from this," he said, squeezing Levy's arm in return.

"Being a Master truly fits you, Levy. You are the absolute best of them. Besides, I wouldn't put you at risk—not with little Levy Jr. on the way."

Mallory snorted, rolling her eyes. "He wishes."

She stepped up to Quinn, rising onto her tiptoes to cup his face in her hands before pressing a soft, lingering kiss to his cheek. Her

Oath Breaker

usual teasing bravado dimmed, replaced by something more earnest, something unspoken.

"Be safe, Quinn," she murmured. "And come back to us, whether you succeed or not. Promise me."

Quinn swallowed hard, blinking rapidly as he tried to push down the emotion threatening to crack his voice. But his glistening eyes betrayed him.

"I promise."

With a final hug for each of them, Quinn turned toward the road stretching ahead. No more words were needed. No more goodbyes.

And, without looking back, he set off.

Brian Tripp

Nesrithil

Andra soared high above Nesrithil, the wind rushing past her as she leaned into the powerful movements of Horacio's wings. His midnight-black scales gleamed under the afternoon sun, each ridge catching the light in rippling waves, while his snowy underbelly reflected the golden hues of the sky.

He was enormous now, far larger than when she had first found him as a hatchling in the desolate Wastes, and with every powerful beat of his wings, she felt the living force of this land beneath her. Nesrithil had become everything they had hoped it could be—and more.

Below her, the landscape stretched out like a dream made real, no longer the barren, cracked husk of a world she had once called home. Rolling fields of deep, endless green sprawled across the valleys, speckled with bursts of wildflowers in shades of violet, crimson, and gold.

Lush trees, thick with leaves in every imaginable hue, stood tall and strong, their branches swaying gently in the breeze. Rivers that had once run dry now surged with crystal-clear water, reflecting the brilliant blue of the sky as they carved pathways through the land, feeding the newfound abundance of life.

Flocks of birds wheeled through the air, their songs a melody that echoed across the revitalized land. Herds of animals—creatures that had long since vanished from these lands—moved through the meadows in great numbers, their coats gleaming with health, their calls blending with the rustling leaves and the babbling streams.

Everywhere she looked, life pulsed in Nesrithil with an energy that was nearly overwhelming. It was as if the land had been waiting, biding its time, until it could finally reclaim what had always been meant for it. It was not just alive—it was thriving. Andra had never seen anything so beautiful.

She guided Horacio lower, skimming just above the treetops, the tips of his wings barely brushing the highest branches. As she inhaled deeply, the air was thick with the scent of wildflowers, damp earth, and the crisp freshness of the rivers that now wove their way through the land like silver veins. It was the smell of renewal, of a future where her people would never again have to fight for scraps of survival.

And for the first time in years, Andra felt something settle within her. A peace she had never truly known.

~~~

Kael watched as Andra landed Horacio on the outskirts of Petram, his sharp eyes taking in the way the wind tangled in her long hair, lifting it in silken waves. There was something about seeing her like this—free, unburdened, alive—that made his chest tighten in a way he couldn't quite put into words.

Every time she flew, it was as though a piece of the weight she carried was left behind in the skies, carried away on the wind. And every time she landed, she looked just a little lighter than before.

Petram had come a long way.

What had once been a settlement barely clinging to survival had transformed into a true city, a beacon of what was possible when perseverance and hope outlasted suffering. Gone were the squat stone hovels that had stood against the cracked, barren landscape of old.

Now, homes of smooth-cut stone and sturdy timber lined the winding streets, their rooftops steep and sloped to weather the seasonal rains that had finally returned.

A sprawling marketplace thrived at the city's center, packed with merchants calling out their wares—woven fabrics dyed in deep Abyssillian blues and reds, golden spices rich with exotic aromas, baskets piled high with fruits and vegetables so fresh they looked unreal.

There were traders from every corner of the world now, not just Abyssillians, setting up shop beneath colorful awnings and intricately carved wooden storefronts. The sound of commerce and conversation filled the air, a chrous of bartering, laughter, and life.

It still astonished him to see how far they had come—not just the land, but the people. The war had changed the world, and for once, it had changed it for the better.

Where once there had been prejudice and distrust, now there

was curiosity, tentative alliances, and slowly, carefully built friendships. It wasn't perfect—there were still places that refused to trade with Abyssillians, still cities that viewed them with wary eyes. But it was better. And every day, it continued to get better.

He and Andra had worked tirelessly with their human allies, determined to bridge the gaps left by generations of strife and resentment. Levy and Mallory had done wonders from Stormhaven, helping to distribute Abyssillian goods and weave their people's history into the broader world.

War stories—some accurate, most embellished beyond belief—had spread far and wide, their heroics shaping public opinion in ways neither of them could have imagined.

Kael smirked to himself, shaking his head. If only the world knew the truth. They hadn't set out to be legends. They had just wanted to survive.

But maybe that was what made it all the more powerful.

He glanced at Andra as she slid from Horacio's back, murmuring something to the Drakon as she stroked his sleek scales. They had survived.

And as he looked out at the city they had rebuilt, at the people bustling through its streets, at the distant glimmer of the mountains where life had taken root once more, he knew that this was only the beginning.

A world of unity was no longer just a dream—it was their future. And for the first time in his life, he knew that future was coming sooner than any of them had ever dared to hope.

Oath Breaker

Back to Where it all Began

The deeper Quinn walked into the cavern, the more the silence pressed against him. His boots echoed against stone, but there was no other sound—no flicker of flame, no whisper of presence, no resistance from an ancient power testing his worth. It was a stark contrast to the last time he had stepped into this place, when he had been a different man. A lost man.

His hair was longer now, brushing against his jaw, his beard fuller than the stubble he used to keep. Ashe would have hated it—would have laughed as she took a razor to his face herself. A pang of sorrow rippled through him, but this time, it did not consume him.

This time, it came with purpose.

The air changed subtly as he stepped fully across the threshold. A familiar pop in his ears told him he had crossed into what remained of the goddess' domain. But it was weak now, little more than a dying ember of what had once burned strong. Hestia was gone from this world, and yet, the place still held something of her, as if the stone itself remembered.

Quinn didn't need light anymore to see. He had spent years bathed in essence, steeped in power far beyond what he once was. His eyes adjusted to the darkness with ease, guiding him forward without hesitation. He moved down the tunnel, toward the place where he had once faced his first trials.

Three archways stood before him.

The bear, once carved into the leftmost passage, was gone—erased from existence. The middle arch, which had once burned with a trial of fire, was nothing but crumbling stone. But the final passage, the one marked with the swirling, jagged symbol of Chaos, remained untouched. It was as if it had been waiting.

Quinn stood there for a moment, staring at the symbol that had defined so much of his journey. This time, however, it was not Chaos pulling him forward. It was his own choice.

He tightened his grip on the pack slung across his shoulders, feeling the weight of it settle against him.

Then, with a steady breath, he stepped into the darkness.

The cold bit into Quinn's skin, seeping through his clothes

despite the thick warmth of his traveling cloak. The cavern was just as he remembered—wide, no visible ceiling, swirling with a ceaseless, frozen wind that carried the scent of old stone and untouched snow. The last time he had stood here, a warrior long dead had risen to warn him away.

There was no warning this time.

No voice echoing through the chamber, telling him to turn back before it was too late. No trial waiting to test his resolve. Just the silence of a world that had already taken too much from him.

Maybe he should have listened all those years ago. Maybe, if he had walked away, if he had not been shackled by a duty forced upon him by Masters who had never truly cared for him, things could have been different.

Maybe Ashe would still be here. Maybe none of this would have been necessary.

But he knew better than to indulge in maybes. The world stood as it did now because of the path he had taken, because of the sacrifices that had been made. He would never know another way.

With slow, deliberate movements, Quinn reached behind him, unshouldering his pack and setting it down in the snow. The fabric was stiff with ice, the buckles frozen at the edges, but his hands were steady as he flipped it open.

His fingers brushed against smooth, solid obsidian.

His breath hitched as he pulled the box free, holding it carefully between his hands. The weight of it was unnatural—not heavy in a way that strained his arms, but dense, as if the power within threatened to drag him into the depths of the earth. He hated looking at it. Hated the way it made his chest tighten, the way it pulled raw, festering emotions from the deepest parts of his soul.

But he couldn't look away.

His fingers traced the edges, searching for a seam, a latch, a hinge—anything that would allow him to open it again. There was nothing. Just smooth, black stone, seamless, unbroken, and utterly final.

Inside this box was everything he had lost.

His heart pounded as he swallowed down the lump rising in his throat, his breath visible in the frigid air.

"Ashe..." he murmured, voice hoarse with the weight of her

name.

For a moment, he simply stood there, the wind howling around him, the frozen world stretching wide and empty.

A low, grating chuckle slithered through the abyss, an unnatural sound, thick with something ancient and vast. The cavern itself seemed to inhale with it, the cold sharpening to a blade's edge as if the very walls were reacting to its presence.

"The hero of the mortal world returns to his humble beginnings," Chaos rasped from the depths, its voice shifting, stretching, coming from everywhere and nowhere. *"Tell me, little Quinn. Did you come to kneel, or to beg?"*

The words dragged through the air like something solid, pressing in on him. Quinn ignored the cold prickle up his spine and stepped to the edge of the abyss, staring down into the infinite black. The presence below curled around him, something *alive*, something watching, tasting the moment.

"I see you brought me a gift," Chaos mused, and though Quinn could not *see* it, he *felt* the abyss shift, drawn toward the obsidian box clutched in his hands.

"Ahhh. I have been missing that for quite some time. Though it appears someone new has taken up residence within."

Mockery dripped from every syllable. Quinn exhaled slowly, forcing himself to stay still.

"You were more entertaining when you let me worm my way into your mind," Chaos sighed. *"I must admit, it was rather amusing to watch you claw and scrape against my influence. But I suppose we must get to business, mustn't we?"*

The darkness thickened, curling around his ribs, the pressure suffocating. *"You wish for me to open it. To unravel the impossible. To undo the binding of a soul in its purest form. But tell me, little Quinn— why should I do such a thing?"*

Quinn tightened his grip on the box. His voice was low, quiet, but firm. *"Because I have something you don't."*

The abyss pulsed, the weight of Chaos leaning forward.

"Hope."

For a long moment, the world was silent. Then, Chaos *laughed*. A deep, splintering sound, something that cracked against the air, like the shattering of a thousand realities. The cavern *shook*. The walls trembled, as if the domain itself recoiled at the sound of it.

"Oh, Quinn," Chaos crooned, a sickly sweet mockery curling through its rasping voice. *"Hope may have been enough to slay gods but it is nothing to me."*

A tendril of darkness slithered up from the abyss, curling lazily around Quinn's ankle before dissipating into mist. A reminder. A warning.

"But I am not without mercy," Chaos purred. *"I will make you an offer. A trade, if you will."*

Quinn's body went rigid. He had known, *known*, this was coming—but hearing the words aloud was like ice in his chest.

"You misunderstand something, little hero. This box does not bind her."

Chaos' voice rasped like old paper, like something ancient unraveling.

"It devours."

The words struck like a hammer. Quinn's grip tightened on the obsidian surface, something twisting inside him, but he forced himself to remain still. To listen.

"This is not a prison. It is a maw," Chaos murmured. "And her soul lingers only because it is unfinished. Suspended. *Waiting."*

Quinn's breath was slow, measured. "Waiting for what?"

"For the price to be paid."

The abyss stilled, as if it were savoring the moment. The shadows curled, retreating just slightly, waiting, *watching*.

"The price is what it always has been," Chaos whispered. *"Your body. Your will. A vessel for me to walk the mortal plane once more."*

A pulse of something *old*, something beyond time, shuddered through the cavern. A promise. A temptation.

Quinn felt the weight of the offer settle over him like chains. His knees nearly buckled under it. He had known. He had always known. But hearing it aloud—hearing it spoken, real, tangible— made it feel so much worse.

"No," he whispered.

"No?" Chaos mused, its voice a lazy drawl. *"You disappoint me, Quinn. For all your pretty words, for all your devotion, you would rather let her rot in the dark?"*

Oath Breaker

Quinn's jaw clenched, his hands curling into fists. "You know I cannot give you that. The world is free from your kind for the first time since its creation. I will not doom it after everything we've done to save it."

The abyss hummed, deep and slow, like something contemplating. *"Oh, but you would, wouldn't you? If only she would forgive you for it."*

Quinn's breath caught.

"I would do almost anything to get her back," he admitted, his voice barely above a whisper. "But I will not damn this world for her. Ashe would never forgive me."

For the first time, Chaos did not laugh.

The abyss did not move.

Something hung between them, heavy and endless.

Then—slowly, *slowly*—Chaos spoke, its voice a thin whisper, curling through the darkness like a blade against silk.

"Then perhaps we might reach another arrangement."

~~~

Quinn exhaled, the weight of his choice already settling over him like a shadow he would never shake. The bargain had been struck—silently, inevitably. He did not like it, but he had accepted it.

One day, the cost of this choice would come due. And when it did, it would not be his burden to bear.

Brian Tripp

Beyond the Veil

She didn't know where she was. She didn't even know *who* she was.

Time moved differently here—fast, slow, or perhaps not at all. There was no beginning and no end, just an endless sea of white that stretched beyond comprehension. She somehow felt *everything*— the weight of eternity pressing in on her, the hush of an existence without meaning—yet, at the same time, she felt *nothing*. She simply *was*.

Had she always been here? Had she ever existed before this place? She couldn't remember.

She drifted, aimless, weightless. There was no sky. No ground. No *self.*

Until—

THUD.

Something *shook*. A tremor ran through the nothingness, so foreign and unnatural that it startled her. But how could something *shake* when there was *nothing* to shake?

THUD.

Another tremor, more forceful than the last. And this time—*a crack*.

A thin, jagged line of translucent light split the empty white expanse above her, cutting through the nothing like a fracture in glass. Her breath—when had she started breathing?—came faster, shallow and unsteady.

Light?

How could there be light in a world that was already made of nothing *but* light?

THUD. THUD.

Two more strikes rattled the void, and the single fracture splintered into a thousand more. A spiderweb of color—colors she had long forgotten existed—spread across the space above her, cracks threading outward like veins of something *alive*.

Then—

SMASH.

The world *shattered*.

Oath Breaker

A deafening *crack* split the silence as shards of white, crystalline light exploded outward, raining around her in a cascade of broken reflections. And beyond them—where there had once been endless nothing—there was only *blackness*.

Abyssal. Infinite. Unknown.

She recoiled. She didn't understand it, but she feared it. It was *new*. It was *wrong*. It didn't belong here.

A hand emerged from the darkness.

It reached forward, followed by an arm, a shoulder, and finally—a face.

A face she *knew*.

Crimson eyes, filled with something deep and aching. Dark hair, disheveled and damp with sweat. A scar that she *knew* the origin of, though she didn't know *how*.

She stared at him, and something inside her broke open.

Her chest tightened, her breath came in gasps, and suddenly she was crying.

She didn't even know why.

Had she been afraid? She *had*, she realized. She had been so afraid.

And now, here he was.

Warmth spread through her, wrapping around her like a presence she had once known but had long since lost. Something deep within her *beat*.

Thud-thud-thud.

A pulse. A sound. A *heartbeat*.

Thud-thud-thud.

Had she always had a heart?

Or had she only just regained it?

The man—*Quinn*—reached for her. His calloused fingers brushed against her hand, *her* fingers—when had they come back? When had she ever had them?—and at his touch, the dam inside her broke.

Like a tidal wave, memories slammed into her.

Laughter in the halls of the Citadel. The heat of battle. The wind whipping through her hair as she soared across the sky on the back of a Drakon. The warmth of a hand holding hers beneath the stars. The searing pain of a blade piercing her chest. The overwhelming agony of choice. Of sacrifice. Of giving everything for the people she loved.

Her breath hitched as it all came back. *All of it.*

Quinn.

Her Quinn.

He had come for her.

A sob tore from her throat as she lunged for him, throwing her arms around his neck, clinging to him as if he were the only real thing in the universe. His arms wrapped around her, crushing her against him, his body shaking just as hard as hers.

She could feel him—*truly* feel him.

The warmth of his skin. The strength in his hold. The way his chest rose and fell, his heart hammering in rhythm with her own.

He was real.

She was real.

And for the first time since she had awoken in this void, she *knew herself.*

She was *Ashe.*

And he had found her.

She didn't know how long they stayed like that, clinging to one another in the darkness, but it didn't matter. Nothing mattered except this.

Finally, she pulled away just enough to see his face.

Tears streaked his cheeks, his crimson eyes raw with emotion. He lifted a hand and gently brushed away her own tears, his touch reverent, his expression something so deep, so full of love and grief and *relief* that it stole the breath from her lungs.

His thumb lingered on her cheek, and in a voice thick with everything he couldn't say, everything he *had* said just by coming here, he whispered—

"Come on, Ashe."

His lips trembled into a smile, warm and unwavering.

"Let's go home."

Oath Breakers

ABOUT THE AUTHOR

My journey into writing began when I picked up reading as a hobby. The way words on a page could create such vivid images in my mind was captivating. The descriptions were so intense, it felt as though I were watching a movie unfold before me. This fascination sparked my desire to write, and I quickly found myself dreaming up my own stories.

Initially, these stories took place within the worlds I had read about, especially the world of *Percy Jackson*, as I had always been drawn to Greek mythology. But over time, those familiar worlds gave way to ones of my own creation. New characters appeared in my mind, each one eager to step into dramatic scenes that played out with a life of their own.

The more I wrote, the more I realized that what I truly wanted was to bring these worlds and characters to life. And so, my writing journey began, and I have no intention of turning back.